Collapsed on Michael's chest, she barely recognized herself. Where was the steady persona that had stood her in such good stead all these years? This man was dangerous. He could make her forget everything.

"What's the matter?" he asked with that odd sensitivity to her thoughts.

"I don't recognize myself."

"How wonderful! Not too many people can lose themselves in lovemaking like that."

"Do you?"

There was a silence. Then he shrugged. "Sometimes."

She wanted to ask if this was one of them, but she was afraid of his answer.

"I don't like it."

That surprised *him*. He turned his face to her. "Why on earth not? People would give anything to achieve it. Those kinds of feelings make legends. Tristan and Isolde. Guinevere and Launcelot."

"I don't want to feel possessed like that."

"Like what?"

"Like someone had invaded my body and taken over my thoughts. I don't know where I am, or who I am. Oh, Michael, this is so frightening."

His arms enclosed her. She was like a volatile gas that had been sealed up in a container until suddenly someone ignited it. A man could not deal with a woman like Sally lightly. He was torn between his selfish need to have her and his fear of having done her irreparable damage.

She cried softly against his bare chest, her tears seeming to burn into his flesh.

"I'm sorry, so sorry," he said softly against her hair.

But that was not what she wanted to hear.

RIVALS

LORAYNE ASHTON

LYNX BOOKS
New York

RIVALS

ISBN: 1-55802-024-1

First Printing/June 1989

This is a work of fiction. Names, characters, places, and incidents are either the product of the author's imagination or are used fictitiously. Any resemblance to actual events, locales, or persons, living or dead, is entirely coincidental.

This book is published by Lynx Books, a division of Lynx Communications, Inc., 41 Madison Avenue, New York, New York, 10010. The name "Lynx" and the logo consisting of a stylized head of a lynx are trademarks of Lynx Communications, Inc.

Printed in the United States of America

0 9 8 7 6 5 4 3 2 1

This book is lovingly dedicated to Norman and Sandra Olesky, two people whose courage, love, and friendship are cherished.

The author also wishes to thank Merby Paine, Dave Hoff, Bill Brett, and Erik Giese, without whose help this book could never have been written. Further thanks to my husband, who was at the computer every morning entering my edits and fixing my facts. The author also wishes to remind readers that this is a work of fiction and in no way should be considered a criticism of the coaching or organizational practices of the United States ski team. In most of the fifty states, skiing, though thought of as elitist and glamorous, is not an important sport, numbering twenty-eight on the list of favorite American sports, just slightly ahead of platform diving. By the same token, it is difficult to find a great basketball or baseball team in the Alpine countries of Europe, where skiing is the number one sport. *Chacun à son gout.*

RIVALS

PROLOGUE

Midnight. A vast silence stretched out through the huge aerospace facility, the only sound the hum of the multimillion-dollar Cray computer. Soporific in its monotony.

The temperature and humidity controlled room, its air filtered so perfectly that it was virtually dust free, was a boon to the man seated at the rolling chair in front of one of the giant monitors, for Max Margolis was allergic to dust, fungus, cat hair, and questions.

Giving himself a push, he moved noiselessly around the room as though on roller skates. He was alone in the empty building and, though he had been at work since early morning, it was for this time that he impatiently awaited. Alone at last with a multimillion-dollar toy that he knew how to play with the virtuosity of an accomplished musician.

Although approaching forty, Max had the look of a perennial college boy seen through the eyes of Washington Irving. As scrawny as a string bean with russet hair which had not seen a comb in several days and stuck up all over his head as if he had touched a live wire, he had eyes narrowed to a permanent squint from peering at computer screens. But his smile was broad and boyish and his brown eyes kind under the bristly eyebrows that rose above heavy horn-rimmed glasses. He was wearing Adidas sneakers, worn khaki pants, a Celtics sweatshirt, and the blue blazer he'd had since the days when he was a freshman in college. He'd grown several inches since purchasing them, so his wrists and ankles stuck out, which only added to his Ichabod Crane resemblance.

Despite his idiosyncratic features, Max was a man of wit, charm, and genius. His mind, like his computer, was filled with mega-bytes of information, ranging from how many home runs Babe Ruth hit in his first season with the Yankees to all the prime numbers from 1 to infinity. Tonight he had the look of a man close to finding Nirvana.

During working hours the Cray was used to simulate and analyze the flow of fluids such as air and water over airplanes, rockets, missiles, and submarines in all kinds of conditions. As an executive engineer at Monroe Aerospace in San Diego, Max Margolis was in charge of the development of the incredibly complex computer programs that ran the Cray.

At the moment his mind was on another type of solid body.

Since he was old enough to slide down a hill in New Hampshire, he had been an avid skier, a top college racer. All his life he had been searching for his personal holy grail: the perfect ski. For months he had been creating programs to tap the vast capabilities of the super-computer to help him with the design.

After painstaking investigation of a number of space-age materials, an alloy of beryllium and copper emerged as the most promising of a number of simulations. Punching in his instructions, he summoned up a chart showing the crucial relationship between the alloy's flexibility and its vibration-damping ability under a virtually infinite variety of snow and temperature conditions.

Because he was an expert skier, Max knew the characteristics needed in a high-performance ski: torsional rigidity, just enough so that the ski can hold an edge under the most demanding conditions but still "snake" through the snow; maximum flexibility so it can absorb bumps without throwing the skier into the air; combined with vibration-damping qualities to prevent the ski from chattering in the lightning changes of terrain a racer encounters not only from run to run but from second to second.

After he touched a few keys the great Cray brain, operating at lightning speed, converted the columns of figures and equations into a three-dimensional representation of a ski moving over the terrain. Using the programs he had laboriously designed during months of after-hours work, Max could, with a few keystrokes, simulate variations in a skier's weight, skill, and speed, temperature and snow conditions, and terrain variations. Despite the legions of designers and engineers the great ski manufacturers employed, what Max could accomplish with the Cray were bound to put him far ahead in terms of ski design.

Watching the computer's graphics system in action gave him more pleasure than looking at great paintings in a museum. Chewing on a fingernail, the only one that had not already been bitten to the quick, he stared.

The ski was behaving exactly as he dreamed it would!

Eureka! He did it! Letting out a whoop, he propelled his chair around the room like a racing car. After the initial flush of excitement, he mentally downshifted to neutral and considered the next steps. There was no question that a huge amount of development work was still needed before an actual ski could be made, but it was clear that a ski of the composition and design he had just seen on his monitor could perform head and shoulders above anything then in production.

With that realization, Max was suddenly hit by a moral dilemma. By all rights, his use of the Cray for personal research, even though all the work had been done on his own time and had no relevance to Monroe's line of business, might entitle the company to possession or ownership of any work done in their employ. Of course, if he erased it from memory, who would know?

The dilemma resolved, he quickly printed out his charts, his equations and calculations, then erased all traces of work from the computer.

The gnawing ethical concerns that continued to trouble Max came to a sudden halt when Monroe was acquired a few weeks later by a rather mysterious raider whose other holdings were totally unrelated to aerospace. In the reorganization that followed the acquisition, Max, along with many of the company's best people, was fired without a review.

Happily grabbing his golden parachute, Max landed on the snowy slopes of Aspen, the perfect laboratory to turn his dream into reality.

CHAPTER ONE

KIT JAMES GAVE A DEEP SIGH AND TURNED TO HER seatmate on the flight to Aspen. They were both returning home after a few weeks of ski training camp on the glaciers of Mount Hood in Oregon. "Do you wonder sometimes if it's worth it?"

Rocky Schneider raised her eyebrows and gave her a weak smile. "I love the racing; it's the training I hate."

"That's what I mean."

"Yeah, but now that we're on the Alpine Select Team . . ."

"World, watch out!"

"Mount Hood was nice," mused Rocky.

"If you like having Hitler for a trainer."

"What? Don't tell me you're looking forward to biking up Independence Pass three times a week and running the Ute Trail full tilt every day, not to mention daily workouts on the weights at the

Aspen Club?" asked Rocky, rolling her eyes in mock horror.

"You make getting back to Aspen sound awful."

The Mount Hood camp had been the final phase of rigorous training until they left for European training before the commencement of the Europa Cup circuit.

"Don't listen to me. You know I love to complain. I'm really looking forward to Europe, aren't you?" asked Rocky.

"I guess so. It's not such a big deal."

"Pardon me, I forgot who I was talking to." Rocky assumed the voice of a bored rich girl. "Paris is so tiresome this time of year, you know. What? London? Again! Oh, the clothes, the jewels, the men. So boring." She stifled a yawn.

Kit jabbed Rocky's ribs with her elbow. "C'mon. Don't be a total shit. You know what I mean." Attempting to snatch victory from the proverbial jaws, she said, "It'll be fun, I'll be your guide."

"One of the girls on the A team said there wasn't much time to go sight-seeing."

"We'll make time."

"Sure. Who needs to sleep?" They grinned and hugged each other.

There was no reason why Kit James and Rocky Schneider should be friends. They were complete opposites in every way: physically, mentally, and socially.

Kit, a classic Princess Di blonde, was the youngest member of what the press referred to tongue-in-cheek as "the James gang." The other members were her half-brother and -sister, Greg and Suzanne. Both had skied on the U.S. Olympic Team and had four silver medals and two bronzes between them.

Kit was a happy-go-lucky girl with the kind of temperament that came from a loving family and a great deal of money. She was a naturally graceful athlete who nevertheless lacked that certain competitive toughness that separates number one from the pack.

On the other hand, Rocky Schneider had competitive spirit to burn. She was a strong, gutsy, daring skier and had been from the moment her father, Pete Schneider, a leading Aspen ski instructor, put her on skis and took her down Ajax Mountain. Her greatest attribute was her concentration, her weakest, her impatience.

She had straight black hair cut in a fringe on her forehead, odd silvery eyes, high cheekbones, and a jaw that expressed her determination. In a few months she'd gone from pudgy girl to strong, well-shaped woman with the defined musculature that seemed to be the hallmark of the young women to whom fitness came before anything.

"Don't you kind of miss having a normal life?" Kit asked her friend.

Rocky watched Kit's eyes get all soft and blurry, the way they did sometimes. "You mean regular school and dates? And being home more? Sure. Who wouldn't? But the chance to get on the Olympic team and win a gold medal. How many people can do that?"

"I guess you're right. You're always right. Still . . . I wonder if I would have bothered if it hadn't been for Suzanne and Greg."

Greg James smiled at his reflection in the mirror, then frowned. Yeah, Suzanne was right, he was getting lines in his face. Probably for the better, he thought. A man didn't need dimples, he needed character.

Although he had never cared for his looks, no one of the feminine persuasion had ever complained. He brushed back the stubborn wave of hair that had sprung from its moussed boundaries to fall in an Elvis Presley lock on his forehead. And smiled. The sulky, pretty-boy face with its quirky lips disappeared. In its place appeared Peter Pan, Peck's Bad Boy, Huck Finn.

An older Russian actress, long defected from the mother country and an avid but awkward skier, had once told him he had a smile that could melt a Bolshevik's heart. He'd used it to remarkable advantage ever since.

He splashed water over his face and head, ran a comb through the thick dark wavy hair again, and slapped some Armani after-shave on his cheeks. In a few minutes he was dressed and ready to go. Downstairs he reached for his suede jacket and pulled it on as he walked to the attached garage.

A new silver BMW awaited. He had pondered its purchase for a long time. Finally, in an attempt to polish his tarnished image, to give himself a more mature look, he had bought it. He had come a long way from the days of being referred to as the Silver Bullet, hadn't he?

In those days, he'd been the heartthrob of the ski groupies. Girls dropped out of the trees into his arms like overripe apples. He wore torn jeans and crazy painted denim jackets, smoked dope, and did coke socially.

Yet, ingratiating as he was (and he could charm both men and women), when the power crowd came to Aspen and wanted a private ski instructor, it was always Tony Frantz they asked for. Not the Silver Bullet, Greg James. They wanted gold, not silver, and Tony Frantz had won many gold medals in his years as the world's number-one ski racer. But he was Austrian and Greg was homegrown.

Recently Greg had decided his playboy image needed taming, at least publicly, so he'd replaced the vintage Corvette and his wild wardrobe with more elegant symbols of his maturity.

He had stopped dating a different girl every night and, up until last week when she had started to make nesting sounds, had semi-lived with Daisy Kenyon, another poor little rich girl ski instructor.

As he slid behind the wheel, the elegant smell of glove leather wrapped around him. It felt as sensuous as a woman's skin. Wait until Kit gets an eyeful of the new machine, he thought. She'd pester him until he let her drive it.

His face softened at the thought of Kit. Outside of the image he saw in his mirror every morning, there was only one other person he truly loved. His half-sister. She was the offspring of his father, the lumber millionaire, and Cee Cee Cromwell, the daughter of the paper tycoon. A merger blessed by Wall Street and the gods of finance. With both parents choosing the English method of nannies and governesses to raise young Kit, it had fallen to Suzanne and him to supply the love. Which, for two inordinately self-centered people, turned out to be surprisingly easy.

Kit had been a wonderful child. Sunny, bright, sweet, affectionate. It wasn't until she'd started racing seriously that Gregory Hamilton James, Sr., took an interest in his youngest. The realization that he might go into the *Guinness Book of Records* with three Olympic medalist children spurred him to a rare expression of fatherhood. But Cee Cee, who'd played doting and beautiful mother for the first six months of Kit's life, was not about to play second fiddle for the rest of her life. She had somehow convinced the senior James that a penthouse in Trump Tower and a *pied-à-terre* in London's Albany was better for both their social and business lives.

So the big house on top of Red Mountain had been given to the children. With Kit skiing all over North America and soon headed for Europe, and Suzanne gallivanting all over the continent in pursuit of fun and games, the house was often empty. But Suzanne, currently between boyfriends, a handsome married senator and a German industrial tycoon, was now home to see if there were any new rich veins to mine that might have materialized while she was away.

And Greg was on his way to get Kit.

Aspen was enjoying one of its rare lazy golden late-fall days. It was quiet, the air invigorating with ozone, the sky an endless bowl of blue. Gone were the hordes of summer, the music festival people, the artists, designers, architects, and humanitarians who filled the small town to overflowing from June until August. Yet to come were the even greater hordes of winter. Locals were taking a big breath and relaxing between the hectic seasons, reclaiming the town for themselves, eating in the good restaurants without making reservations weeks in advance.

There was much grumbling and moaning over what had happened to the sleepy silver town since the world and the developers had found that dry powder, sunshine, and a great mountain was a magnet that drew the rich and famous like helpless iron filings.

In truth the town's commercial coffers bulged with many different kinds of coin of the realm, all easily converted to show a very black bottom line. Culture was proving to be as lucrative as skiing, which was no accident. In the old silver boom days, many of Aspen's first families had been Eastern born and educated, and when they came west to better the family fortunes, they brought their cultural heritages with them. Whereas today they might buy their first BMW, in those days the purchase was likely to have been an exquisitely carved piano from Mr. Bechstein or Mr. Steinway.

There were houses and madams and soiled doves a'plenty then, but there were also six newspapers, an opera house, a literary society, a glee club, many churches—and forty-three saloons. When silver collapsed, culture was put on a dusty shelf. It wasn't until Walter Paepcke and his indomitable wife, Pussy, arrived in the forties that fortunes changed.

All during the Depression the Victorian houses, those elegant symbols of wealth, lay in disrepair, abandoned, shuttered, forlorn. Dusty unpaved roads cracked in the hot dry sun. The opera house was quiet. Even the gaudy Hotel Jerome, known mostly for a powerful drink made with milk and bourbon, had grown faded and shabby. Paepcke, attracted by the town's isolation and purity, saw a dream rise in front of his eyes—a combination of Sparta and Salzburg, culture and nature striding hand in hand to give modern man the benefits of sound mind and sound body.

The down-and-out town was his for a song. Abandoned houses went for back taxes, others were delighted to sell out to the crazy man from Chicago and head for greener pastures.

At a town meeting Paepcke drew up a formal plan to create his modern-day version of Plato's Republic. Unfortunately, not all the cowboys and members of the mercantile establishment were interested in going along with his plans. He was the interloper, the rich stranger, the city "feller," and his autocratic pronouncements and desires were met with the same town-versus-stranger hostility that still exists when the town discusses its future.

If the sunny, dry Aspen winters attracted the

celebrities of Hollywood and New York, the Aspen summers brought in the top business leaders, intellectuals, and artists to perform and partake of the Aspen Institute for Humanistic Studies and Music Festivals. Someone once called it summer camp for the cerebrals.

But now, today, the dusty streets were quiet, the sidewalks along Main Street were filled with nothing more than the last of the burnished autumn leaves, and even the dust motes seemed to be suspended in midair. If you stopped and held your breath, you could hear the measured plops of early-morning runners on the roads and shoulders that stretched out toward the various passes. But those sounds were muffled by the screech of Skil saws, the crack of nails being hammered into wood, and the drawl and twang of the country music stations that Aspen workmen preferred to big-city rock.

A sign of the town's progress was its airport. Once a small jerry-built affair with a single landing strip and daylight-only flying, it had recently undergone a several-million-dollar expansion. Finished only this summer, it was already in need of another expansion.

Ignoring the newly enlarged parking lot that required quarters (which he rarely had), Greg James pulled his car into a no-parking zone without a qualm. Everyone knew his plate, they wouldn't bother him. Besides, he'd be in and out before anyone could notice.

He waved to a couple of people and strode through the waiting room, debating whether to get a cup of coffee at the Pour la France bar in case the United Express plane was late. Before he could make his way there, the loudspeaker announced its arrival.

The usual small crowd debarked. Ranchers in Stetsons and boots probably returning from Greeley and Fort Collins where their feed pens were, Lucy's ladies, a flock of Lucy Smith's single friends who traveled and socialized as a group, just returning from a shopping expedition to Denver. And finally Kit, standing at the top of the rickety steps in animated conversation with a striking dark-haired girl. He squinted at the familiar face.

"It can't be," he said softly. "Last year she was just a pudgy little kid."

"You talkin' to me, mister?" A grizzled old fellow in faded jeans looked at him curiously.

Greg ignored him and walked out the door to wait. He gave Kit a piercing whistle and waved his hand to get her attention. Recognizing the whistle, she looked around. Spotting him at last, she waved in return, a big smile creasing her face.

She raced down the steps and across the field to fling her arms around her brother.

"Hey, take it easy. You'll break the jacket."

"Greg! I didn't know you were going to meet me."

"Would I let a stranger pick up my baby sister?"

Rocky stood to one side and watched the little scene covetously. Greg James was so good-looking. He had a classic skier's body: broad shoulders, lean hips, heavily muscled thighs, and a constant tan. But he was old. Maybe thirty or more.

Kit turned to Rocky and pulled her forward. "Greg, you remember Rocky Schneider, don't you?"

"I remember the name but not the face. You certainly have changed in a year." His eyes were warm in their appraisal. She blushed furiously.

"Oh, oh, did I say the wrong thing?"

"No, it's just that I didn't know . . . that is, I didn't think . . . I mean . . . I don't know what I mean . . ." She trailed off with a lopsided smile.

"That's okay." He put his arm around her shoulders and hugged her. Then, without removing it, he placed his other arm around Kit's. "C'mon, champ, let's get your stuff. I want to hear about training camp."

Rocky tried to match his stride and in her awkwardness got her feet tangled with his. She was about to apologize when he smiled and said, "Is someone coming to meet you?"

"I was supposed to call Mom when I got in."

"Well, call her and tell her not to bother. I'll drop you off on our way home. You live in town, don't you?"

"Midland Avenue," she said, naming the road that meandered around one of the more modest developments in Aspen.

As Rocky went off to phone her mother, Greg said, "You two seem to be pretty thick."

"Yeah, I guess we've gotten to be good friends over the last year. It's so hard to make friends when you're training all the time."

"Tell me," he said fervently, "so how are things going?"

"Okay."

"Just okay?"

Kit shrugged. "I'm tired. It's been a long year."

"You've got a long way to go before Christmas." Abruptly he changed the subject. "What about her?" he gestured with his chin to the absent Rocky. "How's she doing?"

"Oh, she's terrific. Nobody can beat her. I know she's going to make the A team."

"So are you, babe."

"I guess so." Kit looked doubtful, but noticing her brother's expression, forced a winning smile.

"Sure, I will. But Rocky's the best. I mean, one of these days she's going to take a gold, I just know it."

As Kit waxed enthusiastic about her friend's technique, Greg tried to interrupt. "Kit! Kit!"

"What?" she asked plaintively.

"You sound like her press agent. Haven't you forgotten something?"

"What?"

"She may be your friend, but when she's in the starting gate she's just another rival."

The unmistakable yeasty smell of baking bread filled the small house on Midland Avenue. In a chipped earthenware bowl that had once belonged to her grandmother, a lump of dough was rising. Sally Burke Schneider plucked it out, cradling it in the palm of her hands as if it were a small bird. Punching it down, she gave a wry smile and turned to the marmalade cat that sprawled in the sun washing its face. "This feels just like my backside."

The cat turned its face away as if she had heard the complaint too many times.

Sally put the dough back into the bowl for another rising and turned to make a sandwich for her solitary lunch. She slapped mustard on diet bread and thought how much she hated liverwurst and hot-dog relish, but the mountain of unpaid bills on her untidy kitchen counter were a constant rebuke. Visions of smoked salmon and sturgeon on rye with cucumbers and onion slices, a sandwich she had once tasted and loved but was forced to forget when she married Peter Schneider, danced in her head. On a ski instructor's salary the Schneider family ate tasty mystery casseroles and chili. Sally could do incredible things with ground beef and had over three hundred recipes for chicken. With a sigh she began to sort

the bills into several piles: those to be paid immediately or else, those that could wait until the end
of the month, and those that could wait through at
least three months of steadily growing-in-nastiness
reminders culminating in the final admonition
that the matter was being placed in the hands of a
collection agency.

Morosely she looked at her handkerchief-sized
kitchen. The acrylic tile that was meant to look
like expensive Italian quarry tile had so much wax
buildup it had almost turned black, and no amount
of wax remover and elbow grease would clean it.
She should replace it, but that would cost at least
six hundred dollars. Otherwise it was a cheerful
kitchen. The cabinetry was a pine veneer. There
were gay gingham curtains at the windows, kitch-
en herbs and flowering plants on the sills. An old
ice-cream table had replaced the big maple one
after Peter died. With Rocky rarely home, it was
big enough for her and Eric to eat their meals.
Even Eric, that happy-go-lucky extrovert, so much
like his father, was rarely home for meals. He was
a popular kid. His friends all had mothers who
loved having him to dinner because he was such a
good influence on their own rowdy boys.

Stern, loving discipline had been Sally's way of
dealing with her children. She never said no
without giving good reasons for it. She taught that
permission carried responsibility. If Eric was
allowed to go to a hockey game or a movie, it was
up to him to come home when he promised.

It had been tough saying no to Eric and Rocky
when they wanted things, tough because most of
their friends were comfortably well-off. Remembering her own Spartan childhood gave her pangs
of guilt. Most parents today wanted to give their
kids more than they had had. Sally couldn't. Even
holding down several jobs left little over for luxu-

ries. But they had survived, and hope sprang eternal.

Sally idly poked holes in the rising dough, watching it deflate like a tire with a slow leak, which reminded her that she needed to take her car in to have the tires checked before the advent of real winter.

"Hey, anybody home?" Rocky's vibrant voice interrupted her thoughts. "Your favorite daughter has finally arrived."

"Hi, baby!" Sally turned with a huge smile and came to hug and kiss her daughter.

"What are you doing?" Rocky pulled out a chair and slumped into it with a happy sigh.

"The usual. Wondering if I should try robbing a bank or look for a beaded bag and hit the streets."

"You're too old, and besides you have to worry about AIDS. How about the Publisher's Clearing House? Or Lucky Lotta Dollars? Or marrying a millionaire?"

"We should trade places. You be the mother for a while and I'll be the kid."

Although Rocky was a knowledgeable sixteen-year-old in many respects, many of Sally's friends found the frank exchanges between mother and daughter a little too frisky at times. But Sally had never believed in using dainty euphemisms for bodily functions or pretending that life did not have a dark side. What she recognized in her daughter so clearly was herself, not only a physical resemblance but the mind-set as well. Fortunately Rocky's intensity was ameliorated by her light mocking sense of humor.

"How was training camp?"

"The usual." Rocky stood up and stretched, then opened the refrigerator to poke through the shelves. She took out the orange juice container and put it to her lips.

Her mother gave her a warning look. "I don't let your brother do that."

"Sorry. Forgot." She poured herself a glass of o.j., put the container back, and reached for an apple. "Training camp is so boring." She sighed.

"Like practicing scales when you want to play Rachmaninoff?" Sally gave Rocky's knapsack a backward glance as she tripped over it.

"Sorry about that." Rocky picked up the shapeless hulk and hung it on the hook behind the kitchen door, giving her mother a gentle smile. She sat down next to her and picked up Sally's hand, playing with the fingers absently, then took the uneaten half of Sally's sandwich and popped it into her mouth. "I missed home, Mom. Especially when you bake bread. I could smell it before I got to the house. What's the problem?"

"Why does there have to be a problem?"

"Because when you bake bread or clean out your drawers and closets, there's generally something bugging you."

"Nothing special. The usual. Life. And unpaid bills."

Rocky gave a deep sigh and was about to speak when Sally put her finger to her lips. "None of this is your problem. Everything will get paid eventually. I'll get a couple of handbag orders and we'll have some mad money."

"Hang on for another year, Mom. Once I make the A team, we'll be in Fat City. And if I win big on World Cup, I can make tons of money with endorsements, and I'll give it to you."

"You will not! You'll put it in a money fund and use it for college."

"Ma-a-a!" They'd had this discussion before and it always came out the same way. "You spent money so I could race . . ."

"It's part of being a parent. It could have been

piano or ballet or summer tutoring or braces. Instead it was ski racing. That's it and that's all. I declare that this subject has been tabled permanently. Now I want to know what your schedule is for the next couple of weeks." Rocky wet her finger and picked up the bread crumbs from her mother's plate. "You still hungry? Shall I make you something to eat?"

"C'mon, Mom, I'm not helpless. I can make my own sandwich."

Sally carried her plate and cup to the sink and turned on the water to rinse the dishes as the timer alarm sounded.

"Bread's done. Shall I pull it out?"

"Please, but don't turn off the oven. I have another loaf to go in. And you're not to touch it until it cools," Sally warned. Rocky had always loved freshly baked bread, still hot from the oven and slathered in butter and blackberry jam. Sally's mother, who had lived with them briefly before she died, used to warn the child that worms would grow in her stomach from eating food that was too hot. Sally thought briefly about her poor, pitiful, weak mother.

"Who did you say brought you home?" Sally asked. When Rocky called she had simply said she'd gotten a ride and Sally didn't have to bother to fetch her.

"Kit's brother came to pick her up. He offered to drive me home."

"Greg James?" Sally frowned.

"Yeah. You act as if it's a problem."

"No . . ."

"But?"

"But nothing." Sally busied herself with the fresh dough, then asked casually, "Did he say anything to you?"

"You mean other than hello, how are you?" She

shrugged. "No, I don't remember anything else."
The frown had not disappeared from her mother's
face. "What is it, Mom? I mean, has he raped
someone or just gotten out of prison, or what?"

"Nothing, honey. He just has a reputation
for . . ." She stopped.

Rocky blushed. "Well, stop worrying. As far as
he's concerned, I'm just his kid sister's friend."

The fortuitous ringing of the phone ended that
conversation before it became tricky.

Rocky, who was nearest the phone, picked it up
and said hello. "Hi, Daisy, how are you? Yeah, just
a few minutes ago. I'm great. Yeah, me too. See
you soon. Here's Mom."

She passed the phone to her mother and while
Sally spoke Rocky tore the end from the hot bread
and popped it in her mouth. It was like a mouthful
of heaven, resting on her tongue like a snowflake
before it melted in her mouth. Her mother made
the greatest bread in the world. Crusty outside,
chewy, full of interesting things like raisins or nuts
or cinnamon inside.

"Wait a sec, I'll ask her." Sally covered the
phone with her hand and turned to her daughter.
"Daisy needs a fourth for doubles. What do you
think? I hate to leave when you've just come
home."

"Go ahead, have fun. We'll see each other later.
Maybe I'll bike over and watch."

"You sure?"

"Positive."

"Okay, Daisy. I'll be there in a half hour."
Hanging up the phone, she said, "Honey, will you
take the new bread out when the timer goes off?"

"Don't worry, Mom. I'll take care of everything." Rocky shook her head in mock despair.
Ever since her father died, Sally seemed to worry
about everything.

Sally had always been a worrier. Marriage to Peter Schneider had done little to change it. Happy-go-lucky Peter had been an entrancing lover, a perfect travel companion, a superb athlete. But he wanted to live like a millionaire on a ski instructor's salary. When she married him she moved into a higher plane of worrydom. It was only after his death that she realized how desperate their financial plight was. For the last four years, she'd held down several jobs to pay off long-standing bills and keep their heads above water.

She quickly changed into tennis gear. Revving up the old Subaru, she headed out to the Silver Leaf Tennis Club, the most exclusive club in Aspen, owned, as was the famous Silver Leaf Inn and Silver Leaf Spa, by Sophie MacNeal Mallory, descendent of one of Aspen's first families.

Sally was much in demand as a tennis partner. Thanks to Daisy Kenyon, a friend and fellow ski instructor, she was able to play as a guest at a club whose initiation fee was more than she made in a year.

Young, rich, and divorced, Daisy, who had everything but a close friend, had been delighted to find Sally. Reticent at first and a little turned off by Daisy's exuberant possessiveness, Sally had gradually been won over by the other woman's generosity of spirit. It was Daisy who had expanded Sally's horizons beyond the tight clique of ski instructors and wives which had defined her social circle since her arrival in Aspen sixteen years ago, a new bride, married to a man she hardly knew and very pregnant.

After four years without him, Sally could barely remember what her husband had looked like. Her memories were of a man in constant motion, motion that seemed to blur his features and soften the hard edges of her feelings of frustration. Their conversations had never been particularly intellectual or philosophical, although before she'd dropped out of college she had delighted in staying up till all hours debating the finer points of the English Romantic poets or the French Illuminationists.

The poet Rimbaud had been one of her particular favorites. The summer she met Peter in Europe she had seen remarkable similarities between them. His passive resistance and vagabondage was dangerously attractive to a young woman ready to fall in love. And fall in love she did. With Greece, with eye-blinding light, and Homer's wine-dark seas, with the whitewashed island villages, the fresh fish plucked from the sea, the aromatic retsina tasting like pine trees, the grapes that burst in her mouth and ran down her chin to fall on her bare topless chest, and with Peter, who was happy to lick the juice from her salty body. She was a woman drugged with light and love and thousands of years of epic poetry and history.

To think she might not have met him if she had been the dutiful daughter she was expected to be. Much against her parents' wishes, she and several friends from Colby College had decided to bicycle through Europe one summer. It was on a beach in Crete that she had seen the handsome young Austrian ski instructor who was also bicycling around Europe. At the time, skiing seemed enough to draw them together. By the end of the summer they were lovers.

Like most ex-Olympic skiers from Europe, he had a small nest egg from loyal supporters which permitted him the luxury of inviting her to join forces with him and travel farther.

In those days, buoyed with the optimism of

youth, she was sure she could return to real life with him and find success and happiness. When it was time to return, Peter was determined to leave Austria for greener pastures and marry her. She was so wild about him, the thought of finishing college had disappeared from her mind. That was not all that disappeared. Their money had, too. Sally returned to Maine to wait while Peter contacted a cousin living in America who arranged for him to come to Aspen as a ski instructor.

As soon as the arrangements were made, Peter flew to Boston, where Sally met him. Two days later they were married. A month later she discovered she was pregnant, and by the end of November they were on their way to Aspen.

They had stayed with the cousin, Tony Frantz, while Sally looked for a place to live, not the easiest thing for people of modest means to find in Aspen, where tiny run-down Victorian houses in the West End sold for several hundred thousand dollars and rentals, if they existed at all, could run several thousand a month.

At first they had lived in a mobile home in Woody Creek, but with the child about to be born, Peter refused to raise it in a trailer camp. By luck or divine providence, a small two-bedroom house became available in the Midland area and with a down payment borrowed from Tony was bought and presented fait accompli to Sally. Under the circumstances she could barely refuse.

Tony Frantz. She'd never been quite comfortable with her husband's cousin. From the first she'd always felt his cool blue eyes appraising her, and not critically either. But he'd never by word or deed stepped out of line. Over the years they had developed a *modus vivendi* which consisted of her playing Dear Abby, offering unasked-for advice.

He, on the other hand, had adopted a teasing attitude which disguised any real meaning or feelings.

The children adored him, accepting him unequivocally. He was good for them. The male figure that Eric needed and could look up to, the caring father that every girl needed to set the tone for future relationships. With Rocky, Tony had become much more. He was her teacher and her coach. More than anyone else, he had made Rocky the racer she was today.

Despite their cautious, walking-on-eggs friendship, there was nothing Sally wouldn't do for him or he for her. Neither one could possibly realize on that bright sunny day in October that they would have the chance to prove that fact to each other very soon.

CHAPTER TWO

THE DAY FELT AS SOFT AS SUMMER DESPITE THE SNOW on the higher elevations. Those who could were out enjoying the rare late-October days, for there was no knowing when the first real winter storms would blanket the Roaring Fork Valley with snow. The last few seasons had been sparse ones. The snow was late in coming, though the mountain would open in time for Thanksgiving with man-made snow on a limited number of trails. Howev- er, this kind of skiing didn't produce crowds, which was a real hardship for Sally. Ski school classes would be small, and only a handful of instructors would be needed until the Christmas season brought the capacity crowds.

Like most really good instructors, Sally had developed a clientele of faithfuls who returned every year for lessons. She was certainly not in a class with Greg James or Tony Frantz, but with the

recent addition of the four-day intensive Mountain
Master Classes, she was assured of decent tips.

But skiing was the furthest thing from her mind
as she headed her car down Highway 82 toward
the club. The breeze blowing in through the open
window was crisp and sharp with the smell of pine
and sage. These were the kind of days when she
just wanted to point the car's nose in any direction
and follow it, get lost. But it was a fanciful dream
and no matter how bad things got, she was not the
kind of woman who could abandon all responsibility and fly off into the sunset.

The peaks of Daley and Sopris loomed like
painted backdrops in the crystalline, dust-free air,
lending a sense of unreality to a town that already
seemed unreal to her. She had this feeling every
time she was invited to the club—as though she
were setting foot on a stage to act out a part that
had been written for her: the society girl's true-
blue friend with a tart mouth and a loving heart.
Or was it the hooker with a heart of gold? It didn't
matter. Living off Daisy's largesse was practically
the same thing. She had had the temerity to tell
that to Daisy once. The thunderclouds had gathered on her friend's narrow face as tears filled her
hazel eyes. "If that's the way you feel," she'd said,
trying to control the hurt anger, "then fuck off."
Daisy was not shy when it came to using any
expletive that conveyed her sense of outrage. "You
don't know how to be a friend or accept friendship," she'd continued, developing a fine head of
steam as she settled into the task of chewing her
erstwhile friend out. Finally, Sally had put up her
hands in surrender and begged abjectly for forgiveness. But she still wasn't able to get over the feeling
of being the poor relation.

The Silver Leaf Golf and Tennis Club was a
multimillion-dollar facility typical of Aspen. What

other small town could support so many fancy fitness and health clubs when there were hardly enough permanent residents to fill even one? Locals could join the smaller clubs for as little as fifteen hundred dollars a year, depending on whether they played winter or summer tennis, golf, or wanted to include their family in the memberships. Non-locals would have to pay a minimum of five thousand dollars a year, and even short-term visitors could be accommodated for a major consideration of cash.

Sophie's Silver Leaf Club offered everything from baby-sitting to bridge partners, airport delivery and pickup, social activities and seminars, pools indoor and out, ballrooms indoor and out, and the best golf course in the area. There were a first-class restaurant, after-hours club, and cabaret.

But it was the tennis facility that made it so desirable. There were six indoor courts with state-of-the-art lighting that duplicated sunshine without the glare and twenty courts outdoors with underground water systems to keep the har-tru courts playable in the hot, dry, high-altitude atmosphere.

Sally parked her car in Daisy's guest slot and waved to Bee Gee Whitaker, the club's manager. She knew Bee Gee did not approve of Sally's constant appearance at the club but could hardly say anything to Daisy, who was rich, vocal, and active in bringing in more than her share of new members.

Unlike its Victorian counterpart, the Silver Leaf Inn, the Silver Leaf Club was unabashedly Aspen contemporary. A low-profiled series of interconnecting buildings, it nestled amongst the hills, glass-curtain walls facing south and west to catch the winter sun and focus on the splendid sunsets.

The rest of the walls were a combination of river stone and fir beams. Jagged rooflines echoed the profiles of the mountain range that was visible at every turn. The bar and lounge had been done by Sophie Mallory's former daughter-in-law. Rare Navaho rugs from Sophie's huge collection covered the terra-cotta quarry-tile floors. Spaced around the room and creating intimate groups were glove-leather couches and chairs. The vast room was a paean to the best of native Southwestern art. The art on the walls was an ever-changing display of the contemporary Indian artists of the day as well as those of Samantha Mallory, Sophie's daughter, who was rapidly becoming a respected Southwestern artist in her own right.

Pragmatic as she was, there were times when Sally had daydreams about leaving her cramped little house on Midland for the vast spaces and rich appointments of a smaller version of the Silver Leaf Club.

"Here she is!" Daisy Kenyon came to Sally's side, gave her a hug, and pulled her over to the table where several women in tennis clothes sat under the bright blue umbrellas.

Every court was occupied. Most of the players had learned their game from the club's local pro, a former ranking champion from Sweden, and it was readily apparent from the consistency and similarity of their ground strokes. Most hit two-handed backhands and big, looping topspin forehands. They all had the same weakness at net, where the two-handed backhand limited their reach. Sally waved to Tony Frantz, who was changing sides with his partner Richard Farwell. On the next court was the actor Roger Standish playing with his look-alike George Hamilton, while Sunshine Campbell, Roger's longtime significant other, who hated sports of any kind, sat under the umbrella reading a book. Pat and Rachel Mallory, who had recently married after his divorce from his scheming, venal first wife, were playing with Samantha Mallory and her companion, Joe Ferris. Joe, who had been the manager of the Silver Mountain Ski Corp, was now the executive manager of the club as well as the club's ranking golfer.

She also recognized half of the ski school either drinking or playing with Aspen's most prestigious names. She saw Greg James rallying with his sister, Kit, and frowned even though she knew she was being foolish. Just because he'd given Rocky a ride home was no reason to suspect him of anything underhanded. But Sally knew the Jameses all too well.

She and Suzanne had grown up together in Maine.

"Now, don't be mad, but we're playing against Suzanne and her friend."

"Daisy! You know how I feel about Suzanne."

"I couldn't help it."

"Why didn't you call Hildy or Sue or Anne?" She named three other instructors who were excellent players.

"They're out of town. Anyway, we'll beat them in straight sets. That should make you feel good."

Once she and Suzanne James had been as close as sisters, growing up next door to each other in Berwick, a charming old shipbuilding town in Maine filled with gracious houses and fiercely independent people.

The two girls had been inseparable. They'd gone to the same grade school, started skiing at the same time, raced as youngsters. Sally spent more time at Suzanne's house than at her own home, which was not difficult. The senior Jameses were fun, affectionate with each other and their children, while her own father seemed to have stepped out of a dark novel by Hawthorne. He was a cold, forbidding man who never touched her or kissed her but expected her to excel in whatever she set her mind to. Her mother was a shadowy figure, pretty but colorless, fearful, a handmaiden to her father's every request and often on the receiving end of his unprovoked anger.

Her father considered the Jameses frivolous and trivial, accusing them of filling Sarah's mind (he refused to call her Sally as everyone else did) with foolish nonsense and delusions of grandeur. When Christmas and birthdays rolled around, Suzanne would get lockets and pearls and charm bracelets. Sally's father thought such things vain and useless. Sally got pajamas, shoes, or books. When she began to wear lipstick, he had ordered her to scrub her face or he'd do it for her. He was a Fundamentalist, who took religion and sin seriously, a man who could be charming with strangers but never with family. Though she fought him quietly all her young life, she had grown up like him in more ways than she wanted to admit.

While Suzanne was instructed to enjoy life, Sally was forced to abjure pleasure for hard work and excellence. Yet, when Sally brought home perfect report cards or A papers, her father barely acknowledged her efforts. Instead of giving up, she had only forced herself to do better, waiting for the day when her best effort would finally be good enough to coax praise from his narrow lips.

By the time they'd reached high school, the girls' relationship took a sudden turn for the worse. Sally had turned into a driven, intense young woman. Her desire to succeed took precedence over everything else; but it took an inward turn, too. While Suzanne judged her competence in relationship to other people, Sally competed only against her self, setting secret goals and meeting them silently. Soon she had developed the reputation for being a little strange, as she walked around with a smile when there was no reason for smiling.

The friendship, tenuous at best, strained to the breaking point over a boy. In her junior year, Sally had fallen in love with Bryan Blaisdell, a bright, good-looking kid who was number one on the ski team and the star of the baseball team. For some odd reason, he seemed to like her, too. Transformed by first love, Sally relinquished some of her solitary ways and relaxed her unyielding standards. She was just beginning to feel good about herself when Suzanne, privy to every detail of the budding relationship as Sally's best friend, decided to make a play for him.

Suzanne was considered to be the best-looking girl in school. Because of her family's wealth and social position in the town, she hung out with the an older country club crowd and had started to drink and smoke at an early age. In another era, she would have been called "fast."

One toss of her long blond hair and bat of her long-lashed blue eyes and Bryan Blaisdell was silly putty. What made the whole thing so awful was that Sally had planned to go to the Spring Dance with Bryan and had spent months convincing her father that she had to have a formal dress. When days and days went by without Bryan extending the formal invitation, she'd finally swallowed her pride and asked him. He had turned red, developing a sudden fascination with his feet as he tried to stumble through an explanation.

She had not gone to the dance. And she had never thrown away the dress. It hung in her closet, a constant reminder of her best friend's perfidy and the weakness of the male.

Suzanne continued on her merry way stealing

boys and losing girlfriends, barely making passing grades, driving her new Corvette too fast and learning how to talk her way out of trouble. If it were not for her excellence at gymnastics and skiing, her reputation would have been in tatters.

Sally, who enjoyed skiing for its own sake and for the joy of conquering the mountain, watched the competitive Suzanne get so proficient that she was finally named to the women's Olympic team. From the Olympics it had been a mud-puddle jump to international celebrity. They were not to meet again until both came to Aspen.

By that time Suzanne was a self-created legend. She had developed into a tall, slender, silver-haired goddess, the glamour girl of the skiing circuit, the winner of an Olympic silver medal in the slalom, a cover girl, a one-shot movie star, the girlfriend of a host of men whose names were always featured in such magazines as *People*, *W*, *Elle*, *The Tatler*, *Paris Match*, *Stern*, and the gossip columns. At any given moment she was reputed to be engaged to Sylvester Stallone, Don Johnson, Teddy Kennedy, Henry Kissinger, Hulk Hogan, Prince Albert, and/or Prince Rainier. She was the playgirl of the Western world, and with her penchant for other women's men was now called Jesse behind her back. Jesse James! It was an apt sobriquet.

As Daisy and Sally came up to the table and sat down, Suzanne continued talking to her companion for several more minutes before raising her head to acknowledge the other women. She glanced at her watch, then smiled at Sally. "I see you are still a paragon of punctuality," she said, managing to put the compliment in the same class with child molesting.

"Old habits die hard," Sally answered smoothly. "You certainly are the living proof of that."

Marcella Richards gave the two obviously hostile women a glance and raised her eyebrows as if asking Daisy what it all meant. Daisy shrugged in return. Sally put out her hand to Marcella and said, "Hello, I'm Sally Burke. And you're . . . ?"

"Marcella Richards."

"Glad to meet you. Are you visiting?"

Suzanne interrupted smoothly, "Marcella's just bought the Di Lucca house."

With that statement Sally was meant to understand that Marcella was rich, successful, and out of her league.

Sally stood up and took her racket from its cover, thus putting an end to the conversation. "Shall we play tennis?"

As the women walked to their court, they made an odd foursome. Daisy, not even a hundred pounds soaking wet, looked like a twelve-year-old in her white shorts and polo shirt. Marcella, in a jazzy Fila outfit, wore a diamond "tennis" bracelet and Peretti two-carat diamond on a chain around her neck. She carried the newest Prince racket and wore the latest "hot" tennis shoe. She looked every inch the successful lady tycoon. Suzanne, her silver-blond hair held back with a ribbon, wore a black Ralph Lauren outfit that displayed her lean, boyish figure to best advantage, while Sally had on a pair of Rocky's running shorts and one of Eric's old T-shirts. Suzanne gave her a chilly smile. "I'm surprised they let you in the club in that getup."

"I am, too," said Sally. "I guess it's a tribute to my friend."

"Or your game," said Daisy, acknowledging what almost everyone knew. Sally Burke Schneider was one of the best nonprofessional players in town and good enough for Martina to hit with when she couldn't find another partner.

They warmed up for a few minutes, their styles immediately becoming apparent in that short time. Suzanne was anxious to get started while Sally methodically went through each stroke until she was satisfied that her game was in order.

Marcella had a good workmanlike game that once might have been quite a bit better. Nevertheless she was much more consistent than Suzanne James, who expended a great deal of energy running about, overhitting every ball that came to her, and turning the court into a version of Swan Lake. It had the desired effect. Though she won few points, she earned a great deal of masculine attention.

Daisy was a machine and powerful for her size. She was lightning fast at net, poaching every return and more often than not sending it sizzling back out of reach of the slower Marcella. But it was Sally who had the complete game. A big booming kicky serve which she came in behind for a deep approach shot and putaway volley.

It was all over in less than an hour.

Sally, who normally played tennis for the love of the game and not for the win, was, in this case, more pleased than she would let on. Beating Suzanne was as good as a second helping of ice cream.

"You play very good tennis," said Marcella admiringly as she extended her hand in congratulations.

"You play pretty well yourself," said Sally.

"I don't get much of a chance these days," said Marcella, wiping her forehead and gesturing to the waiter with the same motion.

"Marcella's the president of Richco."

"I'm afraid I'm not familiar with that."

Marcella smiled. "Why should you be? It's not IBM."

"Don't be modest," said Suzanne crossly. Then, turning to Sally, she explained as if talking to a slow child, "It's a huge fashion and cosmetics company, one of the biggest in the world. Marcella's developing a new ski line. And of course, I'm working with her."

"Of course," said Sally.

Marcella ordered iced tea for them.

"I'm trying to talk Marcella into doing a ski film out here this winter. You know, like the one that Suzy Chaffee and Willy Bogner did. Like a music video. Lots of flash and glitz."

"Sure, why not?" Daisy said. "Who cares if it's been done before?"

"This would be entirely different." Suzanne colored. "Don't you think Don and Bruce and Martina and Chris would get a kick out of doing it just for fun?"

"Surely, you jest!" said Daisy, rolling her eyes.

"I don't know any stars who do things like that just for fun," said Marcella, who was trying to figure out the exact relationships between these so-called friends.

Aha, thought Sally, the lady is no pushover for Suzanne's brand of bullshit. Well, why should she be? You didn't build an empire before you were forty by being gullible. Sally gave Marcella a covert look. She was probably over forty but not by much, although she had that lapidary hardness that comes from fighting your way to the top. She spoke softly and smiled ingratiatingly, but the voice displayed vestiges of an accent that Sally recognized as New York. And though she appeared relaxed and at ease as she slumped back in the comfortable deck chair, dark eyes darted from face to face, weighing, deliberating, judging, looking for the weakness, the soft spots, the telling gesture. Yes, this was a woman who had learned to make quick and accurate judgments. She wondered if Marcella really liked Suzanne or if

Suzanne were just a convenience for her. After all, if she were going into a new ski line of beauty and fashion, who better to promote it than Suzanne. Though she hadn't won a medal in sixteen years, she was an internationally known celebrity and wherever she went, even to the john, a camera was not far away.

"Good afternoon, fellow athletes."

Four heads turned as Tony Frantz approached their table. He was dripping wet and his soaked shirt clung to his torso, revealing every hard muscular line. He wiped his face and hair with the silver towel that bore the club's name in a darker silver-gray embroidered monogram. He pulled a chair around from an adjoining table but kept his distance, "out of deference to your delicate noses." Then, turning to Sally, he said, "Has our kid returned?"

Marcella gave Suzanne a questioning look, but before Suzanne could offer an explanation, Sally answered. "Not only back, but here." She gestured to Rocky, who was making her appearance around the flower bed. Spotting Tony, Rocky waved and, turning to speak to someone briefly in passing, hurried over to them.

"Hello, champ," he said softly, getting up to give her a bear hug. "Let me look at you." She stood away from him and turned slowly around, giving him her weight lifter's pose. To Marcella's amusement and Suzanne's annoyance, he swatted her bottom, then pulled her onto his knee.

"Phew!" She held her nose. "You smell like a racehorse."

"Rocky!" warned Sally.

"Well, he does, Mom." Then, turning to the others, she said hello, stopping momentarily to stare at the woman she didn't know and the glittering bracelet on her wrist. As an Aspen kid, she was accustomed to seeing women and men, too, in jewels and furs and the glitzy finery that gave the ski resort one of its reputations. But diamond tennis bracelets were new to her.

"Rocky, this is Marcella Richards. Marcella, my daughter."

"I gathered as much. And you have just returned from . . . ?"

"Kit and I were at summer training camp in Oregon."

"Of course, you're the up-and-coming racer."

Suzanne, who hated being away from the center of attention for more than thirty seconds, made an attempt to turn the spotlight back on herself as she addressed Tony. "Hello, darling. Did you have a good game with Richard?"

Without looking directly at her, Tony said, "Not bad." He was deep into conversation with Rocky. The two had their heads together like conspirators.

"Sweetie, excuse me for interrupting, but Marcella would like us to join her at Gordon's for dinner tonight. I said yes. I hope you don't mind."

"Whatever," he said absently.

So this was the famous Tony Frantz, thought Marcella. He wasn't quite what she expected. He was shorter, more rugged-looking, blonder. She knew he was in his mid-thirties, but he looked younger, even though the dark circles under his eyes said otherwise. For the last few years, since she'd been coming to Aspen, she'd wanted to ski with the legendary Olympian, but he was never available. Now she'd finally met him on a tennis court!

Marcella had never fooled herself, and she was not about to now. At her age it was difficult to meet a man. As a highly successful woman with a multimillion-dollar business, her own jet, three homes, and an income in the high six figures, it was almost impossible. Even if the perfect man for her did exist, she had little time to encourage a relationship. She had gotten accustomed to taking romance where she found it.

Once it was the captain of a yacht she had rented on the Riviera, a Frenchman half her age, an accomplished sailor and a skilled lover. They had parted after a week with no regrets, he was thousands of dollars richer, she was replete with satisfaction.

For a while it had been her chauffeur, then the Italian gardener at her weekend house in Connecticut. In Aspen, she'd chosen her ski instructors as much for their ability in the sack as on the slopes. However, the legendary Tony Frantz had been elusive. The fact that he was currently escorting Suzanne bothered her not in the least. She knew Suzanne too well. Currently between the senator and the German industrialist, Tony Frantz was simply filler.

"Excuse me," Marcella interrupted, "I haven't met Tony yet."

Tony looked up. His eyes narrowed. Between that moment and his quick smile he had made a tally of Marcella Richards. She was sleek with long legs, narrow waisted with heavy lush breasts that seemed to want to burst out of the skimpy tennis top she wore. Her best feature was her eyes. They were a deep chocolate-brown, framed with long curling lashes, and there was nothing shy or retiring about the steady way they clung to his. He recognized the invitation immediately. He'd seen that look enough times.

When he was a young racer with nothing but good looks and determination, he'd met a famous actress at one of the World Cup events. She was a gorgeous tawny creature with a lush body. At forty, she had more glamour and sex appeal than all the

kittenish blondes that hung about the skiers' chalet waiting, like music groupies, for the racers to
emerge.

They had met at a party at her chalet. She'd
worn something dark green and very soft, her
yellow hair falling below her shoulders like a
shower of gold. When he'd arrived, shy, awkward,
blushing, she had walked toward him slowly, pin-
ning him with her eyes as if he were the only
person in the room, taken him by the hand and
into her bedroom. There a fire blazed in the great
stone fireplace. On a small nearby table, a bottle of
Veuve Cliquot chilled in the ice bucket. She
poured a glass for him and watched while he'd
made a face as the bubbles burst in his nose.

"I don't like it," he'd said after taking a taste.

Wordlessly she'd taken the crystal flute from his
hand and thrown it against the stone wall. He'd
been shocked, then amused.

"Perhaps you'll like this," she spoke for the first
time. Her voice seemed to contain the same bubbles as the champagne. Then she'd laughed. A low
husky, suggestive laugh that raised the small hairs
on his arms. And then she'd slipped out of the soft
green dress she was wearing, revealing her golden
nude body.

After a week with her, he'd stopped being shy
and awkward. She taught him things he never
dreamed of. She also cost him the downhill. After
that glorious week he'd never seen her again,
except in the occasional film she made. Later he'd
heard that she'd married a Lebanese billionaire.

He'd come a long way since then. And women
like Marcella Richards were a dime a dozen. He'd
married two of them. They'd both been generous,
leaving him with a handsome house on Red Mountain, several sports cars, including a classic
Porsche Cabriolet that spent the better part of the

year on blocks in the garage, and the determination never to marry again.

On the other hand, he didn't think Marcella was looking for marriage, just someone to share her bed with while she was in town. If he was any judge at all, she would make the move soon.

"I've been trying to get some lessons with you for several years now."

"Oh?"

"Believe me, it's easier to get a dinner reservation at Lutèce."

He smiled his most charming, apologetic smile. Sally recognized it and made a low retching sound. He heard it, but his eyes held Marcella's. "Well, the moment you come back this winter, you call the desk and I will leave word that you are a special friend. They'll know what to do."

And so will you, thought Sally. This was what she disliked about Tony, about all the hotshot male ski instructors; but then, she guessed, it went with the territory. Who was she to get upset with what he did with his life? She owed him a great deal. They all did. He had given unstintingly of his time to Rocky. Her daughter had gotten a million dollars' worth of ski training in exchange for a couple of home-cooked dinners.

"Get up, you're getting too heavy." Tony dumped Rocky from his lap. "Besides, I need to talk to your mother."

"You need your ski pants shortened?" wisecracked Sally, one of whose talents was her handiness with a needle.

"No, I need a partner for the Hospital Benefit doubles tournament, and you're it!"

"Wait a minute. You know I hate playing in competitions."

"I know. It's a worthy cause."

"I can't afford the entrance fees."

"I've already paid them."

"Now, see here, Tony. You know I hate it when you do things like that. I can afford to pay my own fees."

"You just said you couldn't afford them."

"Well, I meant I don't want to pay them."

"Great! You don't have to. So it's all set. Besides, consider it as partial payment for all the great meals I've eaten at your house."

"What about me? Why didn't you ask me to play with you?" Suzanne said in a sulk.

He grinned at her and reached for the bottle of Olympia in front of her. He guzzled the contents, stood up, grinned again. "I want to win." Then, with a wave of his hand, he was off to the showers.

Greg James, seated at a table nearby, watched Tony Frantz stride away, watched the eager eyes of every unattached and a few attached women follow his path. Cocky bastard, he thought.

"He's a good-looking devil, isn't he?" commented his companion.

Michael Greenfield, who had been watching the matches with the idea of finding a good partner, was no slouch himself. He'd often been mistaken for Michael Douglas. He was a lean, slender man with sleek dark hair and lazy dark eyes that smoldered quietly under heavy dark brows. Like so many of the Aspen fit, he was older than he appeared.

Unlike Marcella Richards, he didn't let his entrepreneurial habits interfere with his obsession for fitness. He was an immoderate man except in what he ate and drank. Like Marcella Richards, he was a New York street kid whose middle-class parents had struggled to send him to Ivy League schools where he had learned to drink, wear clothes, charm mothers, and make lasting contacts. Upon his father's death, he'd inherited his local chain of sporting-goods stores and in ten years turned it into an empire. From retailing, he had turned to manufacturing. Long before the hostile takeover had become fashionable, he had bought or forced to be sold to him many of the most outstanding sporting-equipment makers on two continents.

His interest had recently turned to skiing. Even though the industry's growth curve had flattened out, equipment and clothing sales made it worthwhile to him. For the consumer it was one of the most expensive sports to enter. Once in, the yearly outlay was prodigious. With skis costing as much as five hundred dollars a pair and a good pair of boots up to three hundred dollars, the search for ultimate equipment made it attractive to a player like Michael. Recently he had bought an aerospace company on its last legs because there were rumors that one of the engineers was developing a unique-performance ski, reputed to be so good it could change the entire technique of skiing.

"Hey, Mike, see that kid talking to my sister?"

"Yes, what about her?"

"That's Rocky Schneider. Would you believe she was a pudgy little baby last year? Look at her now. She's grown into a real beauty."

"A sixteen-year-old hardly qualifies to be noticed," said Michael, whose attention had been on the foursome which included Marcella and Greg's other sister, Suzanne. The exotic dark-haired woman playing with Daisy Kenyon was a spectacular player for an amateur. Michael, who was a gifted amateur in his own right, couldn't take his eyes from her. She simply had no weaknesses in her game as far as he could see.

"Who was that playing against your sister? She's not a pro, is she?"

Greg tore his eyes from the animated Rocky and looked over to the court that Michael indicated.

"Oh, that's Sally Schneider. The kid's mother. You know, the one I was just telling you about."

Michael looked back and forth at the two of them. There was a strong resemblance. They both had those intense dark good looks, although the girl was shorter, beefier.

"She's a ski instructor," added Greg. "But her kid's a racer. She and Kit are both on the U.S. Ski Team. They're both racing in Europe this year and trying for the World Cup and Olympic teams."

"How many places are open on the A team?"

"Just one at the moment. Of course, that changes weekly."

"Why is that?"

"Who knows with these kids? It's tough work. They get tired or depressed or start missing being teenagers. Or someone gets hurt or one of the B racers starts winning on the Europa Cup circuit. It's not exactly what I would call a normal life. But the rewards are terrific. All you have to do is want it more than anything else. That's what we want for Kit."

How does Kit feel? Michael wondered. But he wisely kept quiet. Greg and Suzanne, who'd both been Olympic silver and bronze medalists, were trying to keep the family string going. His impression of Kit was that of a dutiful child obeying her older siblings because she'd been taught to do what she was told. He wondered if she had that indomitable will herself. If he were a betting man, he'd guess that the dark-haired girl, Rocky, had it in spades.

"Was the child's mother a racer, too?"

"Sally? No way! She used to play around with local stuff back home, but she never was interested in doing anything with it. Not like Suzanne, who was absolutely determined. I'll tell you this. Sally Burke could have won a gold medal if she'd decided to take it seriously. She had the technique and the balls. She just didn't want to."

"How about her daughter?"

"Yeah, how about her? That's what I'd like to know."

Sally went to look for her daughter, who was hitting tennis balls with Kit. Neither girl was really interested in tennis. There simply wasn't time.

They loaded Rocky's bike into the back of the Subaru and headed for home. Although Sally was anxious to hear all about training camp, she didn't press her daughter. There was plenty of time to talk later. They both enjoyed the companiable silence as Rocky got used to being back home again. When they reached the little house on Midland Avenue—"the little house on the prairie" —as Rocky called it, Eric was home and waiting. He'd already set the table for dinner.

"Thanks, big guy." Sally ruffled his hair.

"Watch it, Ma!" He pulled away. Eric hated to have anyone touch his hair. Like his father's, it was dark and wavy and he wore it in dignified punk style like Andre Agassi, the young hot tennis player from Las Vegas whom all the kids adored.

He gave his sister a high-five and they immediately started talking with that special vocabulary all the kids used to make adolescent communication totally incomprehensible to anyone over twenty.

"Did you see Tony? Was he there? Who was he playing with?" asked Eric excitedly. Tony was his most favorite person in the world after Bruce Springsteen.

"Yes, yes, and Richard Farwell," answered Rocky.

"I have some news for you guys," Sally broke in.

"About Tony?"

"Sort of."

"Well?" Eric gave his mother one of his long-suffering looks. He hated it when she played these little games.

"He and I are playing in the tournament for the Hospital Benefit."

"Hey, Mom, great! You guys will nerdle them."

" 'Nerdle'? That's one on me."

"Pulverize, smash, destroy, annihilate," offered Rocky.

Sally shook her head. "All perfectly wonderful words. That I and millions of older Americans understand."

She set about making the hamburgers as Rocky peeled potatoes. "Anyway, I had very little to do with it. You know how I feel about playing in tournaments. But Tony made the arrangements first and asked me later. You know how Tony is."

"Yeah," said Eric blissfully. "He's gnarly."

"I couldn't have said it better myself," agreed Sally.

Her kids, who in general were pretty sharp about people and could be counted on to agree with their mother's evaluation, were ga-ga about Tony. Rocky especially. When she'd begun to race for the Aspen Ski Club and it was the parents who were responsible for the clothing and equipment, Tony had been the one who'd used his contacts to get Rocky the best there was. When the coaching had seemed less than adequate, he and Pete had stepped in and taken over. A close relationship had developed among them, a relationship further strengthened when Rocky's father had died so suddenly in the avalanche. Tony had simply taken over the role of surrogate father with the children, although his relationship with Sally had hardly changed at all.

Sally continued to take him to task for this profligate waste of talent and energy, and he continued his efforts to lighten her up. "Chill out, Ma," were Eric's words.

There were times when she would have given anything to do just that.

Max Margolis barely noticed the changes a few short years had wrought in the geography of the Roaring Fork Valley. He was too anxious to get settled and make a phone call to Tony Frantz. Though work had kept him from Aspen for several years, he and Tony stayed in touch by phone or by occasional weekends in San Francisco. Now he was looking forward to spending time in one of his favorite places. Maybe even settle down if it worked out.

Tony had booked him in to the Silver Leaf Inn until he found the right place to rent or buy. Expensive, but what the hell? Tony had offered to put him up but, knowing that cocksman, he would have only been in the way.

Max's room was splendid with antique Victorian furniture and flocked wallpaper. Too splendid for a guy used to sleeping on a cot, when he slept at all. He tossed a silver dollar to the bellboy and shut the door.

He threw his suitcase, his briefcase, and himself on the bed and reached for the phone.

"Tony? Max! Finally here. Yeah. I like the way you spend my money. Listen, I don't want to say too much over the phone. Can you come over? I've got to talk to you. Good. I'll see you in twenty minutes.

When Tony arrived, he found Max sitting at the desk, poring over a foot of computer printouts.

"So what's all the mystery?" By comparison with the tousled inventor, Tony looked almost effete in his white slacks and navy polo shirt. His skin was bronzed by the sun, while Max had the look of a terminally ill patient.

"All here, man." He pointed to the sheaf of papers.

"What?"

"Only the world's greatest ski."

"I don't get it."

"Remember how I always pumped you for what you thought would make the ultimate ski?"

"Yeah, sort of. I remember we talked a bit about edge control and adaptability, flex . . . sure, all that good stuff."

"Well, here it is."

"All I see is a lot of funny numbers."

"Well, look closer." Max flipped through the pages, and a dizzying profusion of computer-imaged drawings of a ski from various aspects and positions jumped out at Tony like one of the flip books that imitated a movie. "There it is. On paper."

"Just like that?"

"It's the beginning, buddy boy. We're going to make this ski."

"We, *kimo sabi*?"

"*We*, white man. I'm going to make it. And you're going to test it. And then we're going to refine it. How does the prospect of great wealth hit you?"

Max was making his head spin. "I'm from Missouri," said Tony with a rueful laugh.

"Hmmm, I thought you were from Innsbruck."

Then Max got serious.

CHAPTER THREE

THE DAY OF THE TENNIS TOURNAMENT WAS WHAT skiers call a "bluebird" day. Perfect high-mountain weather. Dry winy air, cloudless skies, and a crisp pine-scented breeze sweeping upvalley.

Sally lingered over a cup of coffee as her children made their own breakfasts, a ritual she'd established early on when it appeared that every morning they each wanted something different. "If you want it, you make it," had been her directive. After a bit of grumbling, it had become routine. With Rocky not home much of the time, she supposed she could have broken down and made Eric breakfast, but since he had now settled in to cereal, bananas, and milk every morning, she found other ways to show him she was a good mother. Like making him pizza and barbecued chicken or packing extra treats into his lunchbox.

A brown-capped rosy finch perched on her windowsill and peered into the kitchen. It was a sure sign that the dazzling weather would soon give way to snow, for the finches left their timberline nests to winter in the valley, where the insect and seeds were more plentiful.

"Mom, I have to go to the club for a couple of hours, then I'm coming over to watch you and Tony play. When are you scheduled?"

"I don't know, sweetie. Come when you can. There'll be plenty of good tennis. Chris and Martina will be there. So will Bill Cosby. Don Johnson, too, I hear."

"Who's he?"

"Gimme a break, Rocky. You don't know who Don Johnson is?" asked Eric with a mouthful of banana.

"Don't talk with your mouth full," was Sally's automatic response.

"Hey, give *me* a break! When do I get a chance to go to movies?"

"He's on TV," was Eric's lofty, know-it-all response. "He's Crockett on *Miami Vice*."

"A heartthrob," explained Sally, "that men like your brother seem to like."

"Tony likes him, too," insisted Eric. As though that put the Good Housekeeping Seal of Approval on it, Sally thought wryly.

"That's because they ski together," Sally reminded him. "Anyway, it's not worth discussing. Eric, what about you? Are you coming to watch?"

"Sure, Mom. I'll be your coach."

"No coaching allowed," said Sally.

"I'll use hand signals."

Eric was an avid tennis spectator, more interested in what happened on the sidelines than the on-court action. It was he who had told Sally that the European players' coaches were giving illegal advice during matches. Unlike baseball or basketball, where a coach could actively participate, communication during a match was not considered sportsmanlike in tennis. It was an unwritten rule dating back to the days when tennis was still considered a gentleman's game and was never played for money.

Eric, practical as ever, had reminded her that tennis had turned into a money sport, so coaching should be allowed. Tony could find no argument against that.

Tony. Even when he wasn't around, he seemed to figure importantly in their lives. The children's lives, she corrected. She should be happy he cared about them. They missed their father so much. He'd been such a vibrant part of their existence—a wonderful, caring, involved father with far more patience than she. Often as not, Tony had been an integral part of the family get-togethers. It was surprising that with his reputation as a much-in-demand sex object he would choose to be with them. On second thought, maybe not so surprising at all.

Under the circumstances, it seemed completely natural that Tony should care about the family of his cousin. Up to a point, of course.

Daisy Kenyon was convinced that Tony was only waiting for a sign from Sally to step into Peter's shoes. "They don't give awards for celibacy anymore. Even priests and nuns are getting married," she'd reminded her friend.

Sally was not particularly pleased with her monastic existence, but she was not about to fall into bed with the first man who seemed interested in her. Peter had been her first lover, and since his death there had been only one other man in her life: a very brief fling that she had enjoyed when she and Daisy had gone to Mexico to one of the Club Med resorts. Daisy, the perfect bird dog, had spotted him on the beach one morning taking an early walk. By that afternoon they were a threesome, or, she should say, a fivesome, for the children were there, too. Sally had been pleased at their presence, for it protected her from the gentleman's considerable charm. That had worked until the children went off to bed and Daisy disappeared to find her own fun. Then the two of them had been alone. For the first couple of evenings there had been nothing but talk, mostly from him. He was a foreign correspondent whose beat was the world, and she'd been fascinated by his stories. Then one evening the talk stopped and the lovemaking began. A totally voluptuous, completely sensual experience, outdoors, under the stars, with the steady lapping of the waves against the shore and the two of them naked in the dark, surrounded by the perfume of exotic flowers and the faint sound of a mariachi band coming from the distant disco.

Then, all too soon, it was over. He returned to London and she to Aspen. She received a few witty notes, jotted in stacatto phrases as if he were calling in an important story to an editor who would fill in the blank spaces later. She'd written back thoughtful responses. Then the letters stopped and a few months later, she received an invitation to his wedding. She recognized the woman's name immediately as a famous photographer, daughter of one of the peers of the realm. So much for romance with a worldly, fascinating man half a globe away.

Sally carried her coffee cup to the sink and caught a glimpse of her reflection in the small mirror that hung in the mudroom entryway. Her summer tan was turning muddy. Maybe she would listen to Daisy and do something with her hair, learn to use some makeup. She wondered if that worried expression on her face had been there for a long time, then laughed helplessly.

Aspen was so populated with beautiful, exciting women, she'd need a total overhaul just to get one foot on the ladder. Then she berated herself for such negative thoughts. She was what she was, and she wasn't about to change now. Peter had hated it when she gussied up and wore her "war paint," as he called it. She looked at the sink of dirty dishes absently and wondered why thoughts of her little Club Med escapade had brought on these sudden notions of makeovers and makeup.

"Mom?"

Sally turned unfocused eyes from the window to her daughter. "What?"

"Where were you just now? I've been talking and you haven't heard a word I've been saying."

"You were? I wasn't? What? What did I miss?"

"Kit said something about having dinner at their house. Would you mind?"

Annoyance flicked across Sally's face, then disappeared as quickly as it came.

"You do mind. Why?"

"I hate to say no, honey, but after all, I haven't seen you in weeks. You're with Kit every day."

"Forget I brought it up." But Rocky's expression was anything but understanding.

Sally sighed. She hated being the bad guy with her children. Remembering how inseparable she and Suzanne used to be, she was about to give in when she realized the two situations were totally different. Sally had hated going home to be with her own parents, but Eric and Rocky had always enjoyed being with theirs. Besides, where was it written that history had to repeat itself? There was no reason to believe that Kit would turn into someone like her half-sister.

"Mom, you aren't just saying no because of Greg, are you?"

"Don't be ridiculous," Sally said too quickly, too emphatically. "Greg James isn't a problem."

A look of disbelief flashed across Rocky's face. "Whatever you say, Mom."

"Really, baby. In any case, if you have any illusions about Greg James, you should talk to Daisy."

"What's Daisy got to do with it?"

"They've been seeing one another for a couple of months."

"I still don't understand what you're trying to say."

"He's not very nice to her. If she thought she could get away with it, she'd cheerfully have him killed."

"That's her problem. If he's so bad, why does she go out with him?"

"That's what I want to know."

"Well, anyway, don't worry about me. I'll be home for dinner and I'll be at the club to see you play. 'Bye and good luck." Rocky gave her mother a quick kiss and a thumb's-up sign, then grabbed her athletic bag and an apple. Sally watched her retreating back with a mixture of pride and worry. In many ways Rocky was mature and grownup, but where it counted she was still a very sheltered child.

For many parents, the thought of their teenage daughter embarking on a career of ski racing was fraught with peril. Was she old enough to be without parental supervision as she traveled all over the Western world? What kind of trouble could she get into with the more sophisticated Europeans?

Sally's worries followed other paths, opposite paths. She worried that the discipline and dedication required to be a winner would prevent Rocky from developing into a well-rounded adult. While Rocky was running up mountains and spending hours a day in training, other kids were playing tennis, having fun, dating boys, going to dances, all the things that should make their teens the best years of their lives. Sally, who all her life had been accused of being too serious, was concerned that her daughter was getting to be more like her every day.

That was another thing she was beginning to hate about herself. She wore dark clouds of doom the way other people wore jewelry. Soon even her own children would begin to find her presence suffocating. Quickly quelling her morose thoughts, she dressed in the crisp white pleated tennis skirt she'd made the night before and slipped on one of Rocky's team shirts. She tied a bandana around her head, Indian fashion, gave her lips a quick flick of gloss, and ran out the door, determined to play well for Tony's sake.

Her gloom evaporated the moment she walked through the Silver Leaf lobby and out to the courts. There was an unmistakable air of festivity and glamour, and the noise level was greater than usual as people clustered about a buffet table laden with platters of salmon, sturgeon, vegetables, bagels, and bread. Huge pitchers of fresh orange juice disappeared as pros like Billie Jean King, Rosie Casals, Roy Emerson, Martina Navratilova, and Bill Scanlon tanked up and rubbed shoulders with celebrity players Don Johnson, Jill St. John, John Denver, Linda Evans, Wayne Gretsky, Kate Jackson, Suzy Chaffee, Linda Carter, and Julius Irving.

The exclusive club had let down its restrictions in order that the public might watch the events of the first day, but the weekend tickets were expensive, the proceeds going to benefit the Ski Club, the Mental Health Clinic, Martina's Youth Foundation, and the Mountain Valley Hospital. Courtside boxes were going for $500 and included lunch in the VIP tent and cocktails later with the celebrities at the Silver Leaf Inn. For $750, ticketholders would also be treated to a jazz concert and a dinner dance at the club.

The morning had already been taken up by pro-am and exhibition matches which Sally had missed in order to have breakfast with her children.

As she stood on the sidelines watching the famous faces and bodies trying to behave like ordinary people, Tony slipped up behind her and put his arm through hers. "You're late!"

"I am? You didn't tell me an exact time."

"It's all right. We're scheduled to play against Bill Scanlon and Sharon Walsh. How do you feel?"

"Bill Scanlon? He's pretty good, isn't he?"

Tony laughed. "Leave it to you to be worried about Bill Scanlon. You have a partner, remember."

"Are you better than he is?"

"You never know." He gave her a light kiss on the cheek. She pulled away, embarrassed by his public display of affection. She had to admit he looked tanned, fit, and confident enough to take on anyone. With the bright fall sun turning his bleached hair to gold, he could have just stepped down from Olympus for a day of frolicking with the mortals. He wore a navy shirt and immaculate white tennis shorts.

"You look terrific," he said admiringly, meaning every word.

"Not as terrific as you." Said with equal admiration.

As they walked to the sign-in table, she wondered what he'd been like when he first came to Aspen. Peter, who always looked neat, had never been much of a clothes horse, although he'd certainly had the stature for it. Getting him to buy new clothes or even wear the ones she bought for him was like forcing him to walk to his own execution. On the other hand, she'd never seen Tony in anything but the most current of men's fashion. Anyone else might have been teased as a dude or a fop. Not Tony. It seemed to be expected of him.

When he had started to go out with Suzanne, Sally had once commented nastily, "I hope the two of you never plan to live together. You'll be constantly fighting over who gets the mirror."

She wasn't aware that she had been staring at him until he grinned. Two deep dimples dappled his cheeks. "Well, shall we stand here in mutual admiration or go hit some balls?"

He threw his arm loosely around her shoulders, and she was aware of the envious stares that followed their steps. She was also aware that his deep golden tan had not turned muddy or faded. It wasn't fair!

Bill Cosby, the ubiquitous cigar clenched in his teeth, was deep in conversation with Julie Anthony, who with her husband owned the Aspen Club, the Silver Leaf's friendly rival for top spa honors in the Roaring Fork Valley. Julie had met her husband, Dick Butera, when she played for the Philadelphia Freedoms, one of the professional tennis teams that had existed briefly in the mid-seventies and was owned by Cosby and Butera.

They would be one of the celebrity teams playing the afternoon's events.

The play was a little different than most pro-am tournaments in that the teams would play four games, each with a different partner. Bill Scanlon and Sharon Walsh would start out together against Sally and Tony. Then Tony and Sharon would play against Bill and Sally, then Sally and Sharon would play against Bill and Tony, finally ending with the original twosomes. Sally thought it was silly, but for charity she would do her part.

Finally the matches began, with Buddy Hackett and Alan Thicke offering hysterical color commentary.

By the time that Sally and Sharon had joined forces against Bill and Tony, the men had been reduced to helpless laughter. The women pressed their advantage and took the game at love.

During the play, Sally felt an unaccustomed competitive joy surge through her. She didn't know whether to blame it on the perfect weather, the excitement of the day, or the exhilaration of playing with outstanding players. She abandoned herself to the thrill of movement and the sound of hard-hit balls.

When it was all over, Sharon Walsh congratulated her on her play as did Bill Scanlon. Tony shook his head with ill-concealed admiration. "You never cease to surprise me. You know I really had second thoughts about today. I was afraid I had overstepped the bounds of friendship when I arranged to play without telling you. And here you are, breathing fire, looking magnificent, and hitting the ball as if you were in the finals at Wimbledon. And you still insist you hate competition?"

"Don't look a gift horse in the mouth, Frantz. I'm just as surprised as you are. I don't know what got into me. But let's not put it under a microscope. Okay?"

He made a low bow. "I'm your slave."

Tony was not the only one admiring Sally's play. Michael Greenfield, who was waiting to take the court with Suzanne James, had watched the last set of matches in openmouthed admiration. Sally was as fluid as water in her motions, yet her play had that powerful kind of explosiveness that separated the gifted amateur from the professional.

"Your friend is a very good tennis player," he commented to Suzanne.

"Yeah," was Suzanne's grudging reply.

"You've known her a long time, I take it."

"A very long time."

"Greg says you used to race together."

Suzanne wrinkled her elegant nose. She'd been told that little gesture was very adorable. It was not always easy to be thought of as adorable when you were close to six feet tall. "Together is not quite the word I would use. We were on the same ski team at school."

"Was she any good? I mean, obviously you were much better. You were in the Olympics."

Although Suzanne could steer a smooth course around the truth, she hated an out-and-out lie. "She *was* good. In the beginning much better than I was. Skiing came easy to her. I had to work for it. I was always too tall, too awkward. But when Sally got really good, she just gave up trying. She refused to compete."

"Interesting. I wonder why. And now? Are you still friends?"

"Hardly. That ended a long time ago."

"Odd that you should both end up in Aspen."

"Isn't it?"

"So tell me about her. There are children but no husband. Divorced?"

She shook her head. "Widowed. He was a ski instructor. Got himself caught in an avalanche. Four years ago."

"Is there something between them, Frantz and her?"

"Tony and the Village Drudge? The Unmerry Widow? Don't make me laugh. Tony was Pete Schneider's cousin. That's what the relationship is. God knows, if it had been me whose husband had died, I would have been thrilled to have a Tony Frantz waiting in the wings. But not our Sal, she's a stubborn bitch with a holier-than-thou attitude.

Now that I think of it, she was always like that. Even when we were growing up." Suzanne gave a long-suffering sigh. "And a bore. What can I tell you? Life to her is deadly serious, like the prospect of World War Three. I don't think she has the vaguest idea of how to enjoy herself."

"Maybe nobody taught her how."

"Heaven knows I tried. You know, once she was rather attractive. Since Pete died, I think she goes out of her way to look dreary. Listen, her nickname used to be Stony. That should say it all."

Michael didn't think she looked dreary at all, though he was curious to discover why she had warranted such a dreadful nickname. To be sure, she didn't have Suzanne's sleek greyhound body or silvery looks, but she did have something else. She had a grace that came from strength and the kind of looks that would grow more elegant with age. She wore the few gleaming silver threads in her dark hair like a badge of pride while another woman might have panicked at the sight.

As she moved about the court, he'd seen her from every angle and realized she didn't have a bad one. A camera would find her face a never-ending source of interest. Some might say her jaw was too square, her brow too intellectual, her silvery eyes disconcerting, but he found himself filled with a grudging admiration for a woman who chose to ignore the fashionable and superficial expectations of the Aspen cognoscenti.

The more Suzanne said to turn him off, the more interested Michael became, but getting close to the elusive lady was proving to be more difficult than he expected. Suzanne was certainly not going to introduce him. As the new man in town, he really didn't know enough people yet that he could ask. As it turned out, the problem was solved easily, and all it took was money.

The next day there was a silent auction. Those who wished to play in the exhibition games could bid for partners. When Sally arrived, she was immediately grabbed by Daisy and pulled into a corner. "You'll never guess who you're playing with!" she said, barely able to conceal her excitement.

"I wasn't aware I was playing with anyone."

"Well, you are, and he bid a great deal of money for you. You're very much in demand as a partner, in case you hadn't noticed."

Sally frowned. "Daisy, get to the point."

"Michael Greenfield."

Sally looked puzzled. "Michael Greenfield? I don't know a Michael Greenfield. Who's he? Anyone?"

"Take my word for it. He's someone. Rich, good-looking, mysterious."

"If he's so mysterious, how come you know so much?"

"My spies told me. At the moment all I know is that he's rich, good-looking, and available. Isn't that enough? Oh, yes, he's the man who played with Suzanne yesterday."

A sudden vision of a sleek, dark man in white jogged her memory. "I vaguely remember. He has a great overhead."

"Do you know you're impossible? I don't know why I put up with you. Look, he's a very sexy-looking guy. And he wants to play with you!"

"I wonder why." Sally turned away in confusion. Her eyes swept the crowd and stopped when she saw him staring directly at her. She flushed. He'd probably been there all the time, maybe even listening to Daisy's excited recital of his attributes. She had a voice that carried.

He gave her a half smile and pushed away from the wall where he'd been leaning and walked slowly toward her. She watched him cautiously but with undeniable curiosity.

He extended his hand. "I'm Michael Greenfield. I just donated five thousand dollars for the privilege of claiming you as my partner."

She took his hand to give him a quick shake. He ignored her attempt to remove it, looking at it with surgical attention, then turned it over and stared at the palm. "Nice strong hands."

"Mr. Greenfield . . ." She tried to free herself.

"The name's Michael. I think if we're to be partners, we should be on a first-name basis, Sally."

"But why me? There are dozens of players here that you could have chosen."

"You play good tennis."

This was said with such finality, Sally wisely did not try to pursue the subject further.

Why her, indeed? Michael Greenfield didn't know why himself. In spite of his initial fascination, she was clearly not his type. He had had his pick of women since he was eighteen. He was not the first young man to discover that good looks and a little charm went further than brains and money. No matter where he went he had been amused by the blatant sexuality and availability of the women he met. The posher the place, the hungrier the female. In his circles beautiful women were a commodity like soybeans or pork bellies. Sometimes you made a killing, sometimes you took a bath. Most had little to offer besides their perfect profiles and pampered skin.

Sally Schneider was different. Not an ordinary beauty, not man hungry, not readily available. Not even curious about him. Only curious that he had bid for her "services." As he made small talk with her, he was amused by her monosyllabic answers. She wasn't about to give an inch. If her temperature had been zero when they met, she'd warmed only a few degrees as he tried to put her at ease and win her confidence.

There was an aloof dignity that he found more provocative than lowered eyes and revealing necklines. It was like getting water from a stone to squeeze a few noncommittal facts from her.

He smiled. She certainly deserved that nickname.

"You would have made a great spy," he said, interrupting some nonsense she was spouting about the architecture of the club.

Clamping her mouth shut at his interruption, she blushed. "I don't understand . . ."

"So far, the only information you've given me about yourself is literally your name, rank, and serial number."

"I doubt I have anything to say that might interest you."

"Let me be the judge."

He made her feel so uncomfortable she wished she had the nerve to turn tail and run, but just as she raised her stricken eyes she heard their names announced. "I think they want us to play tennis."

"Then let's get to it. I know this is an extraneous observation, but . . . I like winning, Sally." He smiled and turned away. Aside from the little he could see and what Suzanne had told him, the challenge of getting to know her was proving quite difficult.

They had drawn as opponents Richard Farwell, head of the Silver Mountain Ski Corp, and Julie Anthony.

Since Julie was a former ranking professional, they were obviously formidable opponents, but if Michael had been impressed by Sally's play on the previous day, he was astounded today. With a good partner—and he knew how good he was—she was impressive. She was aggressive, smart, and tough. She played even better when they were down a break. Her concentration was so intense, he literally had to tap her on the shoulder when he wanted to suggest a point of strategy. The match went down to the wire, a final-set tiebreaker which she and Michael won by the requisite two points at 14–12.

As word got out about the match, others had drifted over to watch.

When it was all over and they had won, Michael hugged her with shining eyes. "You were positively magnificent."

"Whatever got into you today, Sally?" Richard Farwell kissed her cheek. "You never play like that with me."

Michael raised his eyebrows and said with a smile that barely concealed the truth behind the words, "Maybe she never had a partner that brought out the best in her."

He handed Sally a towel, and the foursome collapsed into chairs. A pitcher of iced tea was brought. As Sally leaned back in her chair, she was assaulted on two sides by her exultant children.

"Mom, you were great," said Eric. "That approach shot and the angled volley, wow!"

"Yeah, Mom. You were awesome, totally awesome."

"Gnarly, bad, the baddest," Eric proclaimed in the argot of the moment.

Michael watched in amusement as Sally's fan club gushed all over her. Her normally severe features relaxed, and Michael, with a catch in his throat, realized she was a beautiful woman. Her fierce maternal feelings were as open as her personal feelings were secret. As he watched Rocky, he could see what the young Sally must have looked like. They could be twins. The boy, on the other hand, must resemble the father. He was tall for his age, gangly and loose limbed. When he filled out and his body caught up to his legs, he would be a handsome man. His dark hair lay in waves over his forehead and he had the dewy dampness that boys of that age usually have. He smelled of sneakers and kid sweat, a nostalgic scent that Michael remembered with a burst of acuity from his street days growing up in New York.

These tender feelings took Michael Greenfield by surprise. He thought he had outgrown them. A tough kid, he had learned to hide his sensitivity behind a barrage of knuckles and muscles, teaching his pals that just because he went to concerts with his mother, he was not a sissy. It was an argument he had been forced to settle on the average of twice a week.

In college, his small size had kept him from the football and basketball teams but not from boxing or debating, two very opposite ways of showing his accumulated strengths.

He caught Sally's children staring at him with ill-concealed curiosity. "Sally, are you going to introduce me to your fan club?"

They giggled. And Sally presented them with a formality that cracked under her own smile.

"You played really well, too, Mr. Greenfield," Eric admitted grudgingly.

"Oh, I was nothing," said Michael modestly. "Your mother carried me through the entire match."

Richard Farwell gave a hoarse laugh.

"You don't have to be modest, Mr. Greenfield. Mom says modesty is the only sure bait when you angle for praise."

"Oh, she does? Tell her Lord Chesterfield would be honored to know she quoted him."

The kids tired quickly of grown-up conversation and twitched like puppies on a short leash until Sally excused them.

"Great kids," he said casually.

"I think so."

"Tell me about your daughter. You know, she looks exactly like you."

"So I'm told."

"I understand she's a ski racer. Serious about it?"

"Why would she race if she weren't?" Sally asked, honestly puzzled by his question.

"It's glamorous; the kids get a chance to travel; it makes them seem special in the eyes of their friends. I don't know"—he shrugged—"there must be dozens of reasons."

"I assure you, if you know anything about racing, it's far from glamorous. I don't think anything that takes that kind of training and strength is particularly glamorous."

"Is that why you never pursued tennis as a career? You know you could have been ranked if you'd wanted to."

"I never wanted to."

"What about you, Michael?" asked Richard Farwell. "You could have been a pro, too. You've got the game. Pat tells me that you used to be a ranking U.S. amateur."

"It never occurred to me. I had a family business to run and plans that didn't leave much room for tennis. Besides, tennis players are like models, they're only good when they're young. I guess if you're a McEnroe or a Lendl you can make big bucks, but it's nothing compared to what you can make when you own a successful business. Besides, I was more interested in why Sally didn't pursue it as a career."

Michael turned to her with a smile and waited,

but she was silent. She was thinking of what he'd said about running a successful business. It always came down to money, didn't it? She wondered what it would feel like never to have to clean a house again, to do the weekly laundry, to try to make nourishing, inexpensive meals, to pay bills on time.

Richard Farwell stood up and looked around. Sophie Mallory, a fine tennis player herself and Bill Cosby's partner that day, waved to him and gestured for him to join her table. "Well, folks, I want to thank you for a fine game. Michael, I'd be pleased to play with you anytime you want." Julie Anthony left a few minutes later, and Sally and Michael were alone at the table.

"Well, I thought we made a pretty good team."

With his sleek good looks and still-pristine whites gleaming against his dark skin, Sally felt that she had just stepped into one of those sophisticated movies of the thirties, the ones where someone like Michael stepped into the room asking, "Tennis anyone?"

She laughed.

"Did I say something amusing?"

"I was just struck with something silly." She stood up. "I should shower and change."

He caught her by the arm. "I was wondering if we might have a celebratory dinner tonight. Say at Gordon's or Pinons?"

She extricated her hand gently. "I don't think so. Thanks anyway. Excuse me."

She could feel his dark eyes boring into her back and wondered if he was angry or amused by her behavior. Gordons or Pinons! What a question. Who wouldn't love to go to dinner there? He would really laugh if he knew the reason she'd turned him down. The age-old cry "I haven't a thing to wear" in her case was the unvarnished truth. She couldn't afford to buy the kind of clothes that women wore to places like that. Even though Aspen dressed informally at night, their casual came at very high prices. Leathers from Smiths that cost in the thousands, designer silk shirts in the hundreds, hand-made sweaters that would pay all her bills for two months, not to mention the hand-tooled boots, the unique jewelry, and the simple but serious furs.

When she returned to look for her kids, Michael was no longer around, but Daisy was.

"What are you staring at?" Sally asked, slipping into a chair next to her friend.

"The two bitches in heat. Look at him, he actually enjoys it."

Sally turned her head and saw Tony, now changed into jeans and a white polo shirt, skewered like a piece of rare beef between two hungry animals. "Suzanne better watch out. I think Marcella has big eyes for her boyfriend."

"Don't worry about Suzanne. Nothing's fair in love or friendship with her."

That was the trouble with Aspen, Sally thought. It's like a big stage here with everyone acting a part. Roles were preordained: After hours, ski instructors had to change into their dancing shoes and play lover; tycoons on vacation were expected not to wheel and deal; celebrities were supposed to drop their famous personas and be just folks.

Which was the real Tony? she wondered. She had seen so many of his guises, she wasn't sure. Was it the consummate professional, legendary owner of three gold Olympic medals? Or Tony the lover of beautiful, rich women? Or was it the caring, gentle man who had been her rock and the children's best friend in those dark, mean days after Peter's death? Or were there still other Tonys she hadn't even met yet?

"I don't know about Suzanne. I think she's met her match in Marcella. I mean, the woman didn't get to where she is by just being cute. She's as clever as Machiavelli when it comes to manipulating a man."

"How do you know so much about her?"

"I've been listening to her conversation."

"And you could hear all the way over here?" Sally looked skeptical.

"Some people have X-ray vision, I have X-ray hearing."

"Hello, darlings. Watching the newest ménage à trois, I see."

"Oh, Madelaine, not you, too," moaned Sally.

Madelaine Laureau shrugged with Gallic precision. "October is so boring, one is forced to dig deep for the dirt."

Madelaine was a Frenchwoman who had come to Aspen twenty years ago with a rich settlement from her lawyer husband. Stunning, witty, clever, and very French, she'd been immediately caught up by the inner circle of divorced and single women who ran the elegant shops and galleries in town, who got invited to, but rarely gave, the best parties, who skied well, played good tennis, and dressed with ineffable chic on relatively little money.

They were shadow thin and on top of every beauty breakthrough from the Bloomingdale diet to Retin-A in their pilgrimage to find eternal youth. They were found in packs, shining in their Lycra armor at every exercise class in every club and spa in town. They were honed, tuned, sharpened, keened and aligned, tucked, trimmed, lifted, and centered. They were bionic, perfect, almost inhuman specimens and they found refuge and protection in the rarefied atmosphere of Aspen's rarefied air. To them it was Shangri-la, and if they ever left, except for quick trips to Denver or any number of West Coast spas, they would probably crumble into dust.

"Rumor has it that Marcella and Suzanne have worked out a time-share schedule with the great one."

"Madelaine, you're making this up," protested Sally.

The Frenchwoman shrugged and tossed her streaky blond hair with a slim hand laden with gold bracelets. She wore a white Chanel T-shirt and navy denim pants and made everyone else look Salvation Army by comparison.

"How do you do it?" asked Daisy enviously.

"Do what, *chérie*? Get my information?"

"No. Manage to look like a million dollars in a lousy ninety-dollar T-shirt?"

"She's French," said Sally with a yawn, mouthing the by now cliché explanation for anything that Madelaine did or said.

"We poor French, we get blamed for everything." Madelaine sighed.

"Yeah, your wine, your perfume, your clothes, your food," teased Sally.

"Do you want me to humble myself?" asked Madelaine.

"I like it better when you behave like General de Gaulle," said Sally.

"So does someone wish to make a bet that Marcella Richards will take full possession of Tony Krantz within a week?"

"You know, this conversation makes me ill," said Sally, standing up impatiently.

Daisy and Madelaine smiled knowingly at each other but kept silent.

"Don't give me that insufferable know-it-all look.

This has nothing to do with anything," she said as two pairs of arms pulled her back into her chair.

"Are you perhaps *un peu jalouse*?"

"I am not a *peu* anything. I just want to know how the two of you know so much about a man I've known for years. I mean, for all I know, this may be wishful thinking on your part."

"I assure you, darling, Tony Frantz is the best-known cocksman in the Roaring Fork Valley. Ask the satisfied customers."

"Are you one of them?" Sally challenged baldly.

"Alas, no. But not for lack of trying," admitted the Frenchwoman with a sigh. "Not rich enough, I'm afraid."

The woman who was rich enough was playing X-rated games in her head. As Tony Frantz traded tit for tat, she played out her scenario. Marcella in her attempt to become a skier decided that the best way to learn skiing was the way she had learned French. Take the instructor to bed. The French had a way of expressing it: *La langue d'oreille, c'est la langue d'oreiller* . . . the language of the ear is the language of the pillow.

But she'd never had luck with the famous Tony. He always seemed to be booked a year in advance or out on a ski jaunt with one of his macho clients. Now, for the first time and because of her newest "friend," she was within striking distance. It seemed she was not meeting resistance. She weighed him against the other men she had known. He was certainly not the best-looking, nor the most charming. Despite the fact that he might do very well for an instructor, she made more money in a week than he could possibly make in a year. Still, there was something about the trim, muscled body and dancer's grace that made her hands itch to explore him.

Marcella was about to spring her little trap on

him, when he suddenly got up and excused himself.

With the last match played and everyone showered and changed, it was time to announce the grand winners of the day, the amount of money raised for charity, and the bestowal of the event's trophies.

No one was surprised when Sally Schneider's name along with her partner, Michael Greenfield, was announced. They accepted their silver bowls and waved to the crowd.

Marcella looked appraisingly at the woman in the khaki safari jacket and trousers. That was a terrible color on her. It made her look even more sallow than she was. But when Tony Frantz came up to her and put his arm familiarly around her shoulders and she turned smiling eyes to him, Marcella felt a frisson of anger. There was something between them! She looked about quickly to see if Suzanne had noticed anything, but the gorgeous Suzanne was deep in conversation with a richly tanned man with silver hair whom she recognized as a well-known Eastern millionaire polo player.

Marcella watched Sally and Tony chat companionably. Sally looked at her watch several times. She obviously had made other plans that didn't include him. When Sally picked up her bag and slung it over her shoulder, that gave Marcella the excuse she needed.

As Sally turned to leave, she heard Marcella Richards call her name. She turned to stare at the other woman, Madelaine Laureau's words still fresh in her mind.

"Sally, I just wanted to congratulate you on your game. You were wonderful. I can't imagine how Suzanne ever expected us to give you and Daisy much of a match."

"I enjoyed that game."

"I can't imagine why. What you were playing out there today was an entire other level of tennis."

"Thank you for the compliment."

Marcella had to hand it to her. No false modesty in this woman.

"By the way, I couldn't help noticing your wonderful bag." That and the fact that you could use a total makeover from the top of your head to your toes, she thought. "Do you mind my asking where you got it?"

"Not at all. I made it."

"You did? My, you are a surprisingly talented woman. Does anyone in town sell them?"

"No, I'm afraid not."

"I don't suppose I could order one from you."

"I can't promise when I can get to it."

"Look, I'll write you a check immediately and you do it whenever you can. Is five hundred dollars enough?"

Sally was about to gulp, when Marcella, misinterpreting her silence, took it to mean that the price was too low.

"Is it more than that? I don't care. Whatever you say."

Sally had never really considered the pricing of her bags. She had made one for Daisy for her birthday and one for Rocky. But she had just started this new endeavor and had no idea where she would go with it. She'd been told the bags were minor works of art. Her inspiration had been Sioux beadwork and she had crafted them with beaded medallions, fringe, bits of silver and turquoise, and the feathers of a hawk when she could find them.

"That'll be fine," stammered Sally. Why not, Marcella could well afford it.

There was an awkward pause as the two women

searched for something more to say. With a quick glance at her watch, Sally gave Marcella a forced smile. "I better get going. I have to make dinner for the kids."

"Well, don't forget to call me when the bag is ready. Suzanne can give you my number." At the sudden tightening of Sally's face, Marcella stammered, "Perhaps it would be easier for me to call you?"

"Yes, it would. I'm in the book. Give me a couple of weeks."

Marcella nodded and turned to rejoin her group. Sally watched for a moment, feeling as she usually did at times like this the gulf between herself and Aspen's hard-playing rich. It's not that she really envied them, but she couldn't help being aware that her clothes were several years older than everyone else's, that she'd worn her hair the same way since she was sixteen, and that social chatter did not come easily to her.

She really should leave Aspen, had in fact thought about it countless times. But it always came down to the same thing. Where? She couldn't possibly go back to Maine. There had never been much there for her anyway. There were no people she cared about. Once away from her father, it was as if he'd never existed. His death had hardly touched her, and when her mother had died last year leaving the house to her, it turned out to be a house sinking in debt. She'd instructed it to be sold, the debts paid, and the pittance that was left put into a college fund for her children.

The good memories were solitary ones. Walks in the woods after a fresh spring rain when the pine-needled floor was carpeted with tiny wood violets so dense her footsteps disappeared in them. Rowing out in the dinghy with a lunch and a book to a tiny uninhabited island in Casco Bay and spending a solitary day with the terns and gulls. Going over to Freeport to shop at L.L. Bean, which stayed open seven days a week, twenty-four hours a day in deference to the fisherman who might pass through in the middle of the night on their way to salmon fishing in New Brunswick or the lakes of northern Maine. Hitchhiking up to Acadia and admiring the porcelain-blue skies, the hot sun, and the cool ocean breeze from the haven of a sleeping bag. Swimming in teeth-chatteringly cold water that remained glacially frigid even on the hottest August day, sometimes becoming decently beara- ble only in September.

Her memories were mostly framed in solitary meetings with nature. Not really so different from the best part of her life in Aspen.

Maybe if she didn't have the kids, she could have gone to San Francisco or Santa Fe, San Diego or Chicago. But she did. And anyway, all she had was a liberal arts degree after years of studying at Colorado Mountain College at night. That was worth next to nothing in an economy where Ph. D.'s were driving cabs or waiting on tables. At least in Aspen, she could hold down several jobs and she had the house. No, leaving didn't solve anything either.

"You look like you're trying to solve the secrets of the universe." Michael Greenfield made a quick sidestep to avoid being run down by a preoccupied Sally.

"Oh, I am sorry. I was thinking of something."

"Apparently."

He took her by the arm. "Come with me. I'm going to buy you dinner."

Sally dug in her heels like a stubborn terrier. She didn't like that imperious tone of voice. "No, you're not." She gently but firmly extricated her- self. "I have other plans."

"With whom?" he challenged.

"That's none of your business." She was surprised by his question. He was obviously used to getting his way, but he didn't seem the sort of man who would take a chance asking a question that was in danger of receiving an unequivocally hostile reply.

"You're absolutely right. I apologize, but you see, I find your behavior provocative. Are you like Cinderella? Must you get back to the scullery before your beautiful gown turns into rags and your Jaguar a pumpkin?"

She gave a bullhorn laugh. "My ball gown is a rag, and as for my Jaguar, it's a Subaru with well over one hundred thousand miles and a terminal case of rust. Now, if you'll excuse me . . . ?"

He saluted her and gave her a smile that never got past his perfect white teeth. In a soft voice that concealed his annoyance, he said, "I warn you, I don't give up easily."

She took a few steps toward the door, then stopped, aware that her heart was beating in a strangely excited way. Why did she always do this? Every time anyone—male or female—offered her the prospect of something pleasant, she got all bristly, like a porcupine. The familiar guilt washed over her. She pasted a humble smile on her face and turned around to call him back, but he had disappeared.

Michael didn't know whether to be annoyed or amused. She was certainly giving him a very hard time. Deliberately? No, he didn't think so. That wasn't her style, he was sure.

From the protection of an umbrella he saw her exit blocked by a disheveled-looking man in wrinkled khaki shorts and a faded blue oxford shirt. He was surprised when she broke into a smile and flung her arms about the man. He was too far away to hear what they were saying.

"What is there about the Widow Schneider that

fascinates you so?'' Suzanne came up behind him and slipped her arm through his.

"Do you know who that is talking to her?''

Suzanne squinted. She, too, started to smile. "My goodness! It's Max Margolis. What's he doing in Aspen? I wonder. It's been years since he's been around.'' Then she turned to appraise him. "Why the interest? Are you jealous?''

"Hardly. He doesn't seem the type to show up at a club like this.''

"Neither is she.''

But Michael didn't hear the snide tone. His mind was elsewhere. Wasn't Max Margolis a senior scientist and computer engineer at Monroe Aerospace? And weren't there rumors about his having come up with some breakthrough product and then been fired before Michael had bought the company? Interesting questions. No answers. Max Margolis would bear watching.

In fifteen minutes, Sally was home, brooding and sorry for her sharpness to Michael, but delighted by the unexpected appearance in Aspen of Max Margolis.

The house was strangely quiet. As she walked into the kitchen the marmalade cat jumped from the windowsill and twined itself around her legs, meowing happily and waiting to be picked up.

She scooped him up and buried her face in his soft fur. "Your mother is a total jerk,'' she said out loud.

"Not to mention totally absentminded.''

"Tony! What are you doing here?'' She whipped around at the sound of the unexpected voice.

"Haven't you forgotten something?''

"What?'' she said, looking around for her tennis racket and gear, but they were on the floor in front of the door.

"Your children."

"The children? Oh, my God. The kids! Where are they?"

"Don't worry, they're here. I brought them home. They're bringing in some things from the car. I've invited myself for dinner. I also brought the steaks. The Butcher Block was having a special."

"I bet. Well, I can hardly say no after you went to all that trouble, and frankly, steak sounds better than eggplant casserole." Then she couldn't resist the dig. "I'm surprised, actually. By the looks of things earlier, I would have thought you might have gotten a better offer."

He looked puzzled.

"Don't give me that innocent look, Frantz. I saw that bandit and her friend dealing for you."

"You mean Suzanne and Marcella?"

"No, Marilyn Monroe and Raquel Welch."

"Are we a little jealous?"

"No, we're a little disappointed."

"That they didn't invite me to dinner?"

"No, that you find them worth spending more than twenty seconds with."

"You're a tough lady."

"No, you're a pushover."

The easy smile left his face. Generally he enjoyed fencing with her, but sometimes she went too far and cut too deep. "Knock it off. You don't know what you're talking about," he said brusquely.

"I know what other people are saying."

"I couldn't care less. Since when do you care about what people say?"

"I don't want to fight with you."

"Good. Let's declare a truce."

Eric and Rocky walked in at that moment, laden with bags. "You know, you two sound like married people," said Rocky.

"Yeah," echoed Eric, "why are you two always picking on each other?"

Tony put his arms around the children. "That's right, kids, tell her to stop picking on me." The easy humor was back, and Sally was happy to smile. This was happening much too often. Some nasty devil kept sitting on her shoulder, prodding her to pick arguments with someone who had never showed her anything but understanding and friendship.

As the kids went upstairs to change for dinner, Tony helped her unpack the groceries. "Why did you run off so quickly? You never even said good-bye to Daisy, let alone me."

"I'm sorry. It was Michael Greenfield's fault."

"What did he have to do with it?"

"The guy's been hitting on me since we met. Every time I take a step he's underfoot, asking questions, inviting me to dinner. I don't understand it. With all the gorgeous women around, why does he pick on me?"

"I can't imagine. You certainly are as homely as a mud fence. As far as your disposition is concerned, alum is sweeter."

"Be serious," she insisted. "He really makes me uncomfortable."

"You don't like him because he's rich?"

"C'mon, Tony, be serious."

If it were any other woman but Sally, he'd be sure that this maidenly protestation was a plea for compliments. But it was Sally. A woman without guile or pretense. She hadn't the vaguest idea what a vital, attractive woman she was. Standing there in her unfashionable clothes, her dark hair wind-blown, she certainly lacked glamour, but she had things that were far more lasting: character and integrity. Someday, someone was going to come into her life and appreciate those qualities. For all he knew, it might even be Michael Greenfield. The fact that he was in pursuit indicated the man was not totally bereft of judgment.

Later, after they had gorged on steaks and salad and baked potatoes with chives and sour cream, the kids went into the den to watch television. Tony and Sally carried their coffee cups to the living room and settled in for an after-dinner chat.

"So what's your opinion of our new man in town?"

He shrugged. "I don't have one. I know he's one of the super-rich, that he's just built the biggest house on Red Mountain, and that he's negotiating for a piece of property in town where he plans to build a mini-mall of expensive sport shops."

"That's enough to make me dislike him. This town is getting impossible. I used to be able to go into Bullock's and buy underwear and socks for the kids. Now I have to drive over forty miles to Glenwood whenever I need anything."

"Aspen doesn't like to be reminded that there are people here who don't have incomes over a million a year."

"How about twenty thousand? And what happens when all the waiters and busboys and cleaning women and other service people decide they can't afford to live here anymore? What are all those rich people going to do then?"

"Learn the joys of hard work?" He smiled, hoping his lighthearted sally might wipe some of the worry lines from her face, but she only looked at him with distaste, a sharp retort forming on her lips. "Hey, I'm on your side. Really," he insisted.

"You don't even remember. You're one of them now."

For the first time he realized how deeply she felt her financial isolation and how wide was the gulf between them. He'd have to do something about that in a hurry or lose the one person in the world he could trust. And the children . . . he didn't even want to consider that. But did she really think that having enough money solved everything?

"By the way, did you see Max today? He was looking for you."

"I must have missed him somehow, but there was a cryptic message on the machine. Did I tell you? He's come up with the greatest idea since the invention of panty hose."

"Panty hose?"

"That's what he said."

She grinned. "What could be greater than panty hose?"

"The perfect ski."

CHAPTER FOUR

THE JAMES GANG MIGHT HAVE STEPPED OUT OF ONE of F. Scott Fitzgerald's novels. Blessed with uncommon good looks, swaggering self-confidence, and plenty of money, Greg and Suzanne were in fact touched by those tragic accidents that ennobled literature but humbled real-life existence. The death in an auto crash of Greg's twin, the lingering death of a beloved mother, the discovery that their jovial but proper father had sired a bastard, his subsequent marriage to a wealthy scatterbrain who preferred her horses to her daughter, Kit. Rather than let these dark devils invade their waking life as they did their dreams, they worked at playing harder, drinking faster, and spending more. This life-style had kept them from forming any significant relationships other than that they had with each other. Neither Greg nor Suzanne seemed to be seriously worried, both professing that the whole idea of marriage even for the purpose of producing children was definitely outmoded.

Suzanne refused to clutter her life or mind with anything that required more than the most cursory consideration. She was not particularly concerned with morality, ethics, or the demands of friend-ship. Her life was her own, her real affection went to Greg and Kit, and with the exception of Sally Schneider, she was blissfully unconcerned with any reminders from the past. Suzanne clung to the old-fashioned double standard that said it was all right for her to write the rules as she went along but not for anyone else. Her current lover, Tony Frantz, seemed unaware of that fact.

As Suzanne paced around the huge living room of the house on Red Mountain, Greg, sprawled in one of the deep leather couches, watched her. "I don't know why you let him get to you."

"It's not him. It's her." Furiously, she amended, "It's both of them."

"It was only a tennis match. What's the big deal?"

Suzanne turned on Greg, blue eyes electric with anger. "It's not the goddamn match! It was Tony wanting to play with her."

"You've got to be kidding. You honestly care what Tony Frantz does?" At the sudden flush that suffused her face, Greg's eyes narrowed. "I told you going out with him was a mistake."

She threw herself into a chair and tucked her feet under her. "Tony doesn't mean anything to me. He's just filler."

"So why are you making such a big deal out of it?"

"Did you see the smug look on her face when they won?"

"Oh, give it a rest. I'm bored with the whole subject of Tony Frantz and Sally Schneider."

Suzanne combed her long silver hair with her fingers and peered into the old silver-framed Spanish mirror. "Consider it changed." But Sally Schneider's flushed victorious face lingered in her memory. For a moment she'd looked almost beautiful. She remembered her first meeting with Sally.

The Jameses had moved in next door to the Burkes. The day of the move Suzanne had been standing outside watching four burly men with smelly cigars parked in the corner of their mouths move in and out of the house with the possessions.

She had looked around in curiosity at her new street and caught the eye of a dark-haired girl about her age watching the proceedings. She had big gray eyes and hair pulled tightly back in a ponytail. While Suzanne wore jeans and a T-shirt, the other girl had on a cotton skirt and shirt in a muddy blue print. The outfit was much too big for her.

From that moment on, she was aware of the girl's eyes following her every move. Finally one day on the way to school, she had allowed the girl to catch up and walk with her. They exchanged names and ages, Suzanne discovering that she was a few months older than Sally. That few months gave her a decided edge, she felt, and carte blanche to turn the younger girl into her slave.

Sally had obviously been mesmerized by Suzanne James, not to mention her wardrobe of circle skirts and Ban-lon shirts. Suzanne, feeling like Lady Bountiful, had given her one of the outfits. Whether it didn't fit or she hadn't liked it, she couldn't remember, but she had never seen Sally wear it. When she asked why, Sally had said that her father would make her give it back if he knew, so she had simply stuck it in the back of her closet, taking it out and wearing it only in her bedroom when she was sure everyone was asleep.

One of Sally's favorite forms of recreation had been to watch Suzanne get dressed for a date. Often, Suzanne would let Sally, who was very good at it, do something interesting with her hair: a pageboy, a French braid, or a chignon. She would allow her to pick out her dress and shoes, for though Sally wore the dreariest clothes in Maine, she had a good eye for color and detail. For Sally, it was sheer joy to fondle the pretty things that she would never own. For Suzanne, it was simply another demonstration of her mastery over the other girl.

At lunchtimes, knowing that Sally lived for a blow-by-blow description of her dates, Suzanne would wring out every detail and word exchanged, often making up outrageous stories that turned the awkward, stammering, sweaty-palmed oaf she had gone out with into a Prince Charming. To Sally, hanging on every word or gesture of Suzanne's casual recital, her eyes shining, her heart pounding, it was like listening to one of the great love stories. As Suzanne related how Sam or Gary or Phil or whoever had held her hand or kissed her or fondled her breast, Sally felt every delicious, dangerous touch and waited for the day it would happen to her.

When it finally did, when Sally had shyly admitted to her that she was in love with Bryan Blaisdell, Suzanne, instead of being happy for her, had seduced the boy. Even though she thought he was a bit of a wimp, she refused her friend this happiness, not because she gave a fig for him, but because she knew Sally was taking her first independent step away from her rule.

And it was, but for a totally unplanned reason. Some so-called Judas friend had told Sally how she, Suzanne, had bragged about her easy conquest of her best friend's boyfriend. When Sally had bitterly confronted her with the information, Suzanne had tried to make it sound as if she had done it for Sally's good, to prove once and for all that Bryan wasn't worth her love or time. She stopped going to Suzanne's house, ending all contact with her. When their mutual friends questioned her, Suzanne would laugh and say she'd gotten tired of dragging around the albatross, but the truth was she felt lost and insecure without the glow of Sally's luminous approval. Years later she realized that she'd never had that unquestioning, accepting relationship with anyone again.

Despite Suzanne's silver medal, her success as a cover girl and as the companion or lover of scores of attractive men and the comfortable fortune she'd made from her celebrity, Sally Burke still had the power to make her feel cheap and inconsequential.

In high school their individual personalities began to take shape, and Sally's seriousness had begun to pay off. Her grades were better, so she made honors lists. Because of the strictness of her father, she had fewer distractions to contend with. She developed formidable powers of concentration that paid off primarily in sports. It was apparent that Sally was a natural athlete: quick, agile, and well coordinated. Those qualities coupled with her intense concentration turned her into a fearless skier. Suzanne, though naturally graceful and a skilled gymnast, was rarely able to beat Sally in any of the local racing events. Later, when Sally dropped off the ski team, leaving her records unchallenged and, deaf to his pleas, leaving her coach tearing his hair, only Suzanne had dimly understood the reasons why. And Suzanne had never said anything to anyone about the reasons Sally had dropped out. Yet though she refused to think about Sally Burke, the specter pursued her

into her Olympic career. If Sally Burke had continued to ski, would she have been the one with the
medal instead of Suzanne?

Whatever real rivalry they might have had years
ago had been muted by time. The knowledge that
she was prettier, livelier, better dressed, and wildly
popular gave Suzanne little satisfaction now because she knew that Sally couldn't have cared less.

That summed it up better than anything. Their
values were totally different and had been since
childhood.

Suzanne felt the stirrings of discontent, an emotion that seemed to plague her more and more
lately. Part of Suzanne's fascination was that she
never stayed anywhere long enough for people to
tire of her. She lived life like a perennial house-
guest, skipping around Europe to ski in Verbier
and Gstaad, and when she tired of that to hop down
to the Caribbean as a guest at someone's private
island or on someone's yacht. Her name and picture
appeared regularly in the gossip magazines and newspapers which found her irrepressible behavior good
copy.

She seemed to have everything: the gilded life,
the flashy image, the golden good looks, and the
nonstop body. She'd never really failed at anything
unless it was her attempt as a sports commentator,
when her peculiar speech mannerisms, her baby-
talk *r*, her rolling *l*'s, and nasality were magnified
with excruciating results.

Greg James recognized the signs in his sister.
Suzanne was about to disturb the peace. He
watched and waited for the explosion.

"God, I hate this place. We should redecorate.
Maybe we should sell it. What do you think we
could get for it?"

The James house was one of the older houses on

Red Mountain, designed in that early Colorado ersatz chalet style, huddled into the red limestone bosom of the mountain, staring over its neighbors like a crouched animal. It was large, rambling, and awkwardly angled inside.

When Greg, Sr., had remarried, his new wife's attempt to inject her Park Avenue style had filled it with pale blue damask and signed English pieces. A year later, when Cee Cee had decided she was not cut out for the sporting life and convinced her husband that a house in the Dominican Republic near Oscar de la Renta would be cunning, she was happy to remove her treasures and hire the services of Liz Mallory, Aspen's popular decorator, to do it over for "the children."

The result was a series of rooms with Liz's signature look of casual clutter planned along heroic lines and with subdued luxury. There were lacquered goatskin consoles and sueded buffalo couches, Spanish tables, and ornately carved benches from Santa Fe. There were stone occasional tables and huge andirons made of old Italian carriage axles, handwoven linen pillows and pale Navaho rugs, an English horn chandelier, and giant yuccas in terra-cotta pots.

At the mention of redecorating, Greg groaned. "Jesus, Suz, I like the place the way it is and so does Kit."

"Well, I'm bored with it."

"Listen, knowing you, you'll be taking off in a couple of weeks. We won't see you for months, and we'll be stuck with your mess. Why don't you just find something else to change? How about the color of your hair or your nail polish?" he suggested hopefully.

"You can forget about my leaving. I plan to be here while Kit trains."

"So do I!"

"Good. You ought to be thinking of what we can do. I'm not going to watch that clone get a step ahead of her."

"You're still fighting a rivalry that hasn't existed for years."

"What about you?"

"What about me? Sally Schneider and her kid don't concern me."

"But Tony Frantz does, and he's the one who's been coaching Rocky all these years."

"So what?" Greg tried to sound offhanded, but Suzanne's words stung him anew. Although Greg and Tony were ostensibly friends and, if not social buddies, at least part of the same rarefied club that the best instructors belonged to, Greg knew he was always considered second to Tony. If Greg got a hotshot Wall Street whiz kid for a private, Tony got his boss, the CEO. If Greg had an ex-governor, Tony had an ex-president. The only fact that made it bearable was that Tony had to work and Greg only worked because it was something to occupy the time. He didn't really need the money.

Tony and Greg had met when both were skiing World Cup and then again as Olympic racers. Month after month, year after year found Greg chasing down courses after Tony's back. With boring regularity it was Tony first, Greg second. At the Olympics, when Tony had been skiing on a strong Austrian team and he on an improved American team, it had seemed that the positions might be reversed, but in the end they had finished in the usual order, even though the times that had separated them were a blink of the eye.

Tony had taken three gold medals that year, an unheard-of feat that only three skiers had ever accomplished. Greg, whose silvers should have been satisfaction enough, had developed a stinging dislike for the cool blond skier, a dislike that was hidden by boisterous camaraderie even as it festered with every passing year.

Greg had come back to Aspen hoping to forget about Tony Frantz, only to wake up a year later to the fact that the Silver Leaf Ski Corp had successfully convinced Tony to make his home in Aspen, offering him a "can't refuse" deal. Tony had arrived in town to the kind of enthusiasm usually reserved for a Robert Redford or the discovery of a new gold vein.

Again Greg was pushed into second position.

Suzanne interrupted his thoughts. "It doesn't bother you that Tony is coaching her?"

"Why should it? We're both coaching Kit. I mean, two Olympic silvers must be worth more than one gold."

"Three golds, and I needn't remind you that Tony is considered the best ski coach in the world," Suzanne said baldly.

"Thanks a lot. Are you saying that because you're sleeping with him, or do you really believe that?"

She was about to hurl one of her choicer obscenities when Kit James burst into the room.

"Listen, you guys, you haven't made any plans for dinner, have you?"

"Hello, Kit. How are you, Kit?" Greg overrode her boisterous entry.

"Sorry," she apologized. "Hi, how are you?" Pausing for a breath, she continued. "Well, have you?"

"That depends. What did you have in mind?"

"I invited some of the kids for dinner. Rocky and I thought we could cook outdoors. Do you mind?"

"Rocky Schneider?"

"Of course, how many Rockys do I know?"

"Kit," began Suzanne worriedly, "I don't think . . ."

Greg interjected smoothly, ". . . you should do all the work. We'll help you. You know, make salad, stuff like that."

"Really, you don't mind?"

Greg was aware that Suzanne was staring at him in openmouthed shock. He gave her a warning shake of his head and continued smoothly. "Mind? Why should I mind? You're my favorite little sister."

"Your *only* one, you mean."

"Who's counting?"

"Great, I'll go shower and change. You're terrific, Grunt."

He smiled at the silly nickname she'd given him when she was little, saying that when he skied bumps he always made that noise.

She bounded from the room, a teenage athlete in superb shape. Hours of torturous training hadn't even made a dent in her prodigious stores of energy.

"What was that all about?" hissed Suzanne.

"What are you going to do? Suddenly tell her she can't be friends with a girl she's been close to all her life?"

"Damn straight."

"Look, let me handle this. We've got a delicate situation here. They've been ski buddies since they could walk. You can't just stop it."

Suzanne clamped her mouth shut. "Oh, no? They're rivals," she insisted, thinking of how it had been between Rocky's mother and herself. Of course, Kit was nothing like her or even Greg. They might all have the same father, but the maternal genes made them as different as strangers. Yet, Kit was not even remotely like the empty-headed Cee Cee. She was fair, open-minded, and reasonable, all qualities that needed to be changed if she was going to compete with the determined Rocky Schneider.

"If you want my opinion, all the training in the world is not going to give Kit the competitive edge," she said, following Greg into the huge kitchen.

"I know you'd like her to use your usual Rambo tactics and wipe out the competition with a single blast, but that's not her style." He took carrots from the refrigerator and pointed them at her as if they were an automatic rifle.

"No, that's not true at all, but I think we have to make Kit realize she can't let friendship interfere with winning."

"We will, but we have to be subtle about it."

"And I'm not subtle?"

"Like a mine field," was his answer. He began to tear lettuce furiously into the salad bowl. Suzanne picked up the chef's knife and sliced tomatoes with cruel deliberation. As he chopped and she sliced, the salad became a simple metaphor for sophisticated methods of torture.

A few miles away and in far less luxurious surroundings, the same conversation was being held between Sally and Rocky. Rocky had just asked her mother's permission to go to Kit's house for dinner.

"You and Kit James seem awfully close."

"We are. We have been for years. You know that. Why does that bother you all of a sudden?" asked Rocky, who was helping her mother fold laundry before getting ready to go to Kit's house.

"It doesn't bother me," denied Sally quickly. "It's just that you see her all the time, you both do the same things. Don't you think it would be nice if you met kids who weren't skiers?"

"And how'm I s'posed to do that? When do I get a chance to meet those kind of people?"

"Honey"—Sally pulled her daughter close—"you don't have to do this, you know. I won't be upset if you decide you want out. You know that."

Rocky pulled herself away gently but firmly. They'd had this discussion so many times. She blamed herself for emphasizing the shortcomings of a racer's life, but once she was on her way to the Olympics and after a year or two of well-paid endorsements, there'd be time for other things, including college and boyfriends. "Don't, Mom. Like, we've had this discussion before. I know what I'm doing. Honest. If I bitch a little, it's okay. It doesn't mean anything. Not really. Besides, it's okay to bitch. Everyone does. You, too. What about when you have a class of donkeys, and after four days they're still donkeys. Don't you bitch?"

"Got me on that. I suppose I keep saying it, because I just want to be sure that you know I only want what's best for you." She rolled her eyes. "Oh, God, I can't believe I really said that."

Rocky laughed. A sudden surge of pure love for her mother ran through her. Sally was the best mother in the world. Even though Rocky had adored her lighthearted, easygoing father, she knew that Sally was the family rock. Fair, strict, objective, demanding, yet loving. Sometimes it was hard to meet her high standards, but she always gave hugs and kisses for effort, even when success proved elusive. "Be the best for yourself," she'd said, "not because anyone expects you to be." It was advice Rocky didn't quite understand, but guessed it had something to do with her mother's past. She'd always wondered why her mother, who was such a great skier, had never raced. Once she'd asked her father about it, but he had changed the subject and somehow she'd been sensitive

enough to realize that it was not a question her
mother would answer easily.

"So do you mind driving me over?"

Although Rocky had a learner's permit, she
hadn't had much opportunity to practice driving,
so Sally was still forced to play chauffeur.

"How will you get home?"

"Don't worry. I'm sure that won't be a problem."

"I hope the boys are good drivers." Sally's
response was automatic. What she really meant
was, as long as it isn't Greg James.

Later, as the racers sat around talking shop and
drinking Diet Cokes, Rocky wondered again why
her mother didn't like the Jameses. Although they
always insisted they told each other everything,
Rocky knew it wasn't really true. She and Kit had
had this conversation recently.

"You and your mom are really close, aren't
you?" Kit had commented enviously.

"Yeah, especially since Daddy died."

"It must be awful not to have a father."

Rocky had shrugged. "Not really awful anymore. Mom tries to make up for it. And now that
I'm older, I realize I tell her things I could never
have told my father, and she tells me things, too.
We tell each other everything," she said loyally,
knowing that wasn't exactly the truth.

"Everything?"

"Well, mostly everything. I mean . . . I don't
discuss sex with her . . . I mean, we have discussed
sex in a general way . . . but, you know what I
mean."

"So if you keep things from her, don't you think
she keeps things from you?"

Rocky bristled. "Like what?"

Kit shrugged and stared at her stubby fingers.
There was an angry hangnail on one of them. She

decided to gnaw on it and avoid an answer, but Rocky persisted. "Like what?"

"Her love life, maybe?"

"Her love life? Mom doesn't have one. Besides, it's none of my business if she does."

"How do you know whether she does or not? You're hardly ever home."

"Eric is. He'd know."

"He's just a kid. And a boy at that. They never pay attention to important things."

Rocky thought for a moment. Somehow she had never thought of her mother having a life outside the one centered on her and Eric. Of course, there was work and her hobbies. With a flash of mature intuition, she realized that her mother was still a young woman and there was no reason for her to behave like an old grandmother. She'd read enough to know that people made love into their forties. It wasn't as if sex was such a forbidden subject; after all, she and her mother had talked about unwanted pregnancies and birth control and AIDS. But it was still a shadowy subject, and she had no idea of what it was *really* like when people made love.

"Have you ever made love with anyone?" Rocky asked abruptly.

Kit flushed. "Kissed, yes, but the other stuff . . . like touching. No. I mean . . ." She was about to qualify her statement, then changed her mind. "No," she said firmly. "You?"

"Tom Platt tried to put his hand up my sweater once." Tom Platt raced first position on the boys' team.

"He did! What did you do? You didn't let him, did you?" Kit, who had suffered the same indignity from the same boy, held her breath for Rocky's answer.

"Are you kidding? I grabbed his hand and practi-

cally broke his knuckles." What she didn't say was
that for a moment she had felt a stab of excitement
before it was replaced by fear, followed by anger.

"You did? Oh." Kit had turned her hot face away
so Rocky couldn't see the awful truth she was sure
was emblazoned on it.

"Don't tell me he tried the same thing on you?"
Rocky's mouth became a thin disapproving slash.

Kit nodded in embarrassment.

"What did you do?"

"Nothing. I let him. I was afraid."

"Afraid of what?"

"I don't know."

"That slime. Now, I'm sorry I didn't break his
arm. Don't worry about it." She put her arms
around her friend, feeling much older and a great
deal stronger. "Now you know, you won't let it
happen again."

"Weren't you the least bit curious?"

"About what?"

"About . . . you know . . . what happens next.
How do you find out about those things? It's not
something you ask your mother, even if she was
around, which mine isn't. I certainly wouldn't ask
Suzanne. She'd kill me."

Rocky had heard rumors about Suzanne and her
sex life. She wasn't quite sure what that meant
exactly, other than having a lot of boyfriends. Did
that mean she made love with all of them? It was
not a question she wanted to ask Kit under the
circumstances. Still, it was all very fascinating.

"You know," complained Kit, "we might as well
be nuns. I'm sure there are lots of sixteen-year-old
girls who know a lot more than we do."

"And do a lot more, too. Oh, well, think of it this
way: They don't give Olympic medals for how
many boys you sleep with."

Kit laughed. That's why she liked Rocky so

much. She could always turn the most serious problem into a joke.

Greg James appeared in the doorway. Looking at his watch, he said, "I hate to break this up, but you guys are in training, remember? You need your beauty sleep. Sorry, Kit."

"It's okay, Greg."

"Did you have the same schedule when you were racing?" asked one of the boys.

"Believe it or not, we did. Only the training was not quite as high tech as it is today and we certainly didn't have facilities like The Aspen Club or the Silver Leaf Spa."

"What do you think our chances are in World Cup?" asked another.

Greg threw up his hands and gave them his boyish, sincere smile. "No comment. Hey, you guys, I'm only an ex-racer."

"Yeah, but you know our record last year was awful," insisted the boy.

"That was last year. This is this year."

"How about coaching us?"

"You have a coach already," Greg reminded them.

He smiled at their boos and catcalls. It was true. They were suffering from lackadaisical coaching. The Development Squad was coached by the U.S. Ski Team coaching staff. Greg had always felt this was the weak link. This was when the racer had the most contact with his coaches and should be learning really high-level racing. But salaries were low; there wasn't a well-defined promotion ladder, and a coach couldn't look forward to a support system—as they could in Europe—when he left coaching. So the level of coaching was low, usually done by ex-racers who hadn't gotten to the top levels.

Once the Olympics were over, the country lost

interest in skiing. The sport had never achieved the exalted status it had in Alpine countries like Switzerland and Austria where skiing was the national sport. It had never even made the inroads that tennis had, because more than half the country lived in areas where it rarely snowed and, even if it had, there were no mountains. Skiing didn't just take a backseat to football or baseball, it just ceased to exist when the snow melted. Along with springboard diving, ski racing was not a choice for a long-range career.

"Do you all have transportation?" he asked.

"Yeah, yeah," they said, breaking into groups and heading for the door.

"How about you, Rocky? You have a way to get home?"

Rocky hesitated, remembering the closed expression her mother got on her face at the mention of Greg James's name. "Uh, I'm sure someone's going in my direction."

"Don't be silly. I'll drop you off. It'll only take a couple of minutes."

"Uh, really, you don't have to."

"Go on, Rocky. He won't bite you. He's really very nice," said Kit.

As Greg slipped into his jacket, Suzanne came down the stairs. "Where are you going?" she asked.

Greg took Rocky lightly by the arm. "I'm going to drop Rocky home. And we're going to have a five-minute discussion of coaching. Aren't we, Rocky?"

The James gang exchanged knowing looks. Rocky felt something unsettling lurking under the friendly raillery of their words, but their faces were innocent, smiling, pleasant, and she chided herself for being influenced by her mother's suspicions.

She didn't see Greg's bold wink to his sister as he followed her out the door.

Rocky was silent as Greg sped down the mountain road. It was a black night, a heavy cloud cover concealing the stars that usually seemed an arm's length away in the dry mountain air. She was glad of the darkness because she didn't know what to say to him. As if that weren't enough, he seemed to give off an aroma of fresh-cut grass and lemons. She had certainly seen plenty of advertisements for men's perfumes, but Greg was the first person she knew who wore them. Inexplicably she blushed, grateful again for the dark cloak of night.

It was seconds before she realized he was talking to her about racing. And to her surprise he seemed to encapsulate all her feelings in a few choice words.

"Oh, yes," she agreed, full of animation. The coaches spoke another language. They didn't have the poetic understanding, this feeling of uniqueness.

"I mean," he continued, "in what other sport does an unprotected body go hurtling down a mountain at speeds over eighty miles an hour? The danger alone and the courage it takes . . ."

"Yes," she breathed. "Were you ever scared?"

"Were you?" he challenged.

She thought for a moment. It never occurred to her to give a girlish squeal and a low breathy answer or that she might even sound immodest. "No, not really."

Now it was his turn to be happy. The little devil was telling the truth. Kit, baby, he thought, you have your work cut out for you.

Greg pulled to a stop in front of her house and reached across her to open the car door. "You know, you've grown up in a year. Last year you were this pudgy kid. Now you're a pretty grown-up girl. Are the boys hitting on you? If they're not, they're crazy."

He let his hand drop over hers for a moment. Then he squeezed it and smiled, keeping his voice friendly, nonthreatening. "Good luck, kid. You're going to be great this year, I just know it."

"Thank you," she said shyly, getting out of the car. Then she bent down to speak. "And thank you for the ride."

"Anytime." He gave her the boyish flash of dimples, leaving her wondering again why her mother's face always looked as if she'd sucked a sour lemon when his name was mentioned.

Greg looked at the gold Rolex on his wrist. Only ten-thirty. Too early to go home, and he felt too restless to watch television. Suzanne was going out with Tony. Kit should be asleep. He turned the car and went out Main Street to Highway 82.

He drove fast, knowing that any moment some beer-slozzled kid in a pickup could come at him head-on and wipe him out in a matter of seconds. Just beyond Snowmass, he turned off. The wind came hustling down across McClean Flats, sending up a whirlwind of devil dust. High up an unpaved road lay an old mining town called Lenado where the actor Don Johnson had just bought a ranch, but he was not looking for star-studded company that night. He was looking for a dark, smelly place where he could joke around with a barmaid and have a few beers.

Along the Roaring Fork was Little Texas, a camp of trailers and worn run-down houses where many of Aspen's service and maintenance people lived. The lights were off and the only sound that rustled through the grasses was the occasional bark of one of the hound dogs shackled to a clothesline out back, probably howling at a jackrabbit or a gopher.

On his left was the Woody Creek Tavern and Post Office. It was an ersatz log cabin with freshly painted red trim. Outside there was an ice machine which worked sometimes, a news kiosk, and a phone.

The tavern had a pool table and a big bar where you could drop in any hour of the day or night and watch ESPN. They served decent chili, ribs, and a handful of Mexican dishes. He pulled his car off the road, parked, and walked in. There were four or five men in plaid shirts and jeans at the bar. They wore Stetsons pushed back on their heads, the heels of their cowboy boots hooked on the bottom rungs of scarred stools.

Vida Sue Buckholtz was a prototypical Western bar girl. She had a tiny waist, swelling breasts and hips, a pile of enraged straw-blond hair that looked as if she had just touched a live wire. She had an innate desire to be pleasing.

Greg sat down and hooked his boots on a rung like the rest of the men. This unconscious wish to look as though he belonged here did not help. Even though he wore the skintight jeans and leather jacket that the others affected, it was obvious that his did not come from the Sears Roebuck catalog. Vida Sue stopped polishing a glass and flashed him a toothy smile. Her voice was breathy and low pitched, which made him smile. He'd heard it plenty of times when it sounded more like a rusty screen door. "Hi, stranger. Long time, no see."

"You say that to all the guys," teased Greg with a broad wink.

"Do I?" She giggled, then leaned toward him to give him the requisite look at her cleavage. "I seem to keep repeating myself."

She had creamy skin, acres of it. A faint tanned vee, the kind that comes when blondes are in the sun for more than fifteen minutes, stained the fair skin. He stared at it, finding it more provocative than the swelling mounds around it. In the red dress she looked like a strawberry sundae with a huge dollop of whipped cream.

"What'll it be?"

"The usual."

She expertly drew a mug of Bud and placed it in front of him, watching as he hefted the glass, then drew it to his lips and took a thirsty sip that reduced its contents by half.

"You musta been doin' somfin' that made you thirsty." Vida Sue had trouble saying her *th*'s. They always came out sounding like *f*'s.

"Not yet." He smiled.

"Ooh," she purred. "That sounds promisin'."

"Where's Rory these days?" Rory Swigart was reputed to be Vida Sue's current boyfriend. He was a dark-haired, good-looking, nasty-tempered ranch hand who seemed to lose most jobs because he let his fists talk when he should have kept silent.

"Oh, him." She turned away and punched the cash register with particular vehemence. "He can go take a flyin' fuck into a rattlesnake's nest for all I care. I haven't seen him in weeks and don't expect to. He got the wrong attitude 'bout us."

I just bet he did, thought Greg, returning his mug for a refill.

"I get off at twelve," she said hopefully, letting her fingertips brush his hand.

"That's an hour from now."

"The longer you wait, the better it is," she promised, deep in her throat.

He thought about it. He wouldn't have to do a thing. Just lie back and enjoy it. Vida Sue's greedy little mouth and strong fingers would do the rest. Vida Sue was a good mindless antidote to overexposure to the Tony Frantz virus, not to mention the chronic problem of how to neuter Rocky Schneider's threat to Kit.

To kill time he shot some pool and watched wrestling and late-night bowling, letting his mind deal with the problem of Kit's training. It wasn't her actual ski training that worried him, it was getting her psychologically hardened. Unlike Suzanne and himself, Kit didn't have the killer instinct. Despite the fact that they had practically raised her, none of their more aggressive patterns of behavior had rubbed off on her. She was good because she was good, dutiful when it came to taking instruction, and a born imitator. All Suzanne or he had to do was demonstrate an aspect of technique and she could duplicate it on the first try.

At twelve o'clock sharp, Vida Sue shooed everybody out to the sound of halfhearted grumbling. Five minutes later they were at her trailer. As her busy fingers undressed him, Greg tried to ignore the pink and white gingham decor, the ersatz maple end tables loaded with china kittens, the artificial paper flowers in a remarkably hideous blue lusterware vase. The air was stale from cigarette smoke and the dregs of wine. In the minuscule sink, a frying pan with congealed bacon grease and bits of fried egg waited for her to wash it.

Greg James was compulsively clean. He hated disorder of any kind. Even in his carefree skiing days, his turtlenecks were neatly folded, his socks nested, his toilet articles arranged like perfect soldiers. He accepted relentless teasing good-naturedly, aware of his compulsion but helpless to change it.

With the lights out Vida Sue's lavender-scented body canceled out the other smells; the sink, the decor, and the clutter was forgotten as soon as she straddled him. She could do things with her mouth that were totally awesome. It was as though the Creator had gifted her with an epiglottal musculature that behaved like some great sucking vacuum cleaner. Once she'd fastened on him, he had visions of being swallowed whole from his cock on up.

"Vida Sue, Vida Sue," he murmured, digging his fingers into the pillowy softness of her buttocks. When he finally invaded that softness, it was like sinking into a down comforter. He was going to suffocate, drown, die. But oh Lordy, what a way to go!

"Where were you last night, you lousy cocksucker?" Daisy's voice carried easily to the next table.

"What do you mean, where was I? And for Christ's sake, keep your voice down." Greg James looked around the half-empty Grill Room of the Silver Leaf Inn.

"We had a date last night, you creep."

"You're kidding, Daisy. We couldn't have."

"Thanks a lot for forgetting." Daisy's face was a swiftly changing road map of emotions. Sally had often told her she knew exactly what cards she was holding when she sat in on the monthly poker games and that it was a good thing she could afford to lose the money. "Thanks a lot for giving a damn. You could have called," she hissed.

"Yeah, I could have called if I had known. Are you sure we had a date?"

"No, I'm making it up, asshole."

"Jesus, Daisy, your mouth is like a goddamn sewer. I can't figure out how anyone who comes from the kind of family you do can talk like that."

"That's how."

He looked at her morose features and felt hardly

a thing. Daisy was getting to be a total pain in the ass. When she'd first come to Aspen and eventually to the ski school, he'd admired her spunk. She was small and as lean as a whippet, with a tiny heart-shaped face, huge hazel eyes fringed with lashes, and lustrous black-stallion hair.

She could outski half the men on the mountain and seemed to be a bottomless pit of energy. She was game for any adventure, any dare, any challenge. When she'd finally gotten around to him, she took one look and bingo! Her endearing persona was immediately exchanged for that of a tearful, moaning shrew who mixed protestations of eternal love with death threats delivered along with painful and colorful descriptions. She was an albatross around his neck.

"Are you going to tell me?"

"Tell you what?"

"Where you were last night?"

"No. What do you want for dinner?" He looked up at the waiter standing patiently at her elbow. They exchanged a look of complicity.

"I'm not hungry. Give me a martini," she said peremptorily, then returned her angry eyes to his. "You don't have to tell me, I already know."

Greg pointed to something on the menu and waved the waiter away. "So why do you ask?"

"You were with that little piece of sleaze, that open-legged trash can, Vida Sue."

"How do you know that?"

"Aren't you afraid of getting a disease? Christ, everything including the Denver and Rio Grande goes through her."

"Put a lid on it, Daisy. You're spoiling my dinner. I asked you how you know I was with Vida Sue."

"Someone saw you at Woody Creek last night." She suddenly switched tactics. Taking his hand, she covered it with kisses. "Greg, honey, why didn't you come to me? You know I love you. How can you be sleeping with someone else when you have me? I'd never do anything like that to you."

He withdrew his hand. "Stop it, Daisy. I think I like it better when you're as mad as a hornet and stinging. Look, you've got to understand something. I never wanted you to give me exclusive rights to you. I hate having a yoke around my neck, so I don't ever intend to put one on anyone I go out with."

"But, Greg, I love you. I thought you loved me!" There was real anguish in her voice.

"I like you a whole lot, you're fun to be with. But love? I never said anything about love."

It was true, he hadn't. Daisy was honest enough with herself to realize she had pushed the easygoing Greg into a relationship that she wanted; she had subtly dictated the terms, and when she received no resistance had assumed that he had wanted it, too. "I just assumed . . ."

"Don't assume," he said firmly. "Look, I don't want to hurt you, Daisy, but I don't love you. I'm sorry, I wish I could. If it's any consolation, I've never told anyone that I loved her. I'm not even sure I know what it is. I only know I've got to stay loose."

"Maybe we should stop seeing each other." The frightening words sprang to her lips so quickly that they were said and over before she could take them back. I don't mean that, she cried silently. You know I don't mean it.

"I think you're probably right."

There was an awkward silence as the waiter put the martini in front of her. "Drink up. Let's finish the evening on a brighter note."

She lifted blazing eyes to him. Gone was the

anguish, and in their place was a murderous hatred that he had seen before. In one sweeping motion, she stood and flung the drink in his face. "Fuck you, Greg James."

He, along with the rest of the room, watched her stormy departure.

CHAPTER FIVE

THE GOLDEN DAYS OF OCTOBER FINALLY GAVE WAY to November. Early-morning mist veiled the higher peaks until, like an ink stain on a blotter, the fog spread out to choke everything in a miasma of white. The damp chill clung to the valley for days on end as those whose livelihood depended on it—and that meant almost everyone who lived year round in the Roaring Fork Valley—looked at the heavens and wondered if this year would be another with poor snow.

The month had gone by too fast for Max Margolis. As he feared, there was a big difference between designing a ski on the computer and actually constructing it. However, he was making progress on his prototype, and now his biggest worry was that there might not be enough snow to test it. Other things bothered him, too. Either he was getting paranoid or someone was following him. Not that he had ever really seen anyone, but he had the feeling strange eyes were watching his every move. He decided to buy a guard dog— especially since he was now living down the valley in a rather secluded cabin. He might as well have an early-warning system as well as company on a cold night.

He advertised for a trained police dog. Surprised by the overwhelming response, he finally settled on one whose name was Jugger for Juggernaut. Now he was able to relax and work. When Tony confronted him after having nearly been torn to pieces by the dog, Max sheepishly told him why.

"I don't know if making this ski is worth your becoming paranoid."

"It's worth it, believe me." And Max went back to work with a vengeance.

For Rocky and Kit November meant work as usual, regardless of the weather. Road work, both running and bicycling, obstacle running, free weights, Nordic pulls to develop upper-body muscle, step running to develop quads, and punching the bag to duplicate the motion of the pole plant, so important to slalom skiing. They wanted to squeeze the juice from every day, for soon they would leave for Alpine training in Europe.

But each departure was put off as it appeared that Europe was being denied its usual early snows. Unusually mild temperatures were being reported from the ski areas of Switzerland, Austria, Italy, and France.

For Sally, it was nail-biting time. The first heating oil bill had already been delivered. Eric needed new sneakers and ski boots and was developing a serious interest in figure skating. Early snows meant work and more money. At the Emporium, where she worked part-time, they were asking her when she expected to leave so they could hire someone to take her place.

She had finished Marcella Richards's bag and accepted her check for five hundred dollars with some guilty trepidation, but when Marcella called her the following week and asked if she could make two more for friends who had admired hers, she stopped feeling guilty and realized that she might have found a lucrative solution to her chronic financial problems.

Tony had accompanied Richard Farwell to Norway to look at a new Swan he wanted to buy and would be gone for another few weeks. The house seemed empty without his boisterous, lighthearted presence, and the children seemed grumpier than usual without him. Sally realized she missed having him to talk to, even if their conversations usually seemed to end with her criticism of his frivolous approach to life. God, they were so different! It was a miracle they were even friends.

Even Daisy had run out on her. After stalking all over town like an angry cat, complaining to everyone who would listen what a shit Greg James was, then moaning how much she loved him, she had gotten fed up and skipped out to New York. Loyally, she'd phoned home every few days to report on the latest new restaurant, the day's purchases, the Broadway shows, and the new man she'd just met: an investment banker, newly divorced, divine, and mad about her. She, unfortunately, could not really fall in love with a man who hated winter and heights, but for a New York quickie, he was a treasure.

Sally had to smile at her friend's antics. Daisy never had trouble meeting men. If she saw someone who appealed to her, she simply went over to him and introduced herself. She got away with it because she was like a bright, frisky, irresistible terrier, boisterously good-natured, funny, and adorable. She fell out of love with the same noisy exuberance with which she fell into it, and instead of moping around with her heartache, she laid it out for all the world to share, thus exorcising it. Her love life was a little like Greek theater, intense, cathartic, dramatic.

Suzanne, whom Sally rarely thought about, was rumored to have gone off with Michael Greenfield, whom Sally did think about from time to time. After his early interest in her, he had apparently grown tired of the pursuit. She'd not heard from him since the tennis matches. The day after their win and her refusal of dinner, he had sent an expensive bouquet of flowers. A note inside proclaimed that the next step was hers. She'd given a shaky laugh and thrown the note away, but the flowers had bloomed for the next two weeks, a constant reminder of his smooth, dark good looks and magnetic charm. She'd had her first dream about him shortly thereafter, a powerfully erotic dream from which she had awakened shaking and wondering. But she didn't call him, thinking of herself as a Cinderella without a fairy godmother, and him as the prince who might be like the storybooks but was more likely not.

Then, as if it would help her to safer ground, she thought again about Tony Frantz. A postcard from Stockholm had surprised her; she thought they had gone to Norway.

It had surprised Tony, too, when Richard Farwell said they would make a quick stop in the Swedish capital. A city of islands, it charmed a first-time visitor with the purity of the many lakes and inlets that surrounded it. He could imagine it sparkling under the brief summer sun, but in November it was gray and bleak. The dark murky light during the short days gave the grave Grimm fairy-tale buildings a phantasmagorical look.

Richard and Tony dined on remarkable smorgasbord at a dazzling restaurant which resembled a palace with its gilded and coffered ceilings and tasted the many flavors of aquavit at still another. The Scandinavian women lived up to their press: tall, blond, beautiful, and friendly.

But the grand surprise was Richard Farwell's announcement that he had booked a week of cross-country skiing for them in Finnish Lapland.

There in the pure white silence above the Arctic Circle, a dazzling expanse of frozen desert bathed in the neon pink and purple of the low polar sun stretched endlessly in front of them. Even with an experienced guide and Richard by his side, Tony had never experienced such a sense of aloneness. He trembled with fear at the sudden vision of himself lost in the trackless waste and slowly freezing to death.

"*Sisu*," said their guide, using the Finnish word for courage. It was a little early, he explained, for such a trip. Usually later was better, but the ice was strong enough to support them.

At first they made short day trips, coming back to a warm fireside and the simple wilderness lodges that offered plenty of hot food, a bed, and little else. Then they set off deep into reindeer country, staying overnight in tiny wooden refuge huts provided by the Department of Forestry. They seemed caught in a constant twilight zone, the sun remaining low or dipping beneath the horizon. Yet the white wastes gleamed with their own reflected light, giving them the look of ghosts as they made their way across the snow.

Herds of reindeer in their winter white pelts lifted curious heads but did not seem particularly frightened by them. "Why should they?" said Richard. "There are only three of us and hundreds of thousands of them."

The food was some of the best he'd ever eaten: thick pea soup, reindeer stew, and lingonberry sauce. Often they would stop and build a sweet-smelling birch log fire where their guide would brew the dark, strong Finnish coffee and they would drink it from wooden cups attached to their belts.

After a week in the icy wonderland, just when Tony was beginning to feel the greatest sense of peace since he had been a child growing up near Innsbruck, it began to snow and suddenly he was caught in a world that seemed without direction, a dream filled with endless quiet, colorless except for the faint shadow of their guide's tunic and tall embroidered native hat. Tony was filled with an exhilarating euphoria, a kind of rapture of the deep such as divers get when they descend too far too quickly, only his was on this dazzling, cold, solid land. He felt like a child without a care or responsibility, happy to forget home and all the unresolved corners of his life.

Tony Frantz was suffering an early midlife crisis. Like most world-class athletes and scientists whose greatest triumphs lay behind them, he was creeping into his late thirties, had never gone to college, and had no special talent for anything but skiing and banging nails. Was that to be his life for the next forty years? He thought of the old Austrian who had been a fixture in Aspen for years, still teaching Arlberg methods, and at seventy still one of the great cocksmen. He could be found every night in one bar or another, cadging drinks and telling the same stories he'd told for years, entertaining the amused and cool young millionaires, who laughed and made fun of him behind his back.

Tony was still one of the most formidable skiers in the world, a legend like the great Stein Eriksen, who, approaching sixty, still was lean, blond, tanned, and handsome.

Admittedly his life was a cut above the ordinary. As the preferred companion of some of the richest, most powerful men in the country, he skied all over the world for free and brought home handsome tips that gave him an income far greater than he might have earned if he had turned professional.

But competition had been his aphrodisiac, his food and drink, and after the torn Achilles tendon, when the doctors had said he would probably have difficulty walking, let alone skiing, everything had changed. He missed the exaltation of competition, a high he couldn't find in social drugs, social drinking, and womanizing.

"How do you do it?" he asked Richard Farwell as the dogsled snaked over the snow to the small landing field where their plane waited to whisk them back to Helsinki.

"Do what?"

"Stay in Aspen."

"I take that to mean how do I stay sane in never-never land?" Richard stroked his chin and the beginnings of a beard. "It's not easy, I admit, but easier for me than you, I suppose. My work is at least real, though it may lack the glamour of yours. I'm sure every red-blooded man in the world thinks he would like to trade places with you."

"For the bullshit, the unreality, the superficiality?"

Richard laughed. "For the glamour, the fun, the gorgeous women, the opportunity to ski instead of work."

"Yes, they don't consider ski-teaching real work. Frankly, I don't either. That's the problem. What's an aging ski instructor to do? I haven't any other skills."

"You don't give yourself enough credit."

Tony sighed. "It's not real, this life, but it's the only one I know. I guess I'm stuck."

"I think if you start thinking of Aspen as a real place and not the dream of some press agent, it will help. After all, Aspen wasn't always a celebrity-ridden ski resort. Once it was a small town with real people and real problems. It still is, although that part of it is buried under the flash and the people that made it real are either dying off or moving out. But it's there waiting for you. You just have to find it."

"What have you decided to do?" The exquisite redhead in the lynx coat looked at her diamond Art Deco watch from Cartier.

"I think I'll pick up the car and drive it to Aspen."

She looked at the sky and frowned. "Looks like it might snow."

"We should be so lucky. So . . ." Greg put his arms around her furry waist and swung her gently back and forth. "I enjoyed it."

"I did, too," she said with a smile that indicated it was time to move on to the next activity.

"Will I see you again?"

"We get up to Aspen several times during the season." The gorgeous woman, who was British and named Jemima, was the wife of Stanley Jamison, President of Jamison Oil. She and Greg had met on the plane from Europe. On the way to Denver they had stopped for a few days in New York where Jemima kept what she called a 'flat,' and which turned out to be a twenty-room town house on Sutton Place.

It had been one of Greg's truly remarkable liaisons. Champagne flowed like water, caviar appeared as if by magic when they were hungry. They rarely got out of bed for three days. She was

skilled—almost too skilled, brilliantly faking orgasm with cries that had been perfected by long
practice. But he didn't care. He'd never made love
to a professional before. He had no proof that she
was, but all signs pointed to it, including her own
carefully edited answers to some of his more
pointed questions.

Now it was over. Still, there was some dialogue
that had to be played out until the curtain fell.

"I'll keep an eye out for you," Greg promised.

"You do that." She blew him a kiss and hurried
away. He stared after her long legs in the impossi-
bly high-heeled shoes striding across the gray-
carpeted floor of Stapleton airport's new wing.

A few hours later, he and his new Porsche were
headed west. The trip by car at this time of the year
usually took from four to five hours. He was
determined to make it in under four if the weather
cooperated.

As he drove the familiar road through the high
Rockies, it appeared he would make it easily. In
Glenwood Canyon the road at times narrowed
between steep cliffs from which dripped or fell the
snow runoff from the higher elevations. The certain sign of a dropping temperature were the
quickly forming icicles.

He passed through Glenwood Springs, where
"Doc" Holliday had lived, practicing dentistry
before becoming a famous drunk and gunfighter.
The movies never mentioned it, but "Doc," reputed to have killed at least eight men in his life-
time, had returned to Glenwood after the Gunfight
at the OK Corral in Tombstone with the Earp broth-
ers, to die of tuberculosis at the age of thirty-five.

As he passed by the red brick buildings that lined
Main Street, he turned into Grand Avenue, where
he could see the rising steam of the famous hot
springs, revered for their medicinal properties by

the Utes. Long before the hotel had sprung up, the Indians would visit the springs yearly as part of the religious rite they believed would make them more skillful hunters and better warriors.

Now Glenwood was just beginning to flourish again after the disastrous shale oil collapse of the seventies. It had all the classic fast-food places— Arby's, Taco Bell, Wendy's, McDonald's—and more auto body repair shops than he had ever seen anywhere, a testament to the uneven driving skills and the tricky winter weather in this part of the state. Sharing this mixture of thriving entrepreneurism were a series of motels with names that seemed to have been borrowed from the early West. The Ponderosa Inn rubbed shoulders with Andre's Redstone, and the Super 8 was within shooting distance of the Antler.

The town also contained two Pizza Huts as well as two huge shopping centers. The local K mart seemed bigger than the entire town of Aspen, and the steady parade of colorless, heavy, dank-haired women wheeling pale-faced crying babies was a far cry from the designer-clad, body-shop–built denizens of Aspen. The two towns were separated by far more than their forty-two miles.

Bob & Alta's diner was but a blink as Greg sped through El Jebel on his way to Basalt.

Basalt was a small Western town that seemed pasted on the side of a mountain. Its name was spelled out in white rocks on a hillside. The nearby Frying Pan River, a legendary trout stream, brought fishermen by the thousand to the neat town which now boasted modern developments along with tidy A-frames and log cabins from an earlier time. In the center was Harry's famous fishing store hunched amid a few tired motels, a bank, and a regional library. Despite the nondescript architecture of Depression America, Basalt still reserved a faint touch of Victoriana.

Beyond Basalt was the real landscape of the West. Thick stands of cottonwood trees, spruce and aspen, old log farmhouses, tilting barns, and rough rail fences strung with rusty, sagging barbed wire. Shiny, well-cared-for snowmobiles were parked amongst the rusting wrecks of old pickups.

By the time he left Basalt, it was snowing heavily. The flakes, big as silver dollars, built up on the cold road quickly, blotting out the red bluffs that rose on either side. All he could see were the shapes and mounds of raw stone and red earth amongst the feathery branches of the leafless cottonwoods.

At Shale Bluffs, a notorious series of blind turns that had destroyed more cars and drivers than any other road in the valley, he was almost blinded by the blanket of white.

He cursed his luck. It had been pleasant and sunny in Denver. Now the swollen gray clouds descended like some miasma from space, spreading out to blot out the landscape. It was like driving in cotton balls. As the road iced up, he slowed, along with the line of traffic in front of him.

Suddenly he heard the crash of metal and realized his car had been solidly hit by a vehicle coming in the other direction. As he fought to keep the spinning Porsche from sliding into the oncoming traffic, his heart leapt to his mouth. He was a superb and experienced driver, but he knew that nothing could ever prepare him for another driver's failings.

When his car finally came to rest, he managed to pry open the jammed door and get out. Peering through the thickly falling snow, he saw a red

Jaguar which had apparently bounced off his Porsche and spun out wildly. It had piled head-on into a wall of the shale which gave that section of road its name, its sleek long whippet nose smashed to a Pekingese snub. Drivers from other cars were racing toward it, all wondering the same thing. Could anyone survive a crash like that, especially in a Jaguar? Luckily, the driver had plowed into the cliffs instead of through the fence on the other side of the road where it was a long way down to the Roaring Fork River.

Greg could only wonder what kind of fool drove a car like that in Colorado in the winter.

Gingerly they pried open the Jaguar's door. Expecting the worst, they found the car's occupant, protected by a seat belt, slumped in the seat. It was a woman, and she seemed to be all right except for a trickle of blood coming from her mouth and a wound on her temple.

"Don't move her," commanded Greg. "Someone should call the police and a doctor. Anyone got a CB?"

"I do," said a young cowboy in a sheepskin jacket.

At the best of times, Shale Bluffs was no place to have an accident. At the worst, it could take hours for the police and an ambulance to arrive in this weather with traffic blocked in both directions.

By now Greg had gotten a good look at the driver and to his horror realized it was Suzanne's friend, Marcella Richards. "Good God, Marcella!"

"You know her, buddy?" asked one of the men who had tried to help.

"Yeah, she's a friend of my sister!" Turning around impatiently, he searched the crowd. "Anyone got a blanket?"

Within minutes two blankets were thrust in his arms and he turned to cover Marcella. If she was alive, she was probably in shock. Until the ambulance arrived, the only thing they could do was keep her warm.

As he drew the covers up, he heard the faint sounds of the sirens. Gradually the cars started to move in both directions until there was a path cleared for both the police and the ambulance.

Now impatient to get Marcella to the hospital, he brushed off Sheriff Marv Rodgers's questions with a peremptory, "I'll make a full report later. I want to get to the hospital. She's a friend."

"Can't let you leave the scene, Greg. Have to ask a few questions."

"Christ, Marv, I'm not going anywhere. Listen, the accident wasn't my fault anyway. Look at my car, look at the impact. You can see it wasn't me. She was coming from town, must have lost control of the car and plowed into me."

"Yeah, you're probably right." The sheriff scratched his chin. "Okay, Greg, you do what you have to do, but make sure you stop by and make a full report. I don't want to have you picked up. In the meantime, we'll tow the car. You'll have to come by and tell us what you want done with it."

Greg looked ruefully at his new Porsche. The car, hit hard on its rear quarter, was unlikely to be salvageable. Forty thousand dollars' worth of trash! "Junk it," he said. "It'll be cheaper to buy a new one."

He got in the ambulance and went to the hospital, aiding in the unconscious woman's check-in. He waited while the emergency-room doctor gave her an initial examination, then came out to report his findings.

"She's alive and breathing. I can't be sure until we examine her more thoroughly and take some pictures, but it looks like it might be a mild concussion. On the other hand, there might be internal bleeding, and that could be serious. You should let me take a look at you, too, as long as you're here."

The earnest young physician looked about sixteen to him. "No, I'm fine. It's my car that needs last rites."

"Well, then, why don't you go home and get some rest? We'll make sure to call you when we know what's going on."

In truth, Greg didn't feel so hot. On top of his anger about the car, he was bruised and shaken. He had not been wearing a seat belt, having unfastened it when the traffic had slowed to a crawl. The unexpected impact had slammed him against the door, and now his shoulder and arm ached. He waggled his fingers. He'd had enough breaks and sprains in his skiing career to know the difference. In his judgment all he'd suffered was a few nasty bruises. He went to the phone and called a High Mountain Taxi to come get him.

When he finally arrived home, it was to a silent house. He felt like a kid who had just been sent home sick from school only to find that his source of comfort and care had deserted him in his hour of need. He walked slowly up the stairs to his suite. In the bathroom, he started the hot tub, and as the comforting steam rose about him, he gingerly pulled off his clothes. His whole body was one big ache now.

He climbed into the tub like a tired old man and sank back against the inflatable pillow with a deep sigh. Soothing steamy water wafted over him and he began to drift, suspended somewhere between sleep and dream. Suddenly he was jolted awake by the slam of the door.

He heard the sound of impatient feet race up the stairs, then Suzanne's voice cut through his befogged brain.

"In here," he called with his last remaining strength.

She poked her head in the door. "What's wrong? Why are you in the bathtub?" She spoke crossly, as if taking a hot tub were some kind of aberration.

Greg scowled. "I'll be right out. Wait for me."

"I'm not going anywhere," she said in annoyance. "I was supposed to . . . but . . ." She couldn't continue.

A few minutes later, Greg, wrapped in a thick white towel, appeared.

She was sitting in Greg's bedroom on a love seat near the fireplace staring out the window. She turned when she heard him. "My God, you look terrible. What happened?"

"There was an accident."

"The new Porsche?"

"Gone. Totaled."

"You're kidding!"

"No. Do you see me laughing?"

"What happened?"

"Your friend Marcella plowed into me."

"Marcella? Was she hurt?"

"Yes, but I don't know how badly."

"My God, I better go to her. Is she at Aspen Valley?"

"Yes, but don't be in such a rush. I went to the hospital with her. They have to do some tests. There might be internal bleeding. The doctor sent me home. Told me he'd call if he had any news."

"Gee, Greg, what a bummer. Are you okay?"

"Thanks for remembering," he said, wincing as he crossed his arms. "Hand me that robe, will you?" She picked up the robe that was folded at the foot of his bed and held it out for him.

As he tried to slip on the robe, he gave a small cry of pain.

"You are hurt!" she cried.

"Just a couple of bruises. She hit me almost broadside." From the look that came over her face, he realized that Suzanne was about to pull one of her righteous-indignation numbers on him. "It wasn't really her fault. The roads were awful. She must have lost control of the car—although I've got to tell you that your rich, successful friend is a little lacking in the smarts department. Anyone who drives a Jaguar in this weather is nuts."

"As crazy as someone who drives a Porsche?"

"I, at least, know how to drive in this stuff."

"I guess you won't be much in the mood to go out for dinner tonight."

"Hardly."

"Well, we have to eat. I'll ask Concheta if she minds making dinner for us."

Later, when Greg joined her in the den, Suzanne was staring out the window, a crystal flute of designer water held loosely in her hand. At his entrance she turned and looked at him long and hard, trying to judge if the time to speak was now or later.

"What's on your mind, Suz? You've had this odd look on your face since you came in. You're not still worried about me, I hope."

"No, that is, yes. But for another reason."

"What is it? Spit it out, for God's sake. I hate it when you get maternal."

She cleared her throat several times and carefully weighed her next words. "It appears that the head coach of the U.S. Ski Team is going to resign."

"Good. Now maybe they can put together a decent coaching staff."

"Wouldn't you like to know whom they're going to ask?"

There were any number of possibilities, Greg

thought. The Mahre boys, Andy Mill, maybe even Bob Beattie. He ran the names through his mind until Suzanne chilled him with one word.

"Tony."

"Tony Frantz?"

"It appears that he's first choice."

"Has he said yes?"

"He's not here. He's still in Europe with Richard. They're waiting for him to come home."

"I don't believe it! That really burns me up."

"I was afraid you'd take it that way, but he is good, you have to admit that."

Greg scowled. "I don't have to admit anything. I don't want Tony Frantz coaching my kid sister. I'm a better coach."

"Don't tell me you would take the job. Greg, it pays peanuts and it would eat up your life." Suzanne looked at her brother as if the injury he'd suffered had affected his brain. She recognized that stubborn, angry face and knew he wouldn't rest until he'd made sure that Tony Frantz's name was mud.

"It has nothing to do with money. It's the prestige. Considering how badly we've done in recent years, do you know what a coup it would be to coach a winning team? As good as Kit and Rocky and the others are, they're not ready for big-time racing yet. But imagine if someone could get them close . . ."

"It'll be a long time before you get a team with the Mahre twins, Billy Johnson, Tamara McKinney, and Cindy Nelson again. That was a fluke."

"Bullshit! The Europeans do it routinely. Not only that, a coach with a hot team could fight for more World Cup events in this country."

Suzanne nodded. That could be beneficial to American skiing in a number of ways. A host country is permitted to enter seven or eight racers in each event, instead of the usual four. That meant they could offer the priceless experience of the "real thing" to twice as many racers and increase the U.S. chances for a good showing. And more World Cup events in the U.S. might arouse the interest of the lethargic American public to the excitement of ski racing.

When Kit came home, they questioned her closely about what she'd heard about the coaching situation. The locker rooms were always a hive of information, even though most of it was more rumor than fact.

She shook her head. "I don't think anyone knows for sure."

"Did you hear other names mentioned?"

"A few."

"Mine?" asked Greg casually.

She looked miserable. "No," she said softly. "Hey, you guys," she pleaded. "I'm beat. Can we talk about this later?"

Suzanne shrugged her shoulders and gave Greg a look of love and sympathy. Once again he had taken a backseat to Tony Frantz.

The truth of the matter was that Greg James was not terribly popular around Aspen. The instructors—that is, the ones who *had* to work for a living—had little use for him in their crowd. He taught only when the mood struck him or the pickings looked good.

Moving into his mid-thirties, Greg James looked into the mirror with self-love mixed with self-loathing. He noticed the lines that were growing deeper and realized he was tired of the daddy's girls. In a weak moment, he'd allowed Daisy Kenyon to take control of his life, but her demands were more than he could handle. She demanded passion from him, but there was none to give. His only real passion was skiing and anything to do with it, and right now that meant making Kit James the greatest racer of the decade.

Marcella Richards still got dizzy when she tried to get up too quickly, but fortunately her injuries were minor. She was out of the hospital now, and Suzanne came over each day to visit or take her to lunch. But it was Greg who'd surprised her. After his first duty call, he had started to drop in when least expected. Gradually, she'd begun to look forward to his visits.

He filled her day with juicy tidbits, gossipy nonsense, and stories she accused him of making up on the spot. He was not only fun but a fund of inside information about Aspen's wheeler-dealers.

When she'd felt well enough, she'd gone back to New York to take care of business and then returned. Deciding to spend as much of the winter as possible in Aspen, she put in computers and telephones to keep her in touch with her empire, which was in the very capable hands of her handpicked and trained executive, Rosalind Byers.

A week before Thanksgiving Marcella was invited to a big party at Michael Greenfield's house on Red Mountain.

To her surprise she found that Suzanne was acting as his hostess while Tony Frantz was escorting one of Aspen's famous resident actresses.

The social scene in Aspen was like a human chess game. She'd gone to New York for several days and come back to find that not only had the board changed, but the players as well.

Daisy Kenyon, whom Greg had described as Krazy Glue, was conspicuous by her absence.

The moment Marcella walked in, Greg appeared at her side to bestow a light kiss and a smile. "I was waiting for you."

A quick retort formed on her lips. He might have

called and offered to accompany her to the party.
But then she reminded herself that Greg was of no
real importance in her life, just attractive filler. He
was certainly mercurial. Faithful as a bird dog for
weeks, then invisible.

As she waited for Greg to fetch her a drink, she
looked idly around the room. Tony Frantz, back
from Europe, sleek and contained, was telling a
group about his cross-country skiing adventure
with Richard Farwell. She watched him carefully,
probing for any chinks in his social armor that
might help her get a bead on him. Marcella had
already decided that Tony was the man who interested her most.

She knew he and Suzanne were cooling down, if
indeed they had ever heated up. She also knew
from gossip that he was a good and close friend of
Sally Schneider's, but she never saw them together
socially, so she assumed the relationship was what
it appeared.

Of all the beautiful women in the room,
Marcella knew none had quite her style or pa-
nache. She had the confident arrogance of a
successful woman. Clothes looked well hanging
from her broad shoulders, and she was a perfect
study of Aspen chic in one of Smith's midnight-
blue suede outfits and matching boots. Her jewelry
was understated: diamond stud earrings from
Peretti and one of Elizabeth Gage's heavy heraldic
rings studded with tourmaline.

By comparison Suzanne seemed almost theatrical in white leather pants and shirt with a white
sleeveless ermine bolero, her silver-blond hair tied
Indian fashion with a white leather cord.

It was Michael Greenfield Marcella couldn't
figure. He still held Suzanne's hand tightly, had not
relinquished it all evening, yet he rarely looked at

her or spoke directly to her. Marcella had a sudden image of a Russian Grand Duke dragging around a magnificent white-coated Borzoi on a jeweled leash.

As luck would have it, she was seated next to Tony Frantz at one of the round tables that dotted Michael's vast dining room. On her right was Aspen's premier resident author, a bombastic man whose books were famous for their violence and sex, but who, according to the grapevine, wrote purely from imagination.

She tried to drown out his comments on current writing while enjoying the excellent venison pâté. Fortunately a salad of tiny gourmet lettuces in a dressing of walnut oil was served, capturing the author's attention and sending him on a round of memories of his childhood in Michigan. The connection was obscure at best.

It wasn't until the perfect rack of lamb was served that Marcella was able to turn to Tony and chat.

"I've tried to get you for private lessons several times," she said, keeping her voice light.

"I'm afraid that tends to get difficult at this time of year," Tony apologized. "Did you call as I suggested and tell them you were a friend?"

"I tried to book you as soon as it snowed."

"And you weren't successful?"

You know I wasn't, you sly bastard, she thought, but her smile was that of a disappointed girl. "You're a very popular man."

He shrugged deferentially.

"When we first met I told you it was easier to get a dinner reservation at Lutèce than a lesson with you." She hoped that would massage his vanity enough to get him to make a verbal commitment. But he remained elusive.

"You flatter me."

She decided to change the subject. "It's an excellent lamb, isn't it?"

Gratefully, he went into a lengthy explanation of why Colorado lamb was the best. She tuned out on his description of feeding, weather, and butchering but kept her eyes fastened on him, her mind having a field day as it flirted with all sorts of possibilities.

When Tony finally ran out of information, she said casually, "I have this marvelous cook from Italy who works for me now. You seem very interested in food. Perhaps you'd join me for dinner one night?"

"That's very kind of you," he said, then turned his attention to the dessert that was just arriving on a pair of silver trays. "May I get some for you?" he asked politely.

She nodded, a sheepish expression on her face. Well, he hadn't refused. On the other hand, he hadn't accepted either. She had a hunch he wouldn't call. He didn't have to. Obviously women called him.

Later, as they gathered in the library for coffee and brandy, Greg came up to her. He was sulking, almost snarling when he said, "You two seemed very cozy at dinner."

"We two?"

"You and Frantz."

"I'd hardly call it cozy."

"Well, you seemed to find a lot to talk about."

"Listen, Greg, dear, what would you do if you were sitting next to that awful man, Ashley whatshisname."

Greg laughed in spite of himself and threaded his fingers through hers.

"Tell me about Tony," said Marcella. "He seems to talk a lot but not say much about himself. Has he ever been married? He and Suzanne seem to have called it quits. Is the actress his new lady friend?"

Greg bristled. So Marcella did have the hots for Tony. Up until this point, he had used Marcella as a transition between Daisy and the next woman who might catch his eye, but when he'd seen Tony Frantz in nonstop conversation with her, she'd taken on a new and interesting aspect. By the time dessert was served he'd convinced himself that once again Tony stood in the way of what he wanted. Was Tony really interested in Marcella or was he just shopping around for a replacement for Suzanne?

Thank God for Michael. Greg had introduced him to Suzanne, hoping that the sophisticated and wealthy businessman would catch her eye, or even more. It was time for Suzanne to stop being the playgirl of the Western world. It wasn't good for her reputation to have her name linked with so many questionable types. He hated seeing her picture in all the glossy magazines with yet another debauched old fart with a title or a fortune. Where the hell was she going to end up?

Suzanne draped herself on the cool linen sheets. She was long and lean, the color of a ripe apricot. With her silver hair spread on the pillow, she was a most appetizing sight.

"It was a wonderful party." She stretched, thrusting up her small breasts.

Michael Greenfield, who was in the process of removing his clothes, bent down and flicked the two puckered cones with his tongue. "I thought dinner was quite good."

"Dessert was better."

"You're dessert," he said too smoothly.

Michael, like most single men with a rich past, had a wide vocabulary of responses for times like these. He'd also developed tones of voice that fit the sensation. Suzanne was not a woman who would respond to inarticulate passion; she would prefer music by Cole Porter or words by Oscar Wilde.

She looked at his gradually emerging body with approval. "You have a great body, Michael. I hate fat. Greg is getting pudgy, don't you think?"

"I hadn't noticed." He pulled off his undershirt and stood in front of her admiring eyes for a moment, then lithely stretched out along her side. His long fingers ran up and down her skin as if he were examining a horse.

"Mmmmm, you've wonderful hands."

He put his mind on automatic pilot and went to work on her body with the expertise of years. It didn't take long to have her at fever pitch. Aside from her wonderful skin, she was not a particularly sensuous woman. Idly he wondered why so many men had fought for her attention.

He turned over on top of her and with an angry growl plunged into her. Suzanne's back arched and she made a low purring sound in her throat, then opened her lips and moaned. It was a creditable exhibition of a woman in the throes of orgasm, but the experienced Michael knew simulation when he heard it. It really didn't matter. As she snuggled into the crook of his arm, she sighed and stretched her length against him. Stroking her long, lean body as unconsciously as he might stroke a cat, he thought of another body. Strong, muscular, far more sensuous. He remembered her on the tennis court; broad shouldered, flat hipped, superb breasts, not these hard little pippins that pressed into his side. His hands twitched. The image of Sally continued to intrude itself, and all the Suzannes in the world could not erase her from his mind.

As if she were capable of reading his mind,

Suzanne gave a little growl and, between the kisses she bestowed on his shoulder, said, "I was afraid you might feel inclined to invite Sally to the party."

He tensed, but his voice was neutral. "Why should you think that?"

"Oh, everybody feels they have to. Poor Sally, poor little widow. How difficult it is to be a woman alone here." She imitated all the backbiting women, her friends!

"What's the real reason you dislike her so?" he coaxed, rolling over to look in her eyes. Lightly he stroked her jaw, looking at her as a fond father would look at an adorable but impossible child. "Did she steal a boyfriend away from you?"

"Just the opposite! I took her handsome ski team captain away from her. Two weeks before the junior prom!"

"Why did you do a thing like that?"

"Because I wanted to."

With these words Michael confirmed what he had suspected since he had met her. Suzanne was an unconscionable bitch. Why did women do these petty things to each other?

"You can't imagine what she was like when she was young. She followed me around like a shadow. I felt suffocated by all that best-friend nonsense."

"Were you best friends?"

"Hardly. I felt sorry for her. Her father was an ogre and her mother was this passive little woman, terrified of her own shadow, a closet drunk. And there was Sally. In her own quiet way, an over-achiever of the first rank. But all she wanted was for me to be her best friend. And she'd do anything for me. . . ."

He waited for her to go on, waited for the explosion when she realized why he was probing into her past.

"Do you mind telling me why we're talking

about Sally? Is this your idea of conversation after making love?"

He put his arms behind his head and looked at her golden boyish body, the silver hair in disarray, the spoiled beautiful mouth. She gave narcissism a bad name.

Suzanne suddenly felt her nakedness under those probing basalt eyes. How could a man make her feel he was undressing her when she was already stark naked? Modestly, she covered her breasts with her arms and saw the fine sensuous lips twitch in the semblance of a smile. She felt a stab of fear in her belly. Suzanne had had a revolving door of lovers, mostly rich and older, all powerful and successful. She'd never been in love in her life, wasn't quite sure what the word meant, but looking at Michael Greenfield, aloof, handsome, and infuriating, she felt her heart beat so rapidly she was afraid she would faint. Could it possibly be?

She searched his eyes for her answers but met the usual opaque wall. Then she felt something else she'd never felt before. Jealousy. What did all that conversation about Sally mean? And in bed! Was Sally going to turn out to be her rival for Michael Greenfield? The irony of the situation did not escape her.

"That Max Margolis. You know, the absent-minded professor type? He was sitting with Daisy."

"We used to call him Mad Max, the mad genius."

"Do you know him well?"

"Actually, yes. I still can't figure out what he's doing here."

Funny, he couldn't, either. He was about to suggest that she ask around when her mouth descended upon him and cut off his breath.

CHAPTER SIX

IT WAS ALBERT BIERSTADT, PAINTER OF THE HEROIC landscapes of the West, who had been responsible for Michael Greenfield's first trip to Colorado. Ironic, he thought, that Bierstadt, German born and trained, should have become the darling of the American upper-middle class, to whom his moody canvases appealed, touching the deeper sensibilities of romance that lurked under the layers of gloss.

Michael Greenfield, a man seeking identification with social history and the semblance of old wealth, found their impressive size and abundance of rich detail, the dramatic lighting effects and theatrical detail appealing, too. In truth his taste leaned more to the sensual Impressionists and the tradition-breaking Postimpressionists. But there was something primitive and elemental in these Beirstadt pictures that piqued his curiosity. Following Greeley's advice and his own instincts, the

Harvard-educated street kid had gone west, too. But those huge canvases had not prepared him for the size of the plains, the grandeur of the mountain ranges, the elemental and quixotic moods of nature.

Like every American boy, even one from the Bronx, he had grown up with cowboy movies and the larger-than-life inhabitants of this land. Baby Doe, Doc Holliday, Butch Cassidy and the Sundance Kid, Kit Carson, Calamity Jane, Bat Masterson, the Pony Express, the Overland Stage, the Santa Fe Trail. All these legendary names thrilled him by their sound alone. One of his first trips took him in the footsteps of such early explorers as Fremont, Pike, and Bridger as he followed their wagon-train routes.

He fell in love with place names, names so rich with imagery it was as if some plains poet had grown drunk on the vistas and flung them into the air in a burst of creativity: Cripple Creek, Purgatory, Trinidad, Durango, mysterious Mesa Verde, Telluride, where Butch Cassidy made his first unauthorized bank withdrawal, Basalt, Rifle, the Frying Pan River. He found a culture that blended Indian and Spanish with hardy American. Yet now it seemed that past had disappeared into the mists and that present-day Colorado began only when gold and silver were discovered in the early Victorian period. It was this same Victoriana that had left its unmistakable mark as much in the gingerbread houses that dotted every town and city, as in the stories of righteous God-fearing citizens capable of the most extreme immoralities, venality, and cruelty. Even then crime rubbed shoulders with culture, murder with morality, vice with the Scriptures.

Michael was fascinated and roamed the entire state seeking the legendary West which still remained in the red-brick saloons, turreted hotels, and balconied fancy houses preserved in places like Aspen, Telluride, Silverton, Creede, and Durango.

Shortly after the party and his night coupling with Suzanne (there were no other words to describe it, certainly not making love), he and Greg decided to take a last overnight hike before the arrival of heavy snow expected any day now. It was unthinkable that Aspen would go dry another winter, especially with Europe still enjoying even balmier weather. If Aspen received early snow, there was a good chance the team would be able to train at home and Greg would be able to keep an eye on Kit.

But Michael was not thinking of snow as he watched hundreds of damselflies circle around him lazily. He was thinking of Sally, and Suzanne's unreasoning hostility toward her. It was apparent to him that Suzanne hadn't the faintest idea of why she really disliked the other woman. But he knew. It had to do simply with depth of character and a crude honesty which Sally had and Suzanne lacked. Sally had no tolerance for lightweights, no time to waste on what passed for social intercourse. He was quite sure that Sally, removed from the economic problems of her life, would probably be a marvelous companion. Dressed becomingly and with her hair styled, she would be a dramatic and arresting-looking woman. He smiled. He wanted to play Pygmalion to this Galatea, but he had a feeling she would be a far from willing subject.

He watched a muskrat make its way across a pond, its wet head turning the water's glassy surface into a flash of white lights. Light reflected in the dewdrops seemed to glitter, reflect, shine, polish, gild, and gleam everything it touched.

Michael was amazed at himself. For a man who loved creature comforts as much as he did, he had willingly agreed to strap on a thirty-pound pack, trudge up five miles of steadily rising trail, and sleep out on a night so cold the streams were turgid with ice!

Yet there were still a few aspens with golden leaves among the bare branches. Summer seemed loath to leave, sneaking in the window when least expected. A sudden gust of warm, sun-dried wind sent a shower of leaves down on him.

He and Greg had climbed to 12,000 feet that morning to one of the great montane lakes that sat like saucers in the high mountain vastness. As they crossed a steep scree of sliding stones, the warm morning suddenly turned gray. A shower of icy pellets rained down on them with the sharpness of needles. His bare legs in shorts and heavy socks grew an angry red from the assault. Greg, looking up at the sky and watching the sullen gray clouds lower farther over them, said in the laconic tones of one of the old mountain guides, "Snow's coming."

They decided it would be better to return to their camp. At the lower elevation the icy pellets changed to delicate flakes that brushed against their faces like shy moths.

Greg blew up the banked campfire and put some kindling on it. It immediately flared up, sending out rays of welcoming warmth. He filled the beat-up enamel coffeepot with water and threw coffee into it when it started to boil.

"I think this is it. The snow will be coming every day now." He sniffed the air like an old hound dog.

Michael couldn't help laughing. "No matter how hard you try, Greg, you'll never resemble one of those grizzled old mountain men."

"When you've lived here as long as I have, you can smell snow on the way," Greg insisted with the air of a spanked puppy.

"Only teasing," said Michael. Greg was a drinking buddy and good fun, but he was not a man for serious friendship or serious thought.

Somehow, though, the word snow opened secret doors of revelation in this happy-go-lucky man. As they hunkered down to drink the coffee, it marked the beginning of a long conversation that centered on skiing. It was the first time that Michael became aware that skiing was more than a sport to Greg James, it was an obsession.

They talked about the rumors that were flying around about Tony Frantz being named as head coach of the U.S. Ski Team, rumors that had not yet been substantiated.

"He's absolutely wrong for the job," said Greg heatedly. He was sitting on his down vest, his legs crossed, his hands clenching and unclenching between them. "He doesn't have the right attitude, and I don't think he really cares about the team per se. Racing came easily to him. He never really had a plan other than to go faster than anyone else."

Michael arched an eyebrow. "You're talking about a man who's won three gold medals."

"I know. But that doesn't mean he would make a good coach. Listen, I was the one they asked last year to coach the women's team. You know why? Because even though I might only have won silver medals"—he said this with a bitter smile—"I know about training."

"So why did you turn it down?"

"I wanted to stay loose, be able to concentrate on Kit. If I handle her right this year, she'll make the A team. You see, it's more than just physical training. You've got to get it here, too." He tapped his head and then his heart. "You've got to have the proper attitude and the love of competition. Some people are born with it, others can be trained."

"You mean brainwashed?" Michael gave him a teasing smile.

Greg shrugged. "Call it whatever you want, but Rocky Schneider has it, the right stuff. She's determined, she has the will, great technique, and concentration. She'll make the team, no doubt about it."

Michael stared at Greg's sulky face. What is this obsession you Jameses have for these people? It was like the Hatfields and the McCoys. Fortunately no one was going around killing one another. At least not yet.

Greg continued, intensity freezing the worry lines on his face. "Kit is good. Thanks to me, she's probably a better technician than Rocky, but she'll never be a champion without that will to win that shuts out everything else."

"Tell me, what makes Rocky so determined?"

"Who knows? Everything, I guess. Suzanne said that Sally was a wimp when they were kids. If she was, and I doubt it, she certainly isn't anymore. I think the kid's simply a chip off the old block. Sally Schneider could have been one of the greatest women racers. If she'd wanted it. Somehow Rocky's picked that up in her gene pool along with the physical resemblance."

"Why didn't she want it? Sally, that is."

"Beats me."

"What was the husband like?"

"Peter Schneider? Tall, good-looking, typical Austrian. Lots of fun, not too much upstairs, likable. Good instructor, but not great. A little lazy, I'd say. Crazy about Sally and the kids. Pretty good racer, I guess. Made a few bucks on the pro circuit. Then the avalanche."

"Seems odd that a man who knew the mountains as he did would have gotten caught."

Greg stood and stretched. "Knowing the mountains is bullshit. No one really knows them. I could recite book, chapter, and verse about guides taking groups heli-skiing backcountry here or in Canada. One minute everything is hunky-dory, the next thing you know you've got ten tons of snow on top of you and you're fighting to stay alive and hoping somebody gets to you before the oxygen gives out."

"Ever get caught in one yourself?"

"Almost. I was in Switzerland, nothing more than a kid at the time, when the great Buddy Werner bought it. Right on the Parsenn in Davos, not even a very steep area. He was skiing off the piste and bingo!"

Michael shook his head. "Amazing how mortal we are. At a certain age we look forward and trust that we won't have heart attacks that will kill us at forty or cancer that will destroy our body. We think of life stretching out until our seventies, even our eighties. And then we step off the curb and get killed by a cab or some drunken, stoned kid drives down the wrong side of the highway and plows into us head-on."

"I don't think of those things," said Greg. "And I'd just as soon not talk about them."

Michael glanced at the sky with a worried look. "Should we start back?"

On the trail back it started to snow seriously. One minute their footsteps were swallowed by the dead-leaf fall, the next all was under a light blanket of snow. Patches of dark gleamed in the disappearing light, and soon they, too, were covered. Michael looked back at their footsteps. Nothing. It was as if their past had been wiped out, as if they had never been here at all. He was filled with a sense of foreboding. The inscrutable mountains, older than time, had always filled him with a kind of exhilarated terror. They were full of stories and memories of everything that had gone before, an inarticulate repository for every kind of human foolishness and courage. The Indian myths, like the Greeks', were full of stories of their gods, disguised as animals, trees, stones, the winds, coming down from their mountaintop homes to wreak vengeance or heap rewards on hapless humans.

He shook himself. What had brought on this black mood?

As if it, too, wanted to know, a gray-headed junco flew to a branch and regarded him curiously, a light dusting of snow on its rusty back. It fluffed its feathers and the snow fell like a tiny shower onto Michael's head.

He felt the solitude sharply, felt winter waiting to pounce on him. It grew colder by the minute, the snow crunched under his boots. He could barely feel his legs anymore. How stupid he'd been to think that the late-fall warmth would go on endlessly.

By the time they returned to town, he felt as if he had died and been frozen, to be revived at some later time. After a hot bath and a very large brandy, the two men settled back to continue their earlier conversation.

Greg seemed unable to stop talking about the imminent threat of Tony Frantz's appointment.

"Tell me, Greg"—Michael settled back on his couch, warm at last, expansive with relief—"why this obsession with the coaching job? Is it that you don't want Tony to have it because he's Tony, or do you really think he's incapable of doing a good job?"

"Yes. That's exactly what I think, and I want Kit to have a chance. Besides, I have the right credentials, and the right connections, too. It should be me."

"You say you think that he wouldn't give Kit the guidance and the attention you feel she needs? What about if you were made coach? Wouldn't the same thing apply to you and Rocky Schneider?"

"I'm a team player, man. I want the best team. That's it."

"Then I think you should go for it. One of my best friends is a member of the U.S. Ski Association board. I'll give him a call on your behalf."

"Great." Greg stood up and extended his hand. "You're a good friend, Michael."

Michael stood as well and shook hands. It mattered not one whit to him if Greg James or Tony Frantz or Lucifer himself was head coach. He'd finally been able to name what had been responsible for his black mood.

Since he'd made up his mind years ago as a ten-year-old, Michael had gotten anything he wanted. By hook or by crook. And it came to him in a blaze of clarity that he wanted Sally Schneider. As a lover, as a . . . no, it was too soon to think of that. Besides, when . . . if he ever married, it would need to be more like a merger of compatible companies than a love match. Better for him, better for business.

Sally's elusiveness reminded him of a small company he had wanted to acquire because it had brilliant young creative personnel. But he had lost interest until he was told that someone else was making a serious bid. So he'd gone after the company, like a well-outfitted army against a weaker foe. The small company had stubbornly resisted. After much time and money spent, he had finally succeeded in the acquisition. The week he'd taken over, the entire management had resigned, leaving him with the shell of a company, worthless, useless, a bunch of empty offices. He smiled at his analogy. No, he wouldn't pursue Sally like a vengeful army, he would seduce her into capitulation.

"Greg, you hear all the local gossip. Have you heard anything about a man by the name of Max Margolis?"

"Max?" He shrugged. "We know Max. A weirdo, like all those computer freaks. Why the interest?"

"Do you know why he'd be in Aspen?"

"He's a skier."

"Any other reason you can think of?"

To Greg, skiing was the best reason. He repeated his question. "Why the interest?"

"I think he has something that belongs to me." He told Greg about his acquisition of Monroe Aerospace, the rumor that Max was working on a highly secret superski when he was fired and that he might have taken the plans with him.

"A new ski?" Greg's eyes lit up. Max was a genius. Maybe he had come up with a high-tech superfast ski. He felt a tongue of excitement lick at him.

"Since you know him, I'd appreciate if you could see what you can find out."

"It would be a pleasure." Greg smiled. The old James luck was holding. Could this be the ammunition he'd always wanted to shoot down Tony Frantz once and for all? If he got his hands on a superski, there was no telling what he could do.

Daisy Kenyon parked her car in the breezeway of Sally's house. She glanced at her watch. Just in time for coffee and something scrumptious baked by Sally herself.

She pushed open the door and called. "Yoo-hoo, anybody home?"

Sally appeared in the hall, wiping her hands on a towel. "I should have known it was you. I just finished baking a carrot cake."

"I figured as much. Why else do you think I came?"

She pulled off her quilted leather parka and hung it on the hook of a Victorian coatrack that stood in the small hall and turned to look at herself in the mirror that hung over a little table. But the mirror was obscured by a huge bouquet of exotic flowers.

"What's this?" asked Daisy.

"Flowers."

"I know that. Who's the secret admirer?"

Sally shrugged and turned away in embarrassment, but Daisy hurried after her and took her arm. "Not so fast. Speak. We have no secrets between us."

"Daisy, you're turning this into a big deal."

"It *is* a big deal." Daisy fairly shouted. "When's the last time someone sent you three hundred dollars' worth of flowers?"

"Three hundred dollars? You've got to be exaggerating!"

"Orchids, rare lilies, and God knows what other unpronounceable species are not cheap. Certainly not in Aspen."

"If I'd known that, I would have sent them back."

"To whom?"

"Michael," she said absently.

"Michael Greenfield? Why, you sly thing! How long has this been going on?"

"Nothing's been going on. The man sent me flowers. A belated thank-you for our tennis victory."

"Oh, yes," Daisy said with exaggerated casualness. "All the men I play tennis with send me flowers months after we play. What's wrong with a hearty handshake and a 'high-ho, Silver, away'?"

"I don't know," Sally said impatiently. "The

man is crazy. He's asked me out to dinner twice already."

"And our brave martyr has said no, hasn't she?"

"Do you want coffee or not?"

"Yeah, I do, but I'd love an answer or two. Jesus, Sally, here I am going through hell over that son of a bitch, Greg James, and one of the richest men in America is in hot pursuit of you. Do you know what his latest bit was?"

"You mean Michael Greenfield?"

"No, I mean Gregory Hilton James."

"Yes, you told me. Several times. I don't understand how you can say you still love him. The man treats his cleaning woman better than he does you. Where's your pride?"

"I'm in love. Lovers don't have pride." She sighed deeply.

"Well, he obviously doesn't love you."

"Yeah, he does. He just doesn't know it. If he spent more time with me, he'd find out how terrific and lovable I am."

Sally shook her head. She loved Daisy like a sister, but when it came to men, her blind spots were baffling. "You say you love him; I call it an aberration in your brain."

"He's so cute, and he's terrific in bed. I love the way he looks in ski clothes, and I've never been so compatible with anyone in my life. When he's in a good mood, he's wonderful and loving and sweet."

"Somewhere in your development, I suspect you were arrested. At about thirteen or fourteen. My daughter has more sense than you."

"You're probably right. Anyway, I want to hear about you and Michael." Daisy took the coffeepot from Sally's hand and poured herself a cup. Spying the cake cooling on a rack, she picked up a knife and cut a wedge.

"That's still hot," Sally protested.

"I know." Daisy took a huge bite and let out a yelp, fanning her mouth with her hand. "Likidisvay." She talked around her full mouth.

"What?"

Daisy swallowed, took a deep breath, then said calmly, "I said, I like it this way. Michael?"

"What about him?"

"That's what I want to know. Why don't you go out with him? I think it's a great idea. You're a real stick-in-the-mud. You don't go anywhere unless it's a PTA meeting or the Ski Club or the Ski Corp. You need to get out and have some fun."

"Stop it!" Sally slammed her hand on the table, setting the crockery to rattling. "Enough already. It's so easy for you to talk. You just go out and buy some ridiculous outfit when the spirit moves you. Well, you know damn well I can't do that!"

"Sal! Is it the clothes? Is that what's stopping you?"

"No! That is, yes! I mean, no. Damn it, Michael Greenfield is an enormously rich man, accustomed to beautiful, elegant women. What the hell does he want with me?"

"Maybe that's just it. Maybe he's bored with all those beautiful, elegant women and wants to spend time with someone who's real. Give him the benefit of the doubt. And listen, kiddo, you don't have to worry about clothes. Half the people who go to those places look like they just stepped out of the thrift shop. Anyway, continue with this fascinating story."

"The flowers are the latest in a steady stream of gifts. Look." Sally opened the pantry door and took out a box of expensive Belgian chocolates, a bottle of fine Burgundy, a steamer basket of exotic fruits and nuts, a coffee-table book of French recipes. "He's smart, I must say. There's nothing here I can really return."

"Yeah, I agree. Too bad it wasn't a diamond bracelet."

"He sends a card with each gift. And it's always the same message." She picked up the stack of ivory cards with his engraved name and the hand-written message *It's your turn* scrawled across the face.

"Well, well, well. Very interesting."

"He hasn't spoken to me directly since the last time I turned him down."

"Then call him. Have dinner at some wonderful place. Then bore him to death, if you want to. But do it. See what it's like to go out with an attractive man for a change. You might even like it."

Sally stared off into space for a moment and then gave her attention to the piece of cake she was cutting. "I can't," she said in a small voice.

Daisy threw up here hands. "I give up."

It was a week before Daisy saw Sally again. When she threw open the door of Sally's house, she was furious.

"What the hell is going on here? You're sup-posed to be my best friend, and all of a sudden all I hear is Marcella and Sally, Sally and Marcella. Since when have you two become such buddies? What happened to Suzanne and Marcella?"

Sally sat in the small workroom off the kitchen, surrounded by hides and skins. Small boxes of colored beads and jewelry findings were stacked neatly on her worktable. She was in the midst of making one of her unusual bags when Daisy burst in. She looked at the tiny angry gamecock with ruffled feathers in leather pants and a bulky white sweater. "Nothing's going on. I'm just trying to make a living while it makes up its mind to snow." She held two bags, one a grainy white cowhide, the other an elegant black suede. "Marcella's given me an order for ten of them."

"Ten! Is she going to wear them all at the same time?"

"I don't know. She can wear twenty at one time if she wants to. I owe Marcella a great deal. She was the one who convinced me I could make some money on this little pastime."

Daisy, who proudly owned and wore two of Sally's bags given to her as birthday and Christmas gifts, had the rich girl's understandably cavalier attitude about money. "You mean she's paying you?"

"Of course. You don't think I'd make them for her any other way? She's not my friend. She's Suzanne's friend, but she's willing to pay me anywhere from four hundred to eight hundred dollars apiece for these."

"Really?" Daisy looked at her friend with new respect. She did a few calculations in her head, then whistled. "If you turned out one eight-hundred-dollar bag a week for the next fifty-two weeks, you'd make forty-one thousand and six hundred dollars."

"That's a lot of money. Unfortunately, I can't make one a week. I don't have the time. Besides, not every bag is eight hundred, some are quite a bit less."

"What if you did nothing else but?"

"I'd probably go bananas."

"Think it over carefully before you say no so quickly. You could give up teaching."

"But I enjoy it. Besides, you told me I don't get around enough. At least when I'm teaching I continually meet new people."

"Yeah, couples from New York or single women who are looking to meet men and figure you know where they are."

"You like the women you meet."

"Some, and we hang out at the Tippler or the

Paragon or The Aspen Club. But I don't have kids, and I'm always looking to meet a man. You just go home and cook dinner and make handbags."

"God, you make me sound so dull, I hate being with myself."

Daisy picked up a covered dish that Sally usually kept filled with nuts. She lifted the cover and peered in. "No nuts? What have you got to munch on? I'm starving."

"Carrots. In the fridge."

Daisy disappeared and came back a few minutes later with a long carrot clutched in her fist. She took a bite and between loud crunches asked, "So what's new with the young lovers?" Before Sally could answer, Daisy said in a conspiratorial voice, "I saw your boyfriend a couple of times this week. Guess who he was with?"

"Melanie Rogers?" Melanie, a lush, small brunette with flawless skin and clouds of black hair, was a gorgeous young local who ran an expensive boutique and gave Suzanne healthy competition in the playgirl department.

"No, sweetie. Our own Suzanne."

"Oh?" Sally squinted her eyes at her work and affected an air of unconcern. Interesting, she thought. What does he want from me if he has her for a playmate? All she said was, "They deserve each other."

"I don't know. The last time I saw them, he was looking at his watch a lot and she was looking into his eyes. I think Suzanne's in love."

"Don't make me laugh."

"Have you heard from him? Any small packages arrive recently with Beluga caviar or maybe a truffle?"

Sally couldn't help laughing. "To you the perfect gift is something you can put in your mouth. I don't know how you keep your weight down. You eat enough to feed a family of four, two of them growing teenagers."

"I worry a lot. I have the metabolism of a hummingbird."

"I noticed more than a passing resemblance, but to answer your question, no. The elegant Mr. Greenfield has apparently grown tired of my silence and given up. Suzanne's a perfect choice. She can talk him to death."

The words were no sooner out of her mouth than the doorbell rang. Sally lifted her eyes in surprise. "I'm not expecting anyone."

"Shall I get it?"

"Would you? I have my hands full."

Daisy reappeared a few minutes later and stood silently in the doorway of the small room. When Sally looked up and saw Daisy's grave face, her heart thudded in her throat. "What is it? What's wrong? Something's happened to one of the kids!" She stood abruptly and a box of tiny turquoise beads spilled and rolled on the floor. They crunched under her feet as she rushed to Daisy. Before she could reach her, Daisy brought her hands from behind her back and proffered a square white box. "Sorry. I didn't mean to scare you. I was trying to be dramatic. Here. This just came for you."

"I could boot your behind," Sally said crossly, taking the box and lifting the lid. Inside, nestled in florist's paper, was the biggest bouquet of deep purple violets she'd ever seen. They were so fresh, there were still drops of dew on them. "Oh, my," she said in wonder. "Violets!"

"I wonder who sent them," Daisy said with a grin, reaching for the white card and whipping it out of the envelope, holding it away from Sally's grasping fingers. "I'll read it, you pick up your beads." Daisy quickly scanned the message. She giggled. Then, striking a pose, she recited in a childish singsong, "Roses are red, violets are blue, I'm running out of flowers, to send to you." She handed the card to Sally. "Cute."

Sally read the card and smiled. It was not quite what she expected, but what had she expected?

"How can you resist a man who does such a cute thing?" Daisy scolded. "Call him. If you don't want to go out with him, invite him for dinner."

"No," gasped Sally. "I don't want him here. With the children."

"He's not going to kidnap them. Do what you want, but do something. Understand? That's an order."

"I'll think about it."

Daisy rolled her eyes in exasperation. "Call me tomorrow."

As soon as she was certain that Daisy was gone, she dialed information and asked for Michael's phone number. With trembling fingers and a swiftly beating heart, she called. She let the phone ring a long time, but there was no answer. She replaced the receiver, surprised to find that she was disappointed.

A short while later reason reclaimed her from Daisy's enthusiasms. For Daisy, life was an adventure. You could turn a corner and there he'd be, the man of your dreams. For Daisy the goal was always a perfect man. Why not? She had everything else. And as for herself? What were her goals? She looked out the window at the lowering clouds, the grim early-November weather. She hadn't had goals in a long time. Happiness and racing success for her daughter, a good education and a chance to be everything he wanted for Eric. No personal aims for herself. Financial security, maybe. Forty-one thousand, six hundred dollars a year. Was that financial security? If she made a bag a day, *that* would be security. She laughed. That was certainly a reachable goal. If she were an octopus. She picked up two skins of stenciled lambskin. Seized by a sudden flash of creativity, she tied them together and then around her waist. They made a perfect skirt. Not something she would ordinarily wear, but, with its uneven hemline, its daring cut, perfect for Aspen. With a pair of dark boots and a black sweater, it could be very interesting.

The phone rang. It seemed unusually insistent. She ran to answer it.

"I had the feeling you might have called me," the smooth voice said after her hello.

"As a matter of fact, I did. To thank you for the flowers. They were exquisite, Michael. Truly."

"And?"

"And what?"

"What's the answer to my rhyme?"

She caught the image of herself in the makeshift suede skirt. "Did you have a particular day in mind?"

"How about tonight?"

"No, I can't."

"Then Saturday. Saturday night is date night, isn't it?"

"In Maine, yes."

"In New York it used to be the night you went to the movies with the guys."

"And what did the girls do?"

"The same thing."

"Would you like to go to the movies?"

"No. I'm taking you to dinner. Is eight o'clock all right?"

"Fine."

She hung up. Well, she had done it. It was six weeks to the day since their first meeting.

Michael poured the champagne into two glasses. Lifting his, he saluted, "Happy anniversary."

A blush stained her face, but in the soft rosy light of Pinons it served only to make her look remarkably young and lovely in his eyes. "It was exactly six weeks ago that we met, you know."

"Is it?" she asked innocently and lowered her eyes. The champagne was an exquisite vintage. Bone dry, properly chilled and full of tiny bubbles that exploded in her nose when she sipped.

Pinons was one of Aspen's newest restaurants, occupying the second floor of the newly renovated Elli of Aspen building. As they'd walked toward the heavy glass doors, she couldn't resist taking a peek in the window of the exclusive new Revillon fur salon that occupied the bottom floor.

"What is that, do you suppose?" She stopped briefly and pointed to a sumptuous fur in the window.

"That's sable," he said knowledgeably.

"Is that what it looks like? I always wondered."

"Would you like to try it on?"

"What for?" she asked practically. "It's not something that I'm in danger of owning."

"You never know," he replied, steering her inside.

The next moment, she was slipping into the softest fur she'd ever touched and marveling at its weightlessness. She stroked it gently, as if afraid that firmer pressure would make it disintegrate.

"How much is it?" he asked of the chic young woman who had been imported from the Paris

salon to help launch the latest arrival in town.
There were already three other fur boutiques in
Aspen but none with the cachet or fame of the
Paris-based salon.

"It is only one hundred fifty thousand dollars,
m'sieur," she answered with a heavy accent.

"Only?" gasped Sally.

"Sally, dear. In a town where homes can go for
sixteen million dollars, that's not a lot for a fur
coat."

"I don't even recognize the language you're
speaking," she said crossly, slipping her arms out
of the fur and handing it to the Frenchwoman with
an apologetic smile. "I can barely cope with
chicken at two thirty-nine per pound."

He laughed. So she did have a sense of humor,
even though it was on the dark side. He had to
remember that the life he now took for granted
was totally beyond her comprehension. How
quickly money makes you forget being poor, he
thought mockingly.

As they waited for the hostess to seat them, he
looked at her with admiration. She appeared surprisingly chic and elegant, even though she was
clasping her hands nervously in front of her. She
had combed her dark hair smoothly back and tied
it with a black ribbon. The severe hairstyle served
only to put the focus on her strongly modeled
face. No, she was not beautiful in the classic sense
of the word. She was arresting with a high, smooth
brow and a strong determined chin. Her lower lip
was full and bowed, the upper a slender line. It was
her mouth that gave her that tight, forbidding look
at times, but when she smiled, it immediately
softened her face and crinkled her eyes. She had a
dusting of freckles over the bridge of her nose
which were barely visible on her tanned skin.

"I like what you're wearing," he said.

"I'm glad. I made it last night."

"Just like that?" He snapped his fingers.

"Just like that!" She smiled. "I'm a jack-of-all-trades. I have to be. I repair leaky washers and broken bike chains, sharpen edges, make curtains, bake bread . . . shall I go on?"

"Well, no matter. You are unquestionably the most attractive woman in this room."

As if she distrusted his words, she gave a quick look around the room. This was a restaurant that attracted Aspen's casual chic. Between the cowhides on the furniture and the leather and suede on the men and women, it appeared as if an entire pasture of livestock had been sacrificed. But as to being the most attractive woman in the room . . .

Michael watched her eyes travel around the room. "You don't believe me?"

She gave him an awkward smile. "I think you exaggerate."

"My opinion. And that's the only one that's important to me."

The silence stretched between them. It had been a long time since Sally had been forced to make small talk. At best, she was unskilled at it.

As if he understood her problem, he said, "I am forty-two years old. I've never been married, never even come close. I like animals, hikes in the woods, Corona beer, flannel shirts, and pickup trucks."

She smiled. "It doesn't go with the image."

"What image is that?"

"Daisy says . . ."

"Ah, yes, Daisy. She's not too fond of me."

"How can you say that? She's the reason I'm . . ." Sally turned scarlet and stopped.

"She's the reason what?"

"Nothing. It's not important."

"Daisy said, let me guess . . . that I'm filthy rich, unprincipled, and not to be trusted."

"Not at all. She said you were . . . uh . . . well, she did say you were wealthy."

"But unlike her, I was not born with a silver spoon in my mouth."

"I take it you're a self-made man, then."

"You might say that. I had the advantage of a good education which helped me make some important contacts."

"Ah, contacts." She took a sip of her champagne and looked around the room. "It's really pretty here, isn't it? If I had all the money in the world, this is the way I would decorate my house."

"Would you? Then you must come and visit mine one day. I think you'd like it if you like this. The same decorator did it."

She let the invitation hang in the air. His eyebrows rose in silent query, daring a response.

The waitress appeared with their menus. Sally flashed her a grateful smile. "What shall we eat?"

As the waitress announced their evening specials, Sally listened in fascination. The woman described ravioli stuffed with elk, paper-thin slices of raw veal, a soup made with three kinds of exotic wild mushrooms.

"What's the matter?" he asked, watching her face tighten.

"Nothing," she said abruptly and gave her order to the waitress.

He smiled and gave his, waiting for the woman to turn away before returning his gaze to her. "Shall I tell you what's bothering you?"

"No."

He smiled and ignored her negative. "You're saying to yourself, 'What am I doing here? I don't belong here. This is not my kind of life.' Am I right?"

"Close enough."

"That's foolish. You belong here as much as anyone else."

"As we used to say in the sixties, this is not my scene."

He shrugged. "Little Annie's is, I guess."

"I feel more comfortable there."

"No one's pointing fingers at you and asking 'What's she doing here?' So I guess they don't feel you're crashing. You know, when I was younger and a great deal poorer, nothing would please me more than going into an expensive, posh place like Twenty-one or The Four Seasons, sitting at the bar, and having a beer or a scotch with the wheeler-dealers. It was an education just listening to them."

"Easy for you to say. And do."

"Darling Sally, it's all cow patty. We're a democracy. There's no such thing as the divine right of kings. The currency in the U.S. is not birth, it's hard cash. When you have it, all doors are open."

"Well, I don't have it."

"Ah, but I do, and you're with me. So relax and enjoy it. I promise it's very easy to get used to. Just trust me."

Peter Schneider had said that to her once. And she had. Look where it had gotten her. But would she have been any better off if he'd lived?

With that uncanny way he had of reading her mind, Michael broke in once again. "Did you love him a great deal?"

"My husband, you mean?" Who else could it be? He had been the only one in her life. "We were both terribly young."

"Is that an answer or an excuse?"

"Of course I loved him."

He heard the asperity in her voice and quickly realized that he was doing just what he had promised himself he wouldn't do. She was prickly and guarded; talking about herself did not come easily. "I didn't mean to suggest that you didn't. Where did you meet?"

"We met in Greece. I was doing Europe with a group on bicycles. We were in Mykonos or Hydra, one of the islands. The air was filled with the smell of herbs and flowers. The Aegean was at our heels. We had glorious sunny days and long romantic nights and he was very handsome. He had money from his skiing days. At least to an eighteen-year-old girl from Maine, it seemed like a great deal of money. We couldn't bear the thought of being apart, so he came to America with me. We ended up in Aspen, thanks to Tony Frantz, who is Peter's cousin."

It was a curiously bloodless recital. There were romantic adjectives in profusion, but not a great deal of emotion. "Ah, he and Tony are cousins. And you two have remained friends?"

Her lips fell into the tight line that he was beginning to recognize as a warning that he was intruding again. "Yes. Why?"

"Just curious. I hear so much of the legendary Tony Frantz."

Detecting a mocking note, she looked at him sharply. "Tony is a local celebrity around here. You've met, haven't you?"

"Yes."

"And?"

"And nothing."

"Good. Can we then change the subject?"

"Anytime you wish." He smiled. The smile displayed fine white teeth, but Sally noticed that it never seemed to travel to his eyes. She found herself wanting to do or say something to annoy him, anger him. Rejoinders went through her mind as she tried them on for size. But, in fact,

Michael Greenfield was doing his best to be a charming, interested, and interesting companion.

"You're very obliging. Why don't we talk about you, since I find my life both past and present fairly uninteresting. Tell me how the rich and famous live. What do they really think?"

He laughed and picked up her hand. Turning her palm over, he dropped a kiss on it and looked up at her, his devil's eyebrows arched with amusement. "You can never be sure."

She pulled her hand away in embarrassment but not before she became aware that those cool, hard lips had left a mark that seemed to sizzle on her palm. She wanted desperately not to like this man. To have this evening over with and her life back on its regular dull even keel. But a strange pulse of excitement went through her. "You're very good at this, you know. I don't have too much experience in dealing with men like you."

Again that blunt honesty. "Then I suggest you don't deal. Or do anything contrived. Why don't we just enjoy the evening, the good food, and each other's company and not look for ulterior motives."

All right, she wanted to say, but you have to promise to keep your hands off me. Instead she made a sign of truce and nodded.

Through dinner he talked of himself, told stories of his early years that made her laugh and try to imagine the sleek well-dressed panther that sat next to her as a dirty-faced loudmouth kid with skinned knuckles who was always fighting with the toughest boys on the block.

When coffee arrived along with a selection of homemade ice creams and sorbets arranged to look like one of Michael's bouquets of flowers, the focus returned to her.

"Greg James said you could have been one of the greatest women racers in the world."

"Greg said that?" she said with disbelief. "I can't imagine why."

"Perhaps because he believes it to be true. What happened?"

"Nothing."

He leaned back in his chair, dying to light up one of his good Havana cigars after such a meal, but proscribed from doing so by Aspen's no-smoking laws. "You can be a most infuriating woman, Sally Burke Schneider. I am not the CIA; you're not being taped."

"You ask questions I can't answer."

"Or don't want to answer?"

"Have it your way."

Over the years Sally's reasons for not racing had altered and blurred in her own mind. The excuse she had fashioned at the time and which was still the easiest to accept was that she didn't care; it wasn't important. What Sally had been unable to accept in herself was her own fear of competition. As long as nothing was on the line, she was a star performer. It gave her a certain bitter satisfaction to know that people could go on saying she might have been, could have been, and she would never have to prove them wrong. What had grown in her instead was an unconscious competition with herself. She had begun to set secret goals for herself and went about meeting them with almost machinelike intensity. It could be something as unimportant as memorizing ten pages of French in a night or skiing a downhill against her own time clock.

"It was never very important to me," she lied weakly. "At least not as important as it was to others."

"Like Suzanne James?"

"What does she have to do with it?"

He saw her back immediately stiffen in protest. "Correct me if I'm wrong, but aren't you and Suzanne contemporaries? Same hometown? Same schools?"

"Yes, but . . ." There it was again. The frigid eyes, the tight mouth.

"Nothing. Just curious. Were you friends then?"

"You know we were." Sally looked away from those probing eyes, biting unconsciously into the remains of one of the crisp tuile cookies served with the ice cream, then crushing the rest into dust.

Once again he surprised her and changed the subject. "How did you feel when your husband died so suddenly and so young?"

She thought about it, remembering the days at the hospital as he clung to life by a thread while she held his hand in a viselike grip, willing him to live.

If he had expected the usual tears and protestations, she disappointed him. "I thought . . . what? What a waste? What a terrible way to die? I don't know. For a long time I hated him for being so cavalier with his life, for leaving us without him. It was terrible for the kids; they adored him. He was a wonderful father."

"And husband?"

She looked at him for a long moment. "I don't know exactly what a good husband is. He was good about chores. We didn't fight much except over money and his lack of ambition. He was wonderful in bed. Good-looking." She recited his qualities as if she were making a shopping list to take to market.

She gave him a weak smile. "I can't believe I said those things. You must think I'm a woman with no feelings or emotions. Peter was a good husband, better than a lot of women in this town have, but if I had met him ten years later, I doubt I would have married him. There, now you know everything, including why everyone refers to me as the Ice Maiden."

"I didn't know that."

"One of the few things I guess that didn't come out in your conversations with Daisy and Greg. You should have spoken to Suzanne about me. Or have you?" She remembered Daisy telling her about Michael and Suzanne.

"Suzanne is no more interested in talking about you than you are about her."

Sally could imagine those conversations. But what she still couldn't understand was why he was bothering with her. Did they have some kind of bet? Was he supposed to seduce her and then report back on how long it took him?

Michael noticed that her cup was empty. Looking up to summon the waitress, he caught Sally staring at a newly arrived couple, a frown tugging at her forehead, and he followed her gaze. Tony Frantz had just walked in with Marcella Richards.

"Isn't that your friend?" he asked.

"Yes. I wonder what he and Marcella are doing together. I thought he and Suzanne were . . ."

"Can't tell the players without a scorecard these days," Michael remarked blandly.

He was curious to see what Tony's reaction would be when he discovered Sally with him. He didn't have long to wait. One moment Tony was bending his blond head to Marcella's, smiling courteously, and then his eyes glanced around the room, slid past them for an instant, then whipped back to stare openly when he recognized them.

He's angry, thought Michael with amusement. There's more here than meets the eye. But he, too, was curious about Tony's appearance with Marcella.

Tony Frantz was wondering the same thing. He had been aware from the first time they met that Marcella had more than just a passing interest in him. A good-looking ski instructor in Aspen would have to be stupid indeed not to be aware of what a trophy he was and how many women came to the great resort just to add another scalp to their belt, especially one as famous and desirable as Tony Frantz.

But Marcella, if nothing else, was Suzanne's good friend. Would she help herself to another's lover? She'd bided her time, and when it was apparent that whatever was between Suzanne and Tony was no more, she'd put herself in his path as frequently as she could.

Tony was not interested, which simply made the pursuit more challenging.

Marcella knew what she was up against. She began to look at Tony as she would a product she wanted to develop or re-image and came up with the following evaluation: Tony was in his mid-thirties, he'd won three Olympic golds, many World Cup crowns; he'd done well as a professional racer, extremely well as an instructor and guide to the rich and powerful men who liked traveling with their pros no matter what their sport. Women dropped like fruit from trees for him; he was still considered a trophy at parties; he seemed to have equal celebrity with the handful of superstars that made Aspen their part-time home. So what was left? Where did you find the new thrills? How did you continue to pump yourself up when it was a major victory to simply get up each morning?

Marcella had an idea. What did it matter if it might be an elaborate ruse just to get a man into her bed? She would be kidding herself if she admitted that she wanted there to be more to it than a temporary affair. Marcella tried to keep herself from thinking as an ordinary woman moving into her forties might think.

"You know," she said, settling into her chair, then lifting her margarita in salute, "you and I are a lot alike."

Tony regarded her with eyes the color of a frozen Norwegian fjord. She was a handsome woman. Hard edged, but handsome. She looked extremely good tonight in pale tawny suedes and heavy gold Florentine jewelry. Everyone in the restaurant was wearing suedes that seemed to blend in with the soft Southwestern decor. Even Sally, he'd been quick to notice. He turned his attention to Marcella, who was talking in that crisp, cultivated voice that he somehow felt was not the one she'd been born with.

"We've both achieved success in our own ways. What's next for us?"

"For me? I have a long way to go before I worry about things like that. I still enjoy what I do." Tony's eyes met hers over the rim of his wineglass.

"Do you really? Don't you wake up on a rotten morning and wish you could stay in bed or have a lazy breakfast by the fire or hop a plane and go to the Caribbean and lie in the sun?"

"But I can do that. Whenever I want. I simply don't choose to."

"Tony?" There was challenge in her voice.

He shrugged. She was reading him too accurately.

"Let's face it. You're an athlete whose great days are behind him." She was pleased to notice a sudden tensing in the shoulders, a frown flickering over his face. "One day you're going to wake up and that small waist is going to have a little tire around it, the chin under the jaw is going to sag a bit. It happens to us all. It's worse for an athlete. After thirty, it's all over. Maybe not for you. Your hunk days are still going on. But for how long?"

"I know you have a point to all this."

"How do you want people to think of you?"

"When I'm dead? I couldn't care less."

"No. Next week. Next year. Ten years from now." She struck a pose like an actress and declaimed, "There he goes. Remember him. The skier. The Olympic champion. Cadging drinks from rich ladies at the Grand Champions Club bar."

Tony kept his face neutral, but inside, his stomach knotted. She was a real bitch. Why had he even bothered? "I doubt that picture you paint so vividly is me."

Unperturbed, Marcella shrugged. "I hope not. It doesn't have to be. I have a proposition."

At his startled expression, she laughed. "Not that kind." Not yet, anyway. "Tony. I'm starting a new men's cosmetic company. I'm calling it The Sports Complex."

"It's a good name. I don't know about for men, though."

"I do. The time is ripe. Men are just as concerned about their looks as women. The spas and salons are full of men doing things for themselves that ten years ago they thought only fags did. It's big business."

"I'll take your word for it. Why tell me?"

"I want you to come in with me. Sort of my resident professional. You'd be the focus of all advertising and publicity, our spokesman. You'd help develop the products, serious products for mountain climbers, skiers, yachtsmen, fishermen. I'd make you an executive vice-president."

"I'm flattered. But why me?"

"Why not? You've got the reputation. People

know your face. I think you're more than just a pretty one, by the way. Suzanne says you're very bright.''

This brought an amused smile to his lips. From Suzanne that was like saying very blond or very tall. "I think you overestimate my publicity value."

"Let me be the judge of that. Besides, we can work on a one-year contract, mutually escapable. If you hate it, you leave, no questions asked. If I don't think you're working out, I'll tell you."

Money had not been mentioned. Obviously Marcella was not looking for a partner in this venture. "I hope you don't expect me to give you an answer between the entrée and dessert," he said. She was a cool customer. There was no chink in her armor, no way of knowing what was going on behind those large luminous brown eyes, but Tony felt distinctly out of his league. Here was a woman just entering her forties who was extremely successful, already arrived at a station in life that very few men of her age could claim. She had been forced, he was sure, to learn very early how to play and win at what had been considered for a very long time a man's game. And she'd made her way into the center of Aspen's most powerful circles, one of the few businesswomen who had. He knew she was respected, but not very well liked because she had little patience with small talk as a path to getting things done.

He knew she had her own jet, took a lot of lessons from a lot of different instructors, although only the best-looking would do, and had been trying to book him for the last two winters. He didn't believe that Marcella Richards was just another wild dame who would try any trick to bed down the local hot instructor. But every now and then, he would find her looking at him hungrily or her pointed tongue would dart out nervously and run over suddenly dry lips. He had the feeling of a hapless fresh-caught trout turning over a fire as a starving fisherman waited impatiently to devour it.

She interrupted his thoughts. "You have certainly given some thought to your future, haven't you?"

"Some," he admitted stingily. It should have something to do with skiing, of that he was certain. That's what he knew better than anyone else. The most interesting prospect was Max's ski.

"I have a few thoughts," he continued, "but I'll certainly consider your offer."

"I'll make it worth your while." Her words were worthy of a bad forties movie and would have been outrageously funny if he hadn't heard the strident pleading that cracked through her carefully cultivated voice, betraying her not-so-high-class beginnings.

He turned his head away and caught Sally's eye. Michael Greenfield had just helped her from her chair and was guiding her from the room, one hand held protectively under her elbow. She lifted a questioning eyebrow as they passed. He returned it with one of his own.

In the mini-spa of the James house on Red Mountain, an exhausted Kit James, her eyes closed, her back against a buoyant pillow, was letting the throb of the Jacuzzi wash over her aching muscles.

Suzanne was sitting on the edge, her legs drawn up under her, watching the younger girl with unsympathetic eyes. Suzanne's sleek boyish body was sheathed in a tight acid-green-and-yellow Speedo swimsuit. She had just finished swimming a hundred laps in their pool. As Greg was so fond of reminding her, "If you had a little more tit, you'd be queen of the *Sports Illustrated* swimwear issue."

"So, tell me again," she said in a hard voice.

"Suz, gimme a break. I'm beat. I've told you a dozen times already. I can't seem to catch up with Rocky. She's just too good."

"That's crazy. And it's simply not true. It's the coaching. I don't know what's going on with those people. How do they expect to field a team without a head coach? Here's Greg just salivating to be named coach, and they keep dragging their heels."

"They're trying to find the right person. I'd rather not have anyone than have a new person every other week."

"Yeah, well, that's what's screwing everything up."

"How come it doesn't bother Rocky?"

"Well, if you had Sally and Tony coaching you practically every hour of the day . . ."

"I have you and Greg."

"Not really, but that's going to change. From now on, we're both getting involved."

"You're not going to be able to just come out and take over, you know." Kit looked up with worried eyes, a sudden picture of her indomitable and aggressive siblings arriving at the ski team practice area in their million-dollar ski outfits with a battery of photographers to the hoots and catcalls of the rest of the team. It was hard enough being their kid sister. At least Rocky didn't have to contend with that. When she needed special attention, she and Tony just disappeared to another part of the mountain and skied. The coaching staff, such as it was, simply looked away. But Suzanne and Greg were not quite as discreet as Tony Frantz.

"Look, what you've got to do is bring home some of your videotapes. We can tell as much from that as from actually watching you. Let's see where she has the edge on you."

"I don't know," said Kit, stepping out of the

Jacuzzi and into the big white terry robe that Suzanne held for her.

"You don't know what, punkin?" Greg appeared at the tail end of Kit's words. He, too, was wrapped in a terry robe and on his way to the pool for his daily laps.

Before Kit could explain, Suzanne had jumped in to tell Greg what was going on with Kit. "She's just not getting the good times."

"How come, punkin?"

"I don't know, Grunt," she snapped. She'd had it with these third degrees from them. There were times when she just wanted to tell them to go out and run the race themselves. It seemed that winning was far more important to them than it was to her. "I guess she's just skiing better than I am."

"That's crap and you know it. You can ski rings around her. You've got better technique, better equipment, better . . ."

"So why is she losing?" interjected Suzanne.

"I don't know. That's what we have to find out."

"Hey, you guys, stop talking as if I weren't here. It's only the beginning of the season. I'm just getting off to a slow start."

"There is no such thing," said Suzanne, her mouth a tight slash across her face. "Not if you want to win. Every time you come in second to her, that means you've got to work twice as hard. Listen, honey, it's bad enough to lose to the Europeans all the time; they expect us to lose. But it's unforgivable at home."

"So I'll come in second. Is that so terrible?" There was a heavy pall of silence as Greg and Suzanne looked at Kit as if she had just spoken blasphemy. "Well, is it? You guys came in second."

"I can't believe you said that," said Suzanne. "Do you think I did that deliberately? That I just went out on that run and said, 'Okay, Suzanne, second's good enough.'"

Greg chimed in vehemently, "That's not going to happen to you. You go for the gold or you don't go at all. Nothing else matters. Not second, not friendship, not anything."

From the dark look on his face, Kit knew she had gone too far. In a small voice, she excused herself with the apology that she was tired and that she wanted a little rest before dinner.

When she was safely out of earshot, Suzanne turned to her brother. "What are we going to do about her?"

Greg pondered for a moment. "Maybe we're going about this the wrong way. Maybe instead of working on Kit, we should be working on Rocky."

"I don't get it. What do you have in mind?"

"I don't know yet. Something. If you can't lick 'em, join 'em. Maybe we need to throw a little monkey wrench into that budding career." What he didn't mention to Suzanne was the possibility of finding out more about that ski. If he could get it for Kit . . . Because if he didn't get it for Kit, he was certain that Tony Frantz would hand it over to Rocky Schneider.

CHAPTER SEVEN

NOVEMBER IN ASPEN WAS GRAY-JITTERS TIME, THE waiting-for-snow time. Ski conversation, which usually started enthusiastically in August whenever lovers of the sport got together in their hot tubs or at the local spas, was filled with dark predictions of disaster by November. Every exercise class or weight workout was designed for one purpose: to get in shape for the winter. In other parts of the country the workouts might be for building better beach bodies, but not in Aspen. Aspenites were going for leg and body strength, agility and endurance. But if there was no winter . . . ? Heaven protect the bottom line!

By mid-November it was obvious that Europe's snow drought was far worse than Aspen's. As soon as the temperatures dropped, the snowmaking equipment on Aspen Mountain lumbered into gear and plumes of spray filled the air, falling like

166

manna on the grasses and weeds covering the slopes. The U.S. Ski Team decided to take advantage of Aspen's early snowmaking and do their preseason training in Aspen instead of Europe. This made Sally Schneider and Tony Frantz particularly happy.

It was profoundly dark. Greg James could not see his hand in front of his face. And it was preternaturally still. Every shadow seemed filled with menace. He cursed the blackness and the icy air and the fear he felt. Using a thin pencil light, he made his way softly through the surrounding woods toward Max's cabin.

He was about to step into the clearing when the air was split with all the sounds of hell. He froze, and feeling like a grounded fox, trembled. The porch light came on and Max appeared in the doorway with a shotgun. "Who's there?" he shouted.

Greg held his breath and remained motionless. Finally, the door closed, the light went out, and the dog, after a few low growls, settled down.

On the next few nights, Greg returned to the cabin. With meat. Gradually, he accustomed the dog to his smell, his presence, and the welcome snack. On a night when he knew Max and Tony were going to be out together, he returned to the cabin. This time the meat was lethally laden with a heavy dose of arsenic. The dog hungrily ate the meat and a short while later lay down as if to take a nap. Greg jarred him with his shoe. The dog didn't make a move.

Greg let himself in with a credit card. He found himself in a large room filled with all sorts of fancy computer equipment. He knew how to turn on a computer, but little else. He had no idea what he was looking for. Stymied for an instant, he realized there was only one possibility. He would put the damn thing out of commission.

Unplugging the computer, he pried open its back and flashed his light into its guts. There was a bunch of wires and some kind of board. He removed them, smashed them, then replaced the back.

When he left, he made sure the door was locked. Then he got back into his Jeep. He deliberately drove cautiously so as not to call any attention to himself. He was trembling with excitement and relief when he called Michael.

Pleased with himself, he dwelled on every delicious detail. But he was hardly prepared for Michael's reaction. "You idiot! I want to wage psychological warfare. You go in like Rambo. Now he knows someone's aware of what he's doing."

"But I broke his computer," insisted Greg.

"He'll buy another. It's the program, the disks that are important. He still has those."

"Then I'll steal the disks."

"You'll never find them now. Leave things to me, will you?"

What disturbed Max more than the broken computer, the invasion of his space, and the knowledge that someone was interested in his work, was the poisoning of the dog.

He dug in to fight this unknown adversary. Then a few incidents followed in rapid succession that were so obvious, he would have laughed if he weren't so furious. First, while he was out walking near his house, a truck had deliberately tried to run him down and he had avoided injury only by jumping into a snow-filled culvert. This incident was followed by hate mail with racial slurs, clumsily formed by the cutout letters from newspapers, like something out of an old-time movie mystery. Amateurs. Max began to relax a little.

It was almost a week before Tony could break free from a couple of his best clients and go down the valley to see Max again. When he walked in, his friend had his arms around a pair of gleaming, copper-colored metal skis. He was dancing them around to the sounds of Mozart on his radio.

It was always a shock to walk into Max's workroom. It was as scrupulously neat and clean as a hospital operating room, a far cry from the environment he himself lived in.

"Hi, pardner," Max said when he caught sight of Tony. "Ain't she a beaut?" And then he burst into song. "I'm in love, I'm in love, I'm in love with a wonderful ski."

"I always knew there was something wrong with you." Tony grinned. "What's this I'm looking at?"

"An alloy of copper and beryllium. It will revolutionize the ski world. I can control all those important qualities we were talking about—tensile strength, flex, et cetera, et cetera—with high-speed induction coil heating."

"Hold on, you're talking to a technical idiot."

"You understand microwave ovens?"

"More or less."

"Same principle. By applying different temperatures to different parts of the ski—the tip, the tail, the center—we can alter the flex easily, as well as the camber and the torsion. I think you'll find it has great recovery. And if the figures are right, I've practically eliminated vibration. But you can find that out by skiing with it on hard snow. It's got great side deflection, and wait until you feel how well it damps. A couple of bump runs should prove that."

Side deflection was the newest aspect of ski

design and as yet not really understood. In a properly curved turn, the entire edge of the ski should pass through the same groove in the snow. Max's ski promised to do this basic trick better, smoother, and faster. At least on paper.

As Max explained, the ski should make high-speed turns on edge much more fluid and give the ski amazing holding power on ice and hard pack. In other words, it would be a super racing ski, perfect for the lightning-fast groomed courses of the racing circuits.

"Anyway, my friend, this all sounds good on paper. But it is you"—he poked his finger in Tony's chest—"oh, great one, who will let me know whether I have done it or we go back to the drawing board and start all over."

"The first thing we'd better do is disguise it. I'm not going to take a ski that looks like it's made of twenty-four-karat gold out on the slopes without creating a lot of curiosity."

"In Aspen? They'll just think Cartier made it for you." He laughed. "So what do you want? K2 graphics, Rossis, Deenies, Mickey Mouse, dirty pictures, hearts and flowers? You name it. I'll do it with my decals and spray paint."

Tony wanted to disguise the ski merely to keep away the curious. Max was thinking. What if he were to tell his friend about all the strange "accidents" that had befallen him and how he was sure that someone was after his ski? Tony would think he was paranoid. Better to keep it to himself.

They finally agreed to do some cartoon characters, that being one of the hot ski designs of the moment.

"I'll run it over to Tiehack and try it out. No one from the mountain ever shows up there."

Everything decided, Max went to the small fridge he had in the corner and popped the tops on two Coronas. He handed one to his friend. "Sorry I don't have glasses or lime to go with it. You'll have to slug it. Pretend you're watching football. So, tell me what's going on in the real world? How's my favorite lady?"

"Which one? You have so many."

"There's only one and you know it." Max looked at his friend oddly. "No, you don't know it. If you did, you would have grabbed her years ago."

"You mean Sally?"

"Give the man a five-dollar cigar. Got it on the first guess. What's with her?"

"Struggling with life and her kids." He brought Max up to speed as he told him about Sally and Michael Greenfield.

"What's she doing with a guy like that?"

Tony shrugged. "Why not? He's good-looking, rich, charming, intelligent. He's almost perfect."

"He's a vulture; he's got questionable business partners; he's bought Monroe, and he's going to destroy it."

"He's the guy who bought Monroe?" asked Tony with a start. "And he's the one who fired you. You never told me."

"I didn't know at first. But I've had some dealings with his lawyers." The idiots had told him that whatever work he'd been doing at Monroe was the property of the company. And that included non-company projects.

"What about?"

"I'm glad they fired me. I would've quit anyway." Max ignored Tony's question. "This way I got all that lovely money to invest. But I don't know as I like the idea of Michael and Sally. Man, what are you beating around the bush for? Are you going to let that creep walk away with the prize?"

"I don't have anything to say about it."

"When are you going to open your eyes?"

"What the hell are you talking about?"

"You don't even know you're in love with her?"

"Don't be an asshole. Sally and I are good close friends. You don't think for a moment I'm going to ruin that?"

"Okay, buddy, whatever you say. Maybe *I'll* propose to her."

Tony grinned. "I'll be your best man if she'll have you."

"First things first. Get my ski off the ground."

"Tomorrow. Is that too soon?"

Max grinned. "Is there anyplace that has nighttime skiing?"

Tiehack lies between mighty Aspen and the beginner's Buttermilk. It is an intermediate mountain with the pitch of some of the more popular Eastern resorts like Stratton or Mt. Snow. There was one run that usually contained enough moguls to make it interesting and enough snow variety to give Max's ski its first series of test flights.

The ski was now disguised with Snoopy and Woodstock figures in black on yellow. Tony hoped that Charles Schulz was not a skier, or if he was that he was not skiing on Tiehack today.

He stood at the top of the mountain and hefted the skis. They felt heavier than those he was used to, but only slightly. He stepped into the bindings and started his descent, changing edge angle and pressure to see how the ski turned in different radii. Immediately he knew the ski felt different. Now he would really put it through its paces. He proceeded down the run, varying his turns, his speed, trying different terrain. The ski performed! He felt its clean reaction. Precise and predictable. There were a few little glitches he noticed, but for the most part, it felt right!

As he put the ski through its paces, his focus grew narrower and narrower until he saw nothing but the ski. Had he not been concentrating so hard, he might have noticed a ski instructor, who had stopped for a moment to give his private a pointer, watching Tony with more than idle curiosity.

That night Tony was back in Max's workshop with a list of questions and observations. Max listened carefully and punched mysterious numbers into his computer. "Okay," he said, "let's do it again. I'll give you a call when I'm ready with the new version. And thanks, buddy. I think we may have a ski here. I said *may*," he warned at the sight of Tony's joyful face. "I didn't say *we have*."

"Guess who I saw at Tiehack today?" said Greg James to his sister, Michael Greenfield, and Marcella Richards. The foursome were sitting in the Jameses' library having a predinner drink. A softly lit lamp in the corner was the only illumination. Below them the lights of Aspen at night glittered in a perfect grid. Under a deep purple sky bulked the dark shadows of the mountain.

"Oprah Winfrey," guessed Suzanne.

"She's still at Buttermilk."

"Who?" asked Marcella. "And what were you doing at Tiehack?"

Greg smirked. "My client requested it."

"And who was this client that obviously wanted to have you all to herself?" queried Marcella, knowing that was the question Greg wanted asked.

"Ever hear of . . . ?" He named a name.

"Who hasn't? He's a trillionaire arms dealer, formerly of Beirut."

"His daughter," said Greg.

"My God!" said Suzanne. "I know her. I met her at a masked ball in Paris. They'd practically had to carry her in, she was wearing so many jewels."

"Does she wear them skiing?" Marcella asked wryly.

"You were saying . . ." interrupted Michael, anxious to change the subject from chi-chi gossip back to Greg's obviously interesting tidbit. "Who did you see at Tiehack?"

"Tony Frantz."

"What was he doing there? He never skis at Tiehack," said Suzanne.

"That's what I wanted to know."

"Was he alone?"

"Just him and his Snoopy skis."

"What's that supposed to mean?"

"That's what I'd like to know. He usually skis Rossis or Atomics."

"Well, maybe he was demo-ing one of next year's skis."

"I don't think so," said Greg uncertainly. He was sure of one thing, though. Tony was so intent on what he was doing, he'd skied right by Greg without recognizing him. Greg, like most professionals, did not watch the skier, he watched the track of the skis to see the way they carved. This ski's track was as precise and narrow as a knife slicing through butter. Was it Tony's expertise, the new ski, or a combination of both? If it was the ski, apparently nothing was going to stop Max from continuing to develop the prototype.

He related his observations to the group.

"You think it could be the new ski?" asked Greg.

"What new ski?" asked Suzanne.

"Well, you know Max Margolis is in town. Remember how he used to say he was going to design a breakthrough ski one day?"

"Max Margolis used to work at the Monroe Space Lab," said Michael.

"So?"

"He's the reason I bought that company a couple of months ago. Somebody fired him."

"Why?"

"Some ridiculous mixup. I had nothing to do

with it. But I heard that he liked working on little projects of his own."

"What was he supposed to be working on before he left?" asked Suzanne.

"Aside from his regular work? A ski."

"Max is one of Tony's best friends," was Suzanne's non-sequitur observation.

"If Max has that ski, I bet he's working with Tony on fine-tuning it," said Michael.

"Everyone and his uncle is always threatening to come out with a breakthrough ski. One day they'll come up with one that you can send out alone to ski for you while you do something else. Or maybe, it'll be computerized. You just set it for bumps, go up to the Ridge of Bell, settle back, and it skis. That'll put us all out of business."

"Don't be a jerk, Greg," said his sister.

Greg tried to stifle his giggles. Apparently, he was the only one enjoying his joke.

Marcella gave him a look of distaste. To think she was sleeping with that!

"I've got to know more about that ski," said Michael. "Nothing's worked so far. Anyone have any brilliant ideas?"

Suzanne raised her arms and stretched. She was almost purring. For weeks now she had been trying to find a way to cut through Michael's armor and the nasty rumor going around that he was obsessed with Sally. To her own great surprise, the woman who had had no trouble capturing the attention and the ardor of an English prince, an Italian Nobel laureate, a French superstar, a philandering senator, and countless other minor celebrities had fallen in love with the elusive Michael Greenfield. At last she could offer him something he really wanted. Who knew where things would go from there?

"I can find out," she said smugly, smiling at Michael.

His own smile was cool and fleeting. She was so obvious! Preening like a long-legged Siamese, sounding like a sleazy Gloria Grahame in one of her 1940s movies.

"Yes, Max had a thing for me back in the old Dartmouth days," Suzanne continued, unaware of the look of distaste on his face. "I bet there's still a little fire left. At least enough to get some information."

"He's not a kid anymore, Suz," reminded Greg.

"Neither am I." She uncurled herself from the couch and, in her path to the phone, stopped to let her lips trail across Michael's face. Only Marcella noticed the way he drew back from her touch.

Perching on the edge of his chair, she dialed a number. The Cheshire-cat grin on her face remained in place the entire time that she spoke.

Amused by the phone call out of the blue, Max decided to play along with Suzanne and arranged to take a few runs with her the next afternoon. First he called Tony, reported the call, and they discussed what he should do. They decided there was no point in denying it, and Tony urged him to give her just enough information to be enticing but nothing solid.

It was easier than Max expected. He watched Suzanne's lips move silently as she tried to memorize every word he uttered. He was careful to drop in a few high-tech phrases that would definitely confuse her. At the end of the day, he bought her a drink and promised to call soon.

That night she reported back to Michael and her brother. "It was something about a new metal and some formula that he'd devised to do something. I'll be damned if I can remember. But he didn't deny it. He's definitely working on something."

"He's supposed to be a genius with new materials. He could be working on something unusual," said Michael, his eyes lighting up with excitement.

"Why are you so interested, Michael?"

"If it's a new ski, it belongs to me. If he developed it on company time. I bought the whole company, including its research."

"So what are you going to do?" asked Greg.

Michael looked out at the gathering darkness. "I think I have an idea or two that might work."

Sally poured Tony a cup of coffee. He had just dropped in, a habit that he had gotten into over the years and that it never occurred to him to break.

"You're angry," he said.

"About what?"

"I don't know, but I recognize that look on your face."

She rattled around the kitchen, moving things that didn't need moving and wiping at spots that she'd cleaned minutes ago. She kept her back to him, allowing her anger to subside to a manageable simmer. "Well, if you must know, I'm annoyed with you."

"What have I done now?"

She whirled around, stuffing her hands into her apron pockets. "Did it ever occur to you to call first before you come over? How do you know that I'm not busy or expecting someone or have a date?"

"So that's it."

"What's it?"

"Michael Greenfield."

"What does Michael Greenfield have to do with anything?"

Defensive and stubborn. Tony would normally have smiled blandly at these familiar postures, but, he was surprised to admit, this time he was annoyed. "I don't know. You tell me. You seem to be thick as thieves these days."

"No thicker than you and Marcella," she said too quickly and blushed. Damn it, she'd sworn that even if challenged she would not mention Marcella's name.

"It may interest you to know that Marcella has offered me a job."

"I'm not interested in the least. What kind of job? Pet lapdog?"

Tony stood up and brought his empty cup to the sink, where he made a fuss about washing it. He was shaking with anger. When he was sure he could control his voice, he said, "I'll pretend you didn't say that."

"Oh, it's all right for you to come in here and make remarks about Michael Greenfield . . ."

He interrupted heatedly, "That's different. Michael Greenfield and you are not in the same league."

"I don't know what that's supposed to mean, but I can tell you that he's a perfectly charming man and an interesting one to boot."

"And why do you think he finds you so interesting?"

"Is it so hard to believe? Am I dull and boring just because I don't hang out in all the posh places and am not on a first-name basis with Barbra Streisand and Don Johnson?"

"He's only interested in one thing from you," Tony insisted.

She laughed without mirth. "Excuse me! For a moment I thought I heard my father talking." She got up so quickly the chair fell over. "What a really dumb-ass remark! Even if it were true, do you think I'd fall into bed with a man just because he takes me to dinner?"

"I don't know," he said gloomily.

"Anyway, it's none of your business." How dare he! She remembered watching Tony and Marcella at dinner that night. She could literally see that hard-boiled career woman melt in the warm glow of Tony's deferential attention. Funny how often she'd watched him in action, marveled at his expertise, and thought nothing of it. He had that one quality common to all great womanizers: He could make you feel that you were the only woman in the room. Except for that one moment when he'd acknowledged her presence, he had kept his eyes and his attention locked on the handsome Marcella. Even without looking at him, Sally knew how the evening was progressing by the subtle changes in Marcella's laughter, which grew deeper and more intimate as the dinner wore on.

"You're right. I apologize."

Tony's technique always worked. Just as she was homing in for a knock-down, drag-out with him, he would suddenly defuse the situation by withdrawing. If she continued to harangue without response, it only made her look and feel like a sour old shrew.

"Well, all right. But I mean it. I wish you'd do me the favor of calling before you drop in. You wouldn't do it to Suzanne or Marcella."

He was about to say, "They aren't friends." Instead he clamped his mouth shut and bit back the words.

"I really came by to tell you about Max's new ski."

Sally's face softened at the mention of Max Margolis. He was the most lovable man she'd ever met, totally nonthreatening. When he was around, it was like having a third child, despite the fact that he was the only live genius she knew.

"New ski?"

He went into some detail, and Sally listened attentively. When he finished, Sally said eagerly, "Can we get a pair and let Rocky ski on them?"

"Exactly what I was thinking. I don't know that

it would do anything for her time. At least, legally. There's no way she can *race* the ski until it gets accepted."

"Still, it would be interesting to find out just how good it is."

"We'll work it out for her to try."

Thoughts of Max's new ski and her angry confrontation with Tony disappeared from Sally's mind when the mountain finally opened officially and she was back at work.

While almost every other ski resort in the country was looking worriedly at the cloudless skies, Aspen had been blessed by the snow gods. By Thanksgiving, the entire mountain was skiable; only some of the double blacks, the most difficult trails, were still closed. Ample snowmaking machinery and below-freezing temperatures combined with good grooming had given them a head start, and nature had obligingly done the rest.

The ski corps had come up with a new marketing twist called Mountain Master classes. These were small, intensive, four-day classes for advanced and expert skiers with top instructors. The idea behind them was to get in as much skiing on difficult terrain as possible with a minimum amount of teaching. It was taken for granted that most of the people who came into the classes needed only refinement and reinforcement of technique. This was not always the case, however, and some of the better instructors—Tony for one —refused to participate in the classes, saying that he felt as if he were back in the nursery again.

Sally rather liked the classes. They generally attracted a wealthier clientele who gave decent tips at the end of the four days, but she could understand why Tony, who was accustomed to skiing with the very best, would find them boring.

When Sally walked into the instructors' lounge before her first class, Daisy Kenyon, with the hangdog look of a basset hound, was telling anyone who wanted to listen about her nonexistent love life. Chuckles Conway, who, despite his monumental size, was as graceful as a dancer, offered himself in exchange. Daisy didn't mind sitting on his lap and blowing in his ear in the locker room, but she wouldn't go out with him. As she said, "I have to draw the line somewhere."

Daisy was amazing. No other woman could get away with her behavior. She could be a pain in the ass, bitchy, morose, and repetitive, but she was so universally loved for her basically sunny disposition and good heart, people tended to forget her latest antics.

As Tony was fond of saying, "If Daisy hadn't existed, we would have been forced to invent her."

Sally walked into the locker room already filled with an attractive group of men and women, busily talking shop. A half-dressed Daisy rushed to her side, suspenders dragging, pushing her arms through a Patagonia quilted undershirt. "Do you believe the latest?"

"Later than yesterday afternoon?" That had been the phone call during which Daisy had sworn never to mention Greg's name again.

"Last night I went to Boogies after the movies, and guess what?"

Sally walked to the coffee maker with Daisy, frisking like a terrier at her heels. "Greg was there. Holding hands with Marcella. God, she's old enough to be his mother."

"Greg and Marcella? I thought Tony was involved with her."

"You kidding? Tony has more sense than that."

Sally frowned, remembering her caustic words. Maybe Tony had been telling the truth about his dinner with Marcella. "He said she had offered him a job."

"Maybe she has." Daisy accepted a cup of coffee from Sally. "You know what else? I hear Greg's campaigning for the head coach's job."

That she hadn't heard. That she didn't like. "You think he has a chance?"

Daisy shrugged. "Who knows? Michael Greenfield is supposed to be helping him. I don't know whether that bodes well for Rocky." Daisy made a little face. "Nah, it'll never happen. They'd be afraid to have him coaching his own sister."

"He's practically doing that now."

"Unofficially, yeah. So they turn their backs. After all, there's nothing that says he can't. And you and Tony work with Rocky."

"I'm not denying it. No, I don't think it'll happen."

"Hope you're right. I don't trust that worm."

"But you still love him."

"I don't know about that anymore, either."

"Then do me a favor. Stop singing those 'done me wrong blues.' Even your best friends are getting tired of it." Sally drained her coffee cup, went to her locker, and pulled out hat and goggles before following the rest of the red-jacketed instructors out to the meeting place.

Sally glanced around at the clusters of skiers. They were a strange mixture of young and old, fat and skinny, well dressed and ill equipped. She'd learned not to prejudge long ago. A man in floppy old gabardine pants and duck-billed cap that cried out 1950 was just as apt to be a sensational skier as the tall, leggy blonde in the silver lurex wet suit and diamond stud earrings.

As she went in search of her group, she saw Michael, apparently angry and arguing with the assistant head about his class assignment.

She walked over, and when there was a lull, interjected, "Problems?"

Michael gave her a cursory glance of annoyance. She could have been a stranger. Then he turned his angry gaze back to the assistant. "First, you tell me there's no one available for a private today. Then you suggest a Mountain Master class, and when I agree to try it, you put me in a class of all women and a woman instructor."

"These women are all excellent skiers. And so is your instructor. Sally Schneider is one of our best."

He turned and found her still standing by his side. Her face was closed, expressionless. "Sally, this is Michael Greenfield. He'll be trying your class today. I promised that if he didn't like it, we'd try to make other arrangements for him. Unfortunately, he wanted a private with Tony and he wasn't available."

That he had tried to get a lesson with Tony surprised her. Other than the brief mention of his name that first night, Michael had never said another word about him on the few subsequent evenings they'd spent together.

"Surely Mr. Greenfield knows that it's easier to get an appointment with the President than a lesson with Tony." She had meant it to be amusing, but instead it had come out sarcastic and patronizing. "We'll have to make sure he gets his money's worth."

She turned away and practically bumped into Marcella Richards. "I'll be in your class, too, Sally. I hope that's okay."

"Everything's just fine with me. Of course, we may have to switch you around, depending on how you ski. But we'll go up and then head over to Sunset. We'll watch you come down and see if we need to make changes."

Sally quickly discovered the names of the rest of the class. Barbara Lowell was a psychologist from San Diego. She was tall, pretty, dark, and voluptuous. Jemima Connors was head of a major advertising agency in Sidney, Australia, a cool, slender Cybill Shepherd–type blonde with an upper-class accent and an Ungaro crinkled silk jumpsuit. Sue Ellen Beauregard was an older woman from Nashville with burnt leather skin and a heavy honeyed accent. Counting Marcella and herself, Michael was indeed the salami between the bread.

By the end of the first day, he had to admit grudgingly that the women were all pretty good skiers. In fact, Sally had been surprised that Marcella skied as well as she did and that Michael didn't ski as well as she expected. She took a consensus of the class to find out how much instruction they wanted, telling them that choice was what differentiated ski class from Mountain Masters. They agreed that Sally would give them specific drills or pointers in the morning and they would then spend the rest of the day practicing.

After their first class, they all headed to the Tippler for an après-ski beer. Michael came up beside her and slipped his hand in the crook of her arm. "I hope you don't feel I was trying to put you down this morning."

She smiled tightly. She had managed to remain aloof from him for most of the day, letting the four of them ride the lifts together as she tagged along with other groups. "Men have that tendency when it comes to skiing. They automatically assume that women don't ski as well as they do. But you noticed, I'm sure, Jemima Connors is very good."

"And I was about to ask you if you thought I might be better off in the top class."

She stopped and looked at him for an instant before replying. "Frankly? No."

"You certainly don't mince words, do you?"

"I try not to."

Over the next few days, Sally watched the group dynamics at work. She insisted that they all get into the habit of positive reinforcement: applauding good runs, urging one another on to better effort, taking turns following her down the mountain. This was primarily for Barbara's benefit. She had a tendency to assume divine right, pushing the others to the rear in her haste to be first down. At first Sally had liked Barbara best of the group, but now that she'd discovered this selfish streak, she went out of her way to avoid her.

Discovering that he was a bachelor, Barbara decided Michael was fair game and seemed determined to land—if not him—at least dinner with him one night. Shamelessly she pulled out all the tricks from her female bag of goodies. Sally was strangely pleased by Michael's resistance to the buxom Barbara.

It was the cool, confident Jemima that Sally grew to like most. Once she had found these high-born English women with their crisp accents intimidating, but when she got to know them, she'd discovered they made good friends, that they weren't torn by petty jealousies, nor were they infuriatingly competitive when it came to men. To Jemima it hardly mattered whether she had a date for dinner or not. She went where she wanted, alone when it pleased her. Although she never said a word, she and Sally obviously shared a disdain for the beauteous Barbara.

Sue Ellen, on the other hand, was a totally lovable scatterbrained Southern grandmother, married to a huge white-haired Kentucky Colonel kind of a man who adored her but wouldn't ski with her. She was game for anything, a real steel magnolia when it came to the toughest trail. She was unaware of the swirls and eddies within the group, interested only in making three perfect turns in a row.

It was Michael and Marcella who surprised her. After the first day, she and Michael still had not exchanged any but the most cursory of words. Still he managed to be at her side often enough to make her realize it wasn't accidental. If he wasn't, Marcella was. They seemed to take turns guarding her. Sometimes she even found herself flanked by them, as if they were bodyguards hired to protect a government witness.

One time as they brought up the rear, the rest of the class filled a gondola, leaving her and Michael to wait for the next one.

Riding up in the glass bubble could be an unsettling experience, suspended as they were, high above the shoulder of Bell Mountain crouching like a snow-covered dinosaur below them.

"I have the impression Marcella has more than a passing interest in you," said Michael.

"Meaning what, exactly?"

Realizing that she had misunderstood him, he quickly qualified his remark. "I don't mean your body, or for that matter, your obvious talent as an instructor. I mean, she indicated you have other talents."

"You mean the leather bags, I guess. Yes, it seems as if she wants to make me rich and famous." This said with a chuckle of disbelief.

"Let her," he said seriously.

"Let her?"

"Of course. Don't tell me it's never occurred to you to take advantage of the contacts you make here? Good Lord, Sally! Here you are at the crossroads of wealth and power. You must meet Marcellas all winter. People who can help you, who want to help you."

She thought of Tony. He had often advised her to do just that, insisting that there wasn't anything wrong with it, that he had reached a fair degree of financial security because of it. All that was necessary was discretion.

"Somehow, I always felt that wasn't cricket."

He shook his head in disbelief. "Are you really that naive? This is the tail end of the eighties; the era when a man's word was his bond and a hearty handshake could seal a contract is over. Anything goes if you can get away with it." At the stubborn expression on her face, he quickly amended himself. "I don't mean that what I suggest is wrong or unethical. I'm just saying that the rules of business have changed somewhat."

"That's too bad. Anyway, I don't play those kind of games too well. I'm simply not cunning enough. I leave that to other people."

"Seriously, you have to realize that you're not taking advantage of Marcella. If anything, she's taking advantage of you. After all, she runs a company that's involved in the most cutthroat kind of competition. She's always looking for new ideas, new products. She's very good at what she does. If she thinks you're worth pursuing, you are. Think about it. You'll never get rich as a ski instructor, but then, maybe getting rich doesn't interest you?"

"Keeping my head above water does."

"Then don't turn down the life jacket when it's offered."

The conversation came to an end when Marcella, noticing the serious conversation continue even after the gondola ride, interrupted them to talk about skiing and compliment Sally on her class. When they reached the bottom of the mountain, Sally excused herself and prepared to go home. As she went to retrieve her car, she heard the crunch of footsteps behind her.

"Good class?" It was Tony.

"Oh, hi. Where did you come from?"

"I was in the Tippler with my private."

"How democratic of you," she teased.

"You and Greenfield seem to be getting along very well."

"He's in my class, along with your girlfriend."

"Oh, which one is that?"

Sally raised her eyes in mock horror. "You mean there are more than ten?"

"I don't know why I put up with your serpent's tongue."

"Neither do I." Knowing that these little ex-changes of theirs could get nasty if allowed to go on, she changed the subject. "Any news about Max and the project?"

He looked around surreptitiously. She laughed at the cloak-and-dagger antics. "*Sshhh.* He's got himself a shop. Probably at work there even as we speak."

She looked at her watch. "I've got to go. It's late. I have to pick up Eric at the ice rink."

"I'll get him for you. Mind if I come by for dinner? I've got a couple of steaks in my freezer that need eating before they go bad."

She flushed. She knew this was Tony's way of making sure that she and Eric were not stuck with what he called Women's Day casseroles. "Tony, really."

"Look, if I'm rude enough to invite myself for dinner all the time, you could be gracious and let me bring the beef. Besides, I can't look at another of your mystery casseroles."

It was on her lips to immediately retort "then don't come," but that would be spiteful. Besides, even if he did drive her wild most of the time, she enjoyed his breezy company and the way he behaved with the children. And with her, she was forced to admit.

On the final day of classes, Sally announced that school was over and they would be receiving their pins and their diploma at a cocktail party at The Aspen Club Lodge. Her sophisticated class was amused by the sophomoric attempt to entertain them, but they made the best of it with a show of comradeship and good humor. Sally handed out the report cards, which showed their progress and what they should work on plus a few personal comments of her own. She did not fill in that section on Michael's card. Over margaritas everyone exchanged addresses and promised to return the following year and take her class again. Barbara whipped out her tiny camera and took pictures, promising to send copies to all.

Believing her presence would not be missed, Sally surreptitiously began to gather her things together.

"Where are you going?" asked Michael.

"Home."

He followed her out to her car. As she bent to unlock her door, he stopped her hand with a light but firm touch. "You're having dinner with me tonight."

"I am? This is the first I knew about it."

"At my home."

The hand under his tightened with resistance.

"I want you to see it," he said softly, insistently.

"Why?"

He shook his head in mock annoyance. "You must have driven your parents crazy with your 'whys.' I'd like you to see it and I would like to see you in it."

"Do I have a choice?"

"None. Dress casually." That earned him a smile. There was no danger of her wearing a designer outfit. "I'll have the car pick you up at eight."

"The car pick me up?"

"I would do it, but I'll be busy cooking."

He took his hand away and smiled at the stunned expression on her face. "Just one of my many talents," he said airily and, hands in pocket, he strode away.

She informed Eric that she would be going out for dinner as she made him his hamburgers and asked him if he minded being alone for a few hours.

"Awww, Mom. Stop treating me like a kid," he answered. "Who you going out with?"

"Michael Greenfield."

"That guy you played tennis with?"

"Yeah. Okay?"

"Sure." He shrugged. If his mother wanted to go out, who was he to say anything about it? He could barely remember what Michael looked like, only that he and his mother had won the tournament, so Eric guessed he must be a pretty decent tennis player.

"Rocky should be home around nine. Tell her there's some meat loaf in the fridge if she's hungry. I'll call you when I get there and give you a phone number in case of emergency." Eric, his nose buried in *MAD* comics, nodded absently.

At exactly eight, Michael's Mercedes arrived at the door. She threw her down coat over the denim Western dress she wore and walked carefully down the icy walk.

As they approached the house on top of Red Mountain, it seemed to rise out of a circle of light against the midnight-blue sky. Its several peaked turquoise roofs echoed the line of mountains that rose in jagged splendor from Independence Pass to Mt. Sopris.

The chauffeur pulled into the circular driveway paved in Colorado redstone, stopped, then ran around to open her door.

She paused for a moment to study the fantastically carved oak doors and knew instinctively that they cost more than the entire house she lived in. Above the door in a niche was a bronze Mercury and eagle.

As she stepped into the foyer, the house stretched in front of her in a glow of pale faded colors. A Heriz rug in faded rose shades over a rosy-tinted marble floor was under her feet.

Flanking the stone fireplace which soared up three stories were a pair of oval windows from which could be seen the dark hulks of the entire range of mountains against the moon-washed sky. "Oh, my," she breathed.

"It took two hundred fifty tons of local red rock to make it," he said proudly.

"It's amazing the house doesn't collapse from the weight."

"Would you like to see the rest of it?"

"Of course, I wouldn't miss it for the world. Anyway, it should give me something to keep Miss Daisy quiet for a few minutes."

"I better be on my best behavior, then. I wouldn't want Daisy to spread any tall tales around town," he said, taking her hand and leading her around the huge living room. Angled hardwood ceilings rose above stone walls, giving the house an even greater feeling of monumentality. Michael, or his decorator, had mixed art with a lavish hand, so that a Remington cowboy seemed perfectly at home with a nineteenth-century Bronze samurai warrior.

The earth-red and blush tones were echoed in

polished granite tables and fabrics the color of sun-baked clay. The floors were paved in the same Colorado rose flagstone of the courtyard. The living room, on varying levels, had intimate corners within the vast spaces, each furnished lavishly and comfortably.

"The master suite is a little baronial, I'm embarrassed to say, but sometimes a man fantasizes about such things." He shrugged charmingly.

She could put her entire house into what he called the master suite. Under a coffered ceiling, his huge bed rose majestically from its platform. It was covered with fur throws and was dressed in white sheets with charcoal braiding. She wondered who did his ironing. She noted with surprise that the room had a small breakfast area that offered an extensive view down the valley and that there were two dressing rooms. "Two dressing rooms?" she said as if his conspicuous consumption were a punishable crime.

He shrugged. "In case I get married."

She moved on, stepping into the shadowy green grotto that was his bathroom. Floors, ceilings, and walls were a black-veined, dark green marble. A huge Roman tub sat in the middle of the floor. Ranged around it were exotic orchids and heavy crystal bowls and jars filled with soaps, creams, and other mysterious male things.

"This is a little overpowering," he said. "I think you'll like the other bathroom much better. It's for the wife or the companion I haven't yet acquired."

Sally gave him a sharp look, not sure how to take his words, but his expression was hidden behind the heavy-lidded eyes that carefully avoided hers.

This room was glass enclosed, hanging like an aerie in space. In the daylight hours, it would be flushed with sunshine. It was decorated like a sitting room with a chaise, shelves for books and flowers, all in a delicate shade of blush pink to match the marble floors and walls. One side was completely mirrored, and the reflection seemed to double the size of the room.

"Look out the window. That's the surprise," he said as he turned on the floodlights.

She moved to the glass doors and saw an outdoor spa: hot tub, lapping pool, Jacuzzi and, under wraps, a rowing machine, a stationary bicycle, and a Nordic pull. "Good heavens," she breathed. "It looks like a mini Silver Leaf Spa. Does anyone use it?"

"Not yet," he said mysteriously. "Are you hungry?"

She looked at her watch, surprised at the time. "I'm starved."

"Come," he commanded.

He led her back, pointing out the guest suites, the library, the formal dining room, the game room, before finally arriving at the huge kitchen of scrubbed blond oak. It was as neat as a pin.

Along one wall was a comfortable banquette upholstered in an Aztec printed linen. He gestured for her to sit as he drew a bottle of Dom Perignon from the refrigerator and popped the cork. He poured the ice-cold, bone-dry vintage champagne into crystal flutes and placed a bowl of caviar in ice in front of her.

"If I had something in marabou, I'd feel just like Alexis Colby," she said in a trembly voice, trying hard not to be overwhelmed.

"Who?"

"Joan Collins. In *Dynasty*."

"Oh. I'm afraid I don't watch television."

"The entertainment of the masses," she said caustically.

"Are you patronizing me?"

"I could ask you the same question."

Michael was not accustomed to women who exchanged tit for tat with such relish.

She relented a bit. "Michael, let's face it. I'm not accustomed to having champagne and caviar on a Friday night, or any night for that matter. I'm certainly not accustomed to marble baths, mini spas, and two hundred fifty tons of Colorado river stone in my living room."

"Neither was I. Contrary to what you might think, I was not born with a silver spoon in my mouth. I just got lucky."

"I don't think I could handle luck quite as well as you've managed to."

"Ridiculous. You'll find out when you get the opportunity."

"You seem very sure of me."

"I wish I were," he said, giving her a long look. "I'm just sure of human nature. Given half a chance, anyone can learn to live quite happily in the lap of luxury."

It was not a subject she wished to pursue further. "What are you making for dinner?"

"Grilled rack of lamb, mesclun lettuces, asparagus, pommes Anna." He tied an apron around his middle and peered at the coals glowing in the large grill adjacent to the restaurant-sized stove. "Perfect," he said. He speared the rack and laid it on the grill. The succulent smell immediately permeated the room and tantalized her taste buds.

The salad was a marvel of shapes and colors. She'd never seen lettuces like these. Curly pale green, jagged oak leaves no bigger than her little finger that were a dense ruby red, slender crisp fingers of romaine, red radicchio. "It's too pretty to eat," she said, watching him expertly mix a dressing of walnut oil and raspberry vinegar.

In less than ten minutes, they were seated comfortably at the kitchen table of scrubbed pine. Heavy linen mats, large white plates, and modern Swedish crystal, his idea of informal, were arranged on the table, along with a fanciful array of yellow and white tulips. Tulips in late November!

It was the best meal she'd ever tasted, and she told him so. The good burgundy and the perfectly prepared food brought her to a state of relaxation she hadn't felt in years. Somehow in the back of her mind, she was aware that she was a willing object in a game of seduction that had begun with the champagne. But she didn't care. She felt like Cinderella who'd not only been given permission to go to the ball, but had extra privileges to stay out late.

A part of her marveled at his technique. He had kissed her once, and only the inside of her palm. He never made suggestive remarks. His conversation was generally free of innuendo. But the casual touches, the preparation of this incredible meal were far more seductive than ordinary foreplay. She wondered at his patience, yet somehow knew that this evening was to be a turning point in their relationship.

They talked desultorily about the previous four days and dissected the women in the class, his testiness at being the only man, and finally, the report card. "I was the only one who didn't receive a personal note from the instructor. Was that an oversight?"

"I didn't know what to say. 'It was nice having you'? 'Keep up the good work'? 'Come back and see me'? You see my problem?"

"Surely I deserved something more original?"

"Probably. But I'm afraid I'm not too glib in these matters. Now if you'd had Daisy Kenyon, I'm sure her remarks would have been memorable."

"But one has to take Daisy along with it. I'm afraid she's too hyper for me. How did you two ever get to be friends?"

"I haven't the vaguest idea. She turned up on my doorstep one day like an abandoned kitten. I took her in and haven't regretted it for a moment." At his raised eyebrows, she laughed. "Well, maybe for a moment."

"I like the way you look when you laugh. You should do it more often."

She was curled up on one of the vast couches in the living room, relaxed, at ease, replete. In her simple denim skirt and shirt, she looked completely right against the pale earth-toned linen. At his words her cheeks turned a becoming rose.

"Do you realize you're blushing? I didn't think women could do that anymore."

"I didn't know I was one of them. I'm not accustomed to flattery."

"You mentioned that."

As they waited for coffee to be brought to them by Michael's houseboy, who had been conspicuously absent all evening, she looked around the room again. Inexperienced and unsophisticated as she was, she recognized a Cézanne when she saw one. The others would prove to be a pair of Hockneys, a smaller Schnabel, a Tinguely, a Kurt Schwitters, and three Ellsworth Kelleys. Later, when she told Daisy about the art, her friend informed her that Michael had one of the great collections of modern American art and was mentioned routinely in the magazine *Art and Antiques*.

What did it feel like, she wondered, to wake up every morning surrounded by art and furnishings like this? What did it feel like to have a library that was almost as big as Pitkin County's? She thought of the kitchen, bigger than some restaurants, the linen closets filled with linens that did not come from Sears or K mart. Some people had two sets of dishes, one for every day, one for company. Michael's armoires had dozens of different patterns, faience from France, majolica from Portugal, earthenware from Italy, china that had been hand-painted just for him by well-known artists.

She fixed her gaze on him, expecting somehow that her unwavering eyes would unfold some grain of insight, give her some information, help her understand where she figured in his life or why.

As the houseboy served the coffee, Michael slipped a CD into his elaborate system and the room suddenly filled with the sounds of Billie Holliday's plaintive voice.

She closed her eyes and listened to the almost whispered words, "God loves the child that's got his own."

"She knows," said Sally.

"Yes, she does. Do you know anything about her?"

"You mean the singer? I don't even know who she is, but she knows about being poor and alone."

"Billie Holliday. Born in a whorehouse. Became one herself when she was a teenager. Started to sing for the customers. Discovered heroin, cocaine, you name it. Sang great music, had a messed-up emotional life and died from an overdose in her forties."

"How sad."

Michael nodded gravely. "She understands the blues."

He got up and changed the discs. Now the music was the kind you listen to in after-hours spots, when it was late and everyone gone but the two of you.

He came to her and pulled her into his arms. She was startled by his unexpected action and was about to resist when he said softly, "Dance with me." She stepped into the circle of his arms, nervous as a doe and ready to skitter away.

He was only a few inches taller than she. Clasped in his arms, their cheeks touched. That close to him, she could feel his hard muscular body under the cashmere sweater. Hard and soft, she thought inanely. That described him perfectly. Her hand on the back of his shoulder brushed his neck. He wore his hair a little longer than was fashionable for the day. Usually it was slicked back against his head, but tonight it was full of springy waves, soft, thick, alive. He smelled good and expensive. "I like to drive too fast and I make up my mind too quickly, but I prefer dancing slowly, especially with someone like you."

He pulled her tightly to him until her breasts were crushed against his chest. As they danced she felt herself grow limpid, caught like a leaf in a brisk wind, helpless to stop the tremors that seized her body. He turned her one way, then another. His leg between hers was insistent, guiding her through the steps, yet doing much, much more.

She'd always found dancing a sensuous experience. Peter and she had danced in the moonlight on the patio of a small taverna in Crete. It was like making love. It was romantic. And though what she and Michael were doing was dancing, too, the movements had taken on another life, a secret life of their own. She knew she was being seduced, that his manipulation of her body was a kind of foreplay.

His grasp tightened. Their bodies became inseparable as they swayed against each other. She let out a small whimper, like an animal that knows it is cornered. For a brief instant she tried to fight him, but seemed to have lost all strength and will. For the next few hours she would just let it happen.

His lips brushed her cheek and murmured

something in her ear. The beat of her heart quickened, her blood raced through her veins. She pulled her face away and with eyes closed turned her mouth to his.

With a soft sound of surprise, he seized the opportunity. His narrow mouth was surprisingly soft as it touched hers, floated over it for an instant, then came down with such demand that she grew lost in it. She felt him stiffen against her almost immediately. He trailed kisses down her throat and behind her ears. Lifting her heavy dark hair, he stroked the pale neck with fingers as cool as snow.

"I'm going to make love to you, Sally, oh, how I'm going to make love to you."

She was too weak to protest. She had denied herself so much for so long. What did it matter if for one moment she was foolish? She felt the past intrude, then drove it away. Her hands reached up to his face and she pulled his mouth to hers in a bruising, demanding kiss. He opened the buttons of her shirt, then pushed her away slightly so he could cup her breasts in his hands. "Beautiful, so beautiful," he murmured. He trailed a line of kisses from the corner of her mouth to the curve of her jaw, down her neck, and into the hollow of her throat. His breath was warm, scented with brandy and coffee. She felt the rush of blood to her face, the sudden dampness under her hair, the convulsing muscles of her stomach.

"Oh, oh," her voice thrummed.

"Are you ready so soon? Just a moment more. I want you melting, liquid."

His words were like fire in her veins. She felt him lead her, still touching and kissing her, to the bedroom. Like a witless statue she let him undress her, a ritual that was accompanied by words and caresses. She was almost mindless with need.

He picked her up and deposited her on the soft furs that covered the bed. It was a feeling that would haunt her dreams. To lie on furs and have this masterful accomplished lover indoctrinate her into the more sophisticated techniques of love was beyond her imagination.

And masterful he was. She had never known lovemaking could be like this. His mouth and hands were everywhere, introducing her to her body's own sensuality, those secret places that brought such rapture. His voice was low and throbbing as he described the places he would touch and kiss. He told her he would make love to her on a sailboat in the Mediterranean. He described nights of love on silk carpets on a houseboat in Kashmir. On the black sands of Kona. In his skyscraping glass-enclosed penthouse in New York, in the rose garden of his estate in Sussex. He wove dreams as sheer as gossamer and she let herself get caught up in them willingly. Sensible, practical, pragmatic, she had never allowed herself to think of a night like this. But now she realized that all her life she had secretly hungered for these words and this kind of lover. She thought it only happened in books, but it had happened to her! Even if it never happened again, she had magic for a moment.

When he finally entered her, she only knew that she could not get enough. She wanted to feel him deeper and still deeper, wanted to feel herself shatter in a million pieces, to forget, if only briefly, that she was plain, ordinary Sally Burke Schneider.

Overcome with a delicious lassitude and feelings that she could barely define, she waited for some magic word from him that would put what they had done into some perspective. But he was quiet, cradling her head on his chest, running his long fingers idly through her hair. When he finally spoke, he said something that took her totally by surprise.

"You know when I first met you, I had the feeling that you and Tony were lovers."

"You what?" She lifted her head and laughed deep in her throat.

"That's the way it seemed at the time. You had some kind of special rapport. I envied him."

"We're good friends," she said. But it wasn't the first time she'd heard that said about her and Tony. What a joke! If they only knew.

He pulled her to him again. Her head bobbed against his chest as he breathed deeply and steadily. She waited for more. When nothing was forthcoming, she broke the silence. "I want to tell you . . ." she started.

He sighed deeply, shaking his head. *"Shhh."*

So he had been as moved as she! This was not just another one-night stand for him. She leaned on an elbow and looked at him with soft, trusting eyes. Reaching out her hand, she stroked his face, watching the path her fingers made on his skin. He was smooth, silky. As she continued to stroke him, he averted his head. She felt a sudden chill, a premonition. She'd gone too far. Even with her body urging her forward, a part of her drew back, thinking as he might. She had eluded him for so long. Would he now think that her sudden capitulation, her puppy-love glances were all a part of a clever plan to trap him?

Her earlier excitement faded, leaving her feeling depressed and foolish. Just because she had felt the world shake, why should she think that he did, too? To a man of his experience, she was just a small hurdle to overcome. He'd said he liked challenges. Was that all she was?

She had stopped believing in fairy tales long ago.

Princes didn't fall in love with scullery maids, and he was obviously extremely capable of avoiding all the romantic pitfalls. He was still single. And why was she even having these thoughts?

She stirred in his arms and tried to get up, but he restrained her. "Where are you going?"

"I should go home."

"Not yet. There's plenty of time."

"For what?" she asked.

His answer was to pull her over on top of him. In the light from the moon, which was high in the sky now, she could see the lines of his body glowing palely. He was lean, well formed, slender, like a thoroughbred greyhound. She touched him tentatively. He seized her hand and drew it down to his penis. It stiffened in her palm. Then he pushed her slowly down, encouraging her to take him in her mouth. For an instant she balked, but his chuckle had a hint of a dare in it. She thought about it, then wrenched herself away. He seemed surprised. But undaunted.

His hands began their dance over her body again, and she was lost. With a cry of triumph, he entered her again. He was like a surging live wire inside her, greedy, insistent, pounding. At her cry of surprise, he fought for control and won. He moved in and out of her tenderly, lovingly, until she felt the world crumble under her. A long sustained cry escaped from her throat. She couldn't believe it was her voice.

Collapsed on his chest, she barely recognized the woman who had just had sex for the second time within an hour, whose body was so sensitive that a mere touch of his hand was enough to set her off. Where was the steady persona that had stood her in such good stead all these years? This man was dangerous. He could make her forget everything. She could hear it now. "Sally's a love junkie."

"What's the matter?" he asked with that odd sensitivity to her thoughts.

"I don't recognize myself."

"How wonderful! Not too many people can lose themselves in lovemaking like that."

"Do you?"

There was a silence. Then he shrugged. "Sometimes."

She wanted to ask if this was one of them, but she was afraid of his answer.

"I don't like it."

That surprised *him*. He turned his face to her, smiling in the way he had—was it only yesterday? —when she still had been mysterious, elusive. "Why on earth not? People would give anything to achieve it. Those kinds of feelings make legends. Tristan and Isolde. Guinevere and Launcelot."

"I don't want to feel possessed like that."

"Like what?"

"Like someone had invaded my body and taken over my thoughts. I don't know where I am, or who I am. Oh, Michael, this is so frightening."

His arms enclosed her. He'd had no idea she would react this way. She was like a volatile gas that had been sealed up in a container until suddenly someone ignited it. The explosion was huge.

A man could not deal with a woman like Sally lightly. She was not an ordinary playmate. He was torn between his selfish need to have her and his fear of having done her irreparable damage.

She cried softly against his bare chest, her tears seeming to burn into his flesh.

"I'm sorry, so sorry," he said softly against her hair.

But that was not what she wanted to hear.

CHAPTER EIGHT

MAX MARGOLIS WAS SPENDING MORE THAN HIS PRO-
digious monthly checks permitted. Damn it, why
hadn't he asked for a lump-sum settlement? Then
he could have invested the money the way he
wanted to and have had the use of it as well.

He needed to borrow money, but what could he
use as collateral? With the exception of real estate
deals, the Aspen banks were not exactly generous.
And even if the ski were a reality, it was still
necessary to keep it a secret until he could patent
it.

The crude attempts to frighten him into ceasing
work on the ski had themselves trickled to an
occasional, halfhearted call or two. He'd gotten
another dog. This one lived on a screened porch,
far enough away to avoid poisoned meat but not
too far to be a presence.

He was so close to success . . . if he watched his
spending, made the money work harder, looked

for alternate and cheaper materials. In all his imaginings it never occurred to him that something could threaten his primary source of supply, those monthly checks.

But it did. On a beautiful bright day Max was enjoying a second cup of coffee and admiring the latest model of his ski when a Fed Ex letter was delivered to him. It was from the legal department of Monroe, telling him that he might wish to consult a lawyer, that Monroe was suing him for restoration of property taken by him when he left their employ.

Naturally, the company would be willing to drop any legal proceedings if Mr. Margolis were to restore the aforementioned property. The company also felt it necessary to add that they would be reviewing his financial settlement with them under the aforementioned circumstances.

He looked up in shock. Damn their "whereases" and "aforementioneds"; could they really have a case against him? And what the hell was he going to do if they cut off his supply of money?

He detected Michael Greenfield's hand in all this. Even though he didn't really know the man, he knew Michael's reputation. He'd stop at nothing to get what he felt was rightfully his. But crude intimidation? Would he stoop that low? Meanwhile, what was he going to use for money?

Thanks to Marcella Richards, Sally had been able to clear up the rest of her overdue bills and make a healthy deposit in her savings account. As a reward for behavior above and beyond the call of duty, she decided to take Eric and Rocky to Lauretta's for supper.

It was not the place she might have chosen for a night out, but she wasn't a teenager anymore; her children were. Lauretta's served pretty decent Mexican food, and the price was certainly right.

As they waited for their chili and enchiladas, Sally looked at the motley crowd. This was a different Aspen. Not the one of glamorous restaurants and furs, $800 glitter-studded denim jackets from Boogies, and multimillion-dollar houses on the mountain.

On her left, swaying to a rhythm only he heard, sat a husky Iowa corn-fed biker in a variety of bandana prints; one wrapped Willie Nelson fashion around his forehead, another tied around his neck, and yet another peeking from the back pocket of his jeans. He wore a studded leather cuff which Eric eyed covetously with a pearl bracelet and a rhinestone-and-jet piece that a girl might wear with a prom dress. Rocky grinned and called her mother's attention to it.

Directly in front of them was a tall lanky girl with dark uncombed hair caught up in one of the currently popular butterfly clips. The heavy shoulder pads on her rhinestone-studded yellow silk shirt kept slipping to reveal bony shoulders. She was painfully thin, able to wear a rhinestone cuff necklace as a belt around her black jeans. Sally and Rocky couldn't help staring at the girl as she stroked the thigh of a boy at least ten years younger than she with one hand and forked up a soft taco with the other.

"Look at those Reeboks, Mom!" stage-whispered Eric.

"What's so special about them?" replied his mother.

"They're pink."

"Are you trying to tell me you want a pair?"

"Pink? Are you kidding?"

Rocky stared out at the passing parade. They were mostly kids her age, out for a cheap meal and the movies. They looked like most kids in their Patagonia jackets and blue jeans, their short cropped hair and gingham shirts, their Wrangler jackets and racing pants. Following her daughter's gaze, Sally marveled at the number of kids that seemed to grow up normally, surrounded as they were by such wealth in a small town that was like no other small town in the world. Once again, Sally asked herself if her family would have been better off someplace else. Following that difficult question was the next one. Where?

"I saw your friend Michael Greenfield today," said Rocky.

"Oh. Did you say hello?"

"I didn't get a chance. He and Suzanne came to pick up Kit."

He and Suzanne. Sally's face tightened. She had to remind herself that Michael owed her no allegiance. Just because they had gone to bed together didn't give her control over his life. But the hurt refused to go away. Sally changed the subject hastily, aware that Rocky was regarding her with curious eyes. She popped the last of her enchilada into her mouth and organized her brood.

"C'mon, you guys. This is a school night. Eric has homework. And I know you have a lot to make up." She pointed at Rocky.

Later that evening as she worked on the new collection of bags for Marcella, she thought of her reaction when Rocky had told her of seeing Michael and Suzanne together. She would have liked to talk to someone about these strange feelings. Daisy, perhaps, but she really wouldn't know how to begin to face the questions of her voluble friend.

Although she had relived that evening in her mind many times, she was still unwilling to give a name to her feelings about Michael. She was long past the love-at-first-sight madness and, since that night, they hadn't seen each other often enough to really develop any deeper feelings. But she knew what her body had felt like. Was she confusing that with real emotion?

She would have another opportunity to test those emotions at Daisy's party.

Just like New York, Beverly Hills, and Palm Beach, Aspen's social life was ruled by a small group of powerful women, those who entertained and who had divided the town into A, B, and C groups.

Daisy Kenyon defied the rules by being welcomed by all groups. The reasons were numerous. Despite her current life as a ski bum, she came from enormous wealth, good bloodlines, and had attended all the right schools. She was fun, witty, unpredictable, and artless with the uncanny knack of making insults sound agreeable.

Daisy herself cared nothing for rules. Her annual pre-Thanksgiving party was for "waifs and wastrels" as she put it. Her guest list contained anyone that interested her. Tonight it would include a bartender from the Paragon, a singing waiter from the Crystal Palace, an English earl, three exquisite black models she had met at a fashion show in Denver, the entire company of Ballet Aspen, two publishers, a senator, three film stars, and her favorite local gentry, the Mallorys, Richard Farwell, Joe Ferris, plus a handful of the ladies who lunched, a group of divorcées from thirty to death.

Daisy's house was a huge Spanish hacienda set in the aspens and pines of West Buttermilk. It sprawled low and lean with as many plantings as the gardener could find that could live at that altitude and atmosphere. The glazed tile roofs sparkling in the sun and snow were a haven for broad-tailed hummingbirds who built minute nests of lichens, moss, plant down, and cobwebs in the cylinders.

The house had originally been built for Daisy's father and mother and their children. The Kenyons usually spent the winter holidays in Aspen and returned in July for the music festival. After Daisy's adored father died suddenly from a heart attack, her mother had lost interest in the place and returned to the East. Daisy, longing to live in Aspen from the moment she'd put on her first pair of skis, had taken over the big house, leaving her grateful mother to discover the pleasant luxury of travel arranged by one of the groups that specialized in rich widowed and divorced women.

Despite her offhanded, rather cavalier behavior, Daisy was an obsessive guardian of her possessions, which were considerable. Her father had been a great collector; masks from Gabon, totems from Alaska, kilims from Turkey, pagan sculpture from pre-Christian Rome, books, bronzes, silver frames, ancient Japanese lacquerware, and first editions. These Daisy tended like a devoted vestal virgin, dusting, washing, cleaning each piece at least twice a month.

Daisy gave marvelous parties with plenty of food and drink. Her friends in the entertainment business were legendary, so it was not unusual to find some well-known performer at the piano, with a group around him singing.

As Sally moved around the room stopping to chat every now and then with people she knew, but not lingering, she snacked on the conversational tidbits around her, rarely joining in. As usual the topics discussed were, in order of importance: real estate, sex, divorce, and ruptured friendships. All subjects Sally had little to contribute to.

Joe Ferris, Samantha Mallory's boyfriend, had apparently just scored a great coup, selling a prized piece of real estate for a madly inflated figure. He had made some shrewd land investments which apparently were paying off, and Samantha's mother, Sophie Mallory, long a staunch defender of zero growth, was furious that he'd sold his corner lot to Michael Greenfield, whose intention it was to build a mini-mall. Obviously Samantha was upset as well, because she and Joe were barely speaking to each other. But Sally knew her friend. Sam was deeply in love with Joe, and although she shared her mother's views on Aspen development, Sally was convinced she wouldn't sacrifice her love for Joe on that particular altar. And now that she knew Michael better, she knew that the building he would put up would be tasteful and in keeping with Aspen's heritage.

And then she heard Sophie Mallory, still on the subject of Joe's perfidy, say, "Not while I have a breath in me. Even if I have to bribe every commissioner."

"She means it," said Richard Farwell, her companion.

"And to think it was Joe who sold it. Knowing how we all feel about another complex of expensive boutiques and restaurants in this town."

"Maybe," said one wag, "Michael Greenfield's planning to put in a K mart."

"Amen," said Sally too softly to be heard.

"Very funny. I think I need a drink," said the elegant, silver-haired Sophie, who looked splendid in her gray suede skirt and shirt. At fifty-five she could hold her own with women half her age. "Are you coming, Richard?" She turned to Richard, then swept away, regal as a queen, still able to strike fear into the bravest heart with that steel-edged voice.

". . . I don't understand why she left in such a hurry," Sally heard Meg Miller say to Daisy.

"If she hadn't they would have run her out on the next railroad car."

"She didn't have a friend left," said another.

Sally realized they were not talking about Sophie Mallory. This conversation centered on the unlamented disappearance of Rosie Sukert, the

social columnist of the *Aspen Times*, a woman who
had once been a good friend to Sunshine Campbell, Sam Mallory, and Sally. Rosie was, at best, a
difficult woman, thin-skinned, quick to take offense and twice as quick to give it.

Then from the corner of her eye Sally caught
sight of Michael Greenfield making an entrance
with Marcella Richards. Suddenly she felt confused, off balance. She knew he had been asked
and she had been surprised that he had not called
to suggest they go together. What was Michael's
game? Why pursue and pursue, why make her
think she was something special, then when she
had capitulated, turn into a stranger? Or was that
the plan? Michael told her he was a collector. Did
that mean of women, too? Was it the pursuit and
not the capture that excited him? If so, she'd
naively walked right into the trap.

The heat of anger filled her body. In the middle
of one of Daisy's moans, she turned on her friend
and practically hissed, "Stop it, Daisy. I'm really
fed up with your boring monologues on the subject of Greg James. You don't know what real
problems are. Rocky just came from the dentist,
and he says she needs orthodontia. Do you have
any idea what that costs? I'll have to rob a bank or
sell drugs. Eric has decided he wants to seriously
work on figure skating. That's another twenty
thousand dollars a year. His coach says he should
go for it. And you tell me Greg is screwing someone's mother or a waitress, or a dog. Good for
him." Sally stormed away before she could say
anything really ugly. Daisy's look of shocked surprise followed her across the room to the open bar.

Sally held out her glass with a shaking hand for a
refill of the white wine she'd been drinking. For
the first time in years, she craved a cigarette.
Instead she watched the crowd circulate in the
huge living room with its heavy Spanish furniture

and the thousands of bits and pieces of Daisy's treasures. Each piece was worth a small fortune. One artifact alone would probably fetch the money for the orthodontist's bill. Ten more would pay Eric's yearly fees for skating lessons for life. Her shoulders slumped as she recalled the conversation she'd had with Eric that morning.

She had been scrambling the last of the eggs when Eric interrupted her. "Mom, promise not to yell."

"I don't promise anything. Why should I yell?"

"You always do when I have to ask you for money."

She turned slowly to face her son. That's what it had come to. They hated asking for things because they knew the answer was always the same. "What is it, Eric?" She kept the edge of impatience out of her voice.

"Well-ll."

She looked at her child. How like Peter he was growing to look. Almost handsome, but with the awkwardness of his age. Long skinny legs and bony fingers, a torso that still had a bit of baby fat. Dark lashes like a smudge across his cheeks, clear, heartbreaker hazel eyes, dark wavy hair that fell over his forehead. He had a rather endearing way of shaking it from his eyes with a toss of his head. She wanted to pull him to her and hug him, muss up his hair, feel the silky skin on the back of his neck, do all the things she had done to him when he was little. But he hated being fussed over, hated kissing, hated her to even caress him unless he was sick.

"Speak, champ. The eggs are getting yucky."

He took a deep breath, then began to rattle off his speech before she could interrupt again. "The class is going to go to San Francisco for the weekend and stay at this hospice and see the parade and do some Christmas shopping, only I don't have to do any shopping, so it shouldn't have to cost a lot, and I have some money saved so it would only be a little." He ran out of steam and looked at her hopefully.

"How much is it going to cost?"

He told her in a small cracked voice, reminding her, "I have some of it saved already."

"How much do you have saved?"

"Enough."

"Eric, how much?" To a kid ten dollars was a lot.

"A lot."

"You're still not telling me how much."

"I only need about seventy-five dollars from you."

"You've been able to save that much? How?"

He shrugged. "I've been doing a lot of errands after school. Sometimes they give me a good tip."

"Who is 'they'?"

"People," he said vaguely.

She'd been stabbed with a feeling of unease. On the other hand, she didn't want to give Eric the third degree. It would sound like she didn't trust him. Instead she decided to take him at his word. He was a good kid, resourceful. Even when he was too little to pull a cart, he'd hung out at the supermarket, offering to help people without cars carry bags of groceries to their condominiums.

"We'll talk about this later," she'd said, happy to see him eating. Then she'd grabbed her jacket and was off to the mountain. The subject had been forgotten.

Now she was berating herself for not taking more time to really talk to Eric. There never seemed to be enough time anymore. Rocky was so busy either training or working out, they'd barely exchanged a half dozen words all week. Tony saw more of her daughter than she did.

Money. It all came down to the goddamn money. Was it possible ever to have enough? Knowing what the answer was by just looking at the assemblage of suede, leather, silks, tweeds, and expensive glitz, she sighed deeply.

"Is it really all that bad?" She heard the silky voice of Michael Greenfield in her ear. "Let me take you away from all this."

"At this point, I wouldn't say no to the devil."

"Well, I'm much less demanding than he is," the voice continued to tease.

"Are you? Yes, I guess you are. One evening seems to satisfy you." She flushed. She had not wanted to say that, to leave herself open and vulnerable. She had been determined to treat that one evening as casually as he appeared to.

She started to walk away, but he pulled her back to face him. "I am sorry for not getting in touch with you. That was not deliberate. Something came up that needed my attention and I had to fly to San Diego."

Liar! she wanted to say. "San Diego? I guess Daisy must be mistaken, then. She thought she'd seen you the other night at dinner. With Marcella."

"She did. We were having a business discussion."

"Oh." Sally wanted to end this conversation before she asked another stupid question. Questions that indicated that she cared more than she wanted him to know.

"And apropos, I did not escort Marcella to the party tonight. We met at the door."

"You don't owe me an explanation."

"Oh, but I think I do. You have every right to be angry with me."

She felt a prickle of pleasure. So he had realized that his behavior was peculiar after that rather extraordinary night of love. She shook her head. Words of explanation weren't necessary. It was enough that he knew.

She was still confused about her feelings for this

man, but again he had appeared at her side at the moment when she'd felt most vulnerable.

"What do you say we leave and go somewhere for a quiet dinner and conversation? Nothing else."

She gave him a grateful look. "I'll get my coat."

As Michael waited for her by the door, he caught Tony Frantz staring at him with a sullen look. A half smile played across Michael's smooth face. When Sally appeared, he took her arm and bent down to say something to her. From across the room, it appeared that he had kissed her temple.

They sat in a candlelit corner at Poppy's, an old Victorian house at the edge of town which served excellent food in a romantic and quiet setting.

"Daisy will be furious with me."

"I doubt that. There are so many people in that convent she calls a house, she won't even know you're gone."

He ordered a bottle of Edna Valley chardonnay for them. "Now, tell me, you looked as if you had been exiled to Siberia without your boots."

She smiled. "That bad, huh?" She leaned her elbows on the table and cradled her chin in her hands. With an audible sigh, she said, "Oh, Michael, don't ever be a parent!"

"So far, so good. But your kids are paragons. At least, that's what you tell me."

"They are. I love them like crazy." And then she went on to tell him about Rocky's teeth and Eric's trip and the mysterious money. One thing led to another and she opened up. It had been such a long time.

He rarely interrupted her, offering only a sympathetic ear, no criticism or judgment. This was a different role than the one Michael had played at dinner at Pinons. This was Michael the friend, the ally, the good companion. He continued to fill her glass with the excellent chardonnay. Her tongue loosened as the alcohol warmed her. She went back to beginnings and told him more about herself and that lonely life in Maine than she had ever told anyone. The floodgates opened and the essence of Sally Burke Schneider came flowing out.

Sally's revelations explained much about her to Michael. That New England reticence to divulge anything personal, the spare, upright character, the competitive nature turned inward. For a moment he regretted that evening in his house, realizing that she was not the kind of woman who could take pleasure in superficial relationships.

Her life was too hard to seek easy indulgences, save for an occasional evening out for dinner or a concert at the Wheeler. Perhaps it would be kinder to her if he stayed out of her life?

"You must find it difficult living here, knowing what goes on and what kind of money gets thrown away."

"Yes and no. In my circumstances I'd find it difficult to live anywhere. The only problem with Aspen is that you can't hide."

"That's important to you?"

"My privacy is. I hate everyone knowing my business. What I do, where I go, whom I see."

"So you do as little as possible?"

"Something like that."

"Marcella's been telling me about your designs. You sound like a one-man workroom. Your bags and sweaters are really unique."

She flushed with pleasure.

"You know I have a chain of very elegant sportswear shops. Only ten, but they're in the best cities in the country. I'm wondering if you might like to design a few lines for us. You could have your own workrooms, your own staff. I don't know how important it is for you to do the actual work."

"It's tedious to say the least, but I'm not sure

how good a designer I am. I've never really sat down and designed, you know what I mean?" She wanted him to understand that she was not a professional.

"Sally, darling"—he noticed her flush at the unconscious endearment—"what do you call what you do now?"

"I don't know. I just put things together out of my head."

"So put them on paper. That's all."

"Is it really that simple?"

"That simple."

"Why are you doing this? You feel sorry for me, don't you?" she said with some acerbity. Then her voice caught in her throat. "I don't want your charity, Michael."

He put his hand on her arm and squeezed it. "Wait a minute, wait a minute. No one ever accused me of being charitable. I think you're a good investment. Marcella, who is a very shrewd and clever businesswoman, thinks you're a real talent. Since she's offered your friend Tony a job, I thought it was only fair that I offer you one."

So Tony hadn't been lying. Marcella *had* been making him a business proposition. She was filled with an involuntary glow of warmth which she quickly replaced with indifference. She didn't care what he did. "Why didn't she offer me a job if she likes my work so much?"

"Oh, she wanted to," he said, "but I told her I'd make you a better offer, no matter what she promised." He gave her a victorious smile, but there was something engaging in it that forced one from her in return. "I also told her she could have anything you created at cost."

"You didn't." She burst into real laughter.

"Yes, I did. After all, she's the one who discovered you."

"Michael, what can I say?" Her eyes were sparkling like the bubbles in her champagne glass. He'd never seen her quite so animated, quite so beautiful.

"How about a simple thank-you?"

She did more than that. She invited him to dinner. When she told the kids he was coming, they insisted that she invite Daisy and Tony, too. Their friends, as they so bluntly put it. Despite the flowers and wine, the killer dessert that Daisy brought and Tony's gallant offer to attend the grill, the evening was a disaster. The children barely spoke to Michael, and when they did, it was in Neanderthal grunts. They went out of their way to show her how much they preferred Tony to him.

Daisy tried to tease them out of their rudeness. Finally she, too, sat back and watched these usually nice kids turn into monsters and blessed heaven that she had none of her own.

Michael withdrew and watched Tony handle them. He was like a lion trainer with a whip. They behaved, performed, rolled over, and did everything but kiss his shoes. Instead of being annoyed, he was amused, wishing that he could reassure them that he had no evil designs on their mother.

When the children got tired of being obnoxious, the evening died a sudden death. Professing an early-morning meeting, Michael asked Daisy if she needed a ride home, then left. His manners had been impeccable throughout. Sally was furious with Tony, her kids, and herself most of all for letting them run roughshod over the evening.

"We didn't like him," said Eric, with his hands on his hips.

"You made that abundantly clear."

"Tony doesn't like him, either," said Rocky.

"Tony has a mouth of his own."

"Why did you invite him?" said Eric.

"Because I wanted to. I'm the adult here, and

we do what I say. You kids were rude. Where did you ever learn tricks like that? Certainly not from me."

"Relax, Sally. They didn't mean anything." Tony tried to intervene.

"You be quiet. I'll get to you later." Then she turned to her children, her voice dripping ice. "Upstairs. Right now. I don't want to see your faces or hear another word out of you. Eric, no television for a week. Rocky, you're grounded. You get home every night by eight o'clock or don't bother to come home at all. That means no hanging out with the gang, no movie dates, no nothing."

"Mother," they wailed in unison.

"Mother? You're not my kids. My kids are nice, cheerful, polite, respectful. Maybe you're just their ugly, mean twins. Upstairs!"

Tony watched the entire scene in a state of shock. In all the years he had known her, she'd never behaved this way.

"Don't you think you're overreacting?"

Sally turned on him. "When I need your advice, I'll ask for it. You were just as bad as they were. In fact, worse. You literally egged them on."

"I did no such thing!"

"You did! You could have stopped them with a word. But you enjoyed it, didn't you? You enjoyed watching Michael squirm. My children were flagrantly rude to a guest, and their beloved Uncle Tony urges them on from the sidelines!"

"Flagrantly? That's a very expensive word." His lips tried to form a smile.

No sooner had he said it than her eyes flashed warning signals. It was not the time for levity. Her hands twitched with the desire to strangle him, to erase that little smile that tugged at his lips. Instead she piled the dirty dishes on a tray to take to the kitchen.

"Here, let me help." He tried to wrest the tray from her hands, but she pulled away, overbalanced, and the tray of dirty dishes crashed to the floor.

Together they stared blankly at the mess. Then the tears started to stream down her face. "Perfect," she sobbed. "Just perfect."

He offered her a tentative smile. "Now you don't have to wash them."

"Damn you, Tony Frantz, I hate you. I don't know why I put up with you. You're in cahoots with my kids, you upset my life, you insult my friends, and now you break all my dishes."

Sally sat down on the floor, leaned against the wall, and wailed.

Tony stared at her in astonishment. "You really like this guy, don't you? Are you serious about him?"

"Leave me alone."

"Don't you see what he's doing? He's playing with you. You're crazy if you get mixed up with him. I don't trust him, even when I can see him. He doesn't have a nice reputation."

"Neither do you," she shot back.

"I don't mess with your head or your emotions. And he does. He is."

"Stop it! Just stop it." She put her hands over her ears. "I don't want to hear another word. You sound like my father. Worse! A jealous lover."

"I'm neither, and you know it. I'm a friend who cares about you and your kids, and I don't want to see you get hurt."

"And you're so sure that's what's going to happen? Well, listen to me, Michael Greenfield has been nothing but charming, attentive, and generous. And he expects nothing in return from me." She crossed her fingers at that statement because she knew he did want something from her. What, she wasn't quite sure of yet. Until this moment she had entertained vaguely romantic thoughts about the man. But she knew, and this came with no small amount of surprise, that it would be easy to fall in love with Michael. He offered a life of fascination, a life of ease.

As she sat on the floor glaring at Tony, she knew what she wanted in a relationship. Trust and independence. A man who would let her be anything she wanted to be and who would make her feel secure in his love. She wanted to be able to talk about anything that bothered her and have him listen to her with respect. A man who would be there for her, but not strangling her. She wanted to be equal partners with him, in life, in bed, in love. Michael could give her that. The question was, what could she offer him?

She put out her hand and he pulled her up. "I'm sorry," he said softly, pulling her into his arms, hugging her. For a moment, she thought he'd been about to kiss her. She disentangled herself gingerly.

"It's all right." Her voice betrayed her weariness. "It hasn't been our first fight, it probably won't be our last." She looked at the mess still on the floor, the gravy congealing, the mashed potatoes like blobs of wet cotton, and said, "Yuck."

"Let me help you."

"No, Tony. Just go home."

"Are you very angry with me?"

"Not very," she answered.

"Sure?"

She let out a deep sigh. He left. The fight had brought her in touch with her emotions. What did she really want? A grown-up Boy Scout! She laughed. Who didn't? And where did you find one these days?

"Mom is so pissed she's barely talking to me." Rocky bit into the pizza and chewed it thoughtfully.

She and Kit were at Pinocchio's. It was late afternoon. The town was filled with a surprising number of skiers milling about, shopping, checking the illustrated maps, looking for a good place for an early dinner or a late drink.

"What happened?"

Rocky told her friend about the previous evening in great detail. "I guess we were both pretty shitty, Eric and me. But there's something about Michael that I don't like." A sudden thought occurred to her. "Doesn't he go out with your sister?"

"She wishes. Greg and he are friends, some business thing, I think. So naturally he introduced Michael to Suz. They went out a few times, but you know my sister. She's a man-eater. I think he got nervous. The funny thing is, I think she's really hooked on him."

Rocky scowled. "I wish he'd leave my mother alone."

"What about Tony?"

"He was just as bad as we were. I heard them fighting after Eric and I were banished."

"No, I mean, what about your mother and Tony? Everyone seems to think they have a thing going."

"Are you kidding? Most of the time they're fighting. It's all our fault."

"That they fight?"

"No, that Tony was there. When Mom told us she was inviting Michael, we told her she had to have Daisy and Tony. I mean, who were we supposed to talk to?"

"That's not the only thing that's bothering you, is it?"

Rocky looked at her friend gratefully. Kit was special. She had this knack of getting inside your head and knowing when things were wrong before you did. "Only everything. Eric wants to go to San

Francisco with his class for Christmas, and he's serious about skating and there simply isn't enough money. I got it all, there's nothing left over for him."

"But the team pays for everything now."

"Yeah, now. But what about all those years when we were starting out? I hate to see him so unhappy."

"He's a good kid. It'll all work out. Didn't you tell me he'd made some money working after school?"

"That's another thing. He won't tell Mom who he was working for."

"Who is he working for?"

"I'm not sure either, but I have my suspicions."

"Drugs?"

"Don't ask me." She pulled the cheese from the pizza and twisted it around her fork, then popped it into her mouth. "Damn it, I have got to make the A team this year and win some big races."

"I'm sure you'll make the team," said Kit loyally. "You're the best we have."

"Not as good as you." Rocky smiled.

Kit gave her a look of disbelief. "Don't I wish?" She paused dramatically. "I can see it now! Rocky Schneider endorsements from chewing gum to cereal. You'll be a zillionaire."

"I'll settle for half a million a year like Phil Mahre."

Phil was one of the legendary Mahre twins, the best ski racers the United States had ever produced. The boys had been able to make legal financial arrangements that allowed them to make a considerable amount of money during their top years as amateurs. They had contracts with ski manufacturers, boot makers, binding, pole, and goggle manufacturers. These contracts included victory payments down to fifth place, bigger payments for bigger races, Olympic races, individual and overall titles, and escalation clauses based on the previous year's earnings. All the money funneled through the U.S. Ski Association and was held in a kind of trust. In the case of TV and print advertisements, the team would receive 90 percent, the skier 10 percent, also in trust.

"Yeah, but the European skiers can make twice as much."

"It's their top sport, that's why. The Alpine countries treat skiers the way we treat football and baseball players. Here the public doesn't even know who the head coach of the U.S. Ski Team is, but I bet they know who coaches the Denver Broncos or the Nuggets. But I don't want to be greedy. I'd just like to start seeing some money so I can pay my mother back and give Eric his chance. I don't expect Hadad to hand over the Ritz-Carlton to me after my career is over or Leslie Wexner to make me a touring pro." She had named two of the wealthier part-time Aspenites.

Rocky thought of the European racers with their wealthy sponsors or hometowns that set them up for life, buying hotels for them to run or giving them sinecure jobs, jobs that gave them money and, for the most part, near-total freedom with little responsibility.

Though Kit James's friendship with Rocky Schneider was a source of irritation to the elder James gang, Kit's heart went out to her friend and her real problems. It offered Kit a touch of reality in a life that was as close to a fairy tale as one can get. Pampered, indulged, catered to, she had grown up remarkably unspoiled, generous, and kindhearted. She had also grown up in the shadow of her two dynamic elder siblings.

Shy and quiet, preferring dolls and make-believe, she had literally been pulled from the nursery one day and thrown on the slopes after her mother had abdicated her maternal responsibilities.

Tough, resourceful, and self-reliant even at that tender age, Rocky had been a magnet to the gentle young girl who viewed this new activity with no small amount of fear. With Rocky shouting encouragement and pushing her to greater and greater feats, Kit had formed a strong bond of friendship with the dark-haired girl.

Sheltered and protected, Kit had never wanted for a thing or been denied any request, so it came as a surprise to discover that everyone did not live as she did.

The first time she had gone to Rocky's house, she'd been shocked by its smallness. After a while she had grown to like it, filled as it was with the noise and laughter of Peter and Sally and kid brother, Eric. There was a great deal of teasing and prank-playing with her often at the center. She had learned to give as good as she got. Mostly she appreciated Sally's down-to-earth acceptance of her.

Sally was not one to make a fuss over her or suffocate her with hugs and soothing platitudes. She was accepted as one of the family. Later she realized that it must have been a hardship to have that fifth mouth to feed so often. So she began to show up for dinner with a smoked salmon, a pâté, a gooey dessert, or some other tidbit in hand. At first Sally had been adamant about not accepting these things from her, but Kit, in a surprising burst of temper, said she would never come back. The shocked Sally zipped her mouth and made grudging acceptance of her gifts.

Kit, too, was anxious to make the A team, but for very different reasons. For Rocky it might mean financial security and enough money to go to college when her racing career was over. For Kit, it meant living up to the impossible expectations of her brother and sister. Despite her retiring nature, she had been brought up to be a winner.

Until this year, the two girls had considered skiing good fun, friendly competition, great exercise. They had made jokes about their future fame and fortune, the interviews on the *Today Show*, dates with famous rock stars, the movie contracts they would sign with Willy Bogner, ski-film-maker extraordinaire and a good friend of Suzanne's.

Now as Kit looked at the clouded face of her friend, she was struck with dread. There were only a few places available on the team. She and her closest, oldest, most trusted friend would be vying for them. What was that going to do to their friendship? Would it be able to survive such pressures?

Rocky, in a one-piece Lycra racing suit that defined her strong skier's body, pulled on her helmet and adjusted her goggles for the practice run. She gave a look around at the other girls, clustered in small groups, their chatter mixed with nervous giggles. Coolly she stacked herself up against them and knew that she could beat most of them standing still. There was only Kit, Pudge Hanson, Dream—that was her name!—Phillips and Sophie Thoerner, who had come from Austria ten years ago with her parents, both ex-racers. Sophie, strong as a Douglas fir and totally fearless, was Rocky's real competition in the downhill. Kit, with her lithe grace and catlike flexibility, was her competition in the slalom. In the Super-G and giant slalom Rocky had no competition.

The downhill course, which was used for both men and women's World Cup competitions with minor variations, was a difficult one. Aztec, though short, was insanely steep and had to be taken at full tilt with a teeth-rattling turn into Dago Road at the bottom of Spring Pitch. Then there was the infamous Airplane Turn and Berlin Wall to contend with. At least half the girls would not finish.

The slalom had been set so it was full of tight turny sections alternating with fast open stretches. The lightning-slick snow conditions coupled with an awkward fall line made it difficult to hold a turning edge. Any race in these conditions would be to the strong.

As Rocky waited her turn for the downhill, she ruefully thought back to the conversation she'd had with Kit. She hated to complain, to sound as if she envied Kit's financial security. She wondered if things would have been easier or different if her father had lived.

Pete had never made a big deal out of Rocky's becoming a ski racer, but there were times when they reviewed old films of his racing days and she could feel that was what he wanted for her. Although he had never achieved quite the greatness of Tony or Greg James, he had developed almost perfect slalom technique. In later years, when Tony had begun to advise her on technique, they would often watch the films together. "Watch, watch! Here! Now! See the downhill ski hold? See how and when he steps onto the uphill ski? Wonderful! Do exactly that." Then Tony would turn and give her cheek a pinch. "It's all right to look like your mother, but you must ski like your father." At which point Sally would throw a pillow at him and they would all collapse with laughter on the floor. They didn't do that anymore, either. Tony and Sally had grown prickly with one another.

Maybe her father's death had only increased her determination to be a successful ski racer. Her year of racing in Europe had given her a seductive glimpse of the world outside of Aspen and increased her desire to leave the small town of her birth. To Rocky, winning meant more than gold medals and her name in the papers and record books; it meant a ticket out. Even though she loved the beauty of the mountains and the crisply scented air, she hated the artificiality and the glitz that was turning Aspen into a fat, glittering stage set, filled with beautiful people playing roles.

In the old days when Sunshine Campbell and Sally used to take her to visit Sunshine's father, Hank, at his ranch, she used to love listening to his yarns of the Old West. She would hunch up on a stool, totally spellbound, while he painted images more vivid than any film she'd seen on the Late Show.

Rocky heard her name called and looked up in surprise. Coach had to call her twice to pull her back to reality. "Better concentration," he said crossly. She took a deep breath, shook every extraneous thought from her mind, and focused on the downhill and keeping her skis on the snow. The video cameras were turned on her and would pick her up as she moved down the run.

She came out of the starting gates like an explosion and the wind tore at her as she picked up speed. It tried to rip her head off, but she laughed to herself, exulting in the feeling of flight and the speed that could reach up to seventy miles an hour. She was a cannonball, a projectile, a missile, and in a final tuck she was at the finish, her cheeks blazing with the frigid cold.

"Not bad time," said the acting downhill coach, looking at his stopwatch.

"Not bad? How fast was I going?"

He shrugged.

"Well, give me an idea, so I can pick up my time."

"You were terrific." She whipped her head around at the strange voice.

Then she heard Kit, who had already made her run and was waiting for her, cry out happily. "Greg, hi. Over here."

Rocky hadn't seen Greg since he'd driven her home that night. Once again she was struck by his good looks. He wore skintight navy-blue racing pants tucked in his Raichle boots and a navy-and-red racer's jacket. The sun and wind had whipped his skin to a glorious bronze which made his sky-blue eyes even bluer. She blushed at her corny image.

"I mean it, Rocky, it was a terrific run. It could—"

"She's so good, isn't she?" Kit interrupted, hugging Rocky.

"Could what?" asked Rocky, detecting an undertone in Greg's enthusiastic compliment and oblivious of his giving his sister one of those wait-'til-I-get-you-home looks. It never occurred to her that he had shown up just to make his own evaluation of how she and Kit stacked up against each other.

He shook his head. "Nothing. It was a terrific time . . . for so early in the season."

The two girls, accompanied by Greg, took the lift back up for another run. While Kit rode with the inarticulate substitute coach, Rocky rode with Greg.

His voice was warm and caressing as he went into detail about her racing form. She was waiting for the "but," but it never came.

"What did you mean 'for so early in the season'?"

Greg smiled. "Nothing more than that."

"That was my best time ever."

"And it was terrific, like I said."

Rocky, always her mother's daughter, was skeptical about Greg's gushing praise. She knew he was paying the same kind of special attention to his sister's skiing as Tony was to hers. So though the words were sweet upon her ears, she accepted them with skepticism.

"Greg, you're not telling me everything. What's wrong?"

"You definitely have an edge over the others," he said finally, but again his tone seemed to imply that he was not saying all.

She had been leaning out over the protective gate, staring at her skis, avoiding his probing blue eyes. At his words, she was forced to look at him. A question formed on her face. Before it was transferred to her lips, he continued, "You ski all four disciplines very well. Of course, there's a danger in that, too."

"I don't see any," Rocky said cautiously.

"Oh," he said airily, "wait until you're racing a few years. To stay on top of one, you have to take something away from the others. It's too tough to train for all four with the same kind of attention. It was bad enough before the Super-G was added and there were only three."

She shrugged and stifled the words of denial. After all, he was an experienced racer. But he didn't know everything. Besides, she didn't find it so difficult to train for all four events; there were common elements in all the races.

On the other hand, maybe he'd noticed something wrong that had slipped past Tony. She'd have to pay more attention in the next practice run.

"Can you come back to the house for a little while?" Kit asked after the day's practice sessions were over.

"I'm still in the doghouse," was Rocky's reply.

"Ooh, cruel and inhuman punishment," she sympathized. "I'll get you home before curfew. Promise."

"Okay." At that moment, facing the James gang was less daunting than dealing with her mother.

Like most girls her age, Rocky was not impressed with furnishings, nor did she recognize styles. But every time she went to Kit's house, she felt as if she were walking into a movie set. First, the size intimidated her. The living room alone was as big as their entire house. Sitting for the first time on the sueded buffalo couches, she had quickly stood and moved to one of the linen chairs, offended by the feeling of the leather, outraged to discover where the material had come from.

But she couldn't fail to be impressed by Kit's quarters: the pretty bedroom, the dressing room, the elegant marble bath, and her den, complete with a soda fountain, jukebox, and collection of vintage movie posters.

This was the room that Kit steered her friend to, knowing that Rocky felt more at ease there than in the rest of the house.

"Now, don't get mad at me," she began.

"You haven't done anything to make me mad."

"But I'm about to."

"Then if you're so sure, don't do it."

"I have to. It isn't for you. It's for Eric."

Kit handed her an envelope. Rocky accepted it suspiciously. The flap was open. She reached inside and pulled out its contents. Inside the folded notepaper was $200. "What the hell is going on?"

"See, I told you you'd get mad."

"C'mon, what's the big idea?"

"It's for Eric. So he can go to San Francisco. Sign a note, and when you get rich and famous you can pay me back."

"I can't do it."

Kit was hurt. "You're my friend."

My friend, she thought. Kit was more than that. Yet she had the awful feeling that it was all about to change. It had nothing to do with their social differences, which were considerable, but which meant nothing to Kit. Rich people were like that, her mother told her. They could choose their friends from any group. Why that was so, Rocky had not quite figured out.

She was about to say something when there was a knock at the door. Before Kit could open it, Suzanne had popped her head in. The smile of welcome froze on her face when she saw that Kit was not alone. Rocky quickly stuffed the envelope into her jeans pocket.

"Oh, Rocky. I didn't realize you were here."

Rocky had the feeling that a rabid rat would have been more welcome.

"Did you want something special, Suz?"

"Just to talk to you. It can wait until Rocky leaves. Are you leaving soon?" she asked coolly.

Rocky flushed. Having money was no excuse for being rude, she thought. She would have liked to say something equally nasty, but what would that get her? Suzanne's hostility was so invasive it made her friendship with Kit difficult at best. And there was the other thing. Today had shown that Kit was improving every day. It was just possible that one day her best friend might be the only one who stood in the way of her realizing her goals. Was ambition worth destroying friendship? Without fully understanding the reasons why, Rocky knew it was not a question to ask her mother. Rocky stood up and shot Kit a grateful look. "I've got to go. You know . . ." She pretended to blow a whistle.

"I'll drive you home," said Kit.

"No, you won't, it's too dark," said Suzanne. "Greg will do it."

Her mother would not approve of that, either.

CHAPTER NINE

INSISTENT SOUNDS OF ROCK FROM THE LOCAL MUSIC
station mingled with the rattle of pots and pans as
Rocky walked in the door of the house on Midland.
The heat from the wood-burning fireplace competed with the icy blasts from ill-fitting doors and
windows.

"Hello, I'm home," she called out tentatively.
The cold war between her and her mother had not
yet thawed. She waited for a response and when
none was forthcoming, she walked to the kitchen
door and poked her head around the jamb. "Mom?
I'm home."

Without turning around, Sally said, "Dinner's in
an hour. We're having meat loaf and mashed
potatoes. Tell Eric when you go upstairs." She
broke an egg into the raw meat, added some
chopped onions, bread crumbs, and a shot of chili
sauce, then dove into the bowl to mix the meat
with her fingers.

"What's he doing?"

"His homework if he knows what's good for him," she said without looking up.

Rocky turned to leave, then stopped. On the edge of tears, her voice was that of a little girl. "Mom, please talk to me. I can't stand it anymore. I want you to be my mother again. I told you I was sorry. Both of us are. How long is this going to go on?"

Sally finally turned around to look at her daughter. Distress and unhappiness were written all over her smooth young face. They were so close, these two; it was unthinkable that the coldness should continue. Sally held out her arms and her daughter rushed to them.

"Oh, honey"—she smoothed Rocky's hair— "I'm sorry, too. I don't know what got into me. Of course, I love you, both of you. It's just that everything seemed to be going wrong and just when I needed some peaceful R and R you and Eric and Tony, too, turned into bad kids. Or so it seemed. You have a right to tell me what you think."

"Look, if you want to go out with Michael Greenfield, you go ahead."

Sally was about to smile and thank her when Rocky interrupted: "Just don't marry him."

Sally was startled and said wryly, "You'll be pleased to know he hasn't asked me."

"Great." Rocky pinched some raw meat and popped it into her mouth. "I'll be down in a little while to help with salad. The meat needs salt and pepper."

Rocky took the steps two at a time and gave a quick knock before going into Eric's room. He was sitting at his desk working on a math problem, his Walkman plugged into his ears, beating time with two pencils and his left foot.

She went up to him and gently removed the apparatus from his ears.

"Hey, cut it out! Don't you believe in knocking?"

"I did, but it would take a cannon to get through that noise. You'll go deaf if you don't turn it down."

"What do you want?"

"Is that the way to talk to the sister who's about to change your life?"

He looked at her skeptically, pulling on a lock of his newly cut Andre Agassi mohawk, a hairdo his mother found slightly revolting. "What do you mean?"

She reached in her jeans pockets and fished out Kit's envelope. "Here."

"What is it?"

"Open it!"

He did. As he pulled out the twenty-dollar bills, his eyes widened. "There's two hundred dollars here."

"I know. Now you can go to San Francisco with the class."

He handed it back. "I don't need it."

"But you told Mom . . ."

He got up and slouched across the room to open his bedroom door. Peeking from left to right, he closed it softly, then whispered, "C'mere. I'll show you something, but you have to promise to keep quiet."

"What are you up to?"

"Nothing," he said with an injured tone. "I just decided that if I wanted things, I'd better get them for myself." He ducked into his closet and came out with a shoe box. "See?"

She saw the bills lying in neat stacks. "Where did you get all that?"

He quickly put the top back on the box and shoved it on the floor of his closet. "I earned it."

"How? Robbing banks?"

Eric scowled and turned his back on his sister. "I didn't do anything wrong."

"I didn't say you did, but that looks like a lot of money."

He refused to say another word, and no amount of insistent questioning would wrest an answer from him.

Later, as they sat around the dinner table, harmony somewhat restored, teasing and joking in their usual fashion, Rocky broached a hypothetical question. "Mom, I need your advice."

Sally, who had been whispering in Eric's ear, gave her daughter her full attention.

"There's this girl I know and she discovered that her brother has a whole lot of money. She asked him where he got it, but he gave her some vague answer, said he earned it or something. She thinks he's lying. What should she do?" Eric's blue eyes smoldered with fury. He got up abruptly and took his plate to the sink.

"Mom, can I be excused? I have to finish my homework."

Sally nodded absently.

"Where do you think he might have gotten it?" Rocky continued.

Sally thought a moment. "Any number of ways, but something tells me your friend suspects her brother of stealing it."

"No, no, he's not a thief. At least I don't think he is."

"Then maybe it's none of her business." Sally's level gaze held her daughter's, but she felt a shiver start along her spine. She stood up abruptly. "Honey, do you mind clearing up? I just remembered I have to tell Eric something."

Sally climbed the stairs, rehearsing what she was going to say to Eric.

She did not bother to knock as she usually did. She found him lying on his bed, his hands under his head. He was wearing his Denver Broncos cap and staring at the ceiling.

Love and fear alternated in her heart. Sally had always tried to level with her kids, give them a sense of self-worth, teach them honesty and respect. She had not wanted to paint the world gray and threatening; neither had she tried to sugarcoat it. It had never occurred to her that she might have to have a conversation like this with her youngest.

"Eric," she said softly.

He averted his eyes. "I'll never talk to her again. She told."

"Where did you get the money?"

"I told you."

"Tell me again."

"Guys gave it to me to run errands for them."

"What guys?"

"Just guys. Regular guys."

"Do they have names?"

"I guess so," he said grudgingly.

"What are they?"

"I don't remember exactly."

"Eric!"

"Something like Capelli or Cavelli or Clavell, something like that."

"Do you know who those men are, Eric?"

He shrugged. For the first time he looked at her and there was rising fear in his eyes.

"I doubt very much that they are nice men. You should not be involved with them. I want you to take that money and give it back to them and tell them you can't work for them anymore."

"But, Mom," he shot up from the bed, "I earned it, it's mine."

"Eric, you could be in big trouble. Don't you understand what I'm saying?"

His face got red, his voice grew high-pitched and obdurate as he screamed at her. "What am I supposed to do when I want something? All the money goes to her." He thumbed in the direction of his sister's room. "She's got everything and there's nothing left for me. So what am I supposed to do? I worked after school. And now you tell me I have to give it back! I won't! I hate you!" And he ran into his bathroom and locked the door. She could hear him sobbing.

Oh, she was tired. Tired of single-parenting. Tired of wondering how much money she would make that season. Tired of having only "no" in her vocabulary when she wanted both her kids to have it all. She thought of Michael Greenfield and his gorgeous house, his impeccable manners, his obvious wealth, and she imagined what it would be like to never want for a thing.

But it was Tony Frantz she called. "Hi, Tony. We've got a problem over here. I need you."

People turned to watch the young boy and the man going up the steps to the gondola. A good-looking father and son, both obviously good skiers. You could tell by the way they walked and carried their skis that they were experts. Maybe the little boy was even one of those hotshot junior racers they'd seen on the mountain.

"So, champ," said Tony Frantz to Eric Schneider. "What's happening? You still in the doghouse with your mom?"

Eric did not answer the question. "Do you have a lot of extra bedrooms in your house?"

"Not a lot. A couple. Why?"

"Would you take in boarders?"

"Depends on the boarder. Anyone you know?" He took Eric's skis and parked them in the rack outside the gondola and scooted in the front. Eric clambered in next to him and hunched forward to watch the ascent.

"Me."

"I don't know, sport. I'm not much of a cook."

"We could eat out," Eric said eagerly. "The Hickory House—I love the ribs—and Little Annie's and McDonald's."

"I don't know. Let's ski a bit and then we'll talk again."

Tony had been on his way out when he'd received Sally's phone call. He canceled his plans and went to her house instead, where she told him about Eric and his cache of money.

The next morning he booked out and called Eric to take him skiing. The boy had puffed up like a peacock. He was not accustomed to having Tony ask him to spend a day skiing with him. That honor was usually reserved for Rocky.

After skiing all morning they stopped for lunch at the Sundeck. Eric basked in the reflected glory of sitting at the "instructors only" table, but his glory was short-lived when Tony's conversation turned serious.

"Your mom told me about the money, Eric."

"You, too?" he said with disgust and turned away.

Tony pulled him toward him gently and put his arm around the boy's shoulders.

"I'm going to talk man-to-man to you. Those men are dangerous, Eric." He related a few sordid stories about Eric's erstwhile employers, sparing none of the details.

The color blanched from the boy's face and his lips pursed in an O of shock. Tony told him of the drug dealing, what was happening to the kids at the local schools, and the dangers of not only using but dealing. "That's why you made so much. You were doing their dirty work for them. You see, a lot of these guys give the stuff to kids to hold or carry. The cops rarely search a kid, but that's going to change soon. We don't want to see you go to jail as an accomplice. Especially when you didn't know what you were delivering."

Eric, who had filled up his luncheon tray with a hamburger, french fries, Coke, and dessert, felt his appetite leave him as Tony talked. Finally he pushed his tray away unfinished. He looked green. "I don't feel very good."

"Then let's get out of here and get some fresh air." Tony's voice was friendly and reassuring. When they were outside, Tony looked at his young charge and a fiercely protective feeling came over him. The Schneider children were the closest he'd ever get to kids of his own. He didn't want anything bad to touch them.

"Tony, I have to return it, don't I?"

"I know it's tough, but yes."

"Could you do it for me?"

At first he was going to say no, that Eric should do it himself. Then he realized he didn't want him to have any more contact with those scum. "Sure, I'll do it. Happy to. And no more strange delivery jobs unless you discuss it with your mom and me. Okay?"

The boy nodded.

The next day Tony returned the money to one of Aspen's more public figures and suggested that he cease using kids to do his dirty work. It was all delivered in a friendly voice with a sincere smile, but anyone who happened to look into Tony's eyes could recognize the unspoken warning.

The U.S. Alpine Ski Team had still not named a head coach, so the coaching was being handled in a somewhat disorganized manner by the assistants, mostly has-been racers in their late twenties who were trying to hold on to the glory years for a few more winters before finding real work. The day of the ski bum—the college dropout who flooded the ski resorts, waited on tables, or cleaned latrines just so he could ski for free, and who crashed with ten others in a shack—were over. These temporary coaches were the last of them.

January brought abundant snows, the annual *Winterschol* festivities, and—since much of the West was still starving for snow—an influx of tourists. Along with shopping at Boogies for $100 T-shirts and seeing how many times they could eat at Gordon's, watching the young women train was a special thrill for many of the visitors.

Early in December the young racers had gone off to Val d'Isere for the first of the Europa Cup races. At Val d'Isere and Tignes the following week, conditions had been marginal; one downhill had had to be canceled. The team then returned to the U.S.A. for Christmas break. Continued poor snow conditions in Europe had caused the cancellation or postponement of some of the races on the circuit, so the team remained in Aspen, waiting, waiting for the heavens to open and real racing to start again.

Without real competition, there was a danger of overtraining—going stale, losing concentration, thinking about other things, even thinking about the real danger of the sport. With their ultimate goal—the race—fading with every cloudless day, emotions ran high. There were arguments, tears, and angry words. The racers had no real outlet, no way of knowing if their training was going to pay off in improved times.

Both Kit and Rocky would arrive home after training depressed and morose, edgy, ready to burst into tears at the slightest provocation. "Racer's PMS," Daisy called it.

Many conversations were held at the James

household and at the Schneiders'. The concerned
adults began showing up casually to watch the
coaches work with the girls. It was an odd sight to
find Greg and Tony, Suzanne and Sally discussing
the shortcomings of the coaching staff as if they
were the best of concerned friends. Concerned
they were—but not for one another.

Rocky was obviously destined to be one of the
finest women skiers ever. Her showing against the
very tough Austrians and Swiss at Val had been
creditable indeed. She had finished in the top ten,
gaining a fourth in downhill and a sixth in giant
slalom. Kit was not very far behind. Their place-
ments would decide whether they would be appointed to the A team and move up to the World
Cup circuit. Other considerations depended on
how well they placed in the next series of European races and how much excitement they generated
in the press. If they made a good showing they
would soon be able to negotiate their own deals
with manufacturers and make some real money.

This was a far cry from the early days when the
girls had been climbing up the tortuous ladder.
Then, equipment would be supplied to the Ski
Club for distribution to the most promising racers.
At the end of the season it was handed down to the
next level until they in turn got good enough to
command first crack. In the case of Kit James,
equipment was never a problem. She always skied
on the best and newest. The James gang would
have it no other way.

To them the fact that Kit had been close behind
Rocky was heartening but not good enough. The
advantage of superior equipment ceased to be a
factor when Tony used his contacts to ensure that
Rocky no longer needed to depend on second best.
That left the quality of training and coaching as the
only potential advantage.

Both girls were in great physical shape, had the best equipment available, and were seasoned by some tough competition under their belt. The only thing that separated them from the Europeans was inspired coaching and fierce concentration. Coaching was of prime importance now, for when World Cup racing started, the coaches would be too busy with administrative tasks. If the kids hadn't learned the technical basics during their Development Squad period, they might as well forget it.

Concentration, on the other hand, was hard to teach.

Shortly after their first casual look-in, Sally and Tony met after ski school classes and went off to the Silver Leaf Club, where they could talk without running into the usual crowd. Most of the instructors usually dropped in at The Aspen Club Lodge bar or the Tippler, maybe even the Jerome before heading home to wives (if they had them) or to dress for the habitual evening on the town.

"I don't like the way things look," said Tony, tossing his parka over a chair and signaling for the waitress.

"Interesting that we all showed up at the same time, wasn't it?" Sally said, slumping into her seat with a sigh of fatigue. She'd had a particularly rough private with a famous movie star who was slightly paranoid about people watching her. It had been worse than working with a particularly active four-year-old, for the star had a habit of taking off on a collision course that put her directly in the path of skiers who had stopped for a breather. Sally was hoarse from crying out, "Runaway skier!"

"We're all worried about the same thing. They're dragging their heels over the head coach's job."

"There was some talk of naming Greg. Did you hear that?"

Tony frowned. "Why on earth him?"

"Because he wants it. And probably because he thinks it would give him a more legitimate excuse to work with Kit."

"It won't help. Not with us on the other side." He squeezed her hand. "I think we should consider going for the job ourselves."

"What about you? Why don't you go for it? You always say the head coach should be a European."

"It's not that I think there's anything wrong with an American. It's just that the Europeans have more tradition, more experience, and the proof is in their skiers. But me?" He shook his head fervently. "Not interested."

"You're interested in Rocky."

"That's different. She's family, and I know how much it means to her."

"How much?"

"Everything. Besides, don't you think it will be kind of interesting? You and I versus Greg and Suzanne. It'll be like the old days."

"Your old days, not mine. Suzanne and I were never rivals."

"Excuse me," he said softly, giving her a hard look. Maybe not in the obvious sense, he thought, but you love beating her just as much as I like getting Greg.

"Are we doing the right thing?" she asked, uncertainty painting worry lines across her face.

"We can't just leave everything to those playboy coaches. Half the time they're horsing around, and the other half, they're trying to figure what to do next. I've heard some of their comments to the kids. It's lucky there's a team at all," he said heatedly.

He was really exercised over this situation, observed Sally. Clearly angry, yet he refused to become actively involved with the team. She wondered why they hadn't approached him. He was an Austrian, an Olympic racer who'd won drawers full of gold, and he was considered one of the best technicians in the world. Was it the money? The pay was really lousy. For a man of thirty-five, the only challenge it presented was of producing a winning team. Was Tony too selfish to give up his rich clients or did he resent giving up four or five years of his life? She felt ashamed of her uncharitable thoughts and remonstrated with herself for having them. But she wouldn't presume to come out and ask him outright.

If Tony wasn't interested in the head coach position, he had thought long and hard about taking a more active part in Rocky's training. It might end up working against her. If she spent all day listening to the coaches, then came home and heard Tony tell her something totally different, it could really screw her up. The best thing to do would be to ask her how she felt about having him work more closely with her. He had been giving her tips for years, but what he was about to suggest was different—and dangerous if the federation ever found out.

"So what do you think?" he asked Sally after outlining what he wanted to do. "Do you think it'll help or just get her in trouble?"

"I think you should discuss it with her. It's her life and her career."

The next day after training, Tony hailed Rocky as she was taking off her skis and putting them in the team van.

"Hi, Rock! Got time for a hot something?"

"Sure!"

"Want to go to Sunshine's place?"

"Great. I can have one of her herbal teas."

He stowed his skis in the instructors' locker room, exchanged his goggles for a pair of Porsche sunglasses and his ski hat for a blue beret.

"Very French." She smiled in approval as he walked out. A cluster of awestruck kids stood off to the side, pointing to them and whispering with excitement.

"I see you have a fan club already." He tossed his chin in the direction of the adolescents.

"Yeah, can you believe they wanted my autograph?"

"Ah, yes! Fame and fortune await. Soon the paparazzi will be following you with their cameras and asking all kinds of intimate questions."

"What's pappa— That word?"

"It's a certain kind of photographer, more like annoying mosquitoes than real photographers."

They walked down Durant Avenue, a striking couple, one blond as a god, the other dark and brown as an Indian. As he draped his arm casually around her shoulders, he was unaware of the envious glances that followed them as they made small talk, stopping every now and then to peek into windows on the Cooper Street Mall. At Mill Street they turned right until they reached Main Street and Sunshine Campbell's restaurant.

Sunshine was one of the last of the original Woodstock hippies, though in the sixties she had been barely a teenager. Her personality had lost none of the ideals of those days, and she was still an outspoken advocate for peace and the preservation of the environment against nukes and development.

In her restaurant, aptly named Sunshine's, she had managed to combine the health-food fad of the sixties with sophisticated California cuisine. She needed no advertising, she had great word of mouth, and Gael Greene often dropped in for a chat and a calamari salad when she was in Aspen. She had described it in one of the sexy reviews she wrote occasionally for *New York* magazine. As a result, the place was rarely empty, and what had once been a well-kept secret rendezvous of the locals was getting the celebrity treatment that was part of the Aspen life-style.

As they settled themselves at a table and gave their order for tea and Sunshine's own carrot cake, Rocky looked around and smiled. "I love the way Sunshine did this place, don't you? One day when I have my own place I'm going to copy it right down to the china."

"You planning to open a restaurant?" he said, his blue eyes twinkling. God, he was crazy about this kid.

From the moment she was born, he had given his heart to that little bundle of dark hair and skin. How homely she'd been! Like a small furry animal. Even at three weeks she had shown signs of the intensity and seriousness that separated her so markedly, not only from her brother, but from her fellow skiers. When she was born and he saw her parents' joy, it was the only time in his life that he regretted not having formed the kind of alliance that could produce the casual comfort and warmth that Peter and Sally had created in that dumpy little house on Midland. When Eric was born, the circle had closed and he had felt like an outsider, despite the fact that they saw each other as frequently as ever.

"What were you thinking of just now?"

"How could you tell I was thinking?" he teased.

"I could smell the smoke."

"Aha, I had better watch myself. I forget how smart you are."

She forked up a huge piece of cake and, opening her mouth wide, wiped the fork clean. Her eyes

closed in sheer bliss. "Ummm, the best. The secret's apple sauce, did you know that?" It was
strictly a rhetorical question. "So, Coach, what do
you want to talk about?"

"Now who's mind reading?" He gave her chin a
chuck. She leaned against his hand for a moment,
thinking, wouldn't it be nice . . . ? Knock it off,
Rocky, she admonished herself, you've got other
things to think about. What will be will be.

Pragmatist that she was, Rocky was just enough
of the romantic to wish that one day her mother
and Tony would get married.

"I want to talk to you about what's going on with
your training."

"Okay."

"Are you happy with it? Do you feel you're
making progress? Do you want help?"

"No, no, yes. I hope I got that right." Wonderful!
If Tony really got involved she could work on those
problems that Greg had so vaguely alluded to. "If
you want to know the truth, the best coaching I
ever had was from you in those years when I was
trying to make it to the team. But how would we do
it?"

"That's not hard. It can be arranged. The problem is that we—that is, your mother and I—don't
want to mess with your head. If you're getting one
set of messages from the coaching staff and another from us, it could be bad. Do you understand
what I'm saying?" Tony could hardly know that
Rocky was already on the receiving end of yet a
third set of messages, from a totally unexpected
source.

"Yeah, but they probably wouldn't notice any
difference anyway. I mean, even I can see things
wrong when we look at the videos, and they don't
even notice."

"That's what I want to do. I can't take the

chance of just appearing casually every day and giving you hand signals or even talking to you without alerting them. So what I want to do is work with you and your videos. That way we can break down each move to a frame-by-frame analysis, and I can show you what's wrong, make suggestions. Then when you go out the next day, you can implement the changes. How does that grab you?"

"It grabs me good."

So they began. First Tony taught her some physics. "Gravity is at least eighty percent of the force accelerating you. Since its pull is pretty constant for all racers at the same point on a given course, you have twenty percent of the rest of the accelerating forces to influence. Your object is to minimize the decelerating forces."

"And how do I do that?"

"Carve turns."

"I know that."

"I know you do. But I want to show you something." He took a piece of paper and drew the tracks of three skiers going through a gate, showing the amount of skidding in each one. The drawings were a series of S's, the perfectly carved turn a skinny S, each one getting fatter as the skier began to skid his turn.

Some days they were able to meet for a surreptitious half hour of skiing. Then he told her about edge lock, how to lock on to a traverse so she made a track like a knife cutting through butter or like a skater cutting a figure.

"In the traverse is where there's the greatest chance of skidding. You've got to get on your edges the instant your skis are pointing to where you want to go. No overturning, no skidding! In slalom when you don't have time, you've got to give a quick edge-set and a forward push at the same time. Let me show you what I mean." He demonstrated. She watched raptly. If she could only ski like that!

In the evening, he and Sally would set up the day's videos and watch whatever Rocky had been doing that morning. By stopping or slowing down the replay, he could show her infinitesimal improvements that might shave off a crucial few hundredths of a second, the difference between winning and not.

He delivered his lessons with a running patter that showed why he was the most in-demand instructor in the country. Tony knew skiing the way Max knew physics. "Listen to your skis talk to you. If you don't hear them, you're making perfect carved turns. Every skier produces his own sound. I want your skis to sing silently to you.

"Now, your best event is probably the downhill. Let's see why." He ran the tape down until he found her downhill run. "See how you are on the straights? Tight, skis a shoulder length apart, but notice what you do on the airplane turn? You come erect, your body automatically finds the position that lets you make a good carved turn. Your coaches told you that's wrong. They want you low all the time. But it's they who are wrong." He quickly backtracked to her downhill. "So what have we learned?"

"I should be more erect in the gates."

"Right. Maybe you sacrifice wind drag, but you're gaining position, and you would lose more by deceleration if you allow yourself to skid. Killy said, 'It's how you make your turns that really decides how fast you go down the mountain.' Everyone is skiing too crouched."

He went into other aspects. Of how the right clothes can reduce wind drag, how a higher stance could permit her to adjust with tailwinds, a lower-than-normal stance for headwinds. He drew her pictures again, showing her the correct aerodynamic position to assume, giving her the example of a headwind of thirty mph on a sixty-mph course.

Again they reviewed her slalom run. It was an event that she was getting better and better in, due mainly to technique. But Tony wasn't completely happy with it. "Here . . ." He stopped and froze the frame. "What's happening here?"

She looked and looked but could see nothing wrong. "I'm not sure. I thought that was pretty good position."

"Not straight enough."

"I don't understand," she said, totally bewildered now.

"Tony"—Sally, who had been sitting quietly and listening, interrupted for the first time and flashed him a warning look—"it's too much at one time. Maybe we should save this for another time."

"No, Mom, not yet." She held out supplicating arms, then quickly turned to Tony. "Tell me."

He pointed up the hill where she seemed to be leaning out too far. "You start the turn too early here. Go straighter. And here"—he stopped the tape and pointed to her position a few feet above the gate—"here you must step to the inside ski to decrease the angle without decelerating. When the gates are set tight, charge the fall line as straight as you can, step on the inside ski to change direction, and give yourself forward motion and don't be afraid, don't make such a wide preparation. Gravity behaves differently at the beginning, the middle, and the end of the turn."

"Tony, does it have to be so technical, so complicated?" Sally interrupted again.

"No, but I want her to understand what the forces are. Rocky, is this too complicated? Am I hindering more than helping?"

"No, no, it's fascinating. You should be teaching physics as well as skiing."

"No, thank you. So, here's the summation." He smiled with encouragement. Sally hadn't seen him so animated in months. He really loves this, she thought. He should be the coach. If he could convey a fraction of his enthusiasm to the kids, they'd be the best team in the world. Then she turned her attention to what he was saying.

"The top of the turn is easy. At the finish there is a tendency to skid. Fight it. When the turn needs a major change of direction, start the turn high, then turn sharply underneath the gate." He went on through the possibilities of gates and the adjustments required for each.

Sally, who had been watching her daughter carefully for fatigue and confusion, saw neither and breathed a deep sigh of relief.

"Oh, one more thing. Even good skiers have a tendency to do this, so you should be aware of it. Don't aim your skis too close to the gates. Give yourself room for angulation and inward lean. Sometimes your ski track might have to be as much as two or three feet from the pole. Do you spend plenty of time looking at the run and picking your line properly to allow for that inward lean?"

"I think so. Let's go back and look."

Again Tony caught Sally's warning glance.

"No, dear heart, it's enough for now. I have a feeling you're going to be running slalom in your dreams tonight." He went over and kissed the top of her head. "You're a good student."

"And you're a great teacher. Isn't he, Mom?"

"I think we can end this mutual-admiration society for tonight, don't you?" said Sally with a laugh. "But yes, he is a great teacher."

They continued their nightly chalk talks until the team was to leave for Europe again. Both Kit and Rocky knew they were getting special coaching, because they had discussed it, even though both had been sworn to secrecy. No casual conversation to each other or to the remaining racers, and no trading of technique pointers. This insistence on secrecy put a damper on their usually open friendship. Rocky decided the best way to avoid it seemed to be to avoid each other. Kit, certain that she had done something to offend Rocky, caught her after practice one night and insisted on discussing the matter.

"I don't like what's happening to us, Rocky."

"What's happening?"

"We used to be as close as sisters. Now, you hardly say a word to me."

"It's the same thing with you," Rocky said, but there was no heat in her accusation. "It's just that . . ."

"What?" Kit's blue eyes glazed with tears. "Is it because of our families? Because Suzanne and Greg are coaching me?"

"Not exactly. I'm getting special coaching, too, you know," she defended. Light dawned. "Did they say anything to you about me?"

"Well, not exactly. That is, I'm not . . ."

"You're not supposed to discuss it with me. And I'm not supposed to talk to you. That's all it is, Kitty-cat." Rocky used her childhood nickname and hugged her friend, feeling years older and wondering how friendships survived such strains.

Kit wiped her eyes and gave her friend a tentative smile. "If that's all it is, I feel much better. Do you think they'll let us bunk together?"

"Why not? Don't we always?"

They parted with a hug and a wave, but both

girls knew that something irrevocable was happening to them.

The weekend before they were to leave, Suzanne decided to throw a party for the team. She and Greg debated whether to invite parents and coaches, but Greg reminded her that Sally would have to be included if she did, so she kept it team only.

"What'll I wear?" moaned Rocky.

Sally had to laugh. Weren't those her very own words the night that Michael had invited her out to dinner? "Is it casual or what?" asked Sally, wondering if she would have enough time to run something up on her machine.

"No, it's not casual. Everybody's sick of wearing racing pants and turtlenecks, they want to get dressed up."

"Well, why not?"

"What do you think, Mom?" Rocky held up two outfits on a hanger for her mother's inspection.

Sally gave them a critical look. They were both a couple of years old and even when new weren't very exciting. "I don't think they'll fit you anymore. Besides they look kind of . . ." She made a disgusting face.

"What'll I do? I don't have time to go shopping, and even if I did, we can't afford it."

"I have an idea. Leave it to me."

So it was that Rocky appeared at Kit's house in an outfit of her mother's making that had every girl green with envy. Sally had made a flounced Western skirt of cornflower-blue suede for her daughter to wear with one of her favorite hand-knit sweaters.

As everyone stood around admiring one another in the unaccustomed mode of dress, Greg watched Rocky from across the room. He, too, had been surprised by the young girl's appearance. She had real style. More, she had poise. Amid the giggles of the girls and the loud teasing of the boys, she stood out like a pool of still water, making comments in a low musical voice, courteous, respectful, and gracious.

When the talk turned to shop, it was Rocky whose comments made the most sense. She was trying to stir up some interest in making short cultural trips when they were in places that had something to see. Most of the girls were in favor. It was the boys who groaned and griped.

The buffet table, catered by Chefs of Aspen, groaned under trays of pasta and barbecued chicken and ribs. There was a huge salad filled with every imaginable vegetable, baskets of crusty breads, and chips. For dessert they had to choose between a gooey rich chocolate cake and create-your-own sundaes.

"I know you guys are into serious carbohydrate loading, but for tonight I thought you could just let it all hang out," said Suzanne. She was trying desperately not to intrude on Kit's party, but that was like hoping you could walk through a den of snakes without getting bitten.

During the evening Rocky would look up every now and then and find Greg James looking at her speculatively. She was too young and inexperienced to put much credence in it, but still it was enough to confuse and distract her. She tried moving around the room, hiding herself within the chattering clusters of her teammates. After dinner Kit put on music, and much to everyone's relief, the elder Jameses disappeared. They danced, and Kip Baily, the most promising junior boy, alternated his attentions between Kit and Rocky, very much to their amusement.

At eleven o'clock, the party started breaking up.

"Don't go, it's early," cried Kit. "I have some movies we can watch." It had been such a wonderful evening, the first one in months that had contained something other than skiing. She hated to see it end. She pleaded with Rocky. "Don't you go, too."

Rocky looked at her watch. "Well, I said I'd be home early. Maybe I could stay just a little while longer, but then I'll have to take a taxi."

"No, Greg will take you home. He won't mind."

"He won't mind what, punkin?" said Greg, sipping his fourth straight vodka as he walked into the living room. "Have you made me a late date?"

"Grunt, you don't mind taking Rocky home in a little while, do you? We were having such a wonderful time, and then everyone decided it was time to leave. I persuaded Rocky to stay a little longer."

"I don't mind if she doesn't mind." His smile was dazzling.

Rocky blushed and stammered. "Well, if you're sure."

Greg's presence had produced the desired effect. He wanted Rocky to be slightly off balance. What he had in mind needed that edge.

From that point on until they finally left, Rocky said hardly a word. She felt a deep sense of uneasiness the moment she was out of the house and buckled into the BMW.

As he carefully manipulated the serpentine curves of Red Mountain Road, she looked at him out of the corner of her eye, finally admitting to herself that she was not only in awe of him but a little afraid of him, too. Despite the wonderful things that Kit had told her about her brother, his warm affection, his patience and his gentleness, this portrait didn't agree with the one that had been painted of him during all her young years in the house on Midland. She couldn't quite figure out how one person could be so many contrary things.

But she couldn't help admiring his strong profile and the way his hair waved over his forehead. His hands on the wheel were strong and certain, too. He wore no gloves and she could see the dark hairs on his knuckles and the way his thumbs curved up, as though he had been hitchhiking and couldn't uncock them. She had seen him race a few times against Tony and some of the other pros at the local competitions held during *Winterschol* and Race Week, and she'd admired his strong, aggressive technique. Lately, he'd been attracted to aerials, a daring wrinkle in the sport, usually performed by those under thirty. These were the somersaults and flips that turned skiers into high divers, only instead of going off a board, they went off snow ramps.

"I saw you last week at the Highlands." Rocky finally broke the silence. "You were really good."

"I was, wasn't I?" He gave her a wink. "Not bad for an older fellow."

"You're not so old," she protested, though she hadn't the vaguest idea how old he really was.

"I'm thirty-five. That's got to be ancient to a youngster like you. Kit calls me Grandpaw."

"I thought she called you Grunt, because that's the noise you make when you do gates."

"Has that child told you all my secrets?" he asked seductively, pleased to see her flush.

"Hardly," she answered in a voice that quavered. She wished he'd stop patronizing her. "Just your nickname and about your Porsche getting totaled. I'm glad you weren't hurt," she offered shyly. "Miss Richards is okay now, too."

"Yes, we were both lucky."

She grew silent again, looking out the window at the luminous night. The stars seemed close enough to touch on this crisp, cold evening. "No snow, I guess."

He leaned forward and peered up. "Not for a while. But you should have some good conditions in Europe this month."

"I hope. It was awful last month. Dangerous."

"You ever get scared, Rocky?"

"No." Funny. He'd asked her that once before.

"You should," he said sharply at her unexpected response. Hell, this kid was well named. Nothing fazed her.

"I should? Why?"

"Because any prudent racer should be aware of the percentages."

"I've had my share of injuries. I guess I'll have more."

"You can't race if you're injured."

She was confused by the bend in the conversation. "I don't understand what you're trying to say."

"Have you ever thought what might happen if you were seriously injured?"

"You mean like a broken hip?"

"A broken back, a broken neck. Paralyzed. It happens, you know."

There was a sharp intake of breath. "But hardly ever. Good skiers don't have accidents like that."

"Just remember what I said. Sometimes in a downhill you know you're going faster than you can handle. You pray that you won't hit a piece of ice or a rut. Sometimes all you can do is hang on by your toes until you get to the finish line."

He gave her a surreptitious glance. Her head was bowed. She was looking at her fingers twisting her gloves into a knot. "Hey!" He reached over and gave her hands a squeeze. "I didn't mean to get you all depressed. You're a terrific skier. You'll be fine.

Just . . . remember . . . no. Just forget everything I said. Chalk it up to an old guy's fears.''

But Rocky couldn't drive his words from her mind. It had never occurred to her to be frightened of skiing. She had started so young. Before anyone had conditioned her to fear. Her mother and father had never used those negative words that made children frightful on snow or in water. Caution was given and rationally explained. Hot stoves burned. Electrical outlets shocked. Icy steps were slippery. Cause and effect. If her mother and father had ever been frightened of anything— heights, closed spaces, tunnels, caves, dark closets, bats, flying—she never knew about it. They taught caution. Not fear.

Now her mind was filled with vague tremors and nebulous anxieties. She saw herself tumbling down a hill in slow motion, then disappearing over the edge into nothingness. She trembled with apprehension.

When he pulled to a stop a few houses from her own, she was still staring at her fingers.

"Hey . . ." He tilted up her chin and looked down into her shadowed silvery eyes. God, she was going to be gorgeous. She had stood out like a tall blue flower in that outfit tonight, making the others seem like gawky adolescents. All that and a phenomenal ability on a pair of boards.

"You know, you looked pretty terrific tonight. It's hard to remember what you looked like in ski clothes. When you go in your bedroom tonight, I want you to look at yourself in your mirror and say to yourself, 'Greg James thinks you're a very pretty girl.' Will you do that for me?" He leaned a little closer, letting his fingers trail down her face.

She could smell his after-shave lotion, feel his breath feather on her face. Her eyelids fluttered in embarrassment. She stiffened, waiting. When he bent down and kissed her lingeringly on the cheek, she gave a little shudder, whether of revulsion or fear, she couldn't be sure.

Greg felt her tremors and smiled a secret smile. He hoped it was working, this little plan of psychological warfare he was waging for Kit's sake. Some small spark of decency in him flickered for an instant, then went out. He wanted Rocky thoroughly confused. He wanted her thinking of him and his words, wanted that awesome concentration of hers broken. Not forever. He didn't want to ruin her life. Just long enough to give Kit an edge.

As she gathered her things together, he raced around to help her out. For an instant she felt panic as his big body blocked the door, but he stepped aside quickly to let her get out.

She scooted past him like a terrified rabbit, then turned and mumbled a hasty good night and thank-you.

"Bon voyage, kid. And remember what I said. Be careful. Don't let those European girls get to you. And . . . good luck."

She ran into the house and up the stairs, holding her breath until she heard the bedroom door close behind her. Then she collapsed against it and let out a deep moan. She did not go and look at herself in the mirror as he had instructed. Instead she brushed her teeth in the dark, flung her clothes on a chair, and slipped under the covers. For the first time in her life, her dreams of skiing were not of victory but of bone-crushing defeat.

CHAPTER TEN

BUSINESS HAD PICKED UP APPRECIABLY FOR SALLY IN early January. Tony was responsible for that. He was directing to her clients he was either no longer interested in or who were willing to accept his recommendation. Although she had made it a point not to date her clients, she had met several attractive and distinguished men who had invited her to dinner. They very honestly told her that they were married, that their wives didn't ski, that they admired her intelligence and would be pleased to have her company for the evening, no strings attached. On several occasions, she had made it a foursome with Daisy.

She continued to see Michael on occasion, usually for dinner dates. He invited her to a party in Starwood given by Rupert Murdoch, an invitation she turned down. It produced angry words between them, but she had stubbornly prevailed, saying, "They just don't interest me, and I never know what to say to them."

"They are the movers and shakers," he insisted.

"I know. But they neither move nor shake my world, which, as you know, is very circumscribed. Why not take Marcella?"

He did. The two were becoming good friends. Sally wondered how long it would be before they discovered how well suited they were to each other. Yet Michael kept coming back, and she was unable to understand why he kept returning.

So was Michael. Especially after the incident over the Murdoch party. At first he thought it was her lack of wardrobe that prompted her to turn down the dinner party invitation. He'd even offered to buy her some things. She'd turned on him savagely for that. It was only after talking to Daisy at that same dinner party that he began to understand what prevented her from breaking down her social barriers. She was afraid! Afraid of walking into a roomful of influential, wealthy people and being ignored. It was not that Sally was socially inept. He'd seen and listened to her when she was with people she knew. She made acute observations and intelligent comments. She was listened to with respect, even eagerness. Unlike Daisy, who had a charming puppy-dog appeal and the ability to put herself in the middle of her own jokes, Sally had an innate dignity and a thin skin. She did not take kindly to criticism or rejection. To avoid either, she avoided the situations that would produce them.

When confronted with his knowledge, she didn't deny it. "If you were me in my circumstances, you'd feel the same way. Don't deny it. We're too much alike, so I know how you'd behave. Damn it, Michael, I barely even finished college. What would I say to them?"

"The same thing you say to one of them when they book you for a private."

"That's different."

"How so?"

"They're on my turf. We talk about skiing and technique."

"Do the same thing when you're on their turf." Her face refused to soften. "Do you think the women they're married to are all brilliant college graduates?"

"Maybe not brilliant, but they belong to the same clubs and do the same charities. I may even be one of their charities for all I know."

"Stop it! I won't listen to that kind of talk from you."

"Michael," she said wearily. "Why are you here?"

"Because I . . ." Words he had never said to any woman were about to slip out, but he caught himself. "Because I want to be."

If she had been expecting to hear something else, she did not show her disappointment.

Sally was still baffled by Michael Greenfield. She knew he was seeing other women. Daisy reported his appearance at the chic parties with Marcella or Suzanne. But when it came to expensive restaurants and intimate dinners *à deux*, she was still his favorite date. By now she had a small wardrobe of suede pieces that she had put together which she could mix about to create new outfits to wear.

For her thirty-sixth birthday the previous week, he had given her a fabulous Indian necklace of colorful fetish birds in coral, lapis, malachite, rose quartz, and hematite, all colors that matched her various suedes. Daisy had given her a four-ply cashmere sweater in a pale gray that matched her eyes, and Tony a contemporary silver bracelet with coral, turquoise, and amethyst inlays by Charles

Loloma, a Native American silversmith. One of her
wealthy steady clients who had taken a great fancy
to her because she reminded him of his dead
daughter had given her an antique pottery bowl
from the Coyote clan of Hopi potters. She was
touched to tears.

When Michael informed her that he had to go
out of town for a week, she broke down and invited
him again to dinner. To her surprise he refused,
telling her instead that he wanted to take her to
Abettone, a fine Italian restaurant whose decor, he
told her, reminded him more of New York than
Aspen.

As they settled down to their lobsters fra diavolo
and an exquisite Vino Nobile de Montepulciano,
she remarked, "This feels like the last supper
somehow."

"It does? I certainly hope not. Why do you say
that?"

"I don't know." She shrugged. "The ghost of my
Sicilian grandmother."

"You had a Sicilian grandmother? That accounts
for the Mediterranean coloring. Was she a witch?"

"Probably. Aren't they all?"

He was very quiet after that. He toyed with his
wineglass, picked at his food, took two bites of the
excellent semi-freddo, and tossed his espresso
down in a gulp.

"Michael," she said finally, "this isn't like you.
I've never seen you treat such good food with such
cavalier indifference. What's the matter?"

"I don't really know. Business?"

"Are you asking me?"

He shrugged and picked up her hand. Threading
his fingers through hers, he turned it over and
kissed her palm. Then, as he felt her resistance, he
trapped it with the other. "Stay with me tonight,"
he said softly, his voice husky with barely con-

trolled desire. "I want to make love to you all
night."

She blushed and tried to pull her hand away.
"Michael, you know that's not possible. What
about Eric?"

"He's a good kid. He can take care of himself."

"But what do I tell him? Mother is not coming
home because she's spending the night with her
lover?"

"Am I your lover? I want to be your lover."

"No, you don't," she said crossly. "Who would
you take to all those fancy dinner parties on the
mountain?"

"You." He turned her hand over and put his
tongue to the inside of her palm. It was hot and
demanding and reminded her of another time and
place. She squirmed uncomfortably in her chair.
"Michael, people are staring."

"I don't care. Let them. I have an unquenchable
desire to devour you. That's why I haven't been
able to eat all night."

"You are really making me angry," she said
testily.

"Good. Any emotion is acceptable." With that he
snapped his fingers for the bill. When it came, he
added a tip and scrawled his signature, then
rushed her out of the restaurant and into his
Mercedes.

The moment they got to the house he pulled her
into his arms. Feverish kisses rained down on her
as he carefully separated her from her clothes.
With each step toward his bedroom, he divested
her of another article of clothing. By the time they
reached the door she was shivering in his arms, so
he picked her up and deposited her on the fur
coverlet. "Did anyone ever tell you that you are not
a feather?" He smiled tenderly.

She shook her head in despair, uncertain whether to laugh or run for her life. His burst of uncontrolled passion had shocked and thrilled her. She'd wanted to protest but instead had felt herself caught up in the vortex of his cyclonic desire and knew it was foolish to fight it.

He talked to her softly as he slowly stripped off his own clothes. In retaliation for the feather remark, she said, "Has anyone ever told you that you sound like an X-rated movie?"

The laugh that bubbled low in his throat was both thrilling and dangerous. He stood in front of her, his tanned body faintly gleaming in the starlight that came into the dark room from the window. His body was hairless, sleek, a swimmer's body. No, a bullfighter's. Lean, hard muscled, satiny, cared for, a body that belonged to a man with money.

She felt the bed give slightly as he joined her. His dark eyes seemed secretively veiled so that she could read nothing but desire in their depths. His lightning-swift passion slowed to a simmer. Now he began to kiss her all over, lazily savoring her as he had not the sumptuous meal that he had pushed away uneaten. He feasted on her flesh, licking her with his tongue, taking small spicy bites from her breasts.

She caressed his hard thigh with her bare foot and sank her hands into the thick dark hair, dragging him up to her mouth. He plunged into it like a man dying for water.

"Michael, Michael," she gasped, "I can't breathe."

"Can't help it," his voice rasped between breaths. "Wanted to do this all night."

As her body responded mindlessly to his demands, her rational mind thrilled with fear. She was still relatively inexperienced in sexual matters. Nothing had ever prepared her for a man like

Michael Greenfield. On the outside he was a coolly controlled, almost calculating kind of man. But inside he was an active volcano threatening to explode when least expected. He seemed to be obsessed with her, reveling in her flesh, unable to satiate himself in the ways she knew. In his drive to possess her—or something in her—he sent her farther away from her own controlled self, threatening to release emotions she didn't even know she had.

Although his pursuit of her was not full of heavy breathing and romantic protestations—after all, they had not actually made love more than a few times—once they were in bed, there were no holds barred. Time after time he would lift her to moaning climax, only to stop and start again. She had no idea how he could bring himself to such a state and then deny himself. By the time they were both ready for orgasm, she was almost delirious with want, exploding in a million pieces, breathless and exhausted.

Breathing hard in his arms, her body flayed and sensitive, she was just catching her breath, when she felt his fingers trail lightly over her back. His lips followed; his hard legs held her in a death grip. Then he rolled his full weight on her. Trapping her hands over her head, his mouth descended to take hers in a bruising kiss. She was flooded with panic. It was like being buried alive. Sex with Michael was the closest thing to death she could imagine. Sex with Michael stole the breath from her, melted her bones, stopped her heart.

Later, when she was safely at home in her own bed, she would remember these analogies and wonder if other women reacted to Michael the way she did. Yet, he continued to fascinate her and she felt herself drawn to him like the proverbial moth.

In the morning, when she was more rational,

with a cup of strong coffee in front of her, she would realize that no matter how intense he got, how verbal, how sense inflaming his words, there was one word that never crossed his lips, even when the heat of passion made all things possible. In his prodigious vocabulary, the word *love* had no place.

She was torn between wanting to hear it pass his lips and grateful that it didn't. It freed her from a responsibility she didn't want to face just yet. In the cool, sober light of dawn, she was forced to wonder what she would do if Michael Greenfield was interested in making a commitment. Right now he was satisfying all sorts of short-term needs and unconsciously helping her to build the self-confidence she'd been lacking since her teenage days when Suzanne James had stolen her boyfriend away from her.

Although she waited to hear love words from him, she was not quite sure if she was ready to offer them in return.

As Sally walked into the familiar hubbub of the instructors' lounge to have her coffee and change into her clothes, the conversation suddenly stopped. Curious eyes turned on her. There were a few whispers, then the noise started again. This time there was a difference. She knew the talk was aimless, meaningless, to cover up what they were afraid she had heard when she walked in.

She fixed a group of women with a stony stare and watched them turn away in embarrassment.

Daisy, who was scowling at herself in the mirror of her locker and trying to do something with her runaway hair, avoided her eyes. "What's going on?" Sally asked as she opened her own locker. "Have I suddenly got leprosy?"

"What do you mean?"

"I walk into this usually friendly locker room expecting the usually friendly hellos, and instead I run into a wall of stares and conversation that stops in mid-sentence. Would someone like to tell me what's going on?" The words which were directed at Daisy were loud enough for the entire room to hear.

"Forget it," said Daisy. "It's the usual locker-room bullshit. You know . . . she saids and he saids . . . and did you hears? . . . and I heard that . . . It's all bullshit!"

Sally swung Daisy around to face her. "Daisy, I've known you too long for you to hide things from me. Look at me!" she ordered when her friend tried to avert her gaze. "You're not telling me something."

Daisy sat down on a chair. The locker room had grown oddly empty during their exchange.

"I'm waiting."

Daisy shrugged. "There was just some talk about the girls on the racing circuit."

"And?"

"It doesn't mean anything. You know, one day one of the kids wins, the next day, another one does."

Sally shook her head in frustration. "Would you stop dancing around and give it to me straight."

"They said that Kit has been making a very strong showing."

"What about Rocky?"

Daisy gave her a placating smile. "It doesn't mean anything. She's probably having a bad week, the flu or something."

"Rocky is doing poorly? How come I didn't know?"

"Look, for all we know it's the James gang propaganda machine at work. To make you crazy."

But it wasn't. The papers were full of it. There

was a small note in *The New York Times* as well as a column by one of the feature writers about the heating-up rivalry between the two Aspen friends. The Denver papers gave it even more space. It was the same kind of hype that had produced headline rivalries between tennis greats Navratilova and Evert.

Sally was barely able to concentrate on her class the whole day. At four o'clock she said a hasty good-bye and went off in search of Tony. But he had taken a small group heli-skiing out of Marble and wasn't expected back until dark. She left a message for him at the "privates" desk to see her when he got back to town.

She was nursing a cup of tea and looking gloomy when he burst into the kitchen. "What's the matter? Mats said it was urgent."

She passed him the newspapers. She had circled the offending articles with a red pencil. He quickly skimmed them. "So?"

"Don't you find it odd that Rocky is being beaten race after race by someone she routinely beats?"

He shrugged. "Not necessarily. It happens."

"Did it ever happen to you?"

"Well, I didn't win everything."

"But did you ever lose frequently to someone you had consistently beaten?"

"Look, maybe those ex-Olympians are not such bad coaches after all."

"Or maybe Greg and Suzanne were more effective than you and I."

His head snapped up. "Now, you're going too far."

She scooped up the papers and threw them in the garbage. "I knew this was going to happen. Sooner or later. You pushed her too hard. She's cracking under the pressure."

"I think you're the one who's cracking. Just

calm down, Sal. Everything will sort itself out." He came over to her and knelt at her feet, lifting her downcast head with a finger and looking kindly into her stricken eyes. "When was the last time you spoke to her?"

"That's just it. She hasn't called in over a week. It's not like her." She burst into tears. He scooped her into his arms and tried to comfort her. She leaned against his familiar chest and wailed, "Oh, Tony, I'm so worried. There's something wrong. I just know it."

He wiped the tears from her eyes. For the first time he noticed, really noticed, how silvery they were behind the veil of tears. An odd feeling seized him and he bent his lips to place a kiss on one, then the other. His hand on the back of her head felt the perfect curve of bone, the silky sense hair that licked at his fingers like live flames. With a shaky laugh, he withdrew and stood up. "Don't worry, Sal," he said with mock gruffness, "I know she'll call and we'll find out that it isn't anything serious."

"Promise?" she said in a little-girl voice that she had never used even when she was small.

"Promise."

"I don't like it," Tony admitted later that week to Max Margolis. There was no reason to put up a false front with his friend. "It's not like Rocky to play second to anyone. Especially Kit James. She's too good."

"But everyone loses sometime," reminded Max, who knew the feeling quite well.

"We've taught her that. As well as how to be a good loser. But she's used to winning and she doesn't take defeat too well. That's what makes her a champion. Losing makes her angry, makes her want to do better. You should see her after a race. She sits for hours watching her runs on videotape, analyzing every move. Then she goes out with a checklist and works on every weak point."

"So what do you think it is?"

"I don't know. But they are televising the races Saturday on ESPN, and I'm making sure I watch."

"Let's do it together. You want me to ask Sally?"

Tony scratched his head. He was torn. If she knew they had watched without her, she'd be furious. On the other hand, it would be agony for her to be so far away from her child, unable to help with a cheery word or her soothing physical presence. "No, let's not. She's got enough to worry about right now. I can always say something later if it ever comes up."

Saturday, Tony canceled his regular private with Richard Farwell, who, when the reasons were explained, was sympathetic. He drove out to Max's house and together the two men watched the races beamed by satellite from Austria.

By the time it was Rocky's turn to take her downhill run, the course was beginning to show deep ruts from all the skiers who'd preceded her. It was slick, fast, and dangerous. Half the field already had fallen and been disqualified.

They saw her in the starting gates. Normally, Rocky timed her breathing to the countdown.

"Look at her. What's wrong?" said Max, leaning forward.

"She's not doing the synchronized breathing I taught her."

She finally took one big breath and shot out of the gate, immediately dropping into a tuck, her legs wide apart, arms in front of her like a diver about to take the plunge.

"Good speed position," said Max.

"Yeah, but she's holding it too long. Straighten up, Rocky, c'mon baby, straighten up." No sooner were the words out of his mouth than she hit one of the speed bumps and became airborne. She fought for control, coming down on one ski, balancing on an edge, fighting to bring the other ski to the snow.

"That's going to cost her," said Tony, his forehead paved with worry lines.

And it did. She didn't even finish in the top ten. Kit came in a respectable fifth.

"She'll make up for it in the GS, you'll see." Max tried to sound reassuring, but both men felt their hearts grow heavy with despair for the young racer.

Again Kit drew a good early starting position and ran a careful, technically correct giant slalom. The icy conditions demanded a certain amount of care. But Rocky was good on ice. Tony had trained her by setting courses for her using "stubbies," short slalom poles that were flexible and light. A skier could get as close to them as necessary without fear. Besides, Rocky didn't have a fearful bone in her body. She did better, but Kit still beat her and the GS wasn't really her event!

In the slalom the bad luck of the draw had Rocky racing on a severely eroded, rutted course that grew icier as the temperature dropped. When she finally appeared in the starting gate the camera zoomed in for a close-up.

"God, she looks like she hasn't had a decent night's sleep in a week." Max pointed an accusing finger.

"That's not all. Look how tense she is. They've called her name twice and she hasn't paid any attention. Max, I'm really worried. I have a feeling I should get myself on a plane and go find out what's happening there. That girl is not our Rocky."

Max grabbed his arm. "Shh, she's off!"

Silently Tony ran the gates with her, trying to reach her mind over the thousands of miles to give her confidence and advice. The first couple of gates were a piece of cake. One third of the way down the course was a series of flush gates set in a straight line, on the steepest part of the course. These gates demanded of the skier the utmost in technique and daring. Holding an edge here was impossible except for the best of racers.

Rocky entered the gates too fast. She hooked a tip, spinning out, but recovering in time to enter the next gate. Now her timing was totally off. She finished the flush tentatively and attacked the rest of the course, trying to make up the lost time.

Tony shook his head. "No use, baby. You were seconds behind the field at the half. What rotten luck." He turned to Max. "You saw it. Her timing's shot to hell. She's tense and distracted. She's in trouble."

"You think the new ski might help? I mean later, not now. Maybe when she comes home, she can give it a try. Maybe it'll help her over the slump."

"I'll have to discuss it with Sally."

Max flicked off the TV set. "How about something to eat?"

Tony nodded absently, his mind far from food although Max made the best five-alarm chili in the west. He always made plenty and kept it in the freezer for moments like this. He took out a container and emptied it into a pot. As Tony chopped onion and shredded Monterey Jack cheese and iceberg lettuce, Max gave his friend a sly look. "Seems to me your concerns for this kid are a little odd, boychick. Are you picking on nymphets in your old age?"

"That isn't even slightly amusing," said Tony, brandishing the knife. "You're spending too much time with your fantasies."

"Maybe the child is only an excuse to get closer to the mother. Or are you perhaps getting wise in your old age and beginning to realize what a special lady she is?"

"I've always known that. But you know me, Max," he mocked, "the bee always searching for the sweetest flower."

"Well, Sally may not be the sweetest flower, but she won't fade. Nosirree, Bob, when the bloom is off those other little rosebuds, she'll be getting better and better. Remember, you heard it here first."

"Don't I always?" Tony popped the top of a bottle of a beer and hovered over the stove, watching Max stir the red mess in the pot. Delicious smells were beginning to fill the kitchen. "When's that stuff going to be ready? And just how hot is it?"

"Hot enough to stop you in your tracks, buster, which takes a lot of hot."

The phone shattered the peaceful scene with an ominous ring.

Max reached for it lazily. With a big wink, he joshed, "One of my admirers, no doubt."

But as soon as he answered it, his face turned white. "You can't do that," he exploded after listening to the voice on the other end. "They can't do that," he echoed.

"Can't do what?"

Max looked at him with anguished eyes. "Tony . . ."

"Talk. What's happening?"

"Someone wants this ski very badly."

"What's that mean? You're not getting death threats, are you?" The idea was so farfetched it was laughable.

"Shit! I wanted to solve this myself." With that admission he brought Tony up to date on the strange accidents that had befallen him in November and early December. "Now Monroe claims the ski is theirs. They've cut off my golden parachute payments pending a thorough investigation."

"They can't do that," Tony said heatedly.

"They can and they are. Legal action would take too long and cost me much too much. I still have enough for a while. But . . ." He rubbed his head vigorously, trying to erase the painful picture his mind was drawing.

"Don't worry about money . . . partner." Max opened his mouth to protest. "I've got plenty. It's yours. If it will make you feel better, we'll have formal partnership papers drawn. Look, we might even make a few bucks." He laughed, but it was a nervous laugh. Christ, he wasn't Richard Farwell or Pat Mallory with a bottomless trust fund. "Listen, we'd better tighten security until we find out who's masterminding this."

"Greenfield," said Max morosely.

Tony's mind was bubbling as he headed up Highway 82 to his house on Red Mountain. Worried thoughts of Rocky, of Sally, of his rash offer to Max, and the very real prospect of violence raced through his head.

In a town like Aspen, which more resembled a South American country with its "haves and have-nots," the amount of petty crime was considerable. Whereas urban crime tended to be more violent, crime in Aspen was rarely personal. Hotel rooms, condos, houses, businesses were all treated democratically when it came to breaking and entering. But the stealing of a radical new ski could be as dramatic in this town as the theft of state secrets.

Such a crime would be front-page news no matter who committed it. Like when Claudine Longet shot Spider Sabich, a local ski hero. Maybe it didn't stay front page for long, but there was plenty about the case to keep party tongues wagging for the season. Well, he was a far cry from Vladimir "Spider" Sabich, and Sally was not Claudine although she might be mad enough to wreak mayhem on him when he broke the news about Rocky to her.

The next evening, Tony invited himself to Sally's for dinner, telling her there was something important to discuss.

From the moment she realized he was not going to say anything until after dinner, she had shown admirable control. Eric's presence at the dinner table gave them a different focus for a change, and the young boy, who rarely had the spotlight fully on him, took full advantage of their attention. Both were grateful not to speak. Finally even Eric got tired. He'd run out of stories and was not clever enough to invent new ones. He excused himself and went to his room, leaving Tony to help with the cleanup.

Tony gathered the dirty dishes from the table wordlessly. When they were all in the sink and soaking, she finally turned to him, dried her soapy fingers on her apron, and said, "Well?"

"Dinner was delicious."

"What are we going to do about Rocky?"

"What do you want to do?"

"I want to bring her home."

"That's crazy. You can't do that."

"Watch me. I'm going to call the woman's coach and tell him to send her home. She can rejoin the team later if she wants to."

"You'll ruin her chances to make the team. Kit will win by default."

"Isn't that what's happening now? I know my daughter. She can't be happy."

"So you're going to let the James gang win by default. Just give up. Hand them the prize. After she's worked so hard."

"After you've worked so hard, you mean." Sally's voice rose in intensity. They were about to have another fight. "Why is it so important to you?

To prove that you're still better than Greg? That you can not only out-ski him but out-coach him, too?"

"Aren't you getting it a little wrong?" The fire in her voice was matched by the cold steel in his. "I don't have to prove myself to Greg James or anyone. It's Greg James who's still trying to prove himself. And what about you?" He pointed an accusing finger.

"Me? Don't be ridiculous. I have nothing to prove."

"Don't you? All your life you've let Suzanne James get away with what she wanted to. Why, I'll never even begin to understand, because I know that you're just as competitive as the next guy, only with you it comes out in a different way."

She stormed out of the kitchen with him close on her heels. "I don't know why we're having this discussion. I don't want to talk about me, I want to talk about my kid."

"And we are."

"I should never have given you such free rein with her. You planted this idea in her long ago. You and your gung-ho spirit of competition. She had to fight, to learn, to win. Always to win. She doesn't know what it means to fail. How is she going to handle it? She's failing now, and it's getting worse."

Tony did not say a word. Now was not the time to tell Sally just how bad it was. Even though the papers would gleefully report this newest slide, at least Sally hadn't been there to see it with her own eyes.

"It's not good for her, Tony. You're a man, competition is meat and drink to you. . . ."

"Hey, wait a minute!" he interrupted. "Am I hearing right? Is this the woman who keeps telling me there are no differences between the sexes except biological ones? A man gets the competitive spirit along with his balls, is that it?"

"Don't be vulgar."

He grabbed her arm and squeezed it until she winced. "I find what you're saying vulgar. And ridiculous. For God's sake, Sally, you're letting your own neurotic fears—I don't know what else to call them—affect your judgment. Rocky isn't you, not by a long shot. She loves competition. She wants to win, and there's nothing wrong with it."

Tears flooded Sally's eyes. "I don't want her to be another you. Or another Suzanne James. Or God forbid, another me. It's bad enough we have to live in Aspen, where life is like a TV miniseries. God, I was raised in a town where there was an ice-cream parlor and a five-and-ten and a football stadium and you knew all your neighbors and the most expensive car was a 'fifty-two Cadillac. I want her to get a taste of real life and go to college, meet interesting people who do things besides ski and chase . . ." She stopped short and clapped her hands over her offending mouth. The look on Tony's face was anguished.

"Is that what you really think, Sally?" All the anger drained from his voice, all the life. "That I'm just another has-been athlete, a thrill-chasing, burnt-out case with nothing left to offer?"

"Oh, God, I'm sorry. I didn't mean to say that."

"I'm glad you did. Now, at last I know what you really think of me. And if you're having nostalgic thoughts about your ideal childhood, let me remind you of what it was really like."

"No, you've got it all wrong. You're absolutely right. I'm fighting those battles again with my daughter. Trying to protect her from what hurt me." She clenched her fists and beat at herself until he took them in his own hands and unfolded the tense fingers, smoothing them until they relaxed. She averted her gaze and whispered, "You've been wonderful. To all of us. It's just that when she calls I hear something in her voice and I recognize it. She sounds sad and depressed. Something's happened and she can't or won't tell me. Oh, Tony, please, let's not fight anymore." She threw her arms around him and clung to him as if he were a piece of driftwood and she about to sink beneath the waves.

What he said was all true. She was using her own phobic fears of competition to stop her daughter from making her own mistakes. Like her father, she thought with a grimace. With a sudden flash of understanding she realized that he had raised her the way he'd been raised. Her grandfather had been a cold, distant autocrat, too. She remembered the sound of her grandfather's voice—dry as paper—intoning his own "thou shalt nots" to his son. Thou shalt not have fun, thou shalt not find amusement in life, thou shalt not express feelings or kiss your daughter or wife or relax or dance or waste time. What else could her glacial father do but follow in the old man's footsteps? She balked at the thought that she, too, was in danger of following in his. And then she shivered as she remembered the murderous feelings she'd had when she was young!

Lizzie Borden took an ax, gave her father forty whacks. When the forty whacks were done, she gave her mother forty-one. The old child's refrain buzzed around in her head. She'd wanted to do it to him. Not to her mother, who was a basket case of anxiety, fearfully begging Sally to be a good girl and listen to her father. Just to preserve the peace.

If she had been guilty of all those violent feelings, would her own daughter feel the same way about her one day? No, their relationship was totally different. Loving, warm, confiding. Maybe not confiding enough. For now Rocky was suffering and not talking.

Tony held Sally quietly in his arms, a victim of her own tortured thoughts. His mind was in turmoil. Tonight had been a turning point in their lives. For the first time he realized how ambivalent her feelings for him were and wondered if he were exacerbating them by remaining so close to this family he considered to be his own. He could even understand this fiercely protective mother wanting more for her daughter and feeling frustrated because she couldn't do enough.

Her voice came out haltingly, muffled by his shoulder. "Tony, please forgive me. Try to forget every nasty thing I've said, if you can. We love you and we need you. All of us."

The words jolted him until he realized the spirit in which they were offered. He drew himself away gently and held her at arm's length. "Look, for some reason, you're behaving very emotionally about this whole thing. I think there's more to it than just Rocky losing races. I'm afraid you'll have to work that out for yourself. In the meantime, I think it would be a good idea if I hopped a plane and spent a few days with Rocky. You know, take her to dinner, see if she says anything revealing, get her to relax a bit." When she was about to protest, he said, "Alone. You stay here. I'll take care of it. Besides, Eric needs you and you need him."

Tony returned within the week. While he couldn't put his finger on exactly what was affecting Rocky's skiing, his visit seemed to have a positive effect. There definitely was a marked improvement in her skiing. She still hadn't retrieved her winning form, but she seemed to be concentrating better. Now it was only a question of time. Sally and he

decided to treat the strange lapse like some kind of
flu bug that would simply have to run its course.
Tony fervently hoped it was not too late to ensure
her a berth on the team.

Of even greater importance was the aftermath
of what had transpired at Sally's house and which,
despite her exhortations, Tony could not forget. He
realized it was true that he was in danger of
becoming some kind of has-been athlete. It was
also true that he had been searching for quick
thrills to match the exaltation he'd felt when
racing. It was more than the racing; it was knowing that your body was at the peak of physical
perfection and then reaching even higher. Ski
racers felt like gods as they defied all the universe's
laws in their search for unhampered speed. That
and the adoration of the crowds, the women
especially, were hard things to give up. He had to
admit grudgingly there had been truth in Sally's
words. He had to stop living from day to day and
start thinking of the future.

On the return flight from Europe, he had made a
decision. It was time to enter a new arena of
competition. It was time to crack the clichéd
image of the skier once again, to prove that they
had brains as well as brawn. Stein Eriksen had
done it. Why shouldn't he? He considered his
options. He'd had the offer from Marcella Richards. The only problem with that was that he
would have to live in New York, and he wasn't sure
he was ready for that. Richard Farwell, who had a
finger in many pies and was willing to slice a
wedge for Tony, had played the familiar litany so
often Tony hardly heard him anymore. Besides,
Richard's offers were always vague, "don't-worry-
we'll-find-something" kinds of offers.

This was the decade of the entrepreneur. People
were looking for the gaps and filling them. From

workshops in the cellar or garages, ideas and products were pouring forth with dizzying speed. That's the way Apple Computer got started. And a fat lady who was tired of diets had come up with the idea of Weight Watchers. Marcella had told him that Estee Lauder got her start by peddling her grandfather's cold cream door-to-door.

Tony identified his strengths. He had a good head for business, he had impeccable contacts, knew dozens of wealthy people, was discreet and respected, and no one knew more about skiing. He had only to put all his strengths to work and he would come up with something. For the first time since he'd swept the Olympic golds, leaving Greg James with snow on his face, Tony felt truly excited.

He'd done a good job of convincing himself. Maybe too good. The next morning he mortgaged the big house on Red Mountain. His financial commitment to Max was now complete.

CHAPTER ELEVEN

To the cognoscenti January was generally the best skiing month of the winter. The lower temperatures kept the snow in perfect condition and the vacationers at home. There was plenty of sunshine. When the big snows came there were fewer skiers carving up the perfect dry deep powder.

But Aspen's problems refused to go away. Even on blue-sky days Aspen air was still a source of concern to the town fathers as they passed increasingly strict clean-air ordinances. More and more low-cost housing was being torn down to make room for bigger and more expensive houses, and the new immigration laws made it difficult to find help. For Sally, January was just another month to get through.

Despite it all, the snows fell, the shops took in plenty of green, and the only red to be seen was on the face of one of Aspen's elite, caught with his pants down in a pickup truck with his contractor's well-endowed wife. It was good for a few laughs at the Silver Leaf bar.

The ski club was celebrating its fiftieth anniversary with a week of festivities. All the legendary names showed up to march in the parade, the highlight of which was the old Tenth Mountain Division from World War II, which included the men who'd literally invented American skiing. They marched in their Alpine white fur-trimmed long parkas and baggy pants and carried skis that looked like barrel staves and poles with baskets as big as melons. All the early names that had started Aspen on its dizzying ascent were there: the Stapletons, the Wards and Sterlings, the Whitcombs and Sapences, André Roch, who'd laid out Roch Run on Aspen Mountain in the 1930s, Friedl Pfeifer, who started the first ski school in 1940. Stein Eriksen, who ran both the Aspen Highlands and Snowmass ski schools before going on to more lucrative pastures. Steve Knowlton, who had the Golden Horn, John Litchfield, who resurrected the Red Onion, and Werner Kuster, who'd owned it for years, were there as well.

There were so many hand-knit Norwegian sweaters from the past that several shrewd boutique owners, detecting a trend, sent out a call to their cottage knitters to take advantage of it.

A young ex-snowcat driver skied 234,000 vertical feet in twenty-four hours to raise money for charity. Translated into miles, it totaled 208, nonstop!

And, of course, there were the upcoming races —from junior to septuagenarian. Aside from events with the past greats in them, the races that held the most interest were those that would involve the two former Olympic rivals, Tony Frantz and Greg James.

A week before the scheduled races, Tony and Max had a meeting in the secret workshop down in the valley.

"This would be a good time to try out the modified ski and see how it performs under real racing conditions," said Tony.

Max nodded his head in agreement. "Do we want to make it public or should we still keep it concealed under phony graphics?"

"I think we should disguise it. It's not a sanctioned race, so I doubt if any of the reps will be around. Can you make it look like my usual Rossignols?"

"Even to the nicks on your edges." Max smiled.

"I never get nicks on my edges," said Tony, clutching his breast with pretended hurt.

"Whatever you say, partner, I'm yours to command."

When Max had learned what Tony's financial commitment was, he was delighted but concerned. He realized that it must represent almost everything Tony had.

Tony reassured him that there were still a few dollars stashed away for his old age and that he intended raising his prices next year to make up the deficit. They laughed, but Max knew that despite the truth to the statement, his friend was risking a lot.

Weeks before the Frantz-James race, the local papers talked up the old rivalry, heaping fresh coals on it until it blazed white hot again. Excerpts from the famous Olympic runs were shown over and over again on the local TV station and a poster had been designed showing the two men, profile to profile, in Roman gladiatorial pose.

Sally felt the town was making too big a deal out of what was supposed to be a birthday celebration. "You'd think it was the Spinks/Tyson fight and the purse was a zillion dollars,'' she commented to Tony after a day of skiing.

Greg James was so amused by the hype, he allowed one of his good skiing buddies to make book on him, complete with daily changing odds.

Tony was the only one who seemed unconcerned by the tumult of conjecture around him. He kept to his appointments, spent evenings with Max, was strangely absent from the scene, including a party that was given expressly for him. Even Sally hardly saw him except coming and going at the ski school office.

Eric was in seventh heaven, basking in the sunlight of the family friendship with the famous local skier. He was even interviewed by his school paper. There were a few boys in the class who were Greg James fans, but he dispensed with them with a few well-chosen words that, had his mother heard them, would have surely grounded him for a month.

Greg slammed his locker shut and spun the combination on his lock. As he was about to leave, he suddenly stopped and looked around, then retraced his steps. To the left of the lounge, there was a large room where instructors racked and tuned their skis. Greg headed in that direction.

In Tony's slot were the skis he usually used. Several pairs of each, neatly stacked. Greg hefted each in turn, looked at edges and bindings, seeking some clue that might tip him off to the mystery ski. The ski with the cartoon graphics was certainly not in the rack. Of course, Tony would be unlikely to leave it here where anyone could see it and ask questions. Where would it be?

At the end of the day, instead of stopping off for his usual beer at the Tippler, Greg headed straight home. The mysterious skis had occupied his every conscious thought, leaving the wealthy young couple from Chicago who'd hired him to wonder why he was considered such a terrific ski instructor when he barely spoke more than a few hasty words to them the entire day.

As he stripped off his clothes, he was struck by a new and horrifying thought. He punched in Michael Greenfield's number and waited. The answering service clicked in. "Damn," said Greg, waiting to leave his message. Nothing was going right today. Why wasn't Michael home at this hour?

"Suzanne? Suzanne?" Clad only in his jockey shorts, he stormed out of his room in search of his sister. The big house reverberated with silence.

By the time he showered and shaved, dusk had fallen in deep folds and the lights of Aspen twinkled below like heaven turned upside down. He looked down on the scene below feeling masterful and in control from his Elysian heights. The phone interrupted his thoughts.

Snatching up the receiver without thinking, he shouted into it without waiting to see who was on the other end. "Michael? Jesus, where the hell have you been? I've been trying to get you for hours."

"It's not Michael, Greg, it's Suzanne. Why are you screaming?"

"Get off the phone, I'm waiting for Michael to call."

"Michael's here. At Marcella's with me. What do you want?"

"Tell him I have to see him. Right away. You, too."

"You sound serious," she said. "We'll be right there."

Michael and Suzanne arrived a few minutes later. Suzanne generally found Greg's dramatics amusing, sometimes irritating, but this time his voice on the phone sounded seriously alarmed.

Michael, looking impeccable and in control with a faint mocking smile tugging at his lips, walked to the blazing fire in the huge stone fireplace to warm his hands, then turned to look at Greg. "Greg, what seems to be the problem?"

"No problem. Just an idea I had about that new ski." He gave a knowing look to Michael, whose relaxed insouciance disappeared and was replaced by an alert wariness.

"What about the ski?" he asked.

Suzanne was really getting impatient. Greg had interrupted a very nice afternoon with Michael, an afternoon that might have led to something more. For the first time in her life, Suzanne was not pushing. She realized if she wanted Michael Greenfield, her old techniques wouldn't work. Then Greg had called. Pleasure postponed again. She sighed.

"I was thinking that if Tony has it, then what if he gives it to Rocky. What if Rocky uses that ski?"

Suzanne's eyes opened widely. "You mean . . . ?"

"I mean, if that ski is so hot, I want to get my hands on it for Kit."

"If it's that hot, I want to manufacture and market it," Michael added grimly. It could be worth a small fortune to him and give him his entry into a tough, competitive market. There was no reason why Rossignol should have it all.

"This is still conjecture," reminded Suzanne. "We don't know for sure if the ski does exist."

"I'm calling Max Margolis," said Michael, a plan formulating in his mind. "It's about time we met."

Michael had considered offering to meet Max at some neutral place for lunch, but realized their conversation could be heard by anyone sitting nearby. When he called to introduce himself and set up a meeting at his house, Max, a poor dissembler, made a few halfhearted excuses and finally suggested that Michael meet him at his home, giving him elaborate directions so he could find the ranch house hidden behind dense underbrush at the end of a tortuous dirt road.

"It's a discouraging road," was Michael's greeting as he stooped under the low doorway to shake hands with the tall gangly man in front of him.

"Deliberately," said Max. "I hate surprise visitors."

"You get many?" Michael looked surprised.

"There are a lot of strange types around who think there's gold and silver in them thar hills." Max gestured with his chin to the ridges which could be seen from his window.

As Michael stepped into the living room, his fastidious nose wrinkled with distaste. How could anyone live this way? There was a musty smell that clung to the room, part cooking odor, part the minglings of the past trapped in the almost airless room. Magazines and newspapers, unopened mail and catalogues of every description occupied every open space and lay in disarray on the tweed couch. One wall contained floor-to-ceiling shelves. Once the books had probably been stacked in neat rows, but use and the addition of many more titles had destroyed that unity. Now they were piled every which way. The man who lived here was not much of an improvement. His nails were ragged from biting, his hair stood on end like a cornfield hit by a tornado. He wore a faded flannel shirt and shredded jeans. His horn-rimmed glasses were held together at the nosepiece with silver duct tape.

Max caught him looking at the disarray. He smiled. "It's a mess, I know, but I can find anything I want. Fortunately, I'm the only one who can."

"Another detriment to those strangers lurking outside?"

Max gave a lopsided smile. "You could say that." He walked over to an ancient gas stove, where a pot of coffee was perking. "Can I pour you a cup?"

"I only drink decaffeinated," said Michael.

"Sorry, this is the cowboy variety, but I do have some instant. I keep it around for guests."

If you ever have any, thought Michael wryly. "No, I'll pass."

Michael watched him pour a cup for himself. It was as thick and dark as mud. He had a sudden image of one of his Jensen silver spoons dissolving on contact in that cup.

"Shall we get to it?" said Max bluntly.

"I take it you know who I am."

Max raised his bushy eyebrows in response.

"So you probably know that I was the one who bought Monroe Aerospace. You're experimenting with a new ski that began in the computers of Monroe on the company's time. True?"

"False."

"What part? The ski or the fact that you developed it at the lab?"

Max played for time. "Where are you getting this ridiculous information from?"

"Do you deny that you worked at Monroe as the chief projects engineer?"

"Of course not." Max blinked at him rapidly behind his glasses. "That's a matter of record."

"Do you deny that you used the Cray computer for things other than lab business?"

He shrugged. "All engineers like to play around with programs on the big babies. There isn't a lab in the country that doesn't have at least a few joystick jockeys. Besides, you never know what you'll come up with when you play. The guys at Bell Labs are always coming up with solid ideas that might have started with play."

"Was that how you came up with the ski?"

"You keep talking about some ski. I don't know what you're referring to."

Michael smiled tightly. Max was good! He might look like an absentminded professor, but his mind was as quick as one of his own computers. As yet he had avoided telling an outright lie, but he had also avoided admitting the truth. "When I bought the company—and by the way, I was not responsible for your being fired. If I had known I would have fired that person. In any case there was a great deal of talk about you."

"That's understandable. I was in charge of some very large and important projects."

"Yes, I know. But the comments were about your strange late-night visits to the Cray computer room."

Michael's gaze, the same that made his associates tremble with fear, bored into Max like laser beams, yet the red-bearded man seemed totally relaxed. Then Michael noticed the telltale pulse beating in Max's temple, the imperceptible tightening of the jaw. He moved in for the kill, certain that persistence would pay off.

"So," Max said at last, "what does that prove? If you knew anything about the aerospace field"—he was pleased to see Michael flinch at that jibe— "you'd realize that we don't punch a time clock. There are times when you're running numbers at all sorts of odd hours."

"I didn't have to know anything about the field to buy the company. That's why one hires managers who do," Michael said acidly, annoyed that he had allowed Max to ruffle his usual control and force him to make such a childish response. This was not the way he liked treating an adversary, which of course Max was. He'd decided that the moment he walked into the disorderly house. "What I want to know is were you working on something personal or were you involved with company business?"

"Your legal department is investigating. Didn't you know?" With the ungainly gait of a long-legged dog, Max got to his feet. His eyes behind the thick rims raked the man in the casual designer clothes, flicked over the smoothly combed hair, and noted the perfect tan. Michael Greenfield reeked of power and authority. Max grimaced with distaste. Men like Michael were taking over the world. It was a game to them. Power plays. Monopoly for grown-ups. With no regard for the people or principles involved. The differences between them went far deeper than the superficial ones of dress and looks. Had things been different, Max might have been curious to find out why Michael was so interested in a ski when he had so many other toys to play with in his industrial sandbox. But they weren't, and it was for this reason that Max decided he would die on the rack before admitting a thing to this too-slick, too-confident man.

He walked to the front door, opened it. "Now, if you'll excuse me, I have work to do."

"Thank you for your time," said a tight-lipped Michael. His eyes would have chilled a snake. Before he went out the door, he turned and added, "Oh, by the way, this discussion may be over, but I'm far from finished."

"Nice to have met you, Mr. Greenfield. Good luck with Monroe. You'll need it now that I'm not there." Max's smile was meant to infuriate.

Michael walked through the door as if Max didn't exist for him anymore. Casually he stuffed his hands into his coat pockets, where he clenched them into tight fists. He was furious, feeling that he had been bested in the exchange and not liking it one bit.

He got into his Jeep and slammed the door hard. The mountains threw back the echo. Anger clouded his eyes so that he almost drove the Jeep off the precipitous road. That brought him to his senses quickly. Once his rational mind took over, he calmed down long enough to concentrate on manipulating the tricky dirt road. Safely back on the highway, his resentment began to bubble again. Max Margolis would not get away with his little hide-and-seek games; Michael would get that ski!

Returning home, he called John Novotny, his chief computer engineer at Monroe Aerospace. "John, somewhere in that Cray computer I know there's a design for a ski. If anyone can find it, you can."

Then he called Sally and made a date for dinner.

Still smarting from the face-off with Max, he once again allowed his impatience to wreck his usual control. Before he could stop himself, he blurted out, "Do you happen to know a man by the name of Max Margolis?"

"Max? Of course, he's a darling man. We love him."

"Oh? Where do you know him from?"

"Oh, for years. Back east. I met him when I was in college. A terribly bright man and a wonderful skier. Used to race for Dartmouth, I think."

Sally's enthusiasm and unqualified affection for Max only added more fire to Michael's long-simmering anger. "There's a rumor around that he's developing a new kind of ski."

A curtain came down over Sally's face. She pretended not to understand. "Oh? Well, with Max, anything is possible." She began to fiddle with her bag and look around, trying to focus her attention on a famous movie star who had just walked in with a coterie of young, handsome men.

"You know something, don't you?" he said sharply, drawing her attention back. "What is it? Is he making the ski? What are his plans for it? Is there anyone involved with him?" He spat questions at her like a relentless prosecuting attorney.

Her eyes narrowed in annoyance. She drew away from him and folded her arms across her chest. He recognized that stubborn gesture. Her voice was low and accusing. "What on earth has gotten into you? Am I on trial or something?" When he persisted in his verbal attack, she made a sound of disgust and half rose from her chair. "Michael, stop! You're making me angry." She'd never seen him this way before. In a split second he'd gone from easy charmer to chilling inquisitor. Was this the real Michael, the one she'd been warned about? Hastily she stood and looked around, seeking the quickest, least obvious way to make her exit.

Michael reached out a hand and pulled her back to her chair. Quietly he apologized, realizing that their exchange had sent many curious glances in their direction. But his apology came too late to still her suspicions. They lapsed into uncomfortable silence. Finally, he suggested that they leave, and she quickly agreed. Knowing that it was best to cut his losses for the evening, he dropped her off at her house.

As Sally watched the lights of his speeding car disappear around the curve, she debated whether to tell Tony about this surprising turn of events. No, Tony would only say I told you so, and she was damned if she'd give him that satisfaction.

John Novotny was unable to report any success to Michael. He requested a little more time. Michael said it had run out. Then he tried to call Sally to apologize for his rude behavior.

Sally did not return his calls.

Finally he resorted to his old tried-and-true method: flowers and an abject note of apology.

When next he saw Greg James, Michael was forced to admit defeat. "There is nothing in the computer. He apparently erased everything before he left."

"That ski exists, I'm convinced of it now."

"And I'm pretty sure I know where it is."

"Where?"

"I paid Max Margolis a little visit. We had a friendly chat which got a little sticky toward the end. I, unfortunately, lost my cool, and directly accused him of using Monroe's labs to develop the ski, which of course he denied. But I saw a garage near the workshop as I left. I bet that ski is there."

"And how do you propose to get them?" Whatever Greg expected Michael to say, it certainly wasn't what finally came from behind those clenched lips with chilling clarity.

"Steal them. I thought I might stage a little break-in. Margolis is pretty well barricaded back there in his patch of woods. When I asked why, he told me there were always strangers around looking for old mines. It seems to me that one of those 'strangers' might just do the job. Anyway, I'll only be stealing back what is rightfully mine. I'm going to need some help with this." He knew Greg was an ally, a man he could trust. "It's not exactly legitimate business practice, you know. Do you know someone we could get to work with us? Someone you can trust?"

"Sure. Me."

"You?"

"Why not? It'll be a gas. Besides, it'll be easier and safer if just one person does the job. And who knows what to look for better than I?"

Michael looked worried. "I don't know, Greg. I

don't like involving you. If Suzanne finds out, she'll be furious."

"She won't find out. And if she suspects anything, she'll forget it when I beat Tony and Kit gets to the Olympics and starts taking all the gold."

"I think you should tell her," insisted Michael stubbornly. "She has a right to know."

That evening they divulged their scheme.

Suzanne, who'd determined that she was going to try a new tack with Michael, which consisted of sweet complicity and virginal charm, exploded out of her chair and with a look that indicated she thought they were both crazy, began to pace the floor. "My God! You've got to be kidding! It won't work."

The two men watched her pace without reply. Finally, she came to Greg and pushed a finger into his chest. "It's too dangerous. They'll suspect you right away. You won't get away with it." Then, aware of how strident she sounded, she lowered her voice and purred, "Why don't you let me butter up Max? I'm sure I could get it out of him."

"Forget it, Suz," said Greg. "He's not going to tell you anything he doesn't want to. And believe me, from what Michael says, wild horses won't pull it from him. Besides, I want to do it. It'll be a kick."

Suzanne continued to grumble, but her protests were countered by their insistence that it was a foolproof plan. Where had she heard that before?

In his own house that night, Michael prowled around the vast and silent rooms, thinking and plotting. He poured himself a snifter of ancient Napoleon brandy to help the process. On the shelf behind him where glasses were stacked saloon style, he could see a picture he'd had framed recently. It showed the group from the Mountain Masters class on their final day. In the middle was

Sally, looking like any other instructor in her blue pants and red-and-white parka. He wondered if he would have given her a second glance if he had first met her as a ski instructor. Then he remembered the abortive evening of a night ago. He wished he had used more discretion with her. But, as the old saying goes, "If wishes were horses, beggars would ride."

Since she would not come to him, he would have to go to her.

Sally's Subaru had developed a terminal cough, so she was forced to depend on Daisy to drive her to the mountain as she contemplated whether to fix it or try to find a new used car. Either way she would have to borrow money.

Today the clouds were swollen and dark, hovering over the town like dirty laundry. Her present mood was a perfect match to the weather.

"Ycck," said Daisy, looking up at the sky. "Great day to be home in bed or shopping in San Francisco."

"I agree."

"You do? Have you caught some dread illness from your afflicted car?"

"Nothing that a large injection of money couldn't fix." She shook her head in mock despair. "It never fails. I just about catch up, even have a couple of extra bucks to put in my money fund or buy something for myself, then another major crisis falls on me."

"Speaking of an injection of money, where's your friend these days?"

"Which one?"

"Oh, you have so many? The dark one. Rich, charming, et cetera, et cetera."

"Don't ask."

"Oh? What gives? Have you two busted up? What are . . . ?"

Sally interrupted, shivering in memory of the last cross-examination she had suffered at the hands of Michael Greenfield. "I said don't ask."

"I know. But when I say it—or any female says it—it means coax me a little, I'll tell you everything."

"Well, I mean it. Ah, saved by the bell," Sally said in relief as Daisy pulled into her black-market parking space at the Aspen Alps. Sally opened the door and headed to the ski desk to check in, turning to say only, "I'll meet you in the locker room at four-thirty."

She found to her pleasure that she'd been booked out on a private for the entire day.

"Who is it?" she asked.

"It says here Michael Douglas?" said Sven at the desk, as disbelieving as Sally.

"The actor?"

"Do I know from actors?"

"Well, what does he look like?"

Another shrug. "He made the reservation on the phone."

"You're a big help. Okay. He can wait for a few minutes. I need some coffee."

"No later than ten o'clock," Sven admonished her with a finger.

"I know, Sven. Relax. He'll get his money's worth." And so would she, if it was indeed the actor. They usually were very generous with their tips. She'd had a few this past year, although the ones who tipped biggest were the beginners. They were so grateful to get down alive, they thought nothing of paying outrageously for the privilege.

Daisy was changing when Sally walked in. "How big's your class today?"

"One," gloated Sally. "A private." Aside from the possibility of a good tip, it was much easier to deal with only one or two in a class. Daisy, on the other hand, was from the the-more-the-merrier school. She loved noise and tumult, and a big class gave her a chance to show off.

As Sally walked over to find and introduce herself to her private, she breathed a sigh of relief. Today, she was in no mood to deal with temperament and group dynamics. She looked around at the assembled skiers, trying to figure out who was likely to be hers.

As usual, the first day of the week brought out the fashion plates. The $2,000 Bogner suits with the broad shoulders and silver patches. There was the usual number of leopard, zebra, and cheetah-striped big suits, all worn tightly belted to show off trim waists. There were even some of last year's rhinestone-studded suits. Wearing these marked their wearers as either sensible or foolish, since the studded look was thought to be tacky this year but the suits were too expensive to throw or give away.

As the groups formed and broke and re-formed again to head off with one of the red-white-and-navy-clad instructors, Sally caught sight of the man who was surely waiting for her. She saw only his back. He seemed to be looking uphill at some descending skiers, probably his wife, she thought.

"Uh, Mr. Douglas . . . I'm your instructor."

The man turned around with a smile, extending his hand. She gave him a closer look, then said angrily, "Michael Greenfield. What are you pulling?"

"It was you who said we resembled each other."

"Yeah, in *Wall Street*," Sally snapped, "and you shouldn't think of it as a compliment."

"Whatever you say."

It was as if their last evening had never happened. Gone was that cold voice, the ruthless questioning, the arrogant power hiding behind the obsidian eyes. He was the old Michael again, full of charm and sly wit, his eyes warm as they caught hers and drew them into his dark depths. "If you don't forgive me, I promise to fall down a hill and break a leg and blame it on you."

She did a double-take but was assured by the broad smile that he was only teasing her.

He put his hand through her arm. "Now, I have a terrific idea. Let's go to Snowmass and get away from all these prying eyes."

Sally very firmly removed her arm from his. Not so fast, mister, she thought. I'm not giving in that easily. Work for forgiveness. Coolly, she said, "Prying eyes? I don't see a single prying eye here. They must have all gone to Snowmass."

"Only on Saturday. Today is"—he looked at his Patek-Phillipe date watch—"Monday. And as the customer is always right, I say Snowmass."

"My car is in the shop."

"Expected to live?"

"Terminal, I'm afraid." She wondered what there was behind his light banter. Wary as he made her, she couldn't help smiling. This was the Michael she liked. Still, under it all, she had the niggling feeling that he was toying with her, jerking her string, setting her up. Had she always been this cynical or was it an attitude she'd recently donned?

"If you can stand my beat-up Jeep, we have transportation."

"It beats walking. But not RFTA." RFTA was the Roaring Fork Transit Association, a very reliable free system with frequently running buses between town, the Highlands, Buttermilk, and Snowmass.

"I'm categorically against public transportation. For thee and me, that is." Before she could utter another word, he steered her to his Jeep.

There had been a large dump of snow a few days ago which usually meant they wouldn't have perfect powder conditions but, with Sally's expert knowledge of the area, they were able to find a quantity of virgin powder.

"Okay, Michael."

"I'm not a great powder skier," he said with a nervous laugh.

"By the end of today, you will be. Today, I'm going to have you eating the stuff."

After their first run, he understood what she meant. He could only watch and marvel as she cut through the thick fluffy stuff as effortlessly as birds flew. "Is there some special trick?" he asked.

Her answer was only, "Follow me." As he let his skis run, the powder blew up in his face. He could taste the icy spume on his lips. It drifted down his neck and piled up to his ankles, obscuring his skis. The first time he discovered them missing, he took an ass-over-teakettle fall and had to be dug out by a highly amused Sally.

To find more of the increasingly elusive unbroken powder, she took him to the Hanging Valley Wall. They had to hike up several hundred yards after getting got off the High Alpine Lift.

"I thought I was in good condition," he huffed. "How do you manage to do it?"

"I live here. I'm used to working out at altitude."

The run was virtually wilderness. Lightly skied, it had broken powder, some moguls, and two very, very steep walls separated by an expanse of gladed trees. She knew Michael was good enough to handle the steep under ordinary conditions, but the Wall was not ordinary. She entertained a few misgivings. As a professional, it was her responsibility to make sure her students were proficient for the terrain she took them on.

"Michael, this is going to be difficult. Can you do it?"

"Of course," he insisted.

"Then make sure you stay behind me. I'll pick the best line down. And no macho stuff. Here, I'm the boss, not you. Agreed?"

"Yes, teach." He smiled, determined to show her how good he was.

Halfway down, on the lower wall, he slid on some crust concealed under the powder and took a spectacular fall. A "yard sale" they called it. Skis, goggles, poles, glasses flew all over the mountain. Sally heard the grunts of surprise as Michael's body bumped down the steep slope, the snap of his safety bindings as they released. Fortunately, she was only a few turns ahead. She pulled to a stop and looked up the hill. It was as if a toy doll had exploded into a dozen pieces.

"Are you okay?" she called as she began to climb up.

"Everything's fine but my ego."

"Good. Stay where you are. I'll gather everything up and bring it to you."

"This time I'm paying attention to every word you say." Michael grinned, rubbing his shinbone where the edge of a ski had clipped him smartly. "I crossed my tips," he offered in the way of explanation.

Sally smiled. "That's a no-no."

By the end of the day, he had finally experienced the nonpareil feeling that drove really good skiers to places they could reach only by helicopters, where there were no lifts, no glittering towns, no streets of gourmet restaurants or trendy boutiques.

This was what the skiing elite dreamed of. Powder. Miles and miles of trackless bottomless slopes like vasts scoops of ice cream set among cones of mountains without end. She described to him the sight of the early-morning sun on dazzling unbroken powder, the feeling of putting in the first tracks. He was spellbound by her recital, wondering if she would ever consider him with that same kind of rapture.

"My God," he said at the end of the day. "I did it, I really did it."

"As advertised," she said with a pleased smile.

"Yes, but you never told me what to expect. It's the most wonderful thing I've ever experienced." His eyes were shining and clear. It was the first time she'd seen him when he didn't seem to be hiding some part of himself.

Then his voice went low, taking on that seductive note she remembered from their times in bed. "I wouldn't have shared it with anyone but you. I mean that, Sally. You're a very special woman. I . . ."

But again he stopped. She'd noticed that the few times he'd allowed himself to open to her, when he was about to say something that would lead them down a different avenue, he always stopped. She could even understand why. Every waking moment, she fought to keep tight reins on her own feelings. Mellow times like these were the most dangerous, when defenses came tumbling down. After a great powder day and a glass of wine, the feeling of well-being seemed as if it would go on forever. It was the same after a night of lovemaking. Unlike her and Peter, who had rushed into bed at the least touch, she and Michael did not. There were many times when they'd simply had dinner and gone their separate ways.

Physically attracted to him as she was, she still could not remove all the barriers she had erected to protect herself. Maybe you just didn't do those things at thirty-six. In fact, Sally was grateful that she was not starved for sex the way so many of her friends were. She worried constantly about Daisy, who seemed to be indiscriminate in her choice of bedmates. She'd even brought up her fears to her friend, who had taken great exception to Sally's low opinion and had responded, "I practice safe sex. I'm not a total nerd."

To cover up for his unfinished sentence, Michael picked up her skis and threw them into the Jeep. He returned with her after-ski boots like Prince Charming with the glass slipper, waiting as she handed him first one of her ski boots, then the other. Steam rose from the insides. "See how fast you are? Your boots are still smoking." He pointed to them.

"That's a charming way of putting it." She wrinkled her nose daintily.

"So. Do you have time for a drink at the Snowmass Club, or perhaps we can just head back and stop at Sunshine's for hot chocolate?"

"Hot chocolate sounds good." She scrutinized the heavy-laden skies and shivered as the wind grew colder. "Definitely snow tonight."

"Good, now that I'm a powder skier, I look forward to it."

He'd been a perfect companion that day. As he dropped her off at her door, she realized that she hadn't let a disturbing thought interrupt the peace and harmony of the day. She was so mellow that when he suggested they go to the Golden Horn for dinner, she accepted without a qualm.

By the time she showered and fed Eric it was almost 7:30. When she told him she was going out for dinner, he didn't even look up or ask with whom. There was no one else in her life. If Michael didn't take her out to dinner, she didn't go, except occasionally with Tony, and then Eric came along, too, as well as Rocky when she was in town.

With a guilty start, Sally realized she hadn't heard from her daughter for a couple of days. She checked the team's schedule which hung over her desk in the bedroom and saw they were in transit. They were like wandering Jews this winter, moving from place to place in search of snow. European conditions continued to be spotty. Now it would take a week of heavy snowfall, even blizzards, to give them the kind of cover they needed. Sally worried about the conditions, because in the downhills the girls were scheduled to run, lack of snow cover sometimes resulted in nasty accidents. Meanwhile the newspapers continued to build the rivalry between the two young racers, a fact that Rocky had mentioned in her last letter. But she and Kit were learning to ignore them. In fact, they'd stopped reading the papers altogether and cut off anyone who tried to bring up the subject. Like good politicians, they'd decided to ignore the media hype.

The Golden Horn was warm, perfumed with exquisite cooking smells and filled with expensively dressed people.

As Michael was pouring the lightly chilled bottle of Gerwürtztraminer, Greg James was getting into a battered old Chevy pickup that he'd borrowed from one of the ranch hands who lived in Woody Creek. Whether the vehicle had a license or not was moot because the bumpers were so covered with mud, nothing was visible.

Michael looked approvingly at the turquoise belt he had given Sally for Christmas, a present she had at first refused to accept, until he told her it was a new work and not as expensive as the old Navaho pieces she'd always admired. It was a convenient lie which she decided wasn't worth making an issue over. She wore it cinched around the waist of her favorite blue denim dress, which he thought she looked particularly good in. Again he noted her lack of ease when she was surrounded by obviously expensively dressed women and hastened to tell her how lovely she looked. She smiled gratefully and squeezed his hand.

As they savored the rich wild mushroom soup and hot crusty bread, Greg James was proceeding down the dirt road toward Max's house. He knew Max would not be home. Pretending to be a friend, he had placed a call to him and told him that Tony wanted to meet him at Tony's house around eight o'clock. He then called Tony with a message to meet Max. That should give him at least an hour and a half to do the job.

Max's house was dark except for a dim forty-watt porch light. Greg checked around the house, trying the various windows to see if one might have been left open. They were all tightly locked. But when he got around to the back, he discovered that the kitchen door had one of those locks that opened easily with a plastic card. Greg took his Visa card and slid it down until it met resistance. Then he gave a little twist and the lock clicked back. The door sprang open and he walked through the darkness into Max's mudroom.

"Look at the size of that veal chop!" exclaimed Sally. "I'll never be able to manage that," she said in dismay. On the large plate in front of her was indeed a veal chop as big as her hand, surrounded with Roesti potatoes and string beans amandine on a bed of carrot puree.

"Eat as much as you like."

"No, you don't understand. In my family, you only accepted as much as you could eat and then you cleaned your plate. If you didn't, you got sent to your room, or even worse, were not allowed to have dessert."

"Then we'll take it home in a doggy bag. Waste not, want not," Michael quoted.

"Oh, so you had the same teacher I had."

"Worse. My mother's plates were twice the size of these."

She grinned. He smiled back at her. "You're having a good time. I like that. I was afraid you might not . . ."

She made a face. "Don't spoil it, Michael. I'm willing to make allowances for that . . . that evening. After all, everyone's entitled to . . ."

Greg pulled out a small pencil flashlight and shone it around the mudroom. There was nothing. Then he remembered Michael had said the garage. He opened a few doors until he discovered the one leading out to the attached building. There he saw the usual assortment of skis one saw in Aspen: a slalom, some GS's, a soft ski for powder, and a beat-up pair for late spring when the rocks started to show. The names were the ones that all good skiers used: Volkls, Rossis, Atomics, Dynastars, K-2's. He was not seeing anything unusual. He was about to admit defeat and turn off the light when he saw a ski tucked behind another pair. Its face was turned to the wall. He reached out with greedy fingers and flipped it around. There it was! Funny cartoon graphics and all. He had it!

Max looked at his watch. "It's nine-thirty."

"We've been here for over an hour," said Tony. "I think it's safe to go back."

The two men had been sharing a pizza and Coke at Max's hideaway. They nodded to one another, got up, and pulled on their down parkas. Max doused the lights in the room he now called "the lab" and slipped keys into the elaborate system of locks.

"Want to stop at Woody Creek Tavern for a beer?" asked Max.

"Sure. Why the hell not?"

At eleven o'clock Sally and Michael were makir.g delirious love. Greg James was at home, beside himself with glee and getting a big high on straight vodka.

Max and Tony walked into Max's ranch house and flooded the mudroom with light. Then Max opened the door to the garage and walked to the rack. Rummaging around, he finally turned and said with a big grin, "They're gone . . . But not forgotten." Tony chuckled.

Whoever had stolen the fancy graphics ski had stolen one of Max's five-year-old Rossignols. At Tony's suggestion, a few weeks earlier the prototype models had been moved to Tony's house on the mountain.

The two men broke into delighted smiles and shook hands.

CHAPTER TWELVE

SATURDAY RACE DAY STARTED OUT WITH OVERCAST skies. A blanket of heavy dark clouds lowered over town. Little Nell was blotted from view, but once above Grand Junction, the intersection of Copper and Spar Gulch at 8,500 feet, it was brighter. The clouds, driven by a brisk wind, rushed across the sky, piling up in their haste to flee. Soon, patches of blue were visible and eventually the sun came out, a little sickly at first, but gaining in strength as the morning wore on.

At the bottom of Lift 1-A, a gay blue-and-white striped tent with tables and chairs had been erected. Outside, the smell of piñon and grapewood wafted into the air as impatient cooks waited for the coals to glow white-hot. When the moment was deemed right, huge slabs of ribs and plump chickens in barbecue sauce were hefted onto the grills. The aromatic smoke reached all the way up to Ruthie's Run, where the racers waited.

Women arrived in droves, bringing vats of cole-slaw and baked beans, bright yellow rivers of cornbread, and batons of sourdough bread. There were pies of every hue, cookies, brownies of every description, and urns of hot coffee which willing hands were happy to set up amidst worried discussions of whether there was enough to go 'round. There were no gourmet pizzas and salads, no fancy drinks or desserts, because this was strictly for local consumption. The object was to recall the times past when skiing was for the brave and foolish, when equipment was primitive and one spent two hours herringboning up a hill to come down it in two minutes, break for lunch, and do it again.

In fact, some of the older boys had decided to do just that, dispensing with the speedy lifts, the fancy ski clothes, and expensive skis. Instead they went to attics and garages to rummage for equipment and clothes they hadn't had the heart to throw away. It was a motley crew that arrived on Little Nell for the over-sixty races. Wooden skis with bear-trap bindings, leather lace-up boots that offered no more support than a pair of high-top sneakers, tuck-in gabardine pants that were two feet wide at the knees and reindeer sweaters tucked into them. Leather finger gloves and billed hats with earflaps completed the gear. Watching these curiosities made one realize how much the sport had changed, not just the high-tech equipment but the clothes.

Stories of the past made the rounds. Memories of skiing at Stowe in Vermont or Mt. Tremblant in Quebec, when the temperatures were twenty below zero and the winds that swept eastward made the windchill factor as dangerous as an Arctic blizzard. How they had frozen in their light cotton parkas. Nightmares of frostbitten fingers and toes!

Today there was down and Gore-tex and Thinsulate and padded pants and cashmere underwear, clothes that weighed ounces and protected from cold and wind. Those diehards who still insisted on skiing with the old gear could only look upon the newcomers as pantywaists, a long-forgotten word that had the same context as Eric's favorite word: nerd.

By the end of the day, in a race that had brought everyone out, there was no question who could still show the kids a thing or two about the downhill. Tony, using the disguised superski on a shortened World Cup course, won easily. Greg James came in second, a full three seconds behind, a vast difference when first and second place were usually separated by only a few hundredths of a second. The wins were repeated in slalom and in giant slalom, the margins not as huge but nevertheless impressive.

Later, people were to remember an eerie silence preceding Tony's run, like the dead calm before a tornado hits. Some even reported a kind of Doppler effect, seeing Tony first, then hearing him, as if sound and motion were out of sync. And the sound of his skis was strange, too. A soft, sibilant *shhh* unlike anything they'd ever heard before.

It was all very mysterious, very odd. As Tony modestly accepted his trophy to tumultuous applause, those that knew him very well saw something in his eyes they'd never seen before.

And Greg looked murderous.

That evening in Max's house over a bottle of champagne, Tony did what he couldn't do in front of the curious spectators. He let out an Indian war whoop of victory and lifted the tall gangling Max off his feet and hugged him until he cried for mercy.

The locker room was abuzz after the races. Greg James, his usual teasing smile absent, his wallet skinnier by several thousand dollars from the bet he'd lost, was taking a joshing from two of his cronies. Greg shrugged boyishly to disguise his fury.

None of the other instructors paid much attention to him or found it odd that he seemed less jolly than usual. They had long ago stopped listening to Greg brag about how he was going to take Tony in the local races they habitually entered to raise money for local charities.

Tony wasn't around that day to hear the conversation. If he had been, he would have been smiling for totally different reasons. Today he was off with one of the veteran ski filmmakers and a group of young hotshots to shoot some fancy skiing. Tony, with a lightweight Steady Cam strapped to his body, would give a bird's-eye view of what it felt like to whip through gates, do aerial flips and gainers. It was something he really enjoyed. In fact, he'd once seriously considered becoming a filmmaker until he'd discussed the idea with Willy Bogner and Warren Miller, who'd discouraged him.

The fact that Tony was filming would have upset Greg even more than his loss, for Greg considered himself the best aerialist in the valley. He and his sister had practically invented this technique which combined acrobatics and platform diving with board skiing. Suzanne had carried it a step further and added ballet pirouettes and arabesques.

Greg pushed away from the wall he was leaning

on and laughed when John Stavishky made mention of Tony's "flying bullets," as he called them.

"I would have beaten him if it weren't for those spooky new skis," Greg muttered, slamming his locker door shut.

"You really kill me, Greg. You honestly believe it was a ski that beat you?"

"Hey, listen," said Pooch Herlihy, "it's all over town. This guy Max Margolis has been playing around in a garage. He's come up with a hot ski, a real breakthrough, they say."

"The ski sucks," sneered Greg. He ought to know. He'd lost on it. Unless . . . Could it be? Was he set up? He felt as if he'd been hit in the stomach. The ski was a phony! Tony had skied the real ski.

"Hey, man, everyone says it's great."

"Yeah? Well, where is this famous ski? You were there. You saw the ski Tony skied on. It was a Rossi. And he used his Atomics in the slalom."

"So you're admitting he's better than you?"

Greg wasn't sure what to say. He'd love to lay Tony's victory on the ski, but on the other hand, he didn't want anyone else to know about it. For he was determined to get that ski for Kit. He scowled, and finally said, "I didn't say that. This time he won. I can't call the clock a liar."

Stick Larson, real name Stanislaus, a towheaded Texan nicknamed Stick because he was so tall and skinny, stared down at Greg as though he were a badly behaved puppy who'd just wet the floor. "He wupped you all right, but he wupped you too good for my taste. Now, we all know that I ain't mighty in the brain department, but it 'pears to me that he had a little help to win that big. And I'm willin' to give a lot of credit to the ski. Either that or he's bionic."

"As far as I'm concerned, you're all nuts. Let's

face it, Tony's good," said John with what he hoped
was finality.

"We all know that." The faintly superior tones of
nasal New England could belong only to Taylor
Peyton Daingerfield. Princeton educated, well en-
dowed by both grandparents with a bottomless
trust fund and by an Episcopalian deity with
perfect looks and teeth, Dink, as he was called, was
a man of such dainty refinement that many of the
other instructors wondered about his sexual pref-
erence. That is, until they saw him ski or deal with
the opposite sex. Then it was apparent that he had
the balls of a lion in both disciplines.

As Dink turned to leave, Greg called out to him.
"You've got to stop watching all those reruns of
Brideshead Revisited. You're getting positively
haughty."

"Imagine," tossed the unruffled young man over
his shoulder, "a ski instructor who knows
Waugh." He exited to good-natured laughter from
the rest of the group.

Sally awoke grudgingly to a gray dawn. Turtlelike
she poked her head from underneath the quilts,
shivered in the frigid air of the bedroom, and
withdrew back into the warmth.

She looked up at the water-stained ceiling she
had meant to paint last summer but didn't because
one of the instructors, who was a painter in the
summer months, told her she'd have to spackle it
first.

Her eyes continued their search of the room,
dwelling on the things she was growing to hate.
The scarred floors that needed refinishing, the rag
rugs that no amount of washing and bleach could
restore to glory, the cramped spaces, the nondescript furniture. It was like picking on a scab.

How had she and Peter ever been able to move around this box without bumping into each other? Even the bed that had once been perfect for cuddling seemed small after sleeping in Michael's luxurious king-size. She was growing appreciative of the seductive feeling of French cotton and fur.

With a bitter laugh, she thought of the time Michael had picked her up in his arms and dropped her on the fox throw that covered the bed. The sensation of being enveloped by acres and acres of silky red fox was overwhelming. "You mean people actually cover beds with these?" she'd asked, a regular smalltown bumpkin with eyes wide as saucers, fingers stroking lasciviously. "I could make three coats from this," she'd said, amused when he'd wrapped her in the luxurious folds and made her look at herself in the mirrors. Hundreds of images of her which she barely recognized came hurtling forth.

She had read enough classy trash and watched the usual TV glitz to know that those gorgeous imaginary creatures suffered from insomnia if they weren't sleeping on fur. But in real life?

She frowned. Her relationship with Michael was producing more than occasional dinners and interesting sex. It was making her dissatisfied with her life. When she was with him, it seemed so easy to accept what his money offered. Coming home from his house to hers was like having a date with the handsome prince, but only if she swore to return to the scullery immediately afterward.

Pete would have handled a similar situation much better. He was avid for the good life, constantly coming up with "get rich" schemes to produce it for them. Like buying Ashcroft and turning it into a resort, a project that not even the Mallorys or Richard Farwell had enough money to pull off. And they were the richest people in town.

She reached for her robe and tried to put it on under the covers. When she managed only to stick a leg in its sleeve, she got up and hopped across the freezing floor in her bare feet to the bathroom, the only warm room in the house this early in the day. Under the steaming shower she came slowly awake, letting the hot water tear at her skin, realizing that life was not as bad as she tried to make it.

Maybe she'd find a letter from Rocky today.

Finally Greg was having a good day. Two men, members of the Young President's Club that he had met through Suzanne, had come in from New York to ski with him. They were good skiers, so he wasn't required to do much teaching. They made a dozen nonstop cruising runs, then headed for lunch at Bonnie's, with its great food and expansive deck.

Bonnie's was an institution on the mountain, much in the same way that 21 or The Four Seasons was in New York. It was the lunchtime hangout for the beautiful people and all those who wished to be part of that exclusive group. In February and March, at school break and Race Week, they piled in from all over the country. Lean, blond Californians, looking as if they'd just stepped out of the *Sports Illustrated* bathing suit issue. Sophisticated Easterners and rich Texans, handsome, tall Aussies, their noisy twang focusing all eyes on them. They were a party-loving, joke-playing crowd.

Here one usually saw the ski clothes that the rest of the world would be wearing the following year. The Westerners liked brilliant neon colors in unusual combinations and matching sunglasses with wild frames. It was impossible to look at them with the naked eye, so dazzling were they. The Easterners liked sleek black and navy. The Texans went for white with rhinestones, studs, and fringe. The film stars, depending on how well they skied, wore special designer clothes that no one had ever seen in a shop.

As Greg and his clients clumped up the steps to get in the line that already stretched out the door, Greg saw her.

"Hey, you guys, I think I'm in love." He gestured with his chin at a woman standing in the middle of the line chatting with a cluster of other stunning women.

"With just one?" joshed Monte MacMillan. "I feel like I've died and gone to heaven."

"Well, I saw her first. Just remember that."

"You still haven't said which one," pointed out Rawson Tremont. Of the three, Rawson was the most voracious. Even with a lovely wife in Darien and three great-looking kids, he still couldn't keep his fingers out of the candy dish.

"Not telling you anything, good buddy." But Greg's glance gave him away.

"Oh, yes!" said Rawson, licking his lips and pretending to make a beeline in her direction.

She *was* the most striking woman on the deck. She wore her glossy black hair in a long braid which curled over her shoulder, and she was very tanned. "I bet she's the same color all over," whispered Monte.

"Look at those legs!" Greg sighed. The tight bright blue pants tucked inside white Raichles outlined the shape of her legs as clearly as if they were bare.

"I haven't got past the tits yet," said Rawson, clutching his heart as the girl removed her jacket to reveal superb breasts straining at her matching blue V-neck sweater. There was no question that she was extraordinary in every way.

"But can she ski?" asked Monte.

"Who cares?"

"Is she wearing a ring?"

"None that I can see. But of course, that doesn't mean a thing these days."

"Who cares?" echoed Greg. "Excuse me, you guys. Someone get me some chicken chowder and two heels of Bonnie's bread. I'm going to stake my claim. You know where to find me."

"I hope she can speak English," said Rawson as he went inside to join the line.

Greg gave him a withering glance. "I've never let language come between me and the women I love."

The young lady proved to be a rare find. Not only was she extraordinarily beautiful, she was intelligent and she could ski. Her name was Nora Pemberton and she was a film editor at Paramount. She was well known to the assorted film stars who were sharing tables with friends and their special private instructors. Some of the most sought-after leading men came over to her to say hello and chat.

Greg was surprised that she didn't hang out with the Hollywood group. "I see too much of them as it is," was her reply. "I don't believe in busman's holidays."

"So why come to Aspen?"

"I met you, didn't I?" she said with a disarming smile, deftly avoiding an answer.

He invited her to ski with them for the rest of the day and she accepted with alacrity. She was a ballsy skier, preferring not to make too many turns and not because she didn't know how. They found out she liked to race cars and planes, too. They nicknamed her Speedy, and though Greg was hoping for exclusive rights, she seemed perfectly happy to share herself with all three. It was only on the last run of the day, when she got him alone briefly, that he realized he might have the inside track. "Would you like to come to my place for dinner?" she asked.

"Don't tell me you can cook, too? Would you marry me?"

She gave him a shrewd look. "What would you do if I said yes?"

He looked surprised, wondering if she was serious. The words had slipped out of his mouth unheeded.

Seeing his consternation, she laughed, a rich, intimate sound that made the hairs on his arms stand up. "Don't worry, I won't hold you to it. Shall we say seven?"

"I don't know if I can wait that long."

"I think you can. See you at seven. Ask the gateman at Starwood for instructions," she called over her shoulder, skating off with consummate grace. He watched her tight backside with admiration, then followed her down the run.

At the end of the day, he boogied into his house, humming one of Sting's love songs, wondering what he could do to kill the next two hours.

In the foyer, he found the day's mail lying on the handsome Santa Fe bench. He picked it up and sorted through it. Bills, bills, junk, pleas for money, and a fat letter postmarked Crans-Montana, a ski area in Switzerland.

He leafed to the last page and looked at the signature. It was signed: "Kit sends love, too. Love, Rocky."

He'd been amused when the funny cards started to arrive from all the places the girls either stayed in or skied in. Those had all been from Rocky and Kit, but he knew that Rocky was the instigator, for Kit was a sporadic writer at best, preferring expensive long-distance calls.

He had attached the growing crop of cards to his mirror so Kit could see them when she came home. They would read the silliness together and have a good laugh. But a letter? That was something new. When he read it through, he realized it was indeed from Rocky alone. She went on and on about how improved Kit was and how she was a shoo-in for the team. She dispensed with her own problems in one line, then spoke of how lonely it was on the circuit and how she missed everyone at home and looked forward to coming back in a few weeks. She told him about the coaching and the strength of the Europeans and the weather and the interesting food they'd had in Zermatt. The letter closed with the lighthearted raillery that had marked their mutual postcards to him. But she couldn't resist a final "I hope I'll see you when I get home."

Love, Rocky. That bothered him. His plan to break Rocky's powers of concentration to Kit's advantage seemed to be backfiring. The last thing he needed on his hands was a calf-eyed teenager and a friend of his sister's to boot.

He dropped the letter back on the pile and ran upstairs to shower, his thoughts returning to the lovely Nora.

Later that evening, after he returned from a strange evening with Nora, consisting of some heavy kissing and fondling, but little else, Suzanne was waiting for him.

Brandishing the letter, she yelled, "What is this all about?"

Greg had drunk too much. Her voice had the force of a pile driver on cement. He covered his pounding head with his arms and winced. "Have a heart, sis, someone's already playing heavy metal on my head. What's what all about?"

"This letter. Don't tell me you've been fucking

around with a sixteen-year-old?" She was as outraged as a nun who'd just caught a boy looking
under the skirts of one of her students.

"Hold on," he said, his outrage matching hers.
"Give me some credit, please. Nothing happened. I
never touched her. Maybe a little good-bye kiss on
the cheek, but nothing else, I swear. I was only
trying to throw her off balance. For Kit's sake."

"So why is this letter full of hopeful flutters and
girlish giggles?" She spoke Rocky's shy lines in a
simpering voice whose very tone turned the gentle
words into a mean travesty. "God, I can practically
hear her panting."

"Look, all I tried to do was mess with her head a
little. We both agreed that what separated Kit and
Rocky was Rocky's incredible concentration. So I
just tried to make it less incredible. Kit's been
winning, so I guess it worked."

"Well, they'll be coming home soon. If Sally gets
wind of this, we're in deep shit."

"Don't worry. I've got everything under control.
Listen, I got more important things on my mind."
He took her by the arm and steered her into the
den. "Have you ever met a girl by the name of Nora
Pemberton? Man, she blew my socks off, but I
gotta tell you . . ." For the next two hours he
poured out the details of his confusing evening
with the hot-and-cold Nora.

Rocky and Kit could hardly wait for the plane to
land before they were at the door and waiting
impatiently for the rickety steps to be drawn up to
the hatch.

As they ran down the steps, eyes searching the
crowd for familiar faces, they caught sight of their
welcoming committee. It seemed the entire town
had turned out.

"Look, there's Mom and Tony and Eric," said

Rocky, feeling genuine excitement for the first time in weeks.

"And Greg and Suzanne." Kit waved, jumping up and down like a child. Rocky stole a glance at Greg, who waved at her, too. She blushed. She had agonized for days after sending that letter, afraid to see him face-to-face, afraid of what he might think of a kid writing to him.

Everything was forgotten as she felt her mother's arms tighten around her, then Tony's arms surround them both. She shut her eyes and luxuriated in the strength and protection of those two pairs of arms. Finally she pulled away, and breathless with happiness, looked down at Eric. "God, you've grown in a month," she said in amazement, watching him draw himself up straighter to bask in the approval of his big sister, the star, as he referred to her, often *not* with admiration.

Tony had arranged to take them all out to dinner at The Grill. It was a casual but very "in" place to eat. Eric could have ribs and french fries, Rocky could have her favorite goat cheese salad and grilled chicken, and he and Sally could have the huge veal chops that the chef did so well.

"I never considered what it might feel like having a star for a daughter," Sally said, smiling, after the tenth person had stopped by the table to offer congratulations and continued luck to Rocky. But she was aware that after each polite thank-you, her daughter seemed to grow increasingly quiet.

Later, when they were home and getting ready for bed, Sally knocked on Rocky's door and waited to be admitted rather than just walking in as had been her wont.

The door opened. Rocky's face had settled back into the distracted look it had worn while she was in Europe.

"Hi, honey, can I come in for a minute?"

"Sure."

Sally looked around at the room, seeing the spilled contents of Rocky's duffle bag spread all over the other twin bed. Dirty laundry seemed to outnumber clean five-to-one. "I guess you're too jet lagged to talk?"

"I am kind of tired."

"Is everything all right?" Sally pulled a pillow case from the unused bed and automatically started to stuff it with the dirty laundry.

"You don't have to do that now, do you? I'll take care of it in the morning."

"Habit," said Sally, putting the stuffed case on the bed, then sitting on the edge. "I'm so glad you're home," she said simply, hugging the dirty laundry in lieu of her child.

"Me, too, Mom."

Rocky seemed distracted, unfocused, walking around the room as though she had never seen it before.

"Are you looking for something special, honey?"

Rocky looked at her with opaque eyes. "Uh . . . no. Where's Kermit?"

Kermit was a bright green beanbag frog that Sally had made for Rocky when she was small and enamored of the Muppets. She'd made several of the characters, whichever was the favorite of the moment, but Kermit was the only one to survive childhood. Often, Sally would peek through the half-opened door and see her young daughter lying in bed, Kermit perched on her chest.

"Didn't you take him with you?"

"No. Never mind. You probably stuck him away somewhere. I'm sure he'll turn up."

Sally nodded. Rocky was certainly growing up.

"I'm really tired, Mom. Do you mind?" Rocky started to pull off her sweater. Sally recognized dismissal when she heard it.

"Sure, honey. We'll talk tomorrow. Can you sleep in or do you have to go right out for training?"

"No, we have a day to get used to the time change."

"Can you take care of your own breakfast?"

"Sure. Don't worry."

Sally realized that Rocky was trying to keep a lid on her annoyance. She wanted Sally to go and leave her to whatever was troubling her, to deal with in her own way. But Sally's mother's heart couldn't stand the thought of her daughter in pain. She stood up and gathered her daughter into her arms. Smoothing her hair back, she held the girl's face in her hands and said softly, lovingly, before kissing her forehead, "Remember, we're a team. What hurts you, hurts me."

"I know, Mom. I just need a good night's sleep." As Sally walked toward the door, Rocky said, with a little of the old spirit, "Dinner was fun tonight, wasn't it? I was real glad to see Tony again. Oh, do you have classes all day?"

"I think so. Why?"

"I thought maybe I'd just come out and ski for fun with you."

Sally's eyes were shining. "I could cancel."

"No, I don't want you to do that. How about we ski through lunch?"

"I'll have a big breakfast," promised Sally.

It had been a long time since mother and daughter had skied for the sheer pleasure of skiing. In the gondola they shared a bag of trail mix and a Hershey Bar in lieu of lunch. Gradually, Rocky opened up to her. Her problems were valid ones, the same that had always existed for the women skiers. No female coaches, no understanding older woman to talk to, no time to enjoy the cultural pleasures of Europe, though this year, due to poor snow, there had been plenty of down time. They had tried to get to museums and concerts but, after several halfhearted attempts, stopped bothering because it seemed more trouble than it was worth and the staff was less than enthusiastic about making arrangements for them.

As mother and daughter got out of the gondola, there was a hum of voices. Rocky's presence on the slopes was electrifying. Skiers stopped to stare, knowing they were watching no ordinary skier. "Do you know who that was?" they would ask Sally, who would then reply with pride, "My daughter."

"She's very good, isn't she?" they would add. And Sally would agree.

Although Rocky's spirits had lightened since her arrival home, Sally still had the feeling her daughter was not telling her everything. Later she discussed her fears with Tony, who had also noticed some distraction in the girl. Tony advised waiting before embarking on any course of action. "Let's see how training goes. With the new staff, things might improve."

Despite his desire and the help of Michael Greenfield, Greg James had not been offered the head coach's job. Tony had, but he had turned it down. In the meantime, the old staff had been fired and a former Swiss Olympian hired. Not much hope was held out for fielding a great World Cup team this year. Changing management in midstream always meant adjustments. Though the training period went on through the year, the actual racing season was short. The U.S. Ski Association was trying to build for the future.

Kit's progress continued to be impressive. The James gang could barely conceal their excitement.

As for Rocky, she seemed to have hit a plateau.

Her vaunted concentration had vanished, leading to several incidents that could have been tragic. On one practice slalom run, she hooked a ski on a gate and fell on her thumbs, bruising one severely. Even splinted, she was in severe pain. Then in a fluke accident she sprained her foot. Taping it, she continued to ski. But the incident that almost destroyed her came later that week.

She had just finished another practice run in slalom and was taking off her skis to take the gondola back up when she looked up in surprise to see Greg walking in her direction. Aside from seeing Greg briefly at the airport, Rocky had not spoken to him since her arrival home. Once she thought she saw him with a very beautiful girl with dark hair, but when she tried to follow them for a better look, they had disappeared into thin air.

"Hi, kid, how goes it?"

They were ordinary words, but she felt her cheeks flame. She looked around quickly to see if anyone had noticed.

"Hi, Greg. We haven't seen you around much."

"Oh, I've been here. Giving the kidlet the benefit of my vast experience." He winked at his little jest. "Taking the gondola up?" At her nod, he said casually, "Mind having company?"

They were the only two in the enclosed bubble. Greg threw his arm over the back of the seat and looked out as the mountain went by at their feet. "I just skied the Ridge. It was a dream."

"It does look great," Rocky said wistfully. "It would be nice to ski for fun again. I went out with my mother the other day. I really enjoyed it."

He was silent. When she lapsed into silence, he gave her a covert look. She sat as though she were made of cement, rigid, unyielding, a morose look on her face.

"Are we friends?" he asked.

"I don't know. Are we?"

"Well, you're Kit's friend, and that's good enough for me." He turned to her, looking at her with what he hoped was brotherly concern. "I know how much you want to be on the team, how important it is for you. And frankly, I'm a little worried about you."

"You are?" She choked. Her heart jumped to her throat and lay like a stone, cutting off her breath.

"Before you left I saw you ski a couple of times. You were terrific. The best. Potentially, the best ever." He shook his head despondently.

"What are you trying to say, Greg? That I'm not good anymore?"

"No, no." He took her hand in his and gave it a playful squeeze. "Nothing like that. It's just that" —he made a tiny grimace—"I don't know . . . it's like you've lost your edge or you've gotten uptight. I can't put my finger on it exactly. I just noticed that your slalom technique has gotten sloppy. Looks like you've picked up a couple of Tony's bad habits. No offense." He laughed, pleased to see he was getting to her. He was not about to say anything specific. Better to keep on in this vein. Let her go nuts trying to figure out what he meant.

"Can't you be more specific?" she asked in a pleading voice, on the edge of tears. "I know I'm not skiing as well as I should, but I just don't know what I'm doing wrong."

He patted her hand. "Not to worry so much. The coaches will work it out for you. Don't pay any attention to me. What do I know? I'm just an old has-been myself." He flashed her that heartbreaking grin. It had the desired effect.

When Rocky finished the day's training, she went to the ski desk to inquire as to Tony's whereabouts. Told that he was with a private and would probably be at The Aspen Club Lodge around 4:30, she put her skis away, changed to after-ski boots, and walked over to the pretty fieldstone lodge adjacent to the ski area. Its long oval bar was a favorite after-ski rendezvous for people who wanted to avoid the tumult of Little Nell's or the Tippler. She found a seat in the corner where she wouldn't be noticed but where she would be able to see the door and anyone who came through it. Ordering a Perrier, she settled down to wait.

The place had been practically empty when she arrived. After four, it began to fill up. Rocky looked at the laughing skiers and wondered who they were, where they came from, what they did. She relaxed, feeling as though she had been given a short pardon from the prison of racing, permitted to see life as it was lived—at least for a little while before going back into custody.

She watched a couple sit down, order margaritas, then not say a word to each other. The woman polished her bracelets with a finger, then looked at her face in the mirror of her jeweled compact and frowned. Her husband watched the cluster of young, pretty girls at the bar. They didn't seem to like each other very much.

In the middle of the bar was a large noisy group of well-dressed men in Stetsons with women in flashy ski clothes. They were laughing and joking. Someone pulled out a camera and they started to clown for one another. They were noisy, but they seemed to be having a wonderful time.

In a corner nearby, two women were holding hands and talking in low, serious tones. Rocky turned away in embarrassment. As she looked up again, she saw Greg come in with the most beautiful woman she'd ever seen. They took a table in the middle of the room adjacent to the bar. She could see them in the mirror, but her vision was somewhat obscured by a large group of people who seemed to be playing musical chairs.

Rocky watched Greg order drinks, then return to his companion. When he sat down, she saw him pick up her hand and start to kiss her fingers. The beautiful woman, a lazy smile on her lips, put one of her fingers in his mouth. He pretended to devour it. Then he leaned forward and gave her a lingering kiss on the lips. She kept her eyes open as if she didn't want to miss a moment.

Feeling a violent blush suffuse her entire body, Rocky looked around in panic. She had to get out of there or she would faint. She couldn't wait for Tony. She'd call him later. Crouched in her seat, she kept her head down, trying to avoid looking in the mirror at the couple who were oblivious of everything but themselves. Sooner or later, the place would be so crowded she could leave without being seen.

She was about to take advantage of the crush of new arrivals when Tony came in with Max. As Tony looked around for a place to sit, he spotted her in the corner and began to wave. Saying a few words to Max, he came to her side.

She breathed a deep sigh of relief. Sliding in beside her, he said, "Hi, what are you doing here?"

"Waiting for you."

His face tightened with worry. "What's wrong? Is Sally all right?" At her nod, he asked, "Eric?"

"Everyone's fine. It's me. I need your help."

"Sure. What's the matter?"

"My skiing has gone all to hell again. My timing's rotten. I seem to have forgotten everything you ever taught me."

"That can happen to anyone."

"It's been happening to me for the last month.

You know that Kit's leaving me in the dust. I'm happy for her, really I am," she hastened to add, not wanting to be accused of disloyalty.

As if disloyalty counted at this moment, thought Tony. He couldn't believe what she was telling him. It was Sally all over again, happy for Suzanne. But not quite. Rocky wasn't Sally. She was no martyr to friendship. At least, he hoped she wasn't.

His heart went out to her. She was ready to break in a million pieces, this tough, fiercely honest youngster he loved as though she were his own. It would be a terrible mistake for him to treat this with intense seriousness. It would be like admitting she had a fatal illness. "So why don't we pick a day to meet and see what's going on?" He tried to make it sound as casual as meeting for a quick lunch.

"Could we?" The joy and relief in her voice almost broke his heart.

"Anytime you say, Rock."

"Tomorrow?"

"You bet. Shall I meet you on lunch break or do you want to do it after practice?"

"Practice in the morning. There'll be videotape in the afternoon."

"Do you want to miss that?" he asked skeptically.

"It hardly matters, does it?"

"I think it does."

"Nothing much happens."

"Still. I'll meet you afterward. How about three o'clock at the top of Aztec? I'll wait around for half an hour."

She reached over to give him a hug. "What would I do without you?"

For the next week, Tony worked with Rocky as she tried desperately to regain her lost footing, but no matter what he said, he could not help. It was as though she had undergone some subtle change in physical ability, unable to make the moves that once had seemed so innate. For the first time in his life, he suffered from total frustration. He, the great teacher and she, the great student had floundered somewhere, and he was damned if he had a clue what to do.

"You know," he said later to Sally and Daisy, "it's like someone who's been thrown from a horse. If they don't get right back on, they develop this horrible fear."

"You think she's afraid?" asked Sally. "She's never been afraid of anything in her life."

"Listen, if I didn't know better, I'd say she was being brainwashed," said Daisy. They looked at her as if she had suddenly gone crazy. "I know, I know, I read too many spy stories. But seriously, suppose someone doesn't want her to make the team. She's a youngster, open to suggestion. If they tell her often enough, she starts getting the idea that she's no good, until she isn't anymore." Daisy looked at their disbelieving faces. "Okay, forget what I said. It's pretty farfetched."

Tony pondered Daisy's words, then turned with a shrug to Sally. "I guess anything's possible these days. Someone tried to steal the ski, didn't they?"

"What ski?" asked Daisy.

"Damn it," said Tony, clapping a hand over his mouth.

"Big secret, huh? I wasn't supposed to know about it, I guess. Well, you might as well finish your story. I promise it won't get any further than this room."

Sally turned to Tony. "It can't be such a well-kept secret anymore. Not if someone tried to steal it."

"Would somebody please tell me what this is all about?"

So Tony told Daisy about Max's revolutionary ski, how he had tested it at Tieback in what he assumed was secrecy. "Somebody must have seen me over there. Someone who knows about skis and skiing. They saw something in the way the ski performed and got curious." Tony had long ago decided not to mention Michael Greenfield's name in connection with the ski. Sally would only think he was trying to prove his earlier warnings about Michael.

"Curious enough to steal it? A ski? C'mon, Tony, it's not the plans to a new guided missile," scoffed Daisy.

"No, but someone obviously thinks they can make a lot of money. Anyway, a lot of funny things started to happen to Max. Then about two weeks ago both Max and I got mysterious phone calls to meet each other at the lab. Needless to say, once we arrived, we discovered that neither one of us had called. We put two and two together and returned to Max's house. Someone *had* taken a pair of skis. Only it was a phony model. The real prototypes are not that easy to find."

"I won't even ask you where they are," said Daisy.

"Thank you. I have no intention of telling you."

"In the meantime, what are we going to do about Rocky?"

"Keep trying, until we find out what's really bothering her."

But the harder Rocky tried, the more tense she got. Her skiing reflected it. Finally, she went to her coaches and told them she wasn't feeling well and was going to take a few days off.

Sally decided to take her down to Denver for some R&R, but Tony felt that she should maintain some kind of schedule, even if it was only weight training and running.

"We're pushing her too hard," Sally accused. "I told you that before."

"And I told you that you were saddling her with your own hang-ups."

And they were off again, having one of those fights that seemed to erupt out of nothing. Once again they were at an impasse.

It took Daisy to break it. She was still unwilling to give up on her pet theory that someone had been brainwashing Rocky. While the storm between Tony and Sally continued unabated, she picked up Rocky and took her to Glenwood for the day. There they relaxed in the hot springs, had lunch and talked.

Daisy was one of those women who had the amazing knack of taking on the age of the person she was with. Her empathy for teenagers was just as strong as her sensitivity toward people counting the remaining days of their lives. To her mind, they had something in common, a sense of alienation, a fear of being alone, and the desire for love and friendship.

Instead of asking Rocky a lot of questions, Daisy rambled on about life in general. Then the conversation finally got around to skiing. One thing led to another and Rocky opened up, forgetting for an instant that Daisy was really her mother's friend and not hers.

"I get the feeling someone's messing with your head," said Daisy offhandedly. "You know what I mean?"

Rocky was startled. "I'm not sure."

"But you're smart. You wouldn't fall for something like that, would you?" Daisy sucked noisily through the straw of her thick shake.

"Do you know Greg James real well?" Rocky asked casually, shooting Daisy a quick look before returning to the contemplation of her own shake.

"Oh, please. Book, chapter, and verse on the SOB," she replied vehemently, her eyes snapping sparks. "What's he got to do with you?"

Rocky tossed her hair. "Nothing. Actually, he was very nice to me before we left for Europe."

"How nice?" Daisy asked suspiciously.

"You know . . ." Rocky reported on the few times she'd been in his company and how charming he'd been, how he had wished her luck before they set off for Europe.

"I don't know that Greg James," said Daisy, not bothering to hide her distaste. "What did you guys talk about specifically?"

"We talked about how hard it was on skiers to be away from home. Stuff like that."

"And you thought a lot about it, didn't you?"

"Well, he was right," said Rocky defensively.

"What else?"

"Nothing." The curtain came down.

"Have you seen him since you came home?"

"Only at the airport." She looked away guiltily. Daisy knew she was lying. "That was all?"

"I skied with him one day." A grudging admission.

"And . . ."

"He said I was doing a couple of things wrong. Maybe picking up some of Tony's bad habits." Rocky grabbed Daisy's hands and squeezed them. She was in anguish. "Please don't tell Mom. She hates Greg and Suzanne. If she ever found out . . ."

"What else did he say?" Daisy went on relentlessly. "Spare no details. Tony's bad habits, indeed," she murmured in disgust. "He has no bad habits, not in ski technique, anyway."

So Rocky, relieved at last to share her tortured thoughts, told Daisy everything. And once again swore her to secrecy. But Daisy had her fingers crossed behind her back, which if you still believed in childish rituals, absolved her from keeping her word.

The next day, Daisy arrived early at the ski school to corner Sally and report on her conversation with Rocky. Before doing so, however, she exacted a promise from Sally not to lose her temper or chew Rocky out. When Sally finally gave her word, Daisy looked behind Sally's back to make sure she hadn't crossed her fingers, before she told her.

"What are you doing?"

"You wouldn't understand." And Daisy repeated word for word Rocky's painful confession.

Remembering her promise, Sally tried to keep her voice in neutral. "Do you think she's telling the truth? That nothing happened between them? After all, he's a very persuasive guy."

"Tell me about it," was Daisy's retort. "No, she's not lying, but it doesn't matter. She clearly hero-worships him. After all, he's devilishly attractive."

"But he's twice her age!"

"So, didn't we have crushes on movie stars or rock singers when we were sixteen?"

"It's not the same," insisted Sally. "They didn't try to take advantage of us."

"Stop worrying about what didn't happen. You want my opinion on what's going on?" Without waiting for an answer, Daisy continued, "You laughed when I suggested it the other day, but now I believe it more than ever. I know that bastard better than he knows himself. There are two things he's crazy about: himself and Kit. And he wants Kit to go for the gold and win it. She's a damn good skier, only she has a best friend who's better. So Greg, who is very good at manipulation, has come up with this terrific idea: He'll mess with Rocky's mind. I know he can do it. He always hits where you're weakest. Now Rocky has no apparent physical or technical weaknesses. But Greg is an ex-racer and silver medalist. In her eyes, he's a role model. He skis with her and says, 'not so good' and she immediately starts to worry."

"But Tony and I have always given her positive reinforcement. Before she went to Europe, she was almost flawless. Why listen to Greg?"

"Wouldn't you believe a stranger before your parents?"

"Oh, that bastard, I could kill him!" said Sally, clenching her fists and hitting her locker. "Ouch!" She looked down in surprise at her reddening knuckles.

"See, even when he's not in the same room with you, his diabolical presence is felt. May the next lady in his bed bite off his balls," said Daisy, putting her hands together in prayer.

"What are we going to do?"

"You wait. If you say something to Rocky, she'll know I told you. I want to keep her confidence, because I'm going to do some brainwashing in reverse. I'm going to start telling Rocky what Greg James really is."

That night Daisy went to a party given by one of her Pittsburgh heiress friends. She wanted to turn it down, but she knew Greg would be there and curiosity about his new girlfriend overcame her. Besides, tonight might be the night to meet Mr. Right or beard Mr. Wrong.

So she "duded" herself up, which for Daisy meant wearing silks instead of suedes. Despite her sophisticated St. Laurent outfit, she still looked about fourteen, a kid dressing up in her mother's clothes.

The moment she walked in the door, she saw Greg with the new girl, Nora Whatshername. "Hi, Greg," she went up to him. "Where's Marcella?"

"Marcella who?" he asked blandly.

Daisy turned to Nora Whatshername and flashed a brilliant smile. "Men are such swine. Don't go to bed with him," she warned. "It makes him forget your name. And take it from me, Greg has forgotten more names than there are aspen trees on Ajax."

Daisy hurried away but barely got halfway across the room when she felt her arm being grabbed in a painful grip. "What the hell are you trying to do? Hell hath no fury like a woman scorned, huh?"

"My God, sometimes your erudition surprises me. But your cheap shots, never."

"What's that supposed to mean?"

"Would you like me to tell you in full sound and fury? I'm sure the entire room would love to hear it." She tried to yank her arm away. "You're hurting me."

"I hope so," he said, spitting out the words. He dragged her out of the room and into the library. Shutting the door, he said, "Now, spit it out."

"You're the lowest of the low," she said venomously. "How do you have the balls to play with a young girl's mind?"

Greg knew immediately of whom she spoke. A cocky smile spread across his face. "I kissed her on the cheek a couple of times and the kid thinks I'm in love with her."

Daisy raised her hand and with surprising force slapped him across the face. "You don't deny it?"

He rubbed the red spot her palm had left. "You're a cunt," he said.

"You're worse," she countered. "Why are you doing this?"

"Doing what?"

"You're trying to undermine Rocky so Kit can beat her out, aren't you?"

"Listen," he said defiantly, "I'll do anything short of murder to see that Kit has her chance."

"Bullshit! Since when did you become so altru-
istic? You don't care about Kit. You just want to see
the James gang make the record books. The skiing
Jameses, collectors of more medals than the
Mahre twins. What about Kit and her friendship
with Rocky? Don't you think that's important to
her?"

"I couldn't care less." Then he smiled malig-
nantly. "You know, Rocky is turning into a pretty
piece. I'm thinking we can go past the kiss-on-the-
cheek stage soon. I think we're ready for something more. What do you think?"

Daisy turned white with fury. "I think I should
tell Tony about this whole conversation and let him
cut your balls off. On second thought, that new
lovely of yours has pretty sharp teeth. Maybe she'll
do the job for all of us. You're dangerous, James.
They should neuter you the way they do chronic
sexual offenders." With that she walked from the
room, her back as straight as a plumb line.

She wasn't going to let Greg get away with it,
even if she had to do something desperate.

The heavy snows that had teased in January finally
hit with a vengeance in February. Every morning
avalanche warnings were posted along with the ski
reports.

At the Highlands, Daisy and a young college
student were skiing Sod Buster, an expert deep-
powder run, which had been closed all season
until she and a few other skiers prevailed on
management to open it. They had been skiing most
of the morning in steadily rising temperatures.
Since the area was patrolled, Daisy wasn't as
vigilant as she would have been in an uncontrolled
deep-powder area. With her usual Marines-have-
landed mentality, she was going all out for speed
when suddenly a slab avalanche broke loose and

set off a slide that ran 700 feet. With superb presence of mind she kept her head and managed to "swim" it out. Though her skis remained on, somehow her pants did not. Her student, having descended first, was safely out of the way when the avalanche broke loose. He went for help.

When friends and patrollers got to her, she was buried up to her shoulders in solidly packed snow. "My ass is freezing," she yelled when she caught sight of them. "I mean it," she said in a wounded voice when they started to laugh. "The goddamn avalanche pulled down my pants." They fished her out smiling and grumbling that the torn pants were her best and that her ass felt as if someone had gone over it with a sandblaster.

A few days later, there was another avalanche in Pearl Basin with much more tragic results. The basin, a favorite area for cross-country touring on the route linking Aspen and Crested Butte, stood at over 12,000 feet. Eleven skiers who were planning to climb 14,000-foot Castle Peak were caught in a blinding snowstorm. One of them, Terry Platt, was an old and close friend of Sally's. They had been trying to cross a steep slope when it buckled and crashed down a series of wind-scoured knolls to bury the entire party.

Both Sally and Tony, who were experts in avalanche procedures, joined the combined patrols of Aspen and Snowmass. Armed with long probe poles, they searched grimly, working in seventy-mile-an-hour winds that blinded them and made every step slow and torturous.

As search planes and helicopters braved the gale-force winds, fresh snow continued to fall. Finally, it was decided to abandon the search until the weather settled. By that time the pass, which had been scoured down to bare earth by the avalanche, was completely covered again. It had been exhausting and fruitless work, the relentless storm slowing them to a standstill. Even on snow-shoes or by snowmobile, there had simply been too much terrain to cover.

The event once more made Sally realize how ephemeral life was. First Pete, then Terry Platt. People worried about the wrong things, she thought. Nuclear waste, the Persian Gulf, brushfire wars, all of which had solutions if people could get together to really implement them. But a disaster from nature, random and indifferent, could turn a green land brown, drown a village, set off a volca-no, keep the rains from falling, kill a friend, and there wasn't one damn thing you could do about it. Life in the mountains was not all sunshine and powder snow.

Sally had little heart to go back out and teach, but she had no choice if she wanted to pay the bills. Her concentration was so fragmented these days that she requested "line-busters" classes, people who simply wanted to ski with an instructor to avoid lift lines and were happy not to have her talking.

Eventually, the sun emerged and the skies re-turned to their normal tropic blue. Along with the good weather came a lifting of Sally's depression. Even Rocky seemed to be happier. Her self-enforced layoff had made it imperative for her to play catch-up with the rest of the team, but in the long run proved to be the best thing for her. She retrieved her concentration from the black hole into which it had fallen and applied herself with a zeal worthy of a Christian missionary. Rocky thrived on competition, and Sally was once again grateful that she had kept her own dislike for it from affecting her daughter.

The night before Valentine's Day a foot of light Colorado fluff fell. The fourteenth happened to be

Sally's day off, and she had planned to stay in bed until noon, go to brunch with Eric, then to the movies with both kids and Tony.

When the day dawned bright and beautiful, she gave it a brief look with a half-open eye and turned away to snuggle deeper into the quilts. Just as she felt herself drifting off to sleep again with the curtain about to go up on a promising dream, the phone rang.

"Oh, no," she moaned, fumbling for the offensive thing with closed eyes. "Go 'way. We don't want any," she said sleepily. "Sally's gone to the North Pole. Not expected back until six tonight."

"Can't fool me," said the cheerful and familiar voice. "Get up, sleepyhead. I've rented a helicopter, and I want to go powder skiing. You've been unilaterally appointed as the guide."

"Michael, do you know what time it is?"

"I do. You've got twenty minutes. I'll pick you up. Happy Valentine's Day."

"Where are we going?" she grumped twenty minutes later, trying to force hot, strong, black coffee down to wake herself up without taking the skin from her lips. "Why am I doing this?" she said to the wall.

"I thought we'd go to Marble. Didn't you tell me you had been involved with a short-lived heli-skiing operation there?"

She nodded, then grumpily added, "Why do you look so bright and bushy tailed this early? Your hair is even combed."

He patted her head as though humoring a small child. "So you know it well? Marble, that is."

She nodded again. "But, I don't know. There's been a lot of snow there lately. Conditions are pretty unsettled, and you know avalanche warnings are up all over the place." She looked at him dubiously.

"I can understand your concern under the circumstances. You've seen enough avalanches for this year. And I'm sorry about your friend." The body of Terry Platt had been retrieved a few feet from where they'd been probing. It was a bitter defeat for everyone who had loved the shy young woman. "But I promise you, we'll turn right around if you think it looks dangerous. That makes sense, doesn't it?"

She sighed. "Why do I let you talk me into these things?"

"Because when you're good and compliant"—he winked broadly on that word—"you are rewarded." He handed her a box from one of the elegant new jewelry stores that had just opened in Aspen.

She frowned. "Michael, you still haven't learned—"

"Open it," he commanded.

She did and found an antique pendant on a chain. It had a ruby heart surrounded by old rose-cut diamonds. "I hope this isn't what I think it is," she said.

"I haven't the vaguest idea what you think it is," he said blandly. "I just liked it, went in, and told them to put it on my American Express card."

"How much?" she wanted to know.

He shook his head unbelieving. Only Sally would dare ask a question like that. "I forgot to look," he said with a guilty smile, "but even if I had, you'd be the last person I'd tell. By the way, they won't take it back nor will they give refunds."

"I don't know what to say."

"Thank you will do nicely."

"I give up."

Sally choked down her coffee, then picked up the box. "I'll just run upstairs and put this away. Won't be a moment."

He nodded. As he waited, he prowled around her house, wondering how anyone could stand living in this nondescript, chilly place for more than a moment. God, he could give her so much. Everything she wanted—except the only thing he guessed she really wanted. A sense of permanence.

He had finally gotten a handle on his obsession for her. It was the excitement of creation. To him, she was so much raw clay. His fingers itched to re-form and reshape her. She had all the basic material: a good mind, a strong rugged beauty, a handsome sensuous body, a certain style, and that uncompromising honesty which was both her curse and her strength.

Thinking of that first night she had come for dinner, he remembered how well she had fitted in his home. Her Western looks, his Western house. A perfect acquisition. Like the Asasazi urn or the Hopi dance tablita.

Pipe dreams. She would never live with him. She would worry about what her kids would say, her friends would say, the world would say. She was a strict conformist.

There were plenty of women who would leap at the chance, kids or no kids. Unfortunately, he craved her. Not ordinarily an addictive personality, he could be in a roomful of other women and still want only Sally, to take her home to bed and mark her with his semen, so all other like animals would keep away.

Why couldn't it be Suzanne or Marcella? Either one would be willing. But perhaps that was part of the problem. They were too available. The more often he made love to Sally, the more time he spent with her, the more he became aware of that closed-off part of her. Don't come any nearer. Danger. Stop. *Défense de stationner.* That was her secret. That's what drove him to her again and again, that piece of unattainability.

As he patrolled the room, he looked for clues to her. On a schoolroom desk he saw her entire persona spread before him. Neat, tidy, controlled, no room for disorder. There were three manila folders with headings underlined: Pay Now or Die, By the End of the Month, When my Ship Comes In. He smiled. At least she had a sense of humor about her financial problems!

In the bookshelves he found a surprising number of good books: Jane Austen, Joseph Conrad, Edith Wharton, Tom Wolfe, all paperbacks with dog-eared pages. Not the kind of show books with fancy bindings and gold-leaf titles and unbroken spines that filled the Jameses' library.

Photographs in cheap Woolworth frames, bespeaking happier days, were jumbled wherever there was room. The tall dark man with a tiny clone of himself hanging around his shoulders was obviously Pete with Eric. What a handsome, rugged-looking man he'd been! A man's man. Someone to ski with, hike with, fish with. Michael saw him in his mind's eye striking out alone with a pack on his back, happy in his solitary state, but also happy to come home and find his brood waiting for him.

Michael felt a pang of envy, wishing he had the simplicity of spirit to accept such homely pleasures. When he heard her footsteps on the steps, he returned the picture to its place and scurried across the room, feeling as if he had invaded one of the private corners of Sally's life.

When she opened the door to the mudroom to get her gear, she barely looked at him. Once again he was struck by her diffidence and felt the frustration that their relationship produced in him. That was another thing that drove him wild. Each time he saw her he felt as though he were required to start all over again, that whatever ground he'd gained on their last meeting had been lost. It was like dealing with a clever adversary who understood guerrilla warfare. Like the Cong, who would cede a hill or village to the Americans during the day and then retake it under cover of night.

"Okay, all set." She slipped her arms through her pack and flashed him a smile. He realized how much he looked forward to that rare smile and how infrequently she offered it with such whole-hearted pleasure.

They were about to leave when Eric came down the stairs with his skates slung over his shoulder.

"Good morning, sweetie. Do you have practice today?"

"No, just going out for fun with Eddie. His mom's picking me up."

"Good. We're heading for Marble for some powder skiing. When Rocky wakes up, tell her. I should be home by dinnertime. Okay?" He suffered her hug and kiss with impatience. She smiled at Michael over the boy's head and made a little gesture of surrender with her hands. He raised his eyebrows in knowing complicity, remembering how he had hated to be fondled when he was that age.

"Better take your powder skis," Eric reminded her.

Sally saluted her son. Then to Michael, "I'll have to stop at the ski school to get them."

They picked up the skis, then headed for the airport. Traffic was light in that direction so early in the morning, most of it coming in to Aspen from down the valley. Michael parked the Jeep near the hangar and they went in search of their helicopter.

It was a brilliantly cold day. Colder than usual for February in Aspen. The pilot, Ed O'Neil, carefully loaded their gear in the Alouette, taking pains to keep it in balance in the tricky surface winds. When he gave the go-ahead, they got in, and he revved up the rotors.

As the helicopter gained altitude they were offered a bird's-eye view of the scene below. Aspen, huddled between Red Mountain and Aspen Mountain, was just beginning to wake up. In a moment the jagged, snow-covered peaks behind Snowmass appeared. Dense pines made ruffles of green at the bottom of the white bodice of snow. From this altitude they could see a half dozen frozen lakes tucked into the high peaks and passes. Here the peaks varied between 11,000 and 14,000 feet. At that altitude the wind was fierce, buffeting the aircraft as if it were made from a child's kit. No matter how many heli trips she made, Sally still had an unreasoning fear about them and tensely watched the pilot battle the controls to keep the craft on course.

Michael put his hand on her arm, felt the tenseness, and mouthed, "Relax. He knows what he's doing."

She gave a sick little smile and tried to take a big breath, but the weight on her chest refused to go away.

In the near distance a stand of aspen trees rose like ghostly sentinels, caught in a cloud bank that seemed to have wandered down from the sky and gotten lost. They were at 14,000 feet. Here the air was thin, and clouds at this altitude had a perfect right to be sharing the skies with them. More, she thought. It's the plane and its occupants who are the intruders.

Sally had been watching their progress carefully. Now she leaned over to the pilot and pointed to a ridge. "Can you set us down there, Ed? It's a good place for our first run."

The noise of the rotors and the sound of the wind caught her voice and ripped it to shreds. He gave her the extra headset and she repeated her instructions.

They spent the morning skiing through un-tracked powder, totally alone in a vast wilderness. At the bottom of each run they found the helicopter waiting for them. At Sally's command, it would take them up again to another slope where they could again ski fresh powder. Michael's skiing had improved greatly since his first powder experience with Sally at Snowmass. Today the conditions were perfect, and they reveled in the feeling of whooshing through the light delicate fluff that flew into their faces like a caress. It was a surprisingly seductive experience.

At noon, Michael called a halt and had Ed put down in a sunny, wind-protected valley. He pulled a hamper from the back and announced a picnic.

"I decided we should have food for a kid's Valentine party." Opening the top of the hamper, he flourished a heart-shaped Jell-O mold: shimmering raspberry with slices of banana frozen like golden jewels in it. Sally laughed with delight. Then came the basket of fried chicken, potato salad made with tiny red potatoes, a tomato salad, and heart-shaped rolls. "Thank God you didn't decide to dye them red," she teased.

There was a Thermos of steaming tomato soup and another of Red Zinger tea. "I wanted to get red Oreo cookies, but they don't make them, so the regular ones will have to do. But if you're very good and eat all your vegetables, you can have these." He tossed a package of candies into her lap. They were the tiny red cinnamon hearts of childhood, the ones that were hot and bit your tongue, coating it with a horrendous red dye.

"You think of everything, don't you?" Her delight was so unfeigned, he felt a strange stirring in the pit of his stomach. As she sat on the poncho with their kiddie feast spread before them, he wondered if he had garnered enough brownie points with her to overcome the inevitable discovery of his complicity with Greg James to get Max's ski.

He shook his head in answer to his own conjecture. With her uncompromising integrity, she would never understand his motivations. He didn't really understand them himself. A ski, even one as revolutionary as this was supposed to be, would never give him the kind of profits that a thousand other products could.

But to him skiing was still an elite sport, like yachting or skeet shooting. And the street kid from the Bronx still yearned to be a part of that elite society. Money had bought him a certain entrée into their clubs and homes, but there was a born-to-the manor mentality that still separated him from them, an ease of birth and privilege that gave them the confidence to stride into a room or a country as if they owned it. If he tried doing it, he would be accused of chutzpah.

"You look like you're having a discussion with yourself and you're not happy about it."

He wrenched himself back. "Nothing important. Happens all the time. Sorry. Was I gone long?"

"Not very."

She crawled over and knelt in front of him. Taking his face in her hands, she kissed him lightly on the mouth. "Thank you. I'm glad you called and woke me. I've had a lovely morning. And you skied very well."

He scrambled to his feet and felt himself blush at her gesture. "Thank you. Let's try to make it a lovely afternoon."

As they approached the helicopter, they both looked up at the sky. "We'd better hurry, then," she said. "The weather seems about to change."

"Wind's picked up, too," said Ed, zipping his padded jacket.

"What do you think?"

"Let's go up and see."

They quickly packed away the considerable remains of their picnic and scrambled into the helicopter.

The rotor gathered speed, and Ed lifted them off to another ridge which they hadn't yet skied. He hovered over it looking for a place to set down, then pointed to it for Sally's approval. The plane was rocking in the wind. She nodded, delighted at the thought of being on terra firma again.

Ed swung the 'copter around and aimed for the flat area on top of the ridge. It was very narrow, with the possibility of unsettling updrafts. He would let them out quickly, all the while maintaining his power, then move off to wait for them at the bottom of the run.

He felt the chopper lurch. One of its skis touched down, the other hung awkwardly in the air like an off-balance skier. He was about to correct when a violent gust of wind caught them. One moment they were level, an inch from a smooth landing. The next they were being swept off the ridge, flipped over, and sliding down the wind-packed slope. Inside they heard, then felt the jolt as the rotor blades crumbled. Sally felt only the moment of cold panic then the seat belt grabbing at her middle before her head knocked into something solid and she blacked out.

Their slide started a small avalanche.

Michael was the first to open his eyes. Dazed, he looked around and realized they were buried in snow, how deep he didn't know. But the milky white light that surrounded them seemed to have motion, either that or he had suffered some kind of head wound and was hallucinating. Sally! He whipped his head around, wincing at the pain. Sally, her seat belt intact, was crumpled over in an awkward position, her breathing shallow. Ed, the pilot, seemed to have suffered a whiplash blow; his head was thrown back against the seat.

Slowly Michael extricated himself from his seat belt. Moving gingerly, he cautiously put one foot in front of the other, testing himself. He was unsteady, but uninjured, slightly stiff. His head ached with the intensity of a hangover.

He scrambled to Sally and felt for a pulse. It was shallow and rapid; she was in shock. Then he probed Ed with gentle fingers. His head lolled forward and Michael saw the trickle of blood at Ed's temple. He hoped it was nothing more serious than a shallow head wound.

The first thing he had to do was get them out of there. He took a deep breath and willed himself to stay calm and take stock. The canopy was shattered. He would have to remove the shards to gain entry to the outside. Carefully, he pulled them away, wincing every time a shower of snow hit his head, wondering when the fragile balance of the snow bridge overhead might collapse and send tons of snow crashing down on all of them.

CHAPTER THIRTEEN

"HI, CHAMP." DAISY WAS HEADING FOR HER CAR when she spotted Eric on Durant Street. "Give you a lift home?"

"Sure, that'd be neat."

They chatted about school and skating as Daisy maneuvered through the streets choked with skiers on their way from the mountain.

As they pulled into the small drive in front of the attached garage, she observed, "I guess your mom isn't home yet."

"She went heli-skiing today."

"It was her day off. I'm surprised."

Eric made a face. "That guy. You know, the one who's always hanging around Mom."

"Michael Greenfield?"

"Yeah, he picked her up early this morning."

"Funny, she didn't say a word."

"You wanna come in and wait for her? She

should be home before dinner. That's what she told me."

"And Heidi never lies," said Daisy with a grin.

"Huh?"

"Never mind"—she ruffled his hair, grinning when he pulled away in boyish annoyance at the affectionate gesture—"it's a private joke."

He walked into the kitchen, Daisy at his heels. Opening the refrigerator, he said over his shoulder, "Wanna Coke?"

"You buyin', partner, I'm having."

Eric gave a patient sigh. He liked Daisy a lot, but she was really ditzy at times, especially when she talked funny.

"Wanna watch a video?" he asked, trying to be hospitable.

"What did you have in mind?"

"My skating coach gave it to me. It shows how to skate figures."

"Sure," said Daisy, who had no idea what he was talking about.

So they watched the skating video, which Daisy decided was just the thing she needed for nights when she couldn't get to sleep. Then one of Rocky's runs, then a rerun of *Family Ties*, followed by a rerun of *Magnum P.I.* . . . By then, it was suppertime, dark as pitch, and there still was no sign of Sally.

Eric started getting restless.

"You hungry, baby?"

He hated when she called him baby. "No," he said grumpily. But he was. Gee whiz, he thought. Some mother. Out with some guy and meanwhile it was suppertime and he was starving and she didn't even care.

The fact that he was old enough and had many times fixed himself something to eat when he was hungry was hardly material. Mothers were supposed to be home at certain hours, being mothers, and that was it. His best friend Jimmy Pierson's mother worked, too, but she was always home in time to make dinner. Of course, Jimmy Pierson had a father, and Jimmy had a new pair of K-2's, while he was skiing on Rocky's Rossi hand-me-downs.

"Shall I make some dinner for you? Or maybe we could go out for a pizza and leave a note for her to join us? I think that's a great idea. What do you say?"

"What about Rocky?"

"What about her?"

"She's got to eat, too."

"We'll leave a note for her, too."

"We-lll," he said. She could see that he wanted to go badly, but some loyalty to his missing mother was holding him back.

"Don't worry. I'll explain it to her when she gets home."

The responsibility was taken from his shoulders. "I'll get my jacket."

Daisy scrawled a note and attached it to the refrigerator door with a kitchen magnet in the shape of a purple eggplant.

Michael dug carefully with his fingers, meeting, not with the solid resistance he had expected, but with soft powder snow. With growing excitement, he began to dig like a dog. His gloves soon grew soaked, his fingernails frozen. Light showers of snow rained down on him into his collar. But he was hot with frenzy and the steam from his own body and oblivious of his own discomfort.

Before long he began to see light and realized that they had been inundated but not solidly buried. His heartbeat returned to normal and he continued to work at clearing the snow. Every time he stopped for a breath, he looked at Sally, pausing to listen for her breathing. As he pushed away the snow, he noted that the sky was darkening and the air getting colder.

What an imbecile he was! The radio. He could radio the airfield and tell them what had happened. He clambered down from his work and looked about the smashed cabin at the complicated controls of the helicopter. Finding the radio, he prayed it still worked. With trembling fingers, he pushed the transmit button and started to call in a distress signal. Nothing happened. No light went on, there was none of the reassuring crackle and static that told him the radio was functioning. As if it were only a temporary malfunction, he continued to call and listen for signs of life on the other end. Finally, he gave up. Dusk descended. He looked at his watch and discovered it had stopped at the moment of impact. He had no idea what time it was.

They would have to wait it out. He hoped that Eric was smart enough to call somebody and tell them that his mother had not returned home. But there was little chance that anyone would look for them before morning. In the meantime, they could freeze to death. In his panic and anxiety, Michael was unaware that he was sweating until, reaching for the Thermos, he felt it slide through his damp fingers.

He looked around for something to cover Sally with. Then he remembered he'd brought his old raccoon coat along, stowing it with the food hamper in the back locker. He reached for it. God, it weighed a ton! He hoped it wouldn't smother her. As he carefully covered her, he heard a moan, so soft he thought he might have imagined it. He heard it again. In the gathering dusk he could barely see her face. He put his ear next to her mouth.

"Cold," she said. "Hurt."

"Where, darling, tell me where?" he said, wanting to hold her close in his arms but afraid to worsen her injuries.

"All over," she moaned. "First-aid kit. Under the seat. Aspirin. Get it for me."

"But, darling, you have a bad bump on your head. It might be a concussion."

"No," she said weakly. "Leg, arm. Broken, I think. Terrible pain. Need something." Her voice began to fade.

For an instant he looked at her, paralyzed with indecision.

Were ski instructors trained like patrollers? He hadn't the foggiest. Maybe she'd been a nurse. He was suddenly aware of how little he really knew about her. All he realized now was that her life and the pilot's were in his hands.

Obediently he went in search of the first-aid box. To his everlasting joy, he found flares, a flashlight, and a set of maps.

He brought the aspirin to Sally and helped her take it with a mouthful of tea from the Thermos. Bitterly he realized that they wouldn't starve to death at least; there was plenty of food from their picnic lunch. That seemed years ago. A whole different time.

He settled Sally as comfortably as the cramped quarters would allow and went back to work trying to dig them out. Finally he had cleared a path. As he carefully stepped out on the snow with first one foot, then the other, he waited, expecting the snow to collapse under him. Nothing happened. He watched the North Star appear. Lighting the flare he'd brought along, he had the faint hope that someone might, by luck, see it and realize what had happened.

Then he returned to the 'copter. He turned the flashlight on the map, trying to figure out where they were and whether they might be near civilization.

All of a sudden, Ed opened his eyes and cautiously rubbed his head. "Wow, I feel as if I've been on a twenty-four-hour toot."

Michael looked up and breathed a deep sigh of relief. "Am I glad to hear your voice. How do you feel?"

Ed moved his limbs cautiously. "Everything seems to be working but my head. Where are we?"

"I was hoping you could tell me."

"Here," he said, reaching for the maps. "Hold that flashlight steady, and I'll see if I can figure out where we are." He stared at the map for a few minutes, then looked up. "Okay, this is the ridge I tried to set down on when the wind caught us. So we have to have ended up about here. Did you notice if we're on an incline or a flat?"

"We plowed into a stand of trees. We're shoulder deep in snow. I thought we might be buried, but I managed to uncover the top. Sally's hurt."

"Bad?"

"I think so. Are we near anything?"

Ed reached for his oilskin wallet of hiker's maps. "These show climbing and hiking trails. Sometimes there are small huts where hikers can spend the night when the weather is lousy." Michael followed Ed's finger as if it were God's own. "See, there should be one here. Not too far away. If we're lucky . . ." Ed's voice trailed off.

When Daisy and Eric got back at eight o'clock, neither Sally nor Rocky had shown up. Daisy wasn't that concerned about Rocky. She'd probably gone off somewhere with her team. But Sally was the most conscientious of mothers, and her absence was most unusual.

Daisy began to question Eric carefully. What time did they leave? Where were they going? When did she say she would be home? Had he called the ski desk to find out if there were any messages?

Her tone of voice really frightened him. She saw the tears well up in his eyes. He fiddled with the buttons of his shirt, growing more and more confused with each question. Finally, he sat down on the bottom step of the staircase and let the tears fall. "Where's my mother?" he cried. "Has something happened to her? Mommy, mommy."

Daisy rushed to comfort him. "I'm sorry, darling. I didn't mean to scare you. I'm sure everything's all right." She wiped the tears away from his face. "She's going to walk in here and see us and think we're crazy. C'mon, let's go see if there's any ice cream in the fridge. We deserve it."

Solemn faced, licking the ice cream from the spoon, he played a game in his mind. He would take a big spoonful of ice cream. He would have to give it five licks. By the time the spoon was clean, his mother would be walking in the door. Then he increased it to seven licks, then ten. When the bowl was completely clean, he looked at Daisy with huge eyes. In a whisper he asked, "Where would we go if something happened to our mother?"

Daisy was taken aback. Before she answered him, she looked at the Big Ben kitchen clock on the wall. Almost nine. Now she was really worried. She went to the phone. As she was dialing, Rocky walked in. She took one quick look at Eric's tear-stained face and said tightly, "Where's Mom?"

Daisy hung up and explained what was going on. "Did you call Tony?"

"No, I was just about to call . . ."

Tears started to well up in Rocky's eyes. "Call Tony, please. He'll tell us what to do."

She is like a general under fire, thought Daisy. Cool, collected, organized. "Right," she said and called Tony.

When Daisy heard his familiar voice say "Leave everything to me," she let out a sigh of relief and threw herself into a chair, surprised to find that her knees could not support her a moment longer. Thank the Lord for Tony. Did Sally realize how lucky she was? When . . . if . . . No, she corrected herself fiercely, there is no "if." When she got back, she was going to have a real discussion with her about Tony.

Ed had found a flashlight with a powerful headlight beam. When Michael took it and said he was going out in search of the cabin that was on the hiking map, Ed tried to stop him. But Michael was adamant. They had to get Sally inside someplace where they could build a fire and make her comfortable.

With the moon risen and casting a silvery light on the snow, it was either a scene out of Swan Lake or some Grimm fairy tale. Grimm is more apt, Michael thought, as he made his way across the snow. It was very difficult. Although the snow was light, it was deep and unsettled, like wading through heavy molasses. Several times he sank up to his waist, then had to struggle to get out. In fifteen minutes, he was dripping wet. In an hour, he was exhausted and hallucinating about the great meals he had eaten in the last year. When he fell again, he had the urge to just stay there and sleep. It wasn't that cold, and he was filled with a delicious lassitude. He'd just rest for a few minutes, take a refreshing little nap, then he would get up and . . . his eyes closed. The snow was as soft as a cashmere blanket.

But some strong sense of survival sounded an alarm. He woke with a start, his senses alive and alert to imminent danger. He heard the cry of a wolf. Getting dizzily to his feet, he thought he saw dark shapes around him. For an instant his heart stopped. He picked up the lamp and shone it around. When his eyes picked out the square solid shape of the cabin looming a hundred feet away, he uttered a cry of triumph.

He almost ran the last few yards. Throwing open the door, he looked around. There were a pair of bunks, each with pillow and folded blanket, a wood cookstove, and a stone fireplace with wood stacked by its side.

Michael, his fingers numb, quickly took some logs from the stack and arranged them so they would have plenty of air, placed kindling and some crushed newspaper under them, and lit the fire. It blazed up immediately. He knelt on one leg to watch it for a minute, to make sure it had caught, then tucked the firescreen around it. He basked for an instant in its warm glow, rubbing life back into his stiff fingers, then with a longing look backward, left the cabin.

I hope Ed is strong enough for this, he thought. It was his intention to make a sling from the blanket he carried under his arm and somehow for the two of them to carry Sally back to the cabin.

His footsteps had made a perfect path back to the plane. He followed them gratefully, thinking of nothing but staying awake and getting back to Sally without further mishap.

When he finally scrambled back into the remains of the helicopter and told Ed his plan, it was not met with enthusiasm. "Too dangerous," was Ed's rejoinder.

"Too dangerous to leave her here," Michael said stubbornly. "In the condition she's in, she'll freeze to death. We have to do it. It's the only chance." When Ed still looked unconvinced, Michael reached in his pocket and pulled out a hundred-dollar bill. "There's nine more on top of this if we get her back safely."

"Let's go," said Ed.

Getting Sally out without inflicting further pain and possible damage was almost impossible. She was in horrific pain. Finally, Ed went to the first-aid kit, took out a syringe, and filled it with liquid Demerol. "It's the only way we can do it," he said, scared and miserable at his bad luck. Even the promise of a thousand dollars did little to allay his fears.

With Sally blissfully unconscious, they were able to move more quickly. Michael jumped down and waited for Ed to gently hand the unconscious woman down to his waiting arms.

Together they constructed a makeshift gurney and, following Michael's path, torturously made their way through the snow.

"Have you called anyone besides me?" asked Tony, pacing the floor, three pairs of fearful eyes watching his every move.

"No," they chorused.

"Her friends?" He was reaching at straws. Sally would never drop into a friend's house without letting her kids know. As he questioned them he kept his tone deliberately gruff to cover up his sense of uneasiness and helplessness. If there'd been an accident, where had it occurred? Were they alive? Hurt? They could freeze to death if they weren't already dead. Goddamn Michael Greenfield for suggesting skiing in the first place. And if he ever got his hands on Sally again, he'd kill her for going out in such unsettled conditions when she knew better. His anger filled him with a surge of emotion. Anything was better than this emptiness in the pit of his stomach. When he allowed himself to think about it, he couldn't imagine what his life would be without her in it.

Then, berating himself for maudlin nonsense, he began to make a series of phone calls. First to the ski desk to get her plan, then to the airport to get their flight plan, then to Mountain Rescue to alert them about the possibility of a crash. They decided to start an air search that night in case the 'copter had come down, in case someone had lit a marker flare, in case it began to snow tomorrow and they couldn't fly anymore.

When Tony suggested that he come, too, they politely asked him not to. Tomorrow was time enough.

Tomorrow! She could be . . . He refused to let himself think of it!

"Okay." He turned to the three people who were hanging on his every word, happy that action was being taken and hopeful that it wouldn't be too late. "If it's okay with you guys, I think I'll spend the night here."

Eric's sigh of relief was so vast they couldn't help laughing. Then they looked at one another guiltily. "No guilt." He nodded encouragingly. "We could use a little levity here."

"I'll stay, too," said Daisy. She couldn't bear being home alone, worrying and wondering.

"I have an extra bed," said Rocky, moving to hook her arm through Daisy's. "You can sleep in my room."

"Okay, then that's settled."

But nobody could bear to go to bed, to go off separately to their own thoughts. It was easier to sit around the kitchen table, drinking hot chocolate and remembering all the good times, so many good times. To Daisy and Tony, who had never really sat down and thought about it, it came as a shock how important this often-impossible woman was to them. How her sanity and pragmatism, her honesty and fierce loyalty had kept them all so close.

Later, as Tony stripped down to his jockey shorts and slipped into the cool sheets of Sally's bed, the very act gave him an almost sensual thrill. Her elusive scent of soap and fresh lavender filled his nostrils. With a tiny groan, he rolled over and clutched her pillow to his chest, feeling himself grow hard.

How selfish could a man be, he thought with disgust. This woman we all care so much about could be lying dead in the frozen wastes somewhere, and all I'm thinking of is how much I want to fuck her. The bald-faced admission struck him with force. No, that's not what he wanted. It went deeper than that. Jesus Christ, it went much deeper!

Sleepless for the first time in many years, he went over their lives together for the millionth time. Since Pete's untimely death and his assumption of surrogacy, something had been growing between them. For lack of a better word, they had called it friendship.

With sudden clarity he realized how subtly she'd invaded his being. Forget about the fights, the temper tantrums, the stormy scenes. He'd always come back for more because Sally Burke Schneider excited him. There was nothing more stimulating, not another downhill medal, another beautiful rich widow, another car, than Sally spitting mad, cheeks aflame, silver eyes sparking. God, how beautiful she was at those moments!

He knew that sleep was impossible. He got up and went downstairs in bare feet, afraid of waking the children. In her small liquor cabinet he found a fine bottle of brandy. With a grim smile, he realized that Greenfield had probably brought it. He sat in the dark quietly drinking, thinking black thoughts of the other man. He felt real pain, not anger or shock, real pain.

His heart congealed at what his mind was revealing and he stretched out his hands to emptiness. No, not yet, he cried to an indifferent deity, there's so much yet. . . .

Finally, when the bottle was half empty, he returned to Sally's room. The cat who had been sleeping at the foot of the bed arched her back and gave a mieuw, waiting for him to scratch her behind the ears. He climbed into bed and pushed the pillows behind him. The cat walked up his chest and perched on his shoulder. He could hear the loud, comforting sounds of her purr.

Suddenly he sat up and gave a shaky laugh. Now he understood why he always ran from commitment, why women went in and out of his life with mind-numbing frequency. He was already committed, had been for years. To this woman and her children.

Then he felt the cold fear again. What if she didn't feel the same way about him? What if all she wanted from him was what she'd always had? What if she was dying and he never had a chance to find out?

Just before dawn Tony opened his eyes, happy to realize that he had actually slept for a few hours. He pulled on his pants and shirt and went to the bathroom. He dashed cold water on his face, brushed his teeth with his finger, then went to the telephone.

Luke Pearsal, head of Mountain Rescue and a good friend, answered the call as crisply as if he'd slept all night.

"No luck," he said tersely to Tony's equally terse question.

"When are you going out again?"

"About twenty minutes."

"I'm going with you."

This time Luke offered no resistance.

They began by flying grids across the high elevations, assuming that a downed plane or an avalanche would be easy to spot from the air. But the relentless whiteness played tricks with perception. After several hours of frustration, Tony realized they were working on a wrong assumption. The helicopter might have crashed in the thick stands of pine and aspen trees.

On one of their lower passes, Tony spotted the wreckage. "Look! Down there," he cried. As Luke dropped down, his copilot called in to tell the others where they'd located the helicopter and to organize the search.

They were met by a second helicopter, which dropped well-equipped men as close to the wreckage as possible. The helicopter Tony was in was running on an almost empty gas tank, so they were forced to return to the airport, gas up, and fly back. In less than an hour they were part of the group combing the crash site.

During the night a light snow had fallen, obscuring most of the wreckage. "It's amazing you could see anything," marveled Luke.

Tony grimly agreed. It had been the intensity of his previously unrevealed feelings that had given his eyes the sharpness. That and some blind luck.

One of the searchers came over to them. He

looked weary and morose. "We've covered the area. Nothing."

"Is it possible they could have walked out of this?" Tony asked.

"Anything's possible." Luke shrugged.

"Look for tracks," Tony ordered.

Again it was Tony's sharp eyes that uncovered the faint outline of scuffling feet which the light snowfall had covered.

"Looks like they were trying to pack something," said Luke.

"It's possible that someone was hurt and they were trying to get him or her out of the plane."

"To where?"

"Damned if I know." Tony shook his head. "Hey, wait a minute! Isn't there a hiker's cabin around here? Give me those trail maps." His hands were shaking with excitement.

"Tony, they couldn't have made it very far. At night. And it was snowing, remember."

Tony brushed him away impatiently and studied the maps. "It shows a cabin here, just below treeline. That way." He pointed to the north. "Let's fan out in that general direction and look for tracks."

"Here! Over here," someone called. He'd found a trough through the snow that looked like an animal trail leading away from the wreckage. But boot prints indicated it to have been made by human feet. "There are two sets of tracks."

Not a third, thought Tony. Someone *is* hurt. He prayed it wasn't Sally.

Everyone converged on the path. "Let's go."

As they started on the grim journey, they were joined by a newly arrived team in snowmobiles. Tony donned snowshoes, and with him in the lead they followed the track for almost a mile. Suddenly they caught sight of smoke rising from a cabin nestled under a ridge.

Tony's heart was so full of anxiety it almost choked him. Running through the snow, he started praying that they were not too late.

He was the first one through the door. His eyes flew around the room. At first all he saw was a grateful Michael Greenfield and the pilot. "Where is she?" he asked sharply.

"Over there," said Michael. "She's been out most of the night. Thank God you found us. I don't know how much more we could do for her without a doctor."

Tony ran to her side and saw a Sally he barely recognized. She was so pale, so still! His fingers reached for a pulse. At first he could barely find it, then as if in response to his familiar touch, it came through, faint yet steady. He bowed his head and, taking her hand, lifted it to his lips. The gesture did not escape Michael's eyes.

Tony started barking orders, galvanizing the group into action. A part of Michael's numbed mind applauded. If it were a different time and Tony were a different man, he might even have allowed himself to like the man.

"Tony . . . I want to say . . ." Michael, strangely at a loss for words, began.

"Save it. We'll talk later. There are a few things I want to say, too."

Sally awoke slowly. Somewhere she heard a Mozart sonata and the sound of strange voices talking very softly. She tried to turn over, but an intense wave of pain engulfed her and she cried out with the surprise of it. She realized she was sweating. How odd, she thought. Her last conscious memory was of bitter cold.

When her eyes finally fluttered open, she saw Tony sitting in the chair, unwavering eyes gazing at her.

"Tony?" She was confused, uncertain.

He quickly got up and came to her. Perching on the edge of the bed, he took her hand and brought it to his lips.

"Tony? What . . . ?"

"Everything's okay now. You're safe."

"But . . ." She tried to focus her eyes. "What happened? Where are the kids?" She rubbed her eyes. "My brain's turned off."

"There was an accident. You crashed."

She looked at him, still fighting for memory. Then it started coming back, small pieces, followed by long blanks. "No. The wind blew us off the ridge." She heard the sound of her voice screaming, then the silence. "How did I get here?"

He told her the story. How Daisy and the kids called him when she didn't come home. How he tracked her down, about the rescue. "Michael rigged some sort of sling for you. He and Ed carried you to the cabin. Which was a good thing. The temperature really dropped that night. You might have frozen to death."

"Michael carried me?"

Tony's heart plummeted at the wonder in her voice. He proceeded to relate the full story, not sparing any details which might contribute to Michael's heroism.

"And you found me?" Her eyes rested on him. She stretched her hand out. Thinking she wanted to kiss him on the cheek, he bent his head and was surprised when her hand cupped around it and drew it to her so she could kiss him on the lips. They were dry and parched, but he felt a thrill surge through him that he'd never felt from the dozens of lips he'd tasted in his long life. He had to control an urge to sweep her into his arms and mold those strong bones to his.

"Am I badly hurt?" She released him a little, but her hand was on his shoulder now and they were still only inches apart. He marveled at the surprising intensity of his feelings, but was determined to maintain a studied calm exterior.

"You'll live," he said with a teasing smile.

"Tell me," she commanded.

His smile grew bigger. There was his imperious Sally. His! "Dislocated shoulder." He used his fingers to enumerate. "Couple of busted ribs, bruised spleen, banged-up femur." When he was about to extend another finger, she stopped him. "Enough. It doesn't matter. I won't be able to work for the rest of the winter." She released him and stared moodily at the wall. "I don't believe this is happening to me."

"Don't upset yourself. You've got major medical, workman's comp, and Greenfield's taking care of any other expenses."

"No, he's not," she said firmly.

"Sally! Be reasonable."

"No."

"No, you won't be reasonable, or no, you won't accept his offer?"

"I want to see my kids. Get my kids."

"They're waiting at home. Doctor didn't want them in the room while you were still unconscious."

She was suddenly quiet. Her eyes, dark and brooding now, stared at him. "What day is it?"

He told her.

"How long have you been here?"

He told her.

"But what about . . . ?"

He cut her off and said tenderly, "Nothing else seemed quite as important."

A slender thread stretched between them, linking them together, but it snapped at the appearance of the doctor. "You must be some special lady. This guy hasn't left your side for thirty-six hours. You up to some tests? Nothing serious. Just want to check that bump on your head and make sure there's no subdural bleeding."

"Tony?" She reached out for him.

With odd pleasure he realized he knew what she was going to say. "Don't worry, I'll bring them here as soon as the doctor says it's all right."

"Tell them I love them and I can hardly wait to see them."

"Don't worry about them. Daisy and I are taking them to dinner and then the movies."

"You and Daisy, hmmm."

"Don't worry about that, either."

"I wasn't," she said with some of the old acerbity, which made him smile and long to scoop her up in a bear hug of appreciation.

It was only later, when he was alone again in his own bed—Daisy having volunteered to spend the evening with the children—that Tony felt his blood congeal at the thought of what might have been.

What if he hadn't seen the downed chopper? What if the snowfall had been heavier and covered their tracks? What if? What if . . . ?

Early the next morning Michael came to visit Sally, preceded by a huge bouquet of yellow roses. Behind him was his houseman, Wang Tai, laden with a hamper. "Is it true what they say about hospital food?" he said, handing the roses to the nurse dawdling in the doorway. He pulled a chair next to her bed and motioned for Wang Tai to put the hamper on the table.

At first Michael seemed shy, but when she kept

casting curious glances at the hamper he said with a smile that he had checked with the hospital and they said she had not injured anything that ate or drank.

After an exchange of accident questions, they lapsed into a discomfiting silence, broken finally by his saying, "Your friend, Tony, is quite the guy."

"You two must have a secret-admiration society. He was telling me how courageous and level-headed you were trudging through the snow with me, and reminding me, I might add, that I was no lightweight. The dirty dog." There was a soft warmth in her eyes and voice that he had never felt directed to him. He felt a pang.

She fidgeted under his unwavering gaze. "What?" she asked.

With time and rational mind returned, Michael had been asking himself why the pursuit of Max's new ski had taken on such importance to him. Despite his reputation as a shark, Michael had always tried to avoid "dirty tricks." There were certainly legitimate ways to acquire anything. Sooner or later the whole town would know of his harassment of Max. Sally, too. He wondered if it had been his way of competing with Tony Frantz. From the moment he'd first opened his eyes after the crash, Michael had been acutely aware of how important Sally was to him.

"I thought after you were able to get around, we might fly to New York for a week and see some shows," he said casually, opening the hamper and pulling out a bag of plump nectarines from Chile for her. The trip he planned was anything but casual, yet he had no intention of playing his hand until he had tested the waters first. His new feelings—was it love?—made him feel vulnerable, another sensation he wasn't used to experiencing.

"Michael." Sally stopped his hand with hers. "You know how grateful I am for what you did, what you've done, but let's be honest. There is no 'we.' You know it. I know it. There never really was. Remember that old song 'Two Different Worlds'? Clichéd as it is, it's true."

"It's because of the ski, isn't it?"

"I don't know what you're talking about. What ski?"

"Never mind, it isn't important."

"What ski?" she insisted. Then, with understanding dawning on her face, she said in a strangled voice, "Oh, no."

His silence gave her her answer.

Shaking her head in disbelief, she said in a whisper, "But why? Why would you do such a thing?"

"Truthfully, I've been asking myself that. At first, I thought it was rightfully mine, that Margolis had developed it when he was in Monroe's employ. Then it got to be something else."

"Greg was behind it, wasn't he?"

Knowing how she felt about the Jameses, it would have been easy to put a good deal of the blame on Greg, but Michael, despite his sometimes questionable tactics, was basically an honest man. "I take full responsibility for my own cupidity. I'm not even sure I would have made that much money out of it if I'd gotten it." He stood up.

"Were you ever going to tell me?"

"Probably not. But I knew that sooner or later you'd find out. It was inevitable."

She turned her head to the wall.

"I had hoped you cared enough about me not to be upset when you heard about it."

She still wouldn't look at him.

"One thing I've discovered about you is that there isn't a dishonest bone in your body. Too bad.

A little larceny makes us all human." He gave a rueful laugh.

"It doesn't matter anymore anyway." She turned finally, fixing her silver eyes on him, making him fidget. "Whether you did a dishonest thing or not has little to do with my feelings for you. If I really loved you, I would have probably forgiven you eventually. But there are other things.

"I'm a plain, simple woman. Not very glamorous, not adventurous, kind of dull. You are a very intense man, exciting. You frighten me most of the time. You're unpredictable and moody, and I think you could be dangerous if crossed. I don't know where you wanted to take our relationship, but that doesn't matter either."

"So I was right."

"About what?"

"You and Tony Frantz."

"I don't know if you are or not. But I think I want to find out. We have a history, Tony and I. It's possible it could end in World War Three, but I should find that out, too."

"I wish you luck." In a way, he felt relief that everything was out in the open between them. "I'd like to remind you that I don't give up easily."

She shook her head and gave him a sad smile. "Don't, Michael." She looked at him so intently, he began to twitch under her steady gaze. "There are a lot of things about you that fascinate me, but I'm not about to play Pandora and open the box."

"No, you're much too rational for that."

"You make it sound like a weakness."

He shrugged. "Sometimes it is."

She looked at her watch. He got the message and stood up.

"Since we seem to have said everything, I think I should tuck my tail between my legs and slink away in disgrace." The arrogant little smile lifted his lips. "If I have a problem with my turns, can I still book a private with you?"

"I'm afraid this year is finished for me. Maybe next year, if I'm still here."

"Oh? Do you think you'll really leave?"

"We'll see."

"I suppose you'll have to tell Tony about the ski."

"I have a feeling he knows already."

A few hours later, when Tony brought the children to see her, she was sleeping. Her strong, handsome face seemed soft, vulnerable, infinitely precious. The children sat in awed silence watching this strange, quiet copy of their mother, fear on their faces, questions unasked.

As though she were aware that she was not alone in the room, Sally slowly opened her eyes. In her line of vision was Tony with a look on his face she had never seen before. Their eyes locked and held and then she tore them away to find her children standing uncertainly, waiting for a word from her.

She held out her good arm to them, and they rushed to her. Uncertainty gone, joy restored, they both started to chatter at the same time until she held up her hands and made the time-out sign.

Laughing and enjoying their awkward hospital etiquette, Sally answered their questions one at a time, constantly aware of Tony, standing outside the circle, watching her with that strange contemplative look in his eyes.

Finally, she asked them to leave her alone with Tony. There were things they had to take care of.

"Tell me again what happened," Sally requested.

He did, leaving out the unnecessary details. "Michael saved your life," he said, more grudgingly this time. "He kept his head and did exactly the right thing."

"But it was you that found me," she reminded.

"He and Ed carried you a mile to the cabin."

"You spotted the wreckage and found the tracks."

"Michael . . ."

"Enough about Michael! Are you his press agent or are you playing Miles Standish?" She was suddenly reminded of how many times Michael had suggested that Tony was in love with her and didn't know it. And once he had even suggested that she was in love with Tony. "Why are you looking at me so strangely, as if you've never seen me before?"

"In a way I haven't."

Sally was silent for a moment. "Something's happening, isn't it?"

"I think so."

"Maybe it's because of the accident," she said almost shyly. "And when I get home, everything will return to normal."

"And maybe it won't. I hope not." Tony's laugh was shaky. "But we've got to talk. About Michael. About a lot of things."

She nodded. He came to her and bent to kiss her cheek. It was surprisingly soft for someone who spent as much time outdoors as she did. And she smelled nice, like soap and baby powder. With a finger he smoothed the thick line of her brow ever so carefully, watching her gray eyes widen with surprise, then close as she enjoyed his touch. She had the look of a contented cat.

When he left and she was alone again, she picked up the mirror that Daisy had left for her and stared at her face to see if she looked different. She certainly felt different.

She put the mirror down and felt an adrenaline rush of excitement mixed with uncertainty. Everything was moving too swiftly. They had to talk, he said. About Michael. What about Michael? She had enjoyed her forays into the high life, had certainly enjoyed her newly discovered sexuality. Michael was a versatile and unselfish lover, but she knew with unquestionable certainty that she hadn't ever been in love with him. A guilty flush stained her cheeks.

The admission to herself made her feel oddly calm and sanguine, as though the fever that had been consuming her had finally burnt itself out. Michael had been an aberration. They no more belonged together than Daisy and Greg.

It was not easy to just walk out of Sally Burke Schneider's life without feeling something. Michael discovered that he was spending a lot of time alone playing "should have said, should have done."

One night, after turning down several party and dinner invitations and finding his own company boring, he got into his car and drove down the mountain. As he slowly patrolled the streets, his protesting stomach reminded him that he had not had dinner that evening.

He turned into Durant, noticing that Shlomo's was still open. The thought of a bowl of hot chicken soup seemed comforting and reminded him of his mother's admonition that chicken soup was good no matter what ailed you.

As he walked in he was surprised to find he was not alone.

"Marcella! What on earth are you doing here?"

The startled woman looked up when she heard her name. She was dressed in a black Yves St. Laurent smoking jacket and trousers. Her fox coat lay in a heap next to her. "An awful party. I just couldn't take it anymore. So I left. What about you?"

"Nothing special," he evaded. "Just had a fierce

yen for my mother's chicken soup. Only she's two thousand miles away. So Shlomo's is the next best thing."

"Join me."

Michael slipped into the seat next to her. Playing with the salt and pepper shakers in front of him, he suddenly felt at a loss for words. Marcella looked at him speculatively as she sipped her tea.

"I guess you weren't with Greg tonight."

"You guess correctly," she said drily. "He seems to be smitten with some lovely named Nora, about fifteen years my junior."

"His bad luck."

"Thank you, kind sir. Very gallant of you to say so. No, I don't care. He was just a temporary toy. By the same token I notice the beauteous Suzanne is not hanging from your arm. Or, for that matter, the attractive young widow Schneider. I heard about the unfortunate accident. Is she all right?"

"I think she will be. As for Suzanne . . ." He shrugged.

"So much for the James gang. They were making me weary anyway. I have to keep reminding myself that I am a successful and wealthy executive who doesn't have the time for willful children."

"Too bad, Suzanne could use a good friend."

"She goes through them like peanuts. I don't intend to fill that role for her."

One thing led to another and Michael found himself telling Marcella about the events leading up to the stolen ski. She listened quietly, offering no comment or criticism. He was grateful for that. But, of course, Marcella would not throw up her hands in horror; she was accustomed to stories like his. In today's business they came with the frequency of the daily newspaper.

She put her cup down crisply. "I have an idea."

"I'm listening."

CHAPTER FOURTEEN

EVEN THOUGH SHE HAD NOT TAKEN A FIRST IN months, Rocky's experience in major races was paying off, and her team standing gradually improved. For the last few days, she had listened as Daisy dissected every aspect of Greg James's character. At first she'd been unwilling to accept Daisy's harsh words, chalking it up to her bitterness that their very public affair was over.

Daisy told her about all the others in the past and the several in the present, one of them a silly young rich girl whose father thought he was paying only for private lessons. What he didn't know was that Greg taught the girl skiing in the morning and sex in the afternoon.

The final nail in the coffin was Nora Pemberton's testimony at lunch one day. Rocky recognized her as the beautiful dark-haired companion she'd seen with Greg when she'd first arrived home from Europe. The brazen Daisy had introduced herself to Nora, discovered that the relationship was over, and that Greg was now involved with a still-married French actress. She had enlisted Nora's support in her campaign to discredit Greg in the young racer's eyes. Whatever it took, Daisy was willing to do; in fact, she relished it, discovering that she had a deep capacity for revenge.

Finally, all of their efforts—Daisy's, Sally's, Tony's, and Nora's—were rewarded by the performance of a rejuvenated angry Rocky, ready to climb back into the number-one spot and win her rightful place on the team.

Her concentration improved until it was even better than before. She attacked her technique with the dedication of a dancer. She watched her videos so intently that Sally literally had to pull her away to feed her and remind her that there was a life after skiing.

And then the day it all came together, disaster struck.

Unusually warm weather had produced spring conditions. In the morning the slopes were fast and icy; by noon, it was slush, then fast and icy again when the sun began to go down.

Although no one was permitted on the race practice course, there was still enough traffic from the racers themselves to produce deep ruts and a buildup of slushy mounds which froze rock hard by early afternoon.

Rocky was having a spectacularly fast run when, halfway down, she lost it on a rock-hard bump on the airplane turn below Spring Pitch and crashed into a Willy bag. The inflated poly bags lined the course gates in difficult turns to cushion the impact of falls at sixty to seventy miles an hour. Because of the fast track, Rocky's speed at impact was great enough to twist her right knee, which had already suffered a number of injuries over the years and could not take another one. They brought her down in pain and rushed her to the emergency room. She was lucky; it proved to be only a bad sprain rather than a torn cartilage or ligament. She was told to stay off her feet as much as possible, given a knee brace, and instructed to limit her exercise to swimming to keep up her muscle tone while the sprain healed.

"Mom," she wailed, as Sally, who had just been informed, came rushing into the emergency room, "I can't believe this is happening to me. God must really hate me."

"Oh, baby, are you hurt badly?" Sally looked at the brace. She was still in a great deal of pain herself from the torn shoulder and cracked ribs, but it was nothing to what she was feeling now for her daughter.

"Luckily just a sprain. That same damn knee again." She stuck out her leg in its elastic brace. "I can walk, but they want me to stay off skis for a week."

"A week? And you were doing so well."

"Yeah," she said, totally disgusted. "I'm so mad I took off those couple of days to hang around and mope and feel sorry for myself. Now, I really feel sorry for myself. And they're picking the team in two weeks. Shit."

Rocky rarely cursed in front of her mother; so the use of the four-letter word was an indication of her disgust.

Kit James came to see Rocky every day after practice, reporting the gossip, conjecturing who would make the team. She felt almost as bad as her friend. "Don't worry," she reassured, "you'll make the team. I heard them talking. They know how good you are. They need you more than you need them."

When the James gang found out that Kit was going to visit Rocky every day after training, there was a huge argument.

On the fifth evening of Rocky's confinement, Kit walked into the house around ten that evening.

Big brother and sister were literally pacing the floors like irate parents with a child out past curfew.

As Kit took off her coat, Suzanne pounced on her, grabbing her arm and squeezing it painfully. "Where have you been?"

"Suzanne"—the younger girl pulled away with surprise to rub the angry red indent of her sister's fingers—"I'm not a baby. You don't have to use that tone of voice with me."

"Where were you?"

"I went to see Rocky and we went to the movies."

"'I went to see Rocky and we went to the movies,'" she imitated, her voice as abrasive as a crow's.

"Do you have any idea how ugly you sound?"

Suzanne was about to screech again when Greg interrupted. He put his arm around Kit's shoulders and tried to comfort her, using his softest, most soothing tone of voice.

"C'mon, kidlet, Suzanne's bark is worse than her bite. She means well." He drew her into the den, where a warm fire glowed in the huge field-stone fireplace. "Here, give me your coat. I'll hang it up."

Grateful for Greg's understanding, Kit gave him her things and went to warm herself.

He was back in a moment with a carton of ice cream and two spoons. "Sharesies?" he asked, with a wink.

"What's Suzanne's problem?" she asked, her mouth full of chocolate almond fudge.

"She's concerned. Here you are, about to be named to the team, and you're more worried about your friend than you are about yourself."

"But Rocky's hurt."

"I know, hon, but it isn't serious. She'll be all right." Greg paused and wondered how she'd take his next offering. "You should be taking advantage of the situation."

"What do you mean?" She drew back, startled.

"Concentrate on winning. On beating out everyone else on the team. I think you have to put your friendship on hold for a while. At least until the season's over."

"But why?" she pleaded, trying to understand.

"I can't explain it exactly," he waffled, "but it's important you don't spread yourself too thin, don't try to have too many things to think about. So you can focus on the skiing. Do I make any sense at all?"

"Yeah," she acknowledged grudgingly. "I guess so."

"So, will you do me a favor?"

She nodded.

"Start thinking of you. Let Rocky be. She's strong. Everything'll be cool. You'll see."

Inside Greg was rejoicing. Rocky's accident was the first good thing to happen to them since they found out the stolen ski was a phony.

Tony had given the modified ski every stress test he could invent, skied it on every terrain, in every kind of condition. He was convinced that they had a winner.

"Do you want to give Rocky a chance to ski on it?" asked Max, lovingly running his finger down the sleek surface of his baby.

"Good question," said Tony.

Max waited. "Do you want her on that ski or not?"

"You mean for practice runs?"

"Yeah."

"That could be very tricky. If they discover she's not working with sanctioned equipment, she could be thrown off the team before she even makes it."

"I was thinking of the next couple of days, while they're making their final decisions."

"She could certainly use a little advantage here. She's missed a lot of practice already. She's still playing catch-up."

"So a little assist from her uncle Tony and uncle Max is not remiss?"

"I don't know. It doesn't seem fair, somehow."

"All's fair in love and war, Tony, me bucko. And this is real war. Think of it this way, if it were the James gang who had the ski, what do you think they'd do?"

Tony spent three days mulling things over, then realized he couldn't make any decision without first discussing it with Sally. There were so many unresolved things still between them, he almost wished he could run away and let everything work itself out. His feelings for her, hers for him, Rocky, the ski. Life had been so simple once.

But it was the new, mature Tony that announced on the phone that he was coming over for some serious conversation.

When he presented himself at her doorway, he was surprised to see her open it herself.

"Hey," he exclaimed, lifting her up in his arms, "I thought you were supposed to stay off your feet."

"Put me down, Tony, you've got me mixed up with Rocky. I'm perfectly capable of walking."

He still held her in his arms. "I don't think so. I rather like the way you feel. I also like you defenseless."

"You know better than that!" she said with spirit, although she had stopped struggling and seemed content to be in his arms.

"You look very . . ." He stopped.

"Very what?"

"I don't know. Young, maybe—soft, vulnerable, no, not that."

He looked directly into her silvery gray eyes and watched them soften. Her dark hair was swept back from her face with a velvet ribbon, and he realized that she was wearing a touch of color on her lips.

Still carrying her in his arms, he walked into the room and sat down in the big armchair, settling her into his lap.

He lifted his hand to the one that held him around the neck and drew it to his lips. Then he let his fingers run down the curve of her cheekbones and the strong line of her jaw. He felt her tremble.

"It's time for us to talk," he said softly.

She gave a sigh. Almost of disappointment. Talk could wait a little longer.

His mouth descended. For an instant she felt fear. When she opened her own to say something, he came down upon it swiftly. Their noses bumped. They giggled. He took small nibbles at her lips. Finally his tongue slipped past her teeth and she opened eagerly to him. It was sweet and wonderful and strange. All the years of cheek-kissing and quickies on the lips had not prepared her for the electricity of this moment. He, too, seemed surprised and lifted his head to look at her.

She wrapped her arms around him and pulled

his face down. He nestled in the nape of her neck, then nuzzled the fresh-smelling flesh there with his lips.

"Oh, my," she said.

In response he pulled the zipper of her robe down past the inviting shadow of her breasts. They rose like dark mounds on either side. When he lowered his mouth to take one, she let out a sigh. And when his teeth clamped hard, she bleated in pain.

"Goddamn," he cursed huskily. "I hurt you."

Abruptly, he sat up and gently set her on her feet and zipped up her robe.

"Tony!" she cried.

"I'm sorry, I'm a selfish pig. There's plenty of time for this when you're feeling better."

"No," she said. "Now."

"We should talk first."

"No, now."

She put out her hand and pulled him up the stairs. He went meekly like an obedient puppy, slightly dazed, full of wonder.

In the chilled bedroom, the late-afternoon sun was making long shadows across the room.

She lay down on the bed and put her arms up to him. With a greedy laugh, he was upon her. He zipped open her robe and laid her bare to his eyes. He let out a choked cry, then retrieved the nipple of the breast that had tantalized him so. She moaned with every touch of his tongue. And then, as if he had all the time in the world, he roamed her body with hands and lips, taking care to touch her with the lightest of strokes, though he wanted much more.

He lit little fires up and down her body wherever he touched it. When he pulled her knees apart and covered her with his cool mouth, she could barely contain herself. She thought she called out to him, but she didn't know whether she dreamed the words or said them aloud.

She felt as if she were in one of those kaleidoscopes where every turn set off another pattern, another burst of color.

Her eyes fluttered open and she saw him hovering over her like a dark, winged bird. For a moment she was frightened, a cry caught in her throat, cut off as his mouth covered hers. And then she felt him enter, cool, hard as marble, and her hands reached for him to pull her closer to him. His body was what she expected. Hard, muscular, smooth as silk and warm, faintly tan, covered with a fine mist of perspiration.

Her legs wrapped around him, pulling him tighter, and then she started to move in a rhythm to match his own.

He suddenly stopped.

"What's the matter?" Her question was almost a sob. Was he going to stop again, afraid of hurting her. "I'm all right, really I am."

His laugh was shaky. "I wish I could say the same. I had no idea you were going to affect me this way." He buried his head in her neck, felt the silky tendrils of her hair catch at his face.

"Oh," she said with understanding and stilled her anxious body, giving him a chance to gain control over himself, waiting patiently to start all over. He was still and hard within her, but his pulsing penis was almost as exciting as his mouth.

Finally he lifted her hips and plunged deeply into her again, feeling her shatter under him. He stopped.

"No!" she cried, picking up the beat. "More, more."

His laugh was exultant. Forgotten was the shoulder, the ribs, all the aches and pains. A pleasure greater than anything caught them both, and together they fell over the edge.

Later they lay in each other's arms, peaceful at last, hands roving each other's body, touches gentle and loving.

"What did you want to talk about?" she said from the hollow of his throat where her tongue was exploring.

"I think I have my answer," he said.

"I'm glad," she said simply.

He pulled her tighter. She winced, but when he tried to withdraw she held him. "It's worth all the pain." She leaned up carefully on her elbow. "Don't you think it's all amazing?"

"You mean this? Us?"

"Yes. For years we've known each other. Who would ever dream we'd end up in bed together."

He looked at her soberly. "It's much more than bed with me. I love you, Sally. I guess I have for a long time and never realized it."

"I know. That's part of it, too. The wonder of it. Daisy knew. Michael did, too. Long before I knew or would even admit it."

"You still haven't said it."

"I haven't?" She sulked prettily. "I wanted you to be first."

"Say it," he commanded.

"I love you," she said simply. Then she threw herself into his arms and hugged him fiercely, "I love you, I love you, I love you."

When the children came home, all was sedate and normal once more. Sally watched Tony peel potatoes. They had been cooing like new lovers, discovering things about each other, confessing bad habits. "As if we didn't already know." Sally had laughed.

In the middle of dinner and the pleasure of her

company in this new scenario, he suddenly had a sinking feeling. Sooner or later they would have to address the issue of Rocky and the ski.

The children, sensing some new current in the relationship between their parent and their favorite uncle, said little. Instead they watched the two adults, trying to figure out what was going on.

After dinner, Rocky and Tony, with the help of Eric, cleared the table and did the dishes. Eric said good night and went upstairs to do his homework. Rocky was about to leave when Tony stopped her. "I want to talk to you and your mother about something very important."

"Shouldn't Eric be here?" asked Sally, misunderstanding what he was about to say.

"No, this concerns Rocky and, of course, you."

"Oh?"

He led them to the living room and sat them down, remaining standing himself.

"Rocky, are you going to make the team?"

She shrugged. "I think so. But . . ."

"You could use a couple of outstanding races."

"Certainly wouldn't hurt."

"All right, I want you to listen to me." He turned to Sally. "Hear me out first, then we can discuss this. Like a family." He smiled.

He then proceeded to tell Rocky about the ski that he and Max had been working on. Its potential, its revolutionary capabilities, how he hoped that the U.S. team would be skiing on it by the next season.

"A couple of things have to happen before that becomes a reality, though." He looked from one face to another. Sally had not said a word yet, but he could see the wheels going around as she tried to guess what he was about to say.

"Max can disguise the ski so that it will look like the ski you're currently skiing on."

"You want me to ski on it?" asked Rocky in surprise.

"I want you to make your last practice runs with it."

"But, Tony, that's wrong!" Sally finally interjected.

"Wait a minute, Mom, let me hear what Tony has to say."

"I'm thinking only of you making the team. You've had a couple of bad jolts. I'm offering you a way of getting back to top form in a hurry. I know you can outski anyone on that mountain using any ski, including wooden barrel staves. But you're behind right now." He turned to Sally and pleaded, "All I'm suggesting is helping her get back where she was. And at the same time I'll find out once and for all how good this ski really is."

Sally's heart plummeted. "Is that what this afternoon's seduction scene was all about," she said bitterly.

"Is that what you think?" he replied, sick to his heart and furious that she should think so little of him.

"What's going on? What does she mean, Tony?" Rocky was totally bewildered.

"Rocky, go upstairs," Sally commanded.

"But, Mom. What about the ski?" She looked at one and then the other, concerned about the frozen looks on their faces. She was used to their fighting, but this was something else, far worse. They were eyeing each other like old antagonists.

"Please, what is it?"

"Upstairs," said Sally, her voice steady and unfamiliar.

"Oh, God, I can't stand it when you two behave like this. You're worse than children." Rocky flounced from the room without a backward look.

"She's right, you know."

"How could you, Tony?"

"What am I doing that's so terrible?"

"You want to give her an unfair advantage with a nonsanctioned ski."

"For Christ's sake, Sally! This isn't the Olympics."

She flinched at the curse.

"I mean, what are you? God or something? Keeper of the flame, winner of the 'be honest at any cost' award?"

"Is there something wrong with that?"

"Don't you want your daughter to be a winner?"

"Not at those prices."

"You're impossible. You don't understand."

"No, I don't." She rose to her feet wearily. "But I understand you. You want to win no matter what it costs." And she walked from the room.

Two bodies had lain together in a warm tangle of limbs earlier. They had tasted each other's flesh and breathed each other's breath. Now they lay alone and sleepless, wondering how things could change so quickly and why the other was so stubborn.

When Tony arrived to meet his private for the day, he was surprised to find Michael Greenfield.

"Do you mind if we don't ski? I want to talk with you."

Tony gave him a suspicious look.

"You probably won't like what I'm going to say. At least, in the beginning. But let me get everything out on the table and then tell me if my offer interests you."

"Where do you want to have this discussion?"

"In my car, for all I care."

"Why not my house?" said Tony.

So the two men sat down in Tony's den with a

pot of coffee, separated by more than the distance between their oppositely-facing chairs.

Michael had been surprised at the luxe of Tony's house. The man was no ordinary ski bum. If his library was any clue, his taste and interests apparently went far beyond his calling. The den itself, which contained the requisite trophies, also had a respectable collection of Remington drawings and other memorabilia of the West.

It was the first time they'd had the opportunity to observe each other so closely. Both were obviously reserving judgment. In the beginning only one thing had stood between them, and it was the one thing they had in common. Their feelings for Sally Burke Schneider.

"It's about the ski . . ." Michael began, watching Tony's face warily. He had no idea how Tony would take this confession. He had a reputation for having a hair-trigger temper.

When Michael admitted to being the mastermind behind the theft and the attempts to intimidate Max, Tony's eyes narrowed and Michael saw the big hands flex until the knuckles were white with restraint.

"That was an absolutely ridiculous thing for me to do. And I assure you I don't make a habit of stealing things I want. I don't have to."

"Why are you confessing to me?"

"Because I want to make you and Margolis an offer."

Tony gave a harsh laugh. "I don't think Max will be interested in anything you have to say."

"Then I'm counting on you to change his mind."

"You don't know Max."

"I'll put my money on you. Speaking of money, I'm assuming you're an investor in this ski."

Tony nodded. "Naturally."

"Much?"

"Enough." Tony was not about to tell him that he had sunk all of his savings into the project, even mortgaged his house, and had no idea how he was going to stay solvent through the summer. Out of friendship and his desire to be part of something to do with skiing, he had casually invested it in a scheme that could get stonewalled at any time. And now Tony's worst fears were in danger of becoming harsh reality. Could he handle being poor again? And now there was Sally. He wanted to give her so much.

"There's no such thing. I'd conservatively estimate it will cost a couple of million dollars just to develop the ski. Then you have to buy into the manufacturer's pool if you want to supply the team. And you want to supply the team because they'll win on this ski and winning will make everyone want your ski. Then you'll have to be prepared to supply technicians, vans, support teams, for all of which you will need even more capital. After this phase, assuming it's successful, it will cost millions to develop and market the ski." Michael paused to let the words sink in.

"As I'm sure you are aware, I have the capital. I have the marketing know-how, and I have the outlets for selling—one hundred and fifty sporting-goods stores around the country, the most successful sports stores in the world. And I'm opening more next year, some in this country, the rest in the Common Market countries and Japan.

Tony smiled uneasily. "If you can't beat 'em, join 'em, huh?"

"Something like that. Let me assure you that my offer is straight. I have no takeover desires. I consider it a venture-capital project. I want to help you get this thing going." At Tony's disbelieving smile, Michael said earnestly, "I know, I know. It sounds like a hustle. But I mean it. It's your company, you control it, you always will. I'm offering to make an investment in it for a minority interest. I would act as a consultant. I have a lot of expertise in these fields. It's yours, if you want it."

"What's in it for you?"

"Besides possibly making money? Nothing, really. I just want to be part of it. I don't even know if this ski is worth my trouble and if it can actually make it in a crowded, shrinking consumer market."

"It is and it can," said Tony grimly. But how could he be sure? Not for the first time he realized what a risk he'd taken. He wasn't a kid anymore.

"I have to take your word for it; though your word, I gather, carries terrific clout around here. After all, you're one of the world's best. I would like to see the ski perform. In the open, instead of behind the trees at Tiehack. Greg told me about that."

So it had been Greg James that had seen him that day! Which brought up another disturbing aspect. "What about Greg James?"

"What about him?"

"What does he have to do with any of this?"

"Nothing as far as my deal is concerned. I don't owe him anything. Listen, if you don't want to accept my offer, I'll understand. But I want you to think about it carefully. Discuss it with Max. If he has any questions, he can talk to me. If you agree, I'll have a binding contract which spells everything out written up for your lawyers to examine. Remember, I'm offering you more than just money. I'm offering you an entire vertical operation."

"Was this your idea?" Tony was still looking for hidden motives.

"Frankly? No. It was Marcella Richards's suggestion. She's a very smart woman."

"What's in it for her?"

Michael seemed surprised at the question. "As far as I can tell, nothing." Then he smiled broadly. "Maybe a private lesson with you?"

For the first time since Michael had broached his extraordinary offer, Tony's face fell into relaxed lines and he allowed himself to laugh.

Tony placed Michael Greenfield's offer in front of Max Margolis, who, as Tony had warned, was incensed that his friend would even make such a suggestion.

Tony also told Sally. She found the offer surprising. When they had been seeing each other, she had not been unaware of the talk at parties. Michael was described as a barracuda, a shark, a hyena, and other rather distasteful animals. She, of course, had not experienced any of those aspects of his personality. Still.

"Maybe it's a kind of peace offering. He must feel very guilty about his part in stealing the ski."

"He really got to you, didn't he?" said Tony in a tone of voice that brought her up sharply.

She said nothing in her defense. At the moment she hung suspended, tangled on the line that led to her future. She and Tony had shared a past. Since her narrow brush with death the parameters that defined their relationship had changed. Now they both stood on a strange new threshold, unable to move forward or backward.

Where once there had been camaraderie, now there was icy strangeness. Conversation, once open and unrestrained, became general and circumspect. After the surprising revelation of their newly discovered feelings, they now went out of their way not to touch each other. Fingers that accidentally brushed against one another were withdrawn as if made of fire.

There was an almost unbearable sexual current between them. Daisy felt it almost immediately but said nothing, watching and waiting for the right moment to interfere. Everyone's current concern was getting Rocky back on her feet.

Daisy had taken it upon herself to take over the running of the Schneider household while Sally recuperated. Her housekeeper came by to tidy up and cook the evening meal. Daisy stayed to clean up with help from Eric.

One night as Sally was being made comfortable on the living room couch after dinner, she said, "I really appreciate what you're doing, Daisy, but you don't have to give up your life to take care of us. I'm fine now."

"I'm not giving up a thing. I'm overdosed on festive occasions. One more party or dinner and I'm going to run away from home. So relax. This is like a vacation for me. By the way, Tony called while you were napping."

"Oh, what did he want?" Said with a casualness she didn't feel.

"He said to tell you that he loved you and was going to mount up his white horse and take you away from all this."

At Sally's startled look and red face, she laughed. "Only joking."

"Some joke," Sally grumbled.

"I thought it sounded pretty good."

When Sally did not seize the invitation to talk, Daisy proceeded bravely on. "What's going on with you two?"

"Nothing."

"Yeah, I noticed. Why?"

"How do I know?"

"I have never seen two people—old friends, at

that—tiptoe around each other like you two. Such exaggerated politeness, such gallantry, you'd think you'd just met. What happened to screaming and fighting and holding hands and kisses on the cheek?"

"I just don't know what to say, Daisy. There are times when I want to drop all the pretense and throw my arms around him and drag him to my bedroom. That in itself is a shock. And then I wonder what he really feels, if he feels anything but what he's always felt."

"Look, I saw that man in the hospital when you were unconscious. He didn't leave your side for a moment. That is not friendship. That is real caring."

"I felt something different, too."

"You went to bed with him." It was more a statement than a question.

"Yes. I did. But then he brought up this thing with Rocky. I can't understand him. Nothing matters but winning. It makes me wonder . . ." Sally's voice trailed off.

"What?" Daisy fairly wailed.

"Oh, I don't know." Sally clutched at her pillow. "He's sunk all his money into this ski. It's not just Rocky's winning that's important to him. I'm just not sure where I stand in this whole situation. In Tony's life."

Daisy leaned over to her friend and yanked on Sally's hair.

"Ow! What did you do that for?"

"Sometimes, Sally Burke Schneider, you're a real pain in the you-know-what." And with those parting words, Daisy flounced out of the room, leaving Sally to contemplate the future.

The more he thought of it, the more Tony realized that Michael Greenfield was the man to bring in to supply the money and the marketing expertise. But Max was adamant.

"I don't know why you're being so stubborn if I'm willing to go along with him."

"I tell you he's a barracuda."

"I agree, but the contract he's offered us is as sound as the Japanese yen. I've had Pat Mallory's lawyer go over it. He says we can't lose."

"What about Pat Mallory? Maybe he'd like to invest in it?"

"Sure, he'd be glad to. But what Greenfield offers is more than money. Face it, Max, the crucial thing after making this baby is marketing it; getting it into the manufacturers' pool and onto some racer's feet, and then capitalizing on that in the retail area. We need seventy-five thousand dollars just to be considered for the May trials when the U.S. team selects its equipment. Michael can not only supply the money but, at the right time, his stores would provide the perfect retail environment. At least, think it over."

"All right, I'll think about it."

Rocky knew she was treading on dangerous ground. She didn't know what would happen if her mother found out. But she couldn't understand how both her mother and Tony could be so convinced one was right and the other wrong.

Tony had admitted to her that it might be considered unfair to use the superfast skis, but that he wasn't suggesting that she run a World Cup race with them. He just wanted her to make the team, which was the same thing she wanted.

So Rocky agreed to use the new ski. The fateful day, she was as tense and wound up as a clock spring. She tiptoed around, guilt oozing from every pore, remembering the litany of admonitions all the years of growing up: not to tell lies, to be fair and honest, that truth and integrity were above all. It was torture not to say anything that would give her away.

She had nightmares every night about falling and hurting herself seriously, worried sick that they would discover she was on a ski she shouldn't be on.

She tried to find out if the rule books had anything to say about what she was about to do. She wanted to ask some of the coaches but was afraid. Tony saw her wrestle with her conscience daily and was torn.

Finally he brought Max in as heavy ammunition.

"Look, honey," he said gently. "There's nothing dishonest about it. You're not racing in competition. Well, not exactly. Everyone knows, coaches included, that you're the best. They want you to win. If it takes some special technical expertise to make the team, let us furnish it. No one says you have to ski on any particular ski when you're in training."

So Max's argument prevailed because she wanted it to.

CHAPTER FIFTEEN

IN MARCH A NEW DIVERSION ENTERED GREG'S LIFE. Rather, an old diversion came back into it. A year or so ago, someone had requested him for a private lesson.

The client turned out to be Angeline Bourget, a young starlet married to a much older man, the famous director Paul Galvin. Later he discovered that she and her husband, though not divorced, lived apart. Angel, as she preferred to be called, was far from angelic. After an hour of lessons, she decided there were other sports she was better at. It wasn't difficult to convince Greg to let her show him her expertise.

Her house in Starwood was tucked away behind a heavy screen of junipers, osier dogwood, sage, and elder. It could have been a Malibu beach house with its angles and glass, with its white overstuffed furniture and lacquered tables. But the only room that interested either of them was the bedroom with its view of the mountains stretching down from Independence Pass. They spent a great deal of time in it as Angel introduced Greg to what she called, with a rich laugh, "The French Method."

After a time, she had become possessive and jealous. Finally, he had to call a halt to the romance. She was wasting him with her gamut of emotions. Every time they were together there was a scene. First tears, then pleading, finally bitter anger and obscenities worthy of a truck driver.

There were stories that she'd returned to California and her husband. But in October, when the club had held their pro-am tournament, he had seen her again playing with some hotshot young pro. She was a good tennis player as so many of the Californians were. This time she seemed different, more in control of herself. The gamine-faced French girl had turned into an elegant, provocative, and mysterious woman. He knew she had noticed him, but when he tried to talk to her, she snubbed him.

One evening he had taken Nora Pemberton to a party in Starwood. Nora was beginning to annoy him with her come-hither, go-away games. He recognized the symptoms, having gone through them enough times. It was always the same. He got bored with the easy victory over a woman; he got bored when he had to work too hard for the victory. He was getting to that latter stage with Nora.

What happened next he blamed on her. Chances are he might never have noticed Angel in that crush of people if Nora had not brought her to his attention. "Who is that stunning woman that just walked in? She seems familiar to me, but I can't place her."

Greg had turned and followed her eyes. Angel,

wearing a black outfit that was so severe it had to be fabulously expensive, had just walked in with Bruce Willis. Her hair was sleeked back from her face and wrapped in a Gordion knot secured by a spray of diamonds. In a roomful of tousled-hair blondes, raucous in Smith suedes, expensive boots, and turquoise jewelry, she stood out like a rare jewel on velvet.

Greg felt the old sexual flame ignite. "It's Angel!" he said. "Angeline Bourget."

"You mean Paul Galvin's ex-wife?"

"Is she an ex now?"

"Of course! But how would you know stuck here in never-never land? It was a messy divorce. Paul absolutely adored her, you know. He used to look the other way when she had one of her little affairs. All he wanted was for her to be discreet. They say he was impotent, and though Angel was not averse to his using 'other' methods of stimulation, it was no substitute for the real thing."

"So what happened?"

"She had a small role in one of those summer shoot-'em-ups that Hollywood thinks the kids like. The star of it was this hotshot black actor who they say was really hung." She demonstrated with her two hands, measuring a rather considerable piece of equipment.

He grimaced. He found it offensive when Nora talked like one of the boys.

"Anyway, for whatever reason, a bigger part, for the hell of it, feeling gamey, she came on heavily to the star. He was no fool. He had a fling with her. Unfortunately, Paul caught them in—how do you say?—in flagrante delicto. Like a bad movie, it hit all the scandal sheets. I'm surprised you didn't see them."

"I don't shop in supermarkets."

After that Greg casually made his way around

the room until he was in close proximity to Angel. She was surrounded by a group of heavy hitters, big-money men from the East, entertaining them with stories in that delightfully husky accented voice.

Now whatever unpleasantness that had passed between them was forgotten. He waited on the fringes, moving slowly about her axis until she looked up and saw him.

Slowly she extricated herself from her admirers and came to his side.

"Well, Greg." She trilled the *r*.

"Angel. Long time no see."

She gave a tight smile. "I have been occupied."

"So I hear. Back for a while?"

"A while."

"We should have dinner one night. For old time's sake."

She put a hand on his arm and looked up at him. One of the things that had always excited him was her smallness, her slenderness, and the big tits that stood out like a prow among all the smallness. For a woman who had done a lot of low-down and dirty things in her life, she looked remarkably untouched. Her skin was still clear, her eyes large and luminous. There wasn't a line or puff of dissipation visible.

So they had begun again. Cautiously at first. Greg recognized the game and relished it. She played him like the virtuoso she was. Every night with her had produced a hard-on that made him ache for hours. When she finally capitulated and allowed him to take her to bed, he had embarrassed himself by exploding instantly, like a horny schoolboy. She had only laughed and then they had settled in to a night-long orgy of lovemaking. In their year apart she had come up with some new tricks. He thought that this time he was finally hooked, forgetting that only a month ago he had said the same thing about Nora Pemberton, whose face he could now barely recall.

On the day of Rocky's trials, it snowed. They debated whether to cancel the downhill, but the skiers themselves wanted to race, saying that they needed the experience of skiing in tough conditions. Rocky was nervous, still worried about using the ski and what her mother would say, but it was a thing she was determined to do—not only for herself but for Tony and Max. They were waiting on the sidelines to cheer her on, but Sally, not knowing the importance of this race, was at home. Crossing her fingers, praying she wouldn't get caught, Rocky waited for her name to be called. She came down seconds faster than anyone else. By the time her times were posted for the slalom and giant slalom, there was no question that Rocky Schneider had regained her edge.

Though the conditions caused many racers to be cautious and some to fall, her astounding time did not escape Greg James's knowing eye.

Later that evening, when he thought Kit was out of earshot, Greg had a talk with Suzanne.

"She won on that new ski, I tell you. You realize that ski can mean a lot of money to the person who can produce it, but do you also realize what it can mean if Kit can ski on it? In a couple of weeks she could win her first World Cup race."

"So what do you want me to do about it?" Suzanne sulked. "You and Michael blew it. Anyway, I don't know what good it would have done if you had been able to steal the right ski. If Kit got caught . . ."

"Steal what ski?" Kit James appeared in the door of the library.

"How long have you been standing there?"

Suzanne stood up quickly, spilling the needlepoint she was working on to the floor.

"Long enough. What ski?"

"No ski in particular," said Greg.

"If you don't tell me, I'll find out anyway. Who do you want me to hear it from? What ski?"

"Tell her, Greg," said Suzanne, behind clenched teeth.

So Greg told her.

Kit listened to every word, her eyes growing wider with every sentence. "We've all heard the rumors around the locker room," she finally said. "But Greg, why would you want to steal it? I don't understand." Her blue eyes were dangerously close to tears. "Grunt, how could you?"

He winced at her use of her old nursery name for him. "Honey, I wanted you to have your chance," he appealed.

"Didn't you think I was good enough to do it on my own?" The hurt was clearly written on her face. Her own brother didn't think she was good enough! "You trained me," she protested. "You and Suzanne."

"It's not enough to be just good. We want you to win the gold."

"You didn't win it. Why do I have to? Was winning the silver so bad?"

Again he flinched.

"Is that the reason you've been so awful to Rocky? And why you don't want me to be friends with her? Just for a gold medal."

He seized her hand. "You'll know what I mean when you win it. And it's because we didn't get it that we want you to go for it. For the family."

She stood up and looked at her siblings. "I really feel sorry for you guys." And she walked quietly from the room, leaving Greg and Suzanne to stare at each other in embarrassment and frustration.

* * *

The fact that Sally was unable to earn her living skiing was a source of great concern. Once again Marcella came to her rescue. The sweaters and handbags that Sally designed and made for herself were about to pay off handsomely.

Marcella had called to make an appointment with her, and now the two women sat in Sally's tiny living room on Midland surrounded by a dozen different sweaters draped over all the available furniture.

"Here's what I think we can do." Marcella was crisp and efficient in her delivery. "We'll take these dozen sweaters and I'll have them copied in the Orient. We'll mix around the designs and the colors and create a line called . . ." She stopped and frowned for an instant. ". . . Taos or Pueblo or Navaho, I don't know, something that bespeaks their Indian heritage. Then you come up with a couple of new ideas each season and we'll translate them."

Sally, a bit awestruck, could only say, "It's that easy?"

"Well, nothing's really easy. But you have enough ideas in a given sweater to produce dozens of variations. For example . . ." Marcella picked up a sweater with a desert scene across the front and a series of Anasazi geometrics. "We can make this in blue, black, white, red, yellow. We can replace the sun with a moon. We can put in a sagebrush for the cactus or an Indian on his horse. The geometrics can be in different colors. The same with your folkloric villages and your aspen tree design."

"I see what you mean," said Sally with growing excitement.

"So is it a deal?"

"What kind of deal are you offering exactly?"

"I'll buy the original from you as I do with your bags. Then I'll pay you a royalty for each sweater we produce. I would say you could—this is a conservative estimate, of course—maybe make a hundred thousand dollars a year the first year we're in production. The following year, of course, if the line goes well . . ."

"A hundred thousand a year! You're kidding!"

To Marcella $100,000 did not seem like a great deal of money. She spent that much keeping body and soul together: her designer wardrobe, her shoes, her masseuse, her hair, nails, skin, feet. She had no idea how much money it could be to a woman like Sally Burke Schneider who taught skiing for a living.

"I could send Eric to a good school. And Rocky could go to college."

"From what I hear, Rocky will be making enough money to send herself to college one of these days."

Sally's face tightened. She was still angry with her daughter for going against her wishes. And she hadn't forgiven Tony for being the instigator. What kind of things was he teaching her daughter, and how could she reconcile her feelings for him with the behavior she wanted to teach her children?

When Marcella left, her excitement over the new project waned. Just thinking of Tony produced a fierce hunger in her. They simply had to resolve this thing one way or another. All these feelings were lying out exposed and nothing was happening to them. They would wither away and die if someone didn't start tending them. Wearily she climbed the steps to the small closet she had transformed into a workroom. As she sat down she caught sight of herself in the full-length mirror.

Staring out at her was her father's face. She grimaced. I'm getting to be more and more like him, she thought. Stubborn, hard, unyielding. Forcing my particular set of values on everyone around me. Was it really dishonest of Tony to do everything he could to help Rocky make the team? Was she making an issue out of something that wasn't even an issue?

She shook her head at the forbidding image of herself. How could Tony or any other man love a face that was beginning to look like it belonged with the other stone faces on Mount Rushmore?

She saw herself growing older, she and her iconoclastic character, honest as the day was long (that was a laugh!), stern, unyielding, unforgiving, unloved.

"No, goddamn it!" She stood up so quickly she doubled over from the pain that cracked across her still-taped ribs, then sat back down quickly, taking shallow breaths and waiting for the pain to subside. She couldn't bear her suffocating self-righteousness. But she didn't know how to let go of it.

She tried to remember when it had all started. When had the joy of winning, of achieving died? When Suzanne had come into her life? She'd wanted that friendship so much! When Suzanne had moved in next door, she'd been dumbstruck by that beautiful, bubbling, laughing girl. Slender, fragile, expensively dressed, an instant social success. Maybe by associating with her, some of that spirit would rub off on her. How willing she'd been to hide her own talents in a dark closet so that Suzanne could shine. She remembered all the times she'd felt guilty for her good grades, her athletic accomplishments, her special relationship with teachers. Suzanne had envied those things, but most of all Suzanne had wanted to take first place in skiing.

And so in a supreme act of selflessness Sally had deliberately fallen in that ski race so Suzanne could take a first. And what had been her reward?

Suzanne had turned on her, accusing Sally of trying to make Suzanne look like a fool. Her mouth tightened. Betrayal, fury, scorn, ingratitude. Sally had made a sacrifice and the result was she'd felt like a rejected lover. Down deep she had secretly despised Suzanne for wanting to win a race, a boy, a contest at any cost. But hadn't she been guilty of the same thing in a way? Hadn't she compromised her own value by not only choosing, but desperately wanting the unworthy Suzanne for a friend? She had quit skiing as a result of that experience, and from that day forward had been contemptuous of competition. She had, she thought, put an end to the rivalry once and for all, and never again had she allowed herself to want something so much that its loss would shatter her. Until now. Now she wanted her daughter to win. She wanted Tony. And most of all she wanted to be proud of a self that was whole and centered. She felt suddenly light. All those burdensome restrictions had magically disappeared.

She looked at her watch. It was still early. Tony would be out with a client. Daisy as well. For the first time since she'd come to Aspen, she had a weekday that was not filled with a list of chores. She stood up guardedly and stretched.

Her injury and her narrow escape from death had provided her with some rather remarkable insights. Her cautious approach to life, the shutting off of expectations and rewards, the denial of certain pleasures until they were earned were undergoing scrutiny as she came to the realization that it was possible she might not live long enough to enjoy anything at all.

Pete's untimely death had proved that. Fortunately for him, he had enjoyed every day as it came. While she planned and scrimped for next week, next month, next year, he was living each day to its fullest.

One of her dearest friends had perished in an avalanche, all her hopes unrealized, put off until there was more time, more money.

With a new sense of determination and a great deal of fear, Sally realized it was time to rid herself of some of her more ironclad conventions and relax. The promise of a yearly income of $100,000 or more certainly made that decision a little easier.

She went to her bedroom and quickly pulled on a skirt and sweater and slipped her feet into warm boots. Marcella's check for $2,500 on account was burning a hole in her handbag. First she would deposit that into her checking account.

As she dressed, her heart raced with excitement. She felt like a child with permission to play hooky from school. She would go out on the town, visit all the shops, have lunch at Sunshine Campbell's, maybe run into Samantha Mallory and her sister-in-law Rachel Fulton there.

She and Sam were old friends who didn't see each other enough because neither had time. She wanted to tell her the news about her and Tony. Then she stopped. What news? She and Tony had been strangers for days. Her fault. She accepted that. She accepted, too, that she had to be the one to remedy it.

She called the ski desk and left word that she expected Tony for dinner that night. Then she got into her car and drove to town. She went to Zee's and had her hair washed and cut in a new tousled and—she had to admit—very becoming style. At Freudian Slip she bought a sexy nightgown. She walked up and down the malls: Cooper, Hyman, and Mill, poking into every boutique and shop, fingering the luxury goods, admiring furs and jewelry, suedes and snakeskins. She bought a beautiful belt for Rocky at Chestnut Run and a funky shirt for Eric at Boogies. Then she went to Waterfall Hope and bought a silver belt buckle for Tony and made them engrave it for her while she had lunch.

At Sunshine's, she enjoyed a huge California salad and the crusty bread for which the restaurant was justly famous. Sunshine came over to sit at the table and was persuaded to have a cup of Red Zinger tea while they caught up with each other's lives.

Sunshine remarked on how pretty she looked.

Sally gave credit to the stylist at Zee and being in love.

"In love. You? Does one have the temerity to ask who the lucky guy is?"

"Tony."

"You're joking! After all these years? I'm flabbergasted! But what about . . . ? I mean, didn't I hear you were seeing Daddy Warbucks? You know, Michael Greenfield."

"It's a long, boring story. Yes, I was. In fact, I owe all this happiness to him. He was the one who kept telling me that I was in love with Tony."

"He must have some crystal ball. Does he have office hours?"

They spent a few more minutes chatting, then Sally continued on her way. She stopped at the Butcher Block for shrimp and a rack of lamb, then picked up some exotic cheeses and a bottle of good Bordeaux.

By the time Sally got home, it was dusk and Eric was already home from school. She dumped her packages on the table.

"What's up?" asked Eric suspiciously. His mother looked unusually flushed to him and different. "You look funny."

"Fifty dollars for a new hairdo and he says I look funny. I ask you!"

"Something *is* wrong."

"Nothing's wrong. I just won the lottery. Or a reasonable facsimile thereof."

Eric shook his head in disgust. Since the accident his mother had been acting really strangely. He'd better call Tony and let him know that Mom had blown a gasket. But he didn't need to, for the thought no sooner popped into his head than the front door opened and Tony himself walked in.

"I got your message. What's up?"

"Eric, go upstairs and do your homework."

"Gee, Mom. I don't have any."

"Then watch TV."

"But you never let me watch TV this early."

"Today's an exception. I have to talk to Tony."

"Aw, Mom."

After the boy was finally persuaded to leave, Tony turned to Sally. "What's this all about? What's the question?"

"Do you love me? You said you did. Do you?"

His brown eyes were wary. He seemed poised to run. "Yes, of course. Even though you make it so goddamn hard." He cracked his knuckles nervously.

"I love you," she said matter-of-factly, as she occupied herself with emptying her shopping bags, face averted. "The kids love you. You love the kids. Don't you?"

"That's two questions. But yes, I do. And will you stop doing whatever you're doing and look at me!" He turned her around to face him.

She stopped. Her eyes and voice went soft. "Will you marry me?"

Tony started to laugh. "That's three questions." She stood, hands on hips, in that aggressive stance that always amused him so.

"You haven't answered me."

"This is so sudden." He grinned, stuffing his hands into his pockets and turning his toes in like a shuffling teenager.

Sally shrugged and went to her coat pocket to remove a small box. "Here." She thrust it in his face. "Maybe this will help you make up your mind."

"Bribery?" he asked, opening the box. The engraved buckle winked up at him. "Sally! It's beautiful."

"Well, I'm waiting." She looked ready to cry, even though her voice was brusque.

He came to her and put his arms around her. "You infuriating, intoxicating, unprincipled woman. Of course I'll marry you." He took her lips in a long, sweet, and thoroughly stirring kiss. "Does this mean all is forgiven?" he said softly. "Or are you doing this to make an honest man out of me?"

"Yes and no. You're honest enough. I finally realized you were only trying to help Rocky make up for lost time."

"I'm glad you understand. I wouldn't knowingly do something dishonest."

"I'm sure of that." She smoothed back a lock of blond hair that fell on his forehead. "You realize there will be a lot of broken hearts when I remove you from circulation," she said, looking at him fondly.

"Remove me, remove me. How glad I'll be not to have to worry where my next meal comes from. But you've got to promise to stop making mystery casseroles."

"Starting with tonight?"

"We could go out to celebrate. With the kids."

"How about staying in?" She gestured with her chin to the rack of lamb standing next to the roasting pan.

She brought his head to hers for a long kiss. "I love you so much it frightens me."

There seemed no reason to leave the circle of his arms, so she stayed there until the loud clearing of a throat made her look up with a guilty start.

"Just what are you two up to?" asked Rocky with a curious stare.

"Caught in the act," said Tony, hugging Sally closer to him.

"Where will you be in June?" asked Sally.

"Geez, Mom, how should I know. Why?"

"You're invited to a wedding."

"Yeah? Whose, yours?"

"Right. You don't seem surprised."

"I'm not." Rocky smiled triumphantly. "What took you so long?"

Sally crumpled into a kitchen chair, seized by a fit of laughing.

"Did you tell Eric?"

"Not yet."

"Tonight?"

"Why not?"

Rocky came to Tony's side and stood in front of him shyly. He took her into his arms and dropped a kiss on her forehead. "I take it you're happy with the arrangement?"

"Oh boy, am I! Now I won't have to worry about her so much while I'm away. But are you up to it? She's a handful."

"Please stop talking about me as if I weren't in the room," said Sally crossly.

"Oh, by the way," Rocky said casually. "I have some news of my own."

"Honey, I'm sorry. I got carried away." Sally went to her daughter and hugged her.

"What's going on in here?" Eric appeared in the door, furious to be missing all the fun.

"Glad you're here, little brother. Now I can tell everyone at the same time."

Waiting expectantly, they stared at Rocky. She stared back. Then a huge grin split her face. She was relishing their impatience. Then it came out in a breathless burst. "Kit and I both made the team. I'm on the U.S. Olympic team."

They descended on her with shouts and hugs.

When the tumult died down, Tony put his arms around Rocky and looked into her shining eyes. Softly he said, "That's a hell of a wedding present." Then with a wink at Sally, he added, "Worth celebrating with one of your mystery casseroles."

"No," protested Eric. "Pizza at Pinocchio's."

"No!" said Rocky. "Hamburgers at Little Annie's?"

"Veal chops at The Grill," chimed in Sally.

"Do I have a say in this?" broke in Tony.

"No," they chorused.

He shook his head in mock disbelief. "What have I gotten myself into here, and is it too late to get out of it?"

"Yes!" they screamed and broke up in laughter.

Mealtime at the Jameses' was neither happy nor filled with conversation. Suzanne and Greg watched Kit's every move, worried and wondering how long the deep freeze would last.

Kit, for her part, felt as though she were living in a house filled with strangers. She toyed with her food, her usually zesty appetite gone. The blanquette sauce congealed on her veal and turned an unappetizing gray. She felt her stomach lurch.

"You've got to eat something," insisted Suzanne. "You've got to keep up your strength."

Kit barely heard her sister. She was formulating a plan. She didn't know if it would work, but she knew somebody who would know.

She stood up. "Excuse me."

"But Kit, you haven't eaten a thing. And Jasmine's made your favorite dessert."

The thought of giving up Jasmine's triple chocolate cake almost stopped Kit, but she took a deep breath and reminded herself that there were things far more important than cake.

"This new ski, it's really different?" Kit asked Rocky as they sat in Sunshine's having herbal tea and carrot cake.

"I don't know all the specs on it, but I can tell you it really moves and holds. I've never skied on anything like it before."

"It would be nice if the team had it for next year, wouldn't it?"

"It would be great, but you know what they have to go through to even be considered."

"Yeah, it's a shame. Especially if it outskis all the established ones. What could we do to get it noticed, I wonder?" Kit drew parallel lines in the tablecloth with the tines of her fork, then crisscrossed them in the other direction. Rocky watched her curiously. She knew Kit so well she could smell the smoke as her brain cooked.

People underestimated Kit. They thought she was just another spoiled James brat with a personality defect. Just because she was reserved and didn't hang out much or act rowdy and boy crazy. She was smart, a good strategist, and knew a lot of things for her age. Kit was the one who had introduced Rocky to painting and Mozart and exotic food, had opened her mind to a world outside of Aspen and sports. It was a never-ending source of amazement to Rocky that Kit, with all her other interests, was as good a skier as she was.

"You don't seem very excited about making the team," said Rocky, whose own appointment had been a source of wild jubilation and celebration. Despite her brother and sister's attempts to celebrate, Kit had treated hers as if it were just another day. But then, she had been behaving strangely for the last week or so. Rocky tried to get her to talk, but Kit denied any preoccupation or that there was anything untoward going on in her life. If anything, she was tired, maybe even a little bored.

"I'm pleased. But excited? Suzanne and Greg are excited. They're carrying on like I was chosen to live their lives over again, only this time to get it right and bring home the gold. They're sure I'll win a gold one of these days."

"You probably will. Tony says you're already a better skier than Suzanne was when she skied in the Olympics. Mom says so, too. And guess what? I've been dying to tell you. Mom and Tony are getting married in June. Don't say anything, though. They haven't told anyone outside the family yet."

"They are?" Kit squealed. "That's exciting. Suzanne's going to turn green."

"Why on earth would she? She's got dozens of guys."

"Yeah, but I think she really likes Tony. And you know why? Because he gives her a hard time." Kit was, in fact, unaware that it was Michael whom Suzanne was losing sleep over.

"Just like Mom used to do with him."

"So that's the secret."

"Beats me."

"Anyway, about the ski. How can we get people to know about it?"

"I don't know. I guess someone has to use it in a race and win big with it. But we can't do that. We'd be thrown off the team."

"Well, you certainly can't. Racing for you means money for college and all the things you want."

"That's not the only reason. But anyway, we can't race it. We'll have to think of something else."

It was unusual for the team to have so much training time at home before the big World Cup race in March. But the European ski resorts were still suffering from the balmiest winter on record. Had it been an Olympic year, the army might have been called in to help bring in the tons of snow needed to prepare the runs. So venues were switched whenever possible to resorts in Canada and the U.S.A. For the Aspenites, training at home gave them a tremendous psychological edge.

This was the first time in years the women would race World Cup events in Aspen. For the young American team it was a time of high excitement. Race week in March was a cross between Disneyland, the presidential convention, and the circus. The organizational skills needed were formidable. Arranging for lodging, chaperones, food, and training schedules for ninety athletes taxed the minds and muscles of everyone involved.

Being homegrown was of a double advantage to Rocky and Kit. Good wholesome meals and comfortable beds were two less things to worry about. And, of course, they knew their mountain. Even a screaming blizzard could not stop them from finding their way down. They were prepared for anything.

Max Margolis was not. Especially not the double-barreled assault being waged upon him by his friend Tony Frantz and his strange new bedfellow, Michael Greenfield. They had been haranguing him for days.

"Jesus H. Christ, Max!" Michael was at his wit's end. He had made abject apologies to the man, literally crawled on his belly to say he was sorry, reinstated his monthly checks to convince Max that he was a man to be trusted. Every argument he had made to the creator of the new ski had met with stolid resistance. "No one is taking anything away from the ski, but as the competition gets tougher, you need the technicians, too.

"Rossignol spends between seven and eight million annually on racing, most of it to secure endorsements, the rest for on-site servicing. Without that, your ski could be made of solid gold and it wouldn't matter. Rossi has an Olympic staff of twenty-six, including nineteen technicians who prepare skis for racing and four crack local skiers who test for snow conditions. They have computers to take all that data in and spit out up-to-the-minute information on weather. What are you going to do? Stick your finger into the wind and tell weather?

"They have anywhere from ten to fifteen pairs of skis in the hands of each downhiller, at least a half dozen for the slalom racers. They're ready to prepare them in dozens of different ways. And that's not even mentioning the hundreds of waxing formulas.

"Are you going to stand up on a hill and let a skier decide which ski to use? Not if you want to win, you aren't. You're going to have a chief downhill technician or a slalom technician making that decision based on hundreds of bits of information fed into the computer.

"I know the ski is great. But we're going to have to move in a hurry before some other maker finds out your secret and starts putting their manufacturing and marketing muscle behind their own ski made of this alloy.

"Believe me, that will happen when they discover that this ski can give a racer a real advantage over the pack."

Michael was perspiring profusely after his impassioned speech. The facts were on the table. If Max insisted on having it his way, he would have nothing but a pretty soap-bubble dream. Michael suddenly realized why this project was so important to him. It wasn't the money. It was the thrill of the chase, the creation of something from nothing, the competition. It was mother's milk to him. Like going fast was to a skier.

"Seven million is a lot of bucks, Max," said Tony softly. "Not even Richard Farwell and Pat Mallory would put up that much money."

Max's face was a grim road map of lines as he considered Michael's arguments. He was not the clichéd addle-brained scientist as people liked to think. He was a hardheaded businessman, too. He knew that without money and an organization behind it, the best-intentioned invention was worth no more than the paper it was drawn upon.

Tony waited. There was one last convincing appeal he could make. But he dreaded making it. "Look, Max, I'm in hock up to my ears on this thing. Every cent I have and my house, too. And I don't have a golden parachute to look forward to."

Max looked at him soberly. "Okay," he said at last. "I guess we have a deal." He put out his hand. Three pairs of hands met and clasped.

The day of the downhill dawned gloomy and gray. Swollen clouds hung over the valley. Despite the flags and kites and brightly colored balloons floating in the heavy air, an uneasy silence hung over the mountain as the racers shuffled restlessly through the opening ceremonies. After the speeches, the local high school band played the national anthem. Thousands of people lined the racecourse. Then, as the racers broke ranks to begin their ascent to the starting shack, the sounds of cowbells and shouts, of laughter and whistles shattered the air.

The sun peeked out briefly, then retired behind a particularly ugly cloud and seemed destined to remain there. The light on the course was as flat as a sheet of paper.

Rocky and Kit had drawn terrible starting positions. By the time they took off, the course would be in less-than-perfect condition.

They watched every girl before them make their mental preparations. Some prayed, some chanted their mantra, some hummed, some merely stared into space.

A little-known Swiss girl had drawn the first starting position. They heard her time announced over the loudspeaker at the end of the run. 1:30:28. Not particularly fast. Anyone could beat it. And did. Several times.

Then the course turned mean and icy. Several former Olympians suffered crashes around Norway Island, where speeds reached their highest and the light was the flattest.

A halt was called while several forerunners were sent down to test conditions on the course. They reported it skiable.

The race was resumed. One of the Canadian girls managed to stay on her feet and finish a second faster than any other racer thus far. But the next racer, a Swiss girl, went down in the same compression where one of her teammates had met a similar fate. She was thrown into a fence and suffered a concussion and a knee injury.

After the third Swiss girl went down in the same place, the wags were ready to change the name Norway Island to Suicide Swiss.

The compression in question was like a miniature roller coaster. Because of flat light the racers could not prepare for it in time and thus were thrown off balance and into the air. If they managed to regain their balance, they had lost only time. If not, a promising racing career might just be over.

Two more racers were permitted to finish and then the race was put on hold. As the jury was called upon to make a decision, it started to snow fiercely.

The announcement came soon after. The downhill was canceled for the day due to poor visibility, not because of race conditions.

They would try to run it the next day, although the weather was predicted to be equally gloomy.

It snowed on and off for the next two days. There were reports of crying jags and fights from keyed-up racers, then the development of strange maladies which baffled the doctors called in for consultation. It was decided they were all attributable to nerves and letdown.

Only Kit and Rocky seemed untouched by the delay.

The sun finally came out and the races were rescheduled. Hundreds of skiers came out to foot-pack the slopes. Then the snowcats arrived with their jaws and rollers to smooth it down. The temperature rose to a friendly forty-five degrees during the day and dropped well below freezing at night. On race day, the course was like gleaming satin, smooth and lightning fast.

There was much grumbling that those who had drawn double-digit numbers would enjoy much more favorable conditions than they would have on the original race date. But that was the luck of the draw and the idiosyncrasy of the weather.

Rocky, in her team colors, looked trim and fit. All racers wore tight white one-piece suits that fit like second skins to cut down wind resistance. Although to a casual observer they all looked alike, she was easily recognizable to her family and friends who waited with false nonchalance for her race.

She got into the start shack a few seconds early to adjust her goggles and her space helmet and settle her mind with a mantra that helped focus her mind on the work ahead. She had every twist and turn of the course committed to memory. When she heard her number and name announced, she was composed and ready as she positioned herself at the electronic gate, hips against the timer, upper body outstretched as if she were going off the high board. At "Go" she pushed off with her powerful legs. It was an explosive start that she knew boded well for the run. Then she settled into a tuck and glide-skated to pick up speed. She made a slight fade to the left, coming too close to the fence, but she made a skillful adjustment and felt her outside edge bite into the turn. Sensing a change in wind speed, she straightened and prepared for the difficult turn at the top of Aztec.

She hit it with speed, staying on both skis where others had been thrown. The slipstream rushed past her with a whoosh. Her weight was perfectly balanced in this short but steep pitch that, in a split second, could throw a skier and send her tumbling out of bounds.

She soared into Spring Pitch, made another difficult turn, and stayed aerodynamic. The centrifugal force tried to push her over her outside ski, but she held on, keeping a fine line of balance on her edges.

When she hit the airplane turn which had sent many of the girls to the brink, she prayed. It was a 180-degree turn that seemed to go on forever. She knew it would suddenly flatten out and that she would have to make a direction change without losing time. She took it high and stayed on track, her peripheral vision showing her the wide tracks unsuspecting racers had been forced to make which cost them valuable time.

Rocky came into Strawpile, where the course was so narrow and speeds so great that hitting the fence could sheer off boot buckles. It was hard to turn here, so she hit the air, landing exactly where she wanted to for the high-speed section. Where others might use their turns to give them control, she used them to generate speed, as she would in the slalom.

She hit the air again to make a hard right, then there were two more air turns and the hard compression coming into Norway Island. There she tucked. She could hear the crowd. It was a sound somewhere between the moan of a huge animal and the roar of a train in a tunnel. And she was down! Finished! On her feet! When the time was announced, the crowd erupted. She felt the coaches hugging her, her back pounded on, her face covered with kisses. It was the best time of the day so far and her own personal best.

Rocky joined Tony and Sally at the bottom of the hill, feeling calm yet elated as she waited for the announcement that Kit was in the starting gate.

Instead of watching with the crowd, the trio went into the official's booth and watched on the monitor.

As Rocky watched Kit, she skied the race along

with her, sending out small mind signals to her friend, telling her of ruts and compressions, of terrain and pitch changes. Kit had good technique and natural grace, and she was skiing the course well.

And when Kit's halfway time was announced, it was a full second better than Rocky's. At that point Rocky, with a sad smile to Tony and her mother, left to make the phone call she had agreed with Kit to make.

The next morning, conversation buzzed from one corner of town to the other. It centered on Kit's disqualification from the race and her removal from the team for skiing on a nonsanctioned ski, and the mystery ski itself. Rocky's winning time was small news compared to the ski.

Instructors and expert skiers were wildly elated, happy to talk at length about what the new ski could mean to the sport. The TV networks were delighted to keep the controversial pot boiling.

Shortly afterward, the *Wall Street Journal* reported the formation of a new company to produce "The Max," a remarkable new space-age ski that was creating the greatest flurry in the industry since Howard Head's incredible metal ski in the late fifties. There was already a clamor from investors eager to pump money into the new company.

As Sally headed for the bank to deposit the latest check from Marcella, she reviewed the past few weeks with a sense of wonder. For years nothing much had happened to her. She had energized herself on her enmity for Suzanne and the passive hope that something would happen to change her life. And it had.

Tony's declaration of love, Michael's surprising offer to Max, her new career, Kit's sacrifice for her friend, Rocky's appointment to the team, her own hard-won insights.

For years Sally had let her experiences with Suzanne color her life. And her daughter's, too. All that emotional baggage she had dragged around. All those fears, insecurities, suspicion! Hoping Rocky would not reach too far so she wouldn't be disappointed if she failed. Disapproving of her friendship with Kit because she was a James and Jameses betrayed you. Thank God, Rocky had prevailed.

And Tony, too. He wouldn't allow Sally's fears to affect Rocky's spirit, her will to succeed. Sally would not live her daughter's life. Rocky should have the right to make her own mistakes, to find her own solutions. Agreed? She was touched by his stern concern for her and hers. Now his, she corrected.

In a way Rocky's victory was hers, too. It had finally freed her from the past, shown her the way of her own future. God bless you, baby, you're a hell of a lot smarter than I ever was.

As Sally waited in line, she smiled. Rocky was going to be just fine. She hoped Kit would be, too.

When Kit and Rocky had come to them with Kit's plan, Sally had been firmly against it. She saw, in Kit, a young girl who was making another useless sacrifice. But Kit had explained her reasons to Tony and her in terms that Sally could understand. "I know that someone has to be on that ski, so people will start talking about it. But if it's discovered, that person probably will be disqualified, right?"

"Right," Tony had agreed.

"On the other hand, if the ski isn't used, no one will know how good it is. And it's important to the U.S. team and to American skiing to get the ski into production sooner rather than later. Someone has to use the ski, and Rocky can't jeopardize her career. So she can't be the one to use the ski. If she's discovered, that's it for her." Kit had taken a deep breath and spoke quickly. "That leaves me."

"You?" Tony and Sally had both been dumbfounded. "Why on earth should you take the chance?"

Kit had smiled serenely. "It's no risk, you see. I don't want to race anymore. I used to love it." She smiled wistfully. "But winning was never the important thing to me. What I had was pure and wonderful: the feeling of speed, the wind tearing at my face." Her smile faded and her eyes grew distant. "It's Greg and Suzanne's fault. They've trashed it for me, turned it into something ugly and greedy. I don't want any part of it anymore. So I'm willing to ski on your new ski. More than willing," she added grimly.

"But it's not just the disqualification or being thrown off the team, dear." Sally's tone was gentle and caring. She was some kid. It was hard to believe that she came from the same stock as the other two. She took her hand and covered it. "We couldn't let you do it. There could be some mean publicity."

"I'll simply tell them the truth."

Sally turned to Rocky. "And you agree to this?"

Rocky looked at her mother mournfully. "Not really. But she knows what she wants to do. I can't talk her out of it."

Tony chimed in. "I can refuse to give you the ski."

"But you won't. And you shouldn't. I have to do this. I want to do this," Kit insisted. "It's my way of letting the world know I'm different from Greg and Suzanne. Please, Tony. It's important. To all of us."

Sally's admiration and respect for Kit was honest and heartfelt. But she worried and grieved for her, too. Once the decision was made, there was no turning back. She was terribly young to have to face that kind of scandal. It could affect the rest of her life. She had tried again to talk her out of it, but Kit was adamant.

"I'll worry about my own future. Don't you."

So they had capitulated.

A rustle of raised voices made her look up. Suzanne James, in tight white jeans and a coyote coat, had just walked into the bank. Their eyes met and held.

For a moment Suzanne hesitated. Then straightening her shoulders she strode across the floor. Stopping in front of Sally, she put her hands on her hips and settled on one leg like a model just before the camera flash. It was as quiet as a library as everyone suspended business to watch the confrontation between the two women. Ignoring their curious stares, Suzanne said ungraciously, "I hope you're satisfied now."

Sally shook her head. Wasn't that just like Suzanne? Hadn't that always been like Suzanne? She was a spoiler. She'd always been a spoiler. And then all those hateful words came back to her, the words that had altered her life for so long. "People hate you because you're a smartass, because you always have to be first down the mountain and get the highest marks and win all the prizes. Nobody likes someone who wins all the time. You're lucky that I even speak to you." Those words had turned her into a fearful, silent, eccentric failure. And despite all her attempts to be mediocre, nobody had suddenly found her lovable. Least of all Suzanne.

Now she realized just how vindictive and jealous Suzanne had been.

"Don't you find it ironic that it was your sister

who made the sacrifice this time? I think we've finally come full circle, Suzanne. The debt is paid. I hope it hasn't cost Kit too dearly."

"I don't know what your daughter did to my sister, but she'll pay for it."

Sally looked at the beautiful face. Only it wasn't so beautiful anymore. Envy, frustration, failure had remade its contours. They were setting like fast-drying concrete into the face that Suzanne would have to grow old with.

"I feel so sorry for you, Suzanne."

"Don't you feel sorry for me! How dare you feel sorry for me?"

Sally turned and walked away. She didn't need to deposit that check today. Today was a day to hug her kid, love her life, do something very special for the man she loved.

As Marcella waited for her private jet to be fueled, she stopped for coffee and a croissant at Pour la France, the snack bar at the airport. It was here that Michael Greenfield found her, nose buried in the *Wall Street Journal*.

"Heading home?" he asked.

"It's about time, don't you think? I was just reading about you." She held up the *Wall Street Journal*.

He smiled. She looked quite different in her townie clothes, her hair sleek and shining, her sable coat over her shoulders, the very picture of a successful New York career woman, a handful for any man.

"All's well that ends well," he said.

"Noble thought. And by the way, you acted very nobly in l'affaire Frantz."

"You were quite nice yourself. Sally is very grateful for your generous offer, I hear."

"She deserved it. She's very talented. Do you think they'll be happy?"

"Ask me where you think our ski will be in five years. That I can answer. In affairs of the heart, I haven't a crystal ball."

"Well, it was nice doing business with you." Marcella smiled and got up. "I think I see my pilot looking for me."

"I get back east at least twice a month."

"What a coincidence." Her mouth quirked. "I spend a great deal of time there myself. Perhaps we can have dinner one night."

"First day of May at Lutèce?"

"Seems appropriate for us capitalists to join the Communist Party's May Day celebration."

"Maybe it will be ours."

"One never knows." She smiled and pulled the sable around her shoulders. He noticed that she had very good legs as she walked away in her high-heeled Maude Frizon shoes.

The house on Midland looked sad and strangely forlorn. Packing boxes occupied every inch of available floor. Furniture had either been sold or given away.

The Schneiders were about to make the move to Tony's house on the mountain. Though he and Sally would not be married until June, he insisted that they at least move in where they would be more comfortable.

Eric was thrilled. He would have a room twice the size of his present one. And though Sally was trying to keep a sane head, she, too, was thrilled about the big kitchen in Tony's house, a room that up until now had rarely been used.

As they sat amid the piles of boxes, Sally worked on the guest list for the after-nuptial party that

Samantha Mallory and Daisy were planning to give them. She looked up to find Tony staring at her with a fatuous look on his face.

"What?" she asked, coloring.

"Nothing. Just thinking of how charming you look at your desk."

"Charming? That's not a word I would use to describe me." And her desk was a packing case that she straddled with unladylike abandon.

"Six months ago, neither would I. But love does strange things to a woman and a man." He stretched like a satisfied cat. "Do you realize we haven't had an argument in at least"—he looked at his watch—"twenty minutes?"

"A record, isn't it? Do you believe I used to think you were arrogant and insensitive, a playboy, a Don Juan?"

"You flatter me."

"And all the time you were secretly yearning for me alone."

"Well, don't go completely haywire. I was certainly living from moment to moment without thinking of tomorrow. The thought of becoming an aging ski instructor cadging drinks at the Tippler was something I wouldn't allow myself to consider."

"I worried about you. But I figured it was your choice. There was always some wealthy lady who was ready to make an honest man out of you."

He shook his head ruefully. "I'm reformed, a born-again straight shooter. Of course, I'll have to go a long way to reach your high standards. I hope you'll be patient with me."

"As you said, love does strange things to a person." She crawled over to where he sat. He reached out his arms for her and she settled into them. Shaking her head, she said, "I still can't believe this is happening to us. If I hadn't had the accident, we might never have known."

He tightened his arms around her. "Whatever it took, I am eternally grateful. But I wish it had happened earlier. I could have saved a lot of wear nd tear on the old bod."

"You mean on all those little fly-by-night affairs?"

"They weren't so fly-by-night," he protested, pretending to be aggrieved. "Some actually lasted more than a week."

"Like Suzanne." She felt him start to protest. "Only kidding. By the way, shall we invite her?"

"Sure. Why not? It would serve her right."

They burst into laughter.

"I love to watch you laugh," he said and wrestled her to the floor. When the children came in a few minutes later, they saw them still on the floor, still kissing, and tiptoed up the stairs.

Suzanne picked up the mail and brought it into the den. She was still smarting from her confrontation with Sally. Greg was huddled over a bottle of scotch. He looked as though he hadn't shaved or bathed in a week. He was still in a state of shock from Kit's treachery. Though they occupied the same house, no word had passed between them. Kit was preparing to go east to a tutorial school where she would hopefully catch up on all her high school subjects so she could enter a junior college in the fall.

As Suzanne dropped the mail piece by piece in his lap, Greg looked up in annoyance. "Do you have to be so noisy? My head is killing me."

"Then lighten up on the booze. What's done is done." She stopped at the heavy creamy envelope with their name and address in calligraphy. "It's an invitation from Samantha Mallory," she said, looking at the return address.

"To a wake, I hope. I couldn't stand anything else."

Suzanne ripped open the envelope and took out the folded sheet. "Well, I'll be damned. The nerve It's an invitation to Tony and Sally's wedding par Do you believe it?"

Greg stared at his sister with glazed eyes. Then he started to laugh. He couldn't stop. "That is rich. I love it."

"Oh, yeah? If you like it so much, you go." She flounced out of the room.

A few minutes later he heard the sound of drawers opening and closing, closet doors slamming, then the thump and bump of suitcases being pulled across the floor.

He got up and unsteadily made his way up the stairs to her room. He found her slinging clothes into a suitcase. "Where the hell are you going?"

"Argentina."

"Are you nuts?"

"No. I got an invitation from Antonio Gades-Servan to join him for the polo."

"But you can't stand the guy."

"At this moment, anyone looks good to me. I've got to get out of here." Suzanne was not planning to waste any more time or tears on her kid sister. Gades-Servan would be far simpler to manipulate.

With grudging admiration, she had to applaud Kit. She turned out to have more backbone than either one of them. Looking around the room to see if she had forgotten anything, her eyes fell on the white lacquered desk and the piles of unopened mail. Pleas for money, for her attendance at fund-raisers, for her time, announcements of upcoming summer programs. She gave a sigh. The problem with Aspen winter is that it always led to

Aspen summer. Argentina would be fun this time of year. Anyplace would be fun. Even hell!

"What about me?" Greg bleated piteously, interrupting her thoughts.

"Frankly, my dear, I don't give a damn," she _____. "You made your bed, now you can lie in it _____ your new playmate. You've got Angel, haven't _____?"

_____ilight was about to descend on Aspen Mountain. _____t had been a wonderful day. For the first time in _____ their lives Daisy, Sally, Max, and Tony had taken a _____ day off simply to enjoy themselves on the slopes. Curious skiers stopped to watch the quartet, staring with breathless wonder as the gifted group made the impossible sport seem as elegant as ballet.

Daisy was like a frisky young filly, daring them to more and more spectacular feats. She led them down the Ridge of Bell, literally leaping from bump to bump like an antelope, screaming and yodeling at the top of her lungs. Sally, who was still mending from her injuries, brought up the rear, proceeding cautiously, content just to be moving again.

Later, they returned to Tony's house, where they sat in front of the blazing fire in the living room, awaiting Daisy, who had gone home to change her clothes for dinner. Tonight the four of them were having an intimate celebration at Gordon's.

"How do you feel, babe?" asked Max.

"Not bad, all things considered." Sally was sprawled out on the long sofa, her feet in Tony's lap. He was massaging her toes to her blissful satisfaction. "Had a little trouble breathing with these busted ribs. Daisy certainly led us on a merry chase."

"She's a fast one," Max said with admiration.

"Wasn't she something else on those bumps? I tell you I don't understand how someone so small can find that much energy. She's cute, isn't she?"

They had made some pair, the tiny elfin dark haired Daisy and the lanky inventor, all gang arms and legs and spiky red hair.

Sally sat up with a delighted look on her "Why, Max, is it possible?"

"What?" he said, blushing furiously. "I'm j making a scientific observation."

Sally and Tony exchanged knowing glances.

A minute later a flushed and windblown Daisy burst in, a huge smile on her face. Stripping off her fur coat, she dropped it on the floor and flung herself into a chair. She had a huge grin on her face. "Have you heard the news? Of course you haven't, so I'll tell you."

"What? What?" They chorused.

"Angel Bourget shot Greg James!"

"Where?"

"In the balls!"

There was a shocked silence. They looked at one another. Daisy was wiggling with delight. "Isn't that just poetic justice?"

Max looked at her with fond amusement. Daisy's face was blazing with malice. He leaned back and stretched happily. "Well, as the bard so cleverly put it, 'All's well that ends well.' Anybody for dinner?"

Watch for
the next book by **Lorayne Ashton**
coming soon from Lynx Books!